"I can assure you, Mr. Quick, that I am not in need of your assistance."

"If you would kindly cease hovering—"

"And if you would cease being so obstinate—" Peter let out a curse as she ignored him. "Oh, for the love of—"

Before she could utter a word in protest, he swept her up into his arms.

"What are you doing?" she cried out, clutching at his shoulders as he carried her across the clearing toward a nearby tree stump. "Put me down at once!"

He plopped her down on the stump without ceremony, then knelt next to her feet, reaching for the hem of her skirt.

"Mr. Quick!" Emily swallowed visibly, then lifted her chin before continuing in a haughty tone. "Really, Mr. Quick, this is hardly necessary. I told you, I'm fine."

He was Mr. Quick now, was he? What had ever happened to her words of love, the husky endearments she had once whispered to him?

Peter's mouth curved in a wide grimace. It wasn't as if he didn't know the answer to that. And he was well aware that he deserved every bit of the animosity he could see lurking in those fascinating violet eyes . . .

KIMBERLY LOGAN

A KISS BEFORE DAWN

AVON BOOKS

An Imprint of HarperCollinsPublishers

This is a work of fiction. Names, characters, places, and incidents are products of the author's imagination or are used fictitiously and are not to be construed as real. Any resemblance to actual events, locales, organizations, or persons, living or dead, is entirely coincidental.

AVON BOOKS
An Imprint of HarperCollins*Publishers*
10 East 53rd Street
New York, New York 10022-5299

Copyright © 2005 by Kimberly Snoke
ISBN-13: 978-0-06-079246-6
ISBN-10: 0-06-079246-9
www.avonromance.com

First Avon Books paperback printing: December 2005

Avon Trademark Reg. U.S. Pat. Off. and in Other Countries, Marca Registrada, Hecho en U.S.A.
HarperCollins® is a registered trademark of HarperCollins Publishers Inc.

Printed in the U.S.A.

10 9 8 7 6 5 4 3 2 1

To Pat Shrout, former student teacher extraordinaire, who befriended a little girl who loved to write and showed her that all things are possible, even becoming a published author. My appreciation knows no bounds.

And to my wonderful editor, May Chen, who took a chance on a "newbie" and made her dreams come true. Thank you for believing in me and for always being so patient and encouraging.

Prologue

Oxfordshire, England
1827

Dear Lord, how did I manage to get myself into this?
Clinging to a tree branch at least ten feet above the ground, Lady Emily Knight squeezed her eyes tightly closed and rested her cheek against the rough bark, restraining the hysterical urge to giggle. She had to admit, the situation would have been funny if it hadn't been so dire.

She was well and truly caught. And the Tuttlestons were due home at any moment.

Up until this point, everything had gone according to plan. Having known the Viscount and Viscountess Tuttleston for years, she was well aware of their

weekly Wednesday-night sojourn to the home of Lord Tuttleston's sister. Being a frequent visitor to the estate, she was also aware which suite of rooms belonged to the master and mistress of the house, and the secured window had proven no barrier to someone who had learned to pick locks at the young age of fourteen. Once inside, she had wasted no time in claiming her prize.

It was upon her escape that the trouble had started. As she was shimmying back down the large oak tree she had used to access the upper floor of the building, her breeches had snagged on a protruding branch, and no subtle maneuvering was enough to loosen its grasp. She could see no way to free herself without risking a very dangerous fall.

It served her right, she reflected, biting her lip. Surely she deserved this for what she was doing, no matter her reasons. She felt a sharp tug of guilt as she recalled how kind Lord and Lady Tuttleston had always been to her.

Who would have ever thought that her past would come back to haunt her after all this time?

"Seem to 'ave gotten yourself into a spot of trouble, 'aven't you?"

The voice coming from directly below her caused Emily to gasp and tighten her grip on the branch before looking down at the figure who stood at the base of the tree.

Leave it to Jenna to state the obvious.

"What are you doing?" she hissed at the younger girl. "You're supposed to be keeping watch."

"I was." Jenna shrugged and glanced back over her shoulder. "There's a carriage coming."

Fear, cold and stark, raced through Emily's veins. Sure enough, in the distance, she could hear the approaching clatter of carriage wheels. "And you didn't think to tell me sooner?"

"I'm telling you now."

Emily gritted her teeth. "I have to get down from here."

Her face a pale oval in the moonlight, Jenna tilted her head to study her companion's predicament from a different angle. "You're caught," she supplied helpfully.

"I'm aware of that. What am I going to do?"

There was a pause as Jenna considered the question. "You'll just 'ave to give it a good tug," she said finally. "But be quick about it. They're getting closer."

Her friend was right. There was nothing else for it. She couldn't get caught. If she did, this would all be for naught.

Reaching back, Emily grasped the material of her breeches and gave it a hard yank. It ripped free with a horrible rending sound. At the same time, she lost her balance and tumbled from her precarious perch, taking Jenna to the ground with her.

They landed in a tangle of arms and legs.

"Bleedin' 'ell," Jenna grumbled, struggling to extricate herself. "You're 'eavier than you look."

Ignoring her, Emily scrambled to her feet and lunged for the bag she'd dropped at the base of the tree. The bag that contained the very thing she'd risked so much for.

"You 'ave it?" Jenna spoke from behind her.

Yes, she had it. But at what cost?

Opening the bag, she peered inside. The many facets of the diamond necklace nestled within winked up at her mockingly.

At that moment, the sound of harnesses jingling and the clip-clop of horses' hooves from the courtyard at the front of the house announced the arrival of the Tuttlestons.

"We 'ave to go," Jenna warned, laying a hand on her arm. "Miles is waiting with the 'orses."

Emily nodded and glanced back at the manor one last time. For better or worse, her fate was sealed.

She turned and followed her friend off into the surrounding darkness.

Chapter 1

London

"I want to hire you."

Caught off guard by the surprising statement, Peter Quick blinked, then raised an eyebrow at the man seated across from him. A man who had been like a father to him for the past eight years of his life. "I beg your pardon?"

Tristan Knight, the Earl of Ellington, set aside the snifter of brandy he'd been nursing for the last hour and rose, unfolding his broad frame from the depths of the armchair closest to the hearth. Turning his back to the room, he braced a hand on the mantelpiece and stared into the flames for a long, silent moment before finally continuing, his tone gruff.

"Something must be done. This is the third robbery in less than a month, and the local constabulary is no closer to catching the thief than they were in the beginning." He glanced over his shoulder, the concern plain to see in his expression. "I'm afraid we have need of your expertise."

Propping his elbows on his knees, Peter leaned forward and studied the earl closely. He'd suspected something was afoot when his unexpected guest had arrived on the doorstep of his Fleet Street flat earlier that evening, and he'd known what it was the minute the subject of the Oxfordshire Thief had been broached. But he'd thought Tristan only wanted the benefit of his advice. Never would he have imagined that the man might actually want to engage his services as a Bow Street Runner.

"You say this most recent theft occurred during a dinner party?" he prompted.

"Yes. Several thousand pounds' worth of jewelry was stolen. And the scoundrel managed to do it with at least twenty guests just down the hall in Lord and Lady Fulberry's dining room. Ever since the first robbery at the Tuttleston estate, he's grown bolder and bolder, and the longer the authorities go without coming up with a viable suspect, the more they're pointing fingers." The earl's mouth tightened. "I don't like the direction they're pointing them in."

For Peter, the light suddenly dawned. "The Park?"

Tristan gave a sharp inclination of his head.

Willow Park. It had been the only real home Peter had ever known as a boy, a place where he'd felt safe and accepted for the first time in his life. After years on the street as the leader of a band of young pickpockets known as the Rag-Tag Bunch, it had been a warm haven from the miserable existence he'd known in the rookeries of London. And now it offered the same protection to other children. Children for whom stealing and scrapping for a living had been the only way to survive.

"We have several older boys who have come to us only recently," the earl was saying, moving away from the fireplace and crossing the tiny parlor to stand before Peter. "No one has come right out and accused them of anything, of course, but the insinuation is there, all the same." A muscle flexed in his jaw. "It's starting to upset Deirdre, and I don't have to tell you how much I dislike seeing Deirdre upset."

Peter nodded. "Especially now, I would expect."

"Yes. Especially now."

It was no secret that the Earl of Ellington was madly in love with his beautiful wife. He'd always been protective of her, but after suffering several miscarriages in the past eight years, the countess was currently in the final month of a rather difficult pregnancy, and Tristan was being ferocious in his care of her.

"Of course, it doesn't help that one of the boys they suspect is Benji."

"What?" Stunned by Tristan's words, Peter jerked his head up to meet the earl's gaze, unable to hide his astonishment. "That's bloody ridiculous! Benji would never be responsible for something like this."

"You and I both know that, but the law doesn't." The earl expelled a gust of air and reached up to rake his fingers through his ebony hair in a familiar gesture. "The truth is, Benji has been . . . different lately. Quiet, withdrawn. Deirdre's worried about him, and I don't mind admitting that I am, too."

Benji had been the youngest member of the Rag-Tag Bunch, a sprightly, charming lad who had grown into a young man of integrity and intelligence. His early love of reading had led to a love of academics, and with the proper schooling and the continued support of the earl and countess, the fourteen-year-old seemed well on his way to a bright future, despite his impoverished beginnings.

However, it had been quite some time since he'd seen the boy, Peter had to acknowledge with an inner pang of guilt. His last visit to Willow Park had been well over a year ago. And now that he thought about it, he hadn't had a letter from Benji—who was usually an avid correspondent—in weeks. Could the youth he'd thought he'd known so well, who had been like a younger brother to him, have changed so much?

Lunging to his feet, he began to pace in front of the sofa he'd been sitting on, his strides long and furious. "I refuse to believe it. He's not capable of it."

"I agree, and I needn't tell you that Deirdre won't even hear of the possibility." The earl crossed his arms, watching Peter with those unnerving violet eyes that had always seemed to see so much. "But you can understand why we need your help. The situation is swiftly becoming desperate."

Taking a step forward, he laid a hand on Peter's

shoulder, bringing his pacing to a halt. "Come home," he said softly.

Home. To Oxfordshire. To Willow Park and the Ellington estate, Knighthaven. To the very person he'd been so diligently avoiding for the last four years.

Home to Emily.

Forcefully shaking off his thoughts before they could wander any further in a dangerous direction, Peter turned back to the earl. "I don't know. I doubt the local authorities would appreciate my interference in their investigation."

"I should think they would be grateful for your assistance. Little Haverton isn't London. The law there isn't used to taking charge of cases like this. Petty thievery, certainly, but something on this scale . . . No, if it's left up to them they'll never catch the bloody bounder."

Peter had to concede that Tristan had a point. From what he could remember of law enforcement in the tiny village of Little Haverton, they were ill-equipped to deal with a professional thief of this caliber. Still . . .

He met the earl's gaze squarely. "Perhaps it would be best if you went to another Runner with this. With my ties to those involved—"

But Tristan was already shaking his head. "You're the only one I can trust to look after the interests of Benji and the other boys, to make sure they're not hounded for something they didn't do." One corner of his mouth quirked upward in a slight smile. "We need the best Bow Street has to offer, and from what I hear, that would be you."

The obvious pride in the earl's voice filled Peter with a fierce sense of accomplishment. That was all he'd ever wanted. To make Tristan and Deirdre proud of him. To prove to them that he was worthy of the confidence they'd shown in him over the years.

Even if he didn't always believe it himself.

"I've heard tales of the escaped murderer you managed to track all the way to the Scottish border last year," Tristan told him, clapping him on the back. "And half of England knows about that robbery ring you uncovered in Brighton. The boys at Willow Park seem to talk about nothing but your exploits. They all want to be Runners someday."

He paused for a moment, then bowed his head, scrubbing a hand over the back of his neck with a sheepish expression. "But I must confess that your talents as an investigator aren't the only reason I want you to come home."

Peter's brow lowered. "Oh?"

"It's been years since you've been to Oxfordshire for anything more than a brief visit. You know how Deirdre worries, and the children ask about you all the time. We all miss you."

And what about Emily? Did she miss him?

The thought sprang into Peter's head before he could quell it, and he once again found himself pushing it away. He'd lost the right to ask that question long ago.

With an effort, he struggled to focus on what Tristan was saying. "I know you've been busy, and Deirdre and I are glad you've managed to make a successful life for yourself. But don't forget you have a family who cares for you a great deal. A family who would like to see you every now and again."

Family. Peter felt another sharp jab of guilt. It was because of Lord and Lady Ellington that he even knew the meaning of the word. He owed them both so much, and he hated the thought of them—not to mention Benji and the other children at Willow Park—being subjected to the suspicious conjectures of the citizens of Little Haverton. If there was a way he could help by bringing this thief to justice, shouldn't he be willing to do so? Perhaps he could even get to the bottom of what was troubling Benji.

"You know there's always a place for you at Knighthaven." Tristan clapped him one last time on the back, then turned away to retrieve his brandy from the table next to the armchair. "And I'm certain Emily will be delighted to have her old friend in residence again."

Peter froze, glad that the earl had his back turned and couldn't see the sudden tension that must show on his face. He was immediately flung back in time to a fragrant, moonlit garden. To the taste of soft, sweet lips moving under his own and the feel of silken gold curls wrapped around his fingers.

Barely stifling a groan, he whirled and stalked to the window, staring down at the darkened street below. Bloody hell! He couldn't believe that the memories were still so easily called forth, even after all this time.

"You know . . ." Tristan's voice at his shoulder jolted him from his brooding reverie. "I never asked you why you made such an abrupt departure from Oxfordshire, and I won't ask you now. I'm certain you had your reasons. But if the authorities manage to lay the blame for these thefts on one of the boys, they'll take advantage of the opportunity to close Willow Park for good." His face darkened. "Not only would that devastate the children, it would tear Deirdre apart, as well. I refuse to stand by and watch that happen."

Peter's hands clenched into fists on the window ledge. How could he turn his back on the earl's request after everything the man and his wife had done for him?

He couldn't, and that was all there was to it. After all, Benji and the rest of the children needed him, and it wasn't as if he didn't have the time. He had just finished wrapping up his last case this morning, and there was nothing else pressing that warranted his attention right away.

As for Emily . . . well, he simply couldn't allow the earl's younger sister to factor into his decision in any way.

Shaking off the sudden image of a pair of smoky violet eyes staring up at him, ripe with sensual promise, he turned from the window to face Tristan, his face a mask of resolve. "Very well. Give me a day or two to sort things out at Bow Street and then I'll join you for the trip back to Knighthaven."

Chapter 2

Emily reined in her horse and drew to a halt at the edge of the woods that bordered the Ellington estate. Shifting in her saddle, she released a sigh and reached up to shade her eyes with one hand as she gazed out over the panorama before her.

Earlier that morning, when she'd first set off on this excursion, the meadow behind the house had been shrouded by a thick carpet of fog, but the sun had long ago burned away the mist. Now, the open expanse spread out before her in an endless sea of green. The very air was redolent with the scent of the wildflowers that grew in profusion just beyond the tree line, while the lazy buzzing of insects drifted to her on the breeze.

And perched on a hill in the distance, resembling a regal queen watching over her subjects, was Knighthaven, its mullioned windows winking and glinting in the sunlight.

Emily loved her home with every fiber of her being, and normally she would have looked upon the scene with a sense of fierce pride, would have basked in the sheer beauty of the day. But not now. After the dark pit of despair her life seemed to have fallen into, she had to wonder if she would ever take such enjoyment in anything ever again.

She bit her lip, brushing a tousled curl back off her forehead. She'd been so certain that an early-morning ride would serve to take her mind off her troubles, but she should have known there would be no escaping the nightmare that haunted her every waking moment. It seemed she would never be free of the lies and the guilt.

Just remember you're doing it for Tristan and Deirdre, she reminded herself vehemently. *Not to mention the babe to come, and all the children at Willow Park who rely upon them.* Her brother and his wife were the only true family Emily had ever known, and she loved them dearly. She would not allow them to be torn away from her.

Not for any reason.

Some of her anxiety must have translated itself to her mount, for Artemis suddenly tossed her head and gave a loud snort, pawing the ground. Emily couldn't restrain a slight smile as she laid a calming hand on the animal's neck. "I'm sorry, girl. I'm being a bit of a wet blanket, aren't I?"

She never had been able to hide anything from

Artemis. The chestnut mare had been a gift from her brother soon after they had come to live permanently at Knighthaven, and no one else could read her moods so well. The only other soul she'd ever been as close to had been—

But she halted that thought before it could go any further. There was no use thinking of him. Not now.

Tapping a heel to her horse's side, she started back along the path toward Knighthaven at a sedate walk. Perhaps she should have gone with her first instinct and sent a message along to Adam at Brimley Hall asking him to join her. After all, the dashing, golden-haired Viscount Moreland could be very entertaining, and she usually quite enjoyed herself in his company. But today she had felt the need to be alone with her thoughts, so she had resisted the urge to extend the invitation.

She couldn't keep on this way, she acknowledged in despair, her shoulders slumping under the weight of her worries. But for now she could see no other options open to her. If she did not follow her tormentor's instructions to the letter, there was no telling what the consequences might be. It was quite likely that she could lose the family she was fighting so hard to protect.

The mere possibility filled her with a sense of terror left over from her lonely and neglected childhood.

At that moment, the track Emily had been following broke from the trees and converged with another path that led directly up the hill to the stable yard at Knighthaven. Nudging Artemis into a quicker pace, she suddenly became aware of the sound of thundering hoofbeats approaching much too fast from the rear and glanced back in alarm.

A large black horse came cantering around the bend in the trail, on top of her before she could shout out a warning. The rider yanked back on his reins, barely avoiding a collision, but the near-disaster was enough to frighten Artemis. The mare gave a shrill whinny and reared up on her hind legs, and the next thing Emily knew, she was sliding from the saddle to land with a jarring thud in the dirt.

Stunned, she lay on her back, staring up at the sky through the thick canopy of tree branches that crisscrossed above her as she struggled to regain the breath that had been knocked from her lungs. Then, through the buzzing in her ears, she heard someone calling her name, and became aware that the other rider had dismounted from his horse and was striding toward her.

"Emily?"

She pushed herself to a sitting position, unable to suppress a soft moan as the landscape seemed to spin around her. After a second or two, however, the world righted itself, and she was able to focus on the figure bending over her.

Her heart shuddered to a stop in recognition.

The man staring down at her was tall and leanly muscled with the lithe, casual grace of a jungle predator. Thick, tawny hair the color of a lion's mane just brushed wide shoulders, and a pair of mesmerizing blue eyes set deep in a face of chiseled planes and angles studied her with the piercing quality of a well-honed sword.

No. It can't be . . .

But it was. She knew there could be no denying it. That striking visage had once been as familiar to her as her own.

Peter Quick had come home.

As Peter gazed down at Lady Emily, noting her shaken expression and dazed eyes, he couldn't help but marvel at the capricious whims of fate. He should have known the one person he wanted most to avoid was bound to be the one person he saw upon his arrival at Knighthaven.

When he had first rounded the bend in the path and seen her on the trail before him, he'd known in an instant of chilling fear at the realization that he might not be able to stop his mount in time. It had been a near-miss, and her tumble from the saddle had set his heart to pounding at a frantic pace that had yet to slow.

"Emily, are you all right?"

"You!"

The word vibrated in the air between them, rife with a mixture of shock and disbelief. The underlying thread of disdain struck him far harder than he would ever admit, and he fought to gather his customary façade of indifference about him as a shield.

"Yes. Me." His tone was soft, deliberate. "And as you appear to be unable to answer my queries regarding your well-being, I suppose I shall have to ascertain your condition for myself." He leaned closer to her in a purposeful manner, lending credence to his words.

Emily gasped and glared up at him mutinously, as if

daring him to touch her. "Don't be ridiculous. I'm fine."

"Are you certain? That was a hard fall."

"Of course I'm certain. It was only a small spill, and it's not as if I've never fallen off a horse before."

"Ah, yes. I seem to remember one incident in particular. It was our first year in Little Haverton, and one of the Willow Park boys had dared you to ride your brother's new stallion. You wound up in the nearest watering trough, I believe."

A becoming shade of pink flooded her cheeks and she grimaced, as if she regretted reminding him of the embarrassing occurrence. "Yes, well, I always did have more nerve than sense. And that just goes to prove my point. I'm rather used to such unfortunate mishaps."

"Yes, you do tend to have a bad habit of getting into trouble, don't you?"

Emily's flush deepened and she started to struggle to rise. Peter instantly shot out a hand to catch her elbow, steadying her as she stood, and though she didn't jerk away from his touch, he felt her stiffen in response.

"Where is Artemis?" she asked, glancing about her with a worried look.

"Right over there." Peter jerked his head toward where the mare stood next to his own gelding, Champion, munching away on a patch of grass. "She seems to have more than recovered."

Emily took a step in her mount's direction, but she suddenly seemed to falter and her breath hissed through her teeth, her brow furrowing with obvious pain.

Peter's grip on her arm tightened. "What? What is it?"

"Nothing. My ankle is a bit sore, that's all."

"Here. Let me help you."

"I can assure you, Mr. Quick, that I am not in need of your assistance. If you would kindly cease hovering—"

"And if you would cease being so obstinate—" Peter let out a curse as she ignored him and took another tottering step forward. "Oh, for the love of—"

Before she could utter a word in protest, he swept her up into his arms.

Dear God, she was so small, so delicate. How easily she could have been badly hurt in their near-collision. The feel of her dainty curves pressed against his chest had his nether regions reacting in a predictable male fashion that he could only pray she wouldn't notice.

"What are you doing?" she cried out, clutching at his shoulders as he started to carry her across the clearing toward a nearby tree stump. "Put me down at once!"

That was probably a very good idea. The sooner he had her out of his arms, the sooner he could distance himself from the powerful effect she seemed to have on him. "Gladly."

He plopped her down on the stump without ceremony, then knelt next to her feet, reaching for the hem of her skirt.

"Mr. Quick!"

He froze and looked up at her. She had changed little in the last four years. She was as beautiful, as luminous as ever. In an elegant riding habit of royal blue with her blond curls swept up under a matching feathered hat, she looked every inch the pure and golden angel he'd always thought she was. A bit of a rumpled angel, to be sure, with her dress dirt-stained and her hat askew, but an angel nonetheless.

She swallowed visibly, then lifted her chin before continuing in a haughty tone. "Really, Mr. Quick, this is hardly necessary. I told you I'm fine."

He was Mr. Quick now, was he? What had happened to her words of love, the husky endearments she had once whispered to him?

Peter's mouth curved in a wry grimace. It wasn't as if he didn't know the answer to that. And he was well aware that he deserved every bit of the animosity he could see lurking in those fascinating violet eyes.

Forcing himself to focus on the matter at hand, he assumed a stern expression. "Whether you like it or not, Lady Emily, I intend to check you for further injury, and it will go much faster if you cooperate. I promise you, I shall enjoy this no more than you will."

Her Cupid's bow lips tightened. But to his surprise, instead of arguing, she crossed her arms and leveled her cool gaze over his shoulder, as if it were no longer worth it to her to fight him.

Taking a deep breath, he bent to his task. Lifting the hem of her skirt, he carefully removed her riding boots and slid his hand along one ankle. Though he tried to remain detached, there was no ignoring the well-shaped turn of that ankle or the warmth of her skin through her stockings. He quickly moved to the other foot and examined it as thoroughly, noticing when she gave a small wince in response to his gentle probing.

"This one?" he asked, his voice hoarse.

She shrugged, but refused to look at him.

He continued to run his fingers over the obviously tender area. "Well, nothing appears to be broken. It seems you've just twisted it." He lowered her foot to the ground before speaking again. "I owe you an apology, my lady."

Her startled gaze finally swung back to him. "For?"

"For frightening your horse and causing your accident. I'm afraid I was lost in my thoughts and was going much too fast, but I had no idea that anyone was on the path in front of me. It never occurred to me that anyone from Knighthaven would be out riding this early."

Emily looked down at her gloved hands in her lap. "Lately I've become a bit of an early riser, and I find that a morning ride sometimes helps me to relax."

"You? An early riser? As I recall, you used to lie abed until almost noon."

She ducked her head, and Peter wondered if she was thinking about all the times he had slipped away from Willow Park and climbed the trellis up to her room at Knighthaven to tap on the glass and tempt her into joining him for an early-morning adventure. She had always grumbled and scolded him for waking her, but she had always forgiven him.

And she had always gone with him.

"More than one thing has changed in the last few years," she said stiffly before meeting his gaze once more, her eyes shadowed and dark with distrust. "Why are you here?"

Peter felt his eyebrows wing upward at her rather curt manner. "You know, one might almost be excused for thinking you aren't pleased to see me."

She shot him a glare. "I beg your pardon, but surely you must agree that I have every right to be surprised by your appearance? On your past few visits to Little Haverton, you haven't ventured near Knighthaven. You've always stayed at Willow Park."

Ah. So she *had* noticed his avoidance of the Ellington estate. And here he'd thought she'd been completely oblivious. He should have known better. "That's true. But I'm sure that my presence here would have only made it awkward for both of us."

"Perhaps. That doesn't answer my question, however. Why are you here?"

"Your brother invited me."

"Tristan? He's home from London?"

"He should be soon. His carriage wasn't far behind me."

When he and Tristan had set off at dawn from the inn they'd passed the night at, Peter had chosen to make the rest of the short journey to Little Haverton on horseback, feeling the need for some time alone to sort out the chaos of his thoughts. It hadn't helped, and running into Emily in such a fashion had only served to unsettle him further.

Frowning, he rose and took a step back from her. "Perhaps we should head for the house if you want to be able to greet Tristan when he arrives."

Emily's expression closed up once more. "Yes, of course."

As she bent to slide her riding boots back on, Peter moved a short distance away. He knew he'd been a bit abrupt, but the sooner he delivered her to Knighthaven, the better off he would be.

If such a brief time in her company threw him this much off balance, he wondered grimly, how in bloody hell was he going to handle staying under the very same roof with her for who knew how long?

Despite his misgivings, he knew there could be no going back now. He only hoped this wouldn't turn out to be the biggest mistake of his life.

Chapter 3

Peter was home.

Her mind awhirl with the implications of his appearance, Emily couldn't help studying the man who rode alongside her as they started their horses back up the trail toward Knighthaven.

What was he doing here?

When she had first looked up to see him looming over her, she'd been certain that she must be dreaming, that she had hit her head in her fall and conjured forth his image from the depths of her muddled brain. But when he'd opened his mouth to speak, she'd realized she wasn't hallucinating. He was really standing there before her, as tall and handsome as ever. True, his shoulders were a bit broader, his square, tanned face a bit harder, but he still affected her just as strongly as he always had, stealing her breath, her wits, and her reason.

Dear God, she'd been so certain all her feelings for Peter were dead, that he had killed them with his abandonment that long-ago night, but it seemed he was still entirely capable of bringing her body to life in a most distressing manner. When he had swept her into his arms, the feel of that muscled chest under her hands had caused her mouth to go dry, and his gentle examination of her ankles with his lean, callused fingers had set her stomach to fluttering.

Remember who this man is, she warned herself. *He is the one who walked away and left you without a second thought!*

She had every right to be wary. Once she had believed they were closer than any two people could be. But she'd been wrong. That misjudgment had caused her a great deal of pain and disillusionment, and that was something she could never forget.

However, at nearly two and twenty, she was a woman now, not a child. Surely she could control these troubling emotions and behave as a proper young lady should. She would be polite, but distant, making it clear in no uncertain terms that whatever had been between them was now firmly in the past.

Turning in her saddle to face him, she schooled her features into a deliberately casual expression. "You know, you never really answered my question."

He glanced at her over his shoulder. "Oh? And what question was that?"

"Why are you here? Why would my brother ask you to come home now?"

He gave a careless shrug and looked away to contemplate the tree-lined path before them. "He seemed to think it would be a nice surprise for Lady Ellington."

Emily waited a few moments, but when no further explanation was forthcoming, she didn't force the issue. It appeared that Peter was no more anxious to converse with her than she was with him.

At that moment, their horses trotted into the stable yard behind the house, and as a groom came forward to take their mounts, Peter swung down from his saddle. Before Emily had a chance to move, he was at her side, reaching up to grasp her waist and lower her to the ground in one smooth motion.

But instead of releasing her right away, his hold seemed to tighten a bit and he leaned his head close to her ear, his eyes searching her face in an unnerving manner.

"Are you certain you're all right?" he asked. "Your ankle isn't paining you?"

Polite, Emily, she reminded herself, feeling oddly breathless as she met his gaze. *Polite, but distant.*

"Yes, of course. I'm quite recovered." It wasn't a complete lie. Right now she could feel nothing but a queer tingling sensation where his fingers spanned her waist.

Peter opened his mouth to speak, but before he could say another word, he was interrupted by the unmistakable sound of a carriage approaching from the road in front of Knighthaven.

Feeling an overwhelming sense of relief, Emily took advantage of his momentary inattention to disengage herself and move away.

"That must be Tristan now." Without waiting for a reply, she turned and started off along the cobblestone path that wound around the building, grateful for the reprieve.

By the time she reached the front of the house with Peter at her heels, the carriage was rolling to a stop at the foot of the wide steps that led up to the front entrance of Knighthaven. Recognizing the elegant equipage with the Ellington crest emblazoned on its side, she hurried forward eagerly.

The coachman hopped down from his perch, swinging open the door to reveal the powerful frame of the Earl of Ellington.

"Tristan!" Emily lunged at him as he stepped down from the conveyance and flung her arms around his neck in a fierce hug.

"Here now. What's this?" His voice was teasing as he bent to press a kiss to her temple. "If I didn't know any better, I might almost believe my little sister missed me."

Her heart lodged in her throat. She and Tristan hadn't always been close. In fact, when he had first returned home to assume guardianship of her upon their father's death when she'd been fourteen, she'd viewed him with anger and resentment. But over the years, their relationship had grown and flourished into a deep and abiding affection.

"As if that were even a remote possibility," she sniffed, releasing her stranglehold on him. "I can't imagine why I would ever miss anyone so vexing."

Tristan chuckled, then his smile faded and he gave a slight start as he focused on his sister's disheveled appearance. "Good God, Emily! What happened to you? You look as if you've been dragged backward through a briar patch."

Aware all the while of Peter watching them quietly from a short distance away, she felt her cheeks flush and lifted a hand to push a tangled curl back behind her ear. "Er, I took a bit of a tumble off Artemis during my morning ride, I'm afraid."

"Are you hurt?"

Before she could reply, Peter stepped forward. "She twisted her ankle," he interjected with smooth aplomb, his tone deep and even. "But otherwise, she appears to be unharmed."

Emily turned to face him. As if she needed him to speak for her! "Yes, Mr. Quick happened by just in time to offer me his assistance," she told Tristan. She met Peter's gaze for a long, drawn-out moment, arrested by the shadows she could see swirling in their blue depths. "I'm most grateful."

The earl grinned, seemingly oblivious of the powerful undercurrents arcing between his sister and the Bow Street runner. Strolling forward, he clapped the younger man on the back. "Ah, Peter. You made it." He glanced back over his shoulder at Emily. "I suppose he told you that he'll be staying here at the house for a while."

Emily's stomach lurched. Surely she must have misheard? "Here? At Knighthaven? Not Willow Park?"

"That's right. He has agreed to lend the local authorities a hand in apprehending the Oxfordshire Thief."

Oh, dear God!

Emily felt all of the blood in her body drain into her toes and her pulse start to pound in her ears as her world narrowed down to Peter's piercing eyes, staring at her with a disturbing intensity. She should have known, should have suspected, but she'd been so caught off guard by his unexpected arrival that the possibility hadn't even occurred to her.

How would Peter react if he discovered that the girl he'd grown up with, the girl he'd once taught to pick pockets for the sheer fun of it, was now using those very skills to rob the good citizens of Oxfordshire?

She was very much afraid she knew the answer. With his newfound sense of duty, he would feel honor bound to turn her in. She doubted he would hesitate for even a moment, for he would never understand her actions, regardless of the reasons behind them. He would arrest her, and everything she'd done in order to save her family would have been in vain.

"Em?"

She looked up to find her brother watching her with curious eyes, and she fought to paste a smile on her face despite her growing panic. "That's wonderful news, of course." She turned to Peter, her smile wavering a little at the corners. "But I am a bit surprised. Surely you must be much too busy to spend your time searching for a simple country thief? You—"

"Far from simple, Em," Tristan cut her off, his jaw setting at a stubborn angle. "The brigand has robbed three homes in Little Haverton in the last month, one of them the home of very good friends of ours. And I needn't tell you what sort of problems he has caused for Willow Park."

"Yes, but—"

"I am never too busy when it comes to aiding my family, Lady Emily." Peter took a step forward, coming to a halt in front of her, his expression serious. "Things are a bit slow at Bow Street at present, so my time is free as I will it. And I plan on using it to bring this thief to justice."

She froze, unable to speak past the lump in her throat. Finally, she forced herself to incline her head in a stiff nod, praying none of her guilt showed on her face. "Of course. I'm certain the constable shall be happy to have your assistance."

Tristan reached out and clapped Peter on the back in a hearty gesture before tucking his sister's arm through his. "There. Now, why don't we go inside and let Deirdre know you're here? She'll be anxious to see you."

Feeling as if she were headed for her own execution, Emily climbed the steps next to her brother, aware the whole time of Peter's powerful presence close behind her. He gave off an almost palpable magnetism that seemed to vibrate through every pore of her body, making it impossible to ignore him.

He's here to find the thief.

The words echoed in her head and she suppressed a shiver at the sudden chill that overtook her. What was she going to do? Peter would be much harder to deceive than the rest of her family. If he was set on finding the thief—and it seemed he was—she knew better than anyone how single-minded he could be once he had decided upon a course of action.

She took a deep breath. She had to stay calm, had to keep her wits about her, no matter what.

As they stepped into Knighthaven's spacious entry hall with its wood paneling, wine-colored carpet, and gilded furniture, they were approached by the butler, Langley, who greeted his master's return with a genuine smile of relief.

"It is good to have you home, my lord," the portly little man said with a bow as he took the gentlemen's hats and gloves.

"Thank you, Langley," Tristan said, nodding in return. "It's good to be back."

"And Master Peter!" The servant's smile widened even more in his plump, ruddy face as he recognized the man standing next to his employer. "Have you come for a visit?"

"You might say that."

The butler looked pleased at the news. "Lady Ellington will be overjoyed. Will you be staying long?"

Emily tensed as Peter looked in her direction, his gaze hooded. "Nothing is certain at this point, Langley. Let's just say that my stay could be indefinite."

His statement had her gritting her teeth in outraged frustration. If she didn't know any better, she'd swear the beast was actually baiting her!

"By the by, Langley," Tristan asked, glancing about with an obvious air of anticipation. "Where is Lady Ellington?"

"Having tea in the parlor with Mistress Lilah, my lord."

"And how has she been this morning?"

"Quite well, my lord." Langley lowered his voice as he cast a brief glance in the direction of the parlor door, which stood ajar. "Though I must admit it has been difficult to keep her occupied so she isn't tempted to push herself. Thank goodness for Mistress Lilah. I——"

At that moment, he was interrupted by the sound of an inquiring feminine voice drifting out into the corridor. "Langley, who are you speaking to? Do we have guests?"

Tristan didn't wait another second, but moved off along the hallway toward the parlor with purposeful strides, his impatience to see his wife evident.

Emily turned and started after him, eager to put some distance between herself and the man next to her, but Peter's hand on her arm brought her to an abrupt halt. She gasped at the frisson of heat that shot through her, and she struggled to bring her fluttering pulse back under control before she faced him with what she hoped was an unreadable expression. "Yes?"

He hesitated for just a moment, regarding her silently before he spoke in a low tone. "Emily, I want you to know that my presence here isn't in any way meant to hurt you. I apologize if the situation is a bit awkward."

She raised an eyebrow. A *bit* awkward? Why, she couldn't think of a way the situation could possibly be any worse. But she had no intention of letting him know how she felt—or of letting him see her fear. "Think nothing of it, Mr. Quick. I assure you that your presence here doesn't affect me one way or the other. I can't imagine why it would."

With that, she whirled and swept off after Tristan, feeling Peter's stare burning into her back as he followed her.

She caught up with her brother just as he stepped into the parlor. Spacious and airy, the room reflected the refined tastes of the lady of the house with its delicate color scheme of blue and ivory echoed in the carpets and the flowered wallpaper. Gauzy lace curtains, chintz-covered chairs, and elegant furnishings completed the picture. On the far side of the room, louvered French doors stood open to the gentle stirring of the spring breeze.

They were greeted by a voice far less dulcet than the one that had called out a few moments ago.

"Well, look who finally decided to come 'ome."

Despite her worries, one corner of Emily's mouth gave a humorous twitch as her gaze went to the woman who stood next to the fireplace.

Tall and statuesque with upswept black hair only faintly touched with silver, Lilah was Lady Ellington's good friend and companion, as well as wife to Tristan's right-hand man, Cullen. A former prostitute who had followed the family to Oxfordshire when they'd left London eight years ago, she still possessed a brassy charm that might have been off-putting to some, but made her a particular favorite of Emily's. She never hesitated to speak her mind.

As she was doing now. "It's about time you decided to get 'ere," she continued, crossing her arms over her ample bosom and leveling Tristan with a stern glare. "Off 'aving a grand old time gadding about the city while we sit 'ere on our bums and twiddle our thumbs waiting for you."

"I can assure you that I was far from enjoying myself, Lilah," Tristan pointed out, his tone dry. "You know how I deplore London. Especially during the Season."

"Tristan."

The one word, softly spoken, was enough to draw everyone's attention to the person ensconced on the sofa closest to the French doors.

Tall and slender with large, speaking green eyes and a tumble of spiraling auburn curls, Lady Ellington was a striking woman with an air of almost queenly grace. No one looking at her would ever have guessed at her harsh childhood as a London pickpocket, and Emily sometimes had trouble believing that she was almost nine months along in a rather delicate pregnancy. Her cheeks glowed with color and her smile was as warm and lovely as ever, the only sign of her condition the obvious mound of her stomach beneath the amber material of her muslin day dress.

Pushing herself up from her reclining position, Deirdre held her hand out to her husband. "Welcome home, darling."

Emily watched as Tristan rushed to his wife and clasped her hand in his, leaning forward to press a fervent kiss on her cheek. "What's this I hear about you not obeying Dr. Brady's instructions?" he asked, his brow lowering in a disapproving manner. "Deirdre, you know—"

"Oh, pish," she interrupted him with a careless wave of her free hand. "Really, Tristan, you must know I would never do anything to endanger our child. I simply rode over to Willow Park a couple of times to check on the children. I assure you, I was very careful, and I didn't stay long."

Tristan glanced over his shoulder at Lilah, who shrugged. "Don't look at me. You know 'ow impossible it is to keep 'er from doing something she's determined to do."

The earl cast his wife a stern look. "Well, now that I'm home, things are going to change. Isn't that right, darling?"

"Yes, Tristan," Deirdre replied sweetly, but Emily wasn't fooled for a minute. Her brother might think he was the one in charge at Knighthaven, but everyone knew who really held the reins.

At that moment, the countess's gaze went past Tristan to Peter, who still stood in the doorway, one shoulder braced against the frame in a casual posture as he observed their exchange in silence. "So, Peter, are you going to come and say hello to me, or are you going to continue to just stand there?"

A broad grin spread over his face, and Emily couldn't help but notice the way it softened his brooding features as he levered himself away from the door and crossed the parlor to Deirdre's side with long, easy strides.

"Hello, my lady," Peter was saying as he captured Deirdre's outstretched hand in both of his and pressed a kiss to her knuckles. "I'm glad to see you looking in such good health."

"I knew you would come," Lady Ellington said, her countenance alight with true pleasure as she looked up at him. "Tristan wasn't certain, but I never doubted it."

"You were so sure of me?"

"I know you, Peter Quick. You protect the ones you love."

Emily felt her heart pick up speed in response to Deirdre's words. It was true. She couldn't deny it. Peter Quick would do anything for the people he cared about, and he would never hesitate to make sure that anyone who hurt them was brought to a swift and suitable justice.

Renewed terror flooded through her at the thought.

"It's about time you brought yourself back 'ere, my boy," Lilah said, moving to join the men next to the sofa. "I'd say your return is cause for celebration."

"I agree, Lilah," Deirdre said with an emphatic nod. "And I think it would be a wonderful idea to mark the occasion with some sort of get-together this evening. There are quite a few people who will want to welcome you home."

"Deirdre—" Tristan began warningly.

"Oh, nothing too large, darling. Just a small dinner party with a few of our dearest friends, like Lilah and Cullen. And the McLeans, of course. I'm certain Angus and Rachel would love to see Peter again, and they could bring Jenna along with them."

Emily suddenly felt quite ill. A dinner party? Where she would have to be in Peter's vicinity all evening long, pretending to be happy he was here when all she wanted to do was retreat to her room and hide?

"Perhaps that isn't such a good idea, Deirdre," she ventured, hoping to dissuade her sister-in-law from her current course by being the voice of reason. "You say a small get-together, but even the smallest event takes planning. You really shouldn't overtax yourself, you know."

To her surprise, it was Peter who rushed to agree with her. "She's right, my lady. A party isn't necessary. And I should most likely use this evening to become familiar with the particulars of the Oxfordshire thefts."

"Nonsense," Deirdre insisted. "No one wants to see that devil caught more than I, but surely one evening's delay shan't hurt? In fact, Tristan can send a note round to the constable and request his presence here at Knighthaven early tomorrow morning. I'm certain he will be glad to offer you whatever insight he may have into the case."

She looked at Emily. "As for the planning, dear, there is no need for anything elaborate. Anyone who is close to us realizes that we don't stand on ceremony here."

Reaching out, she covered Peter's hand with hers, her expression beseeching. "Please, Peter? You are home so rarely, and I would enjoy an opportunity to take my mind off my own troubles." She gave a rueful glance down at her swollen belly before looking back up at him. "We could even invite Benji. I'm certain he wouldn't want to miss the chance to see you."

For just a moment, Emily could have sworn she saw something shift in Peter's face. A shadow seemed to pass over his features before he finally nodded his consent. "Very well. I suppose there's no harm in it. As long as Lord Ellington doesn't object."

Tristan shook his head. "I wouldn't dare. Once she

gets the bit between her teeth, there's no stopping her."
He sent his wife another firm look. "However, I intend
to hold you to your promise that it remain small. No
guests other than those present and the ones we've already mentioned. And I shall be keeping a close watch
on you. If you start to feel fatigued at any time, I expect
to be informed at once so I can call a halt to the proceedings. Is that understood?"

There was no mistaking the seriousness of his tone.
Deirdre might have had the earl wrapped around her
finger, but she knew when not to push him.

"Of course, darling," the countess assured him with a
sunny smile. "Don't I always bow to your superior
judgment in such matters?"

Tristan rolled his eyes.

So, it appeared as if things were all settled, Emily
thought crossly as Lady Ellington and Lilah began to
discuss the forthcoming dinner. Whether she liked it or
not, it looked as if she would have to sit through an evening of pleasantries and idle chatter with Peter and a
roomful of guests. And all the while she would have to
talk and laugh and behave as if everything were all right
when deep down she felt as if her whole world were on
the brink of falling apart.

Across the room, her eyes met Peter's, and a tingle
shot through her at the intensity of his expression.

Dear God, how was she ever going to get through this
night? Or for that matter, the days to come?

Chapter 4

"**A**nd the next thing I know, they're planning a dinner party to celebrate his return home!"

Emily gave Artemis's side another vigorous stroke with the currycomb and looked over her shoulder at Jenna, who stood slouched against a post at the entrance to the stall, arms crossed and peaked cap pulled forward to shade her eyes. "Can you believe it? It's as if they've all forgotten how he just up and left without a thought to us."

As if suddenly realizing how childishly indignant she sounded, Emily turned back to her horse with a careless shrug. "Not that any of that matters to me, of course."

A snort from behind her caused an embarrassed heat to creep into her cheeks. "It doesn't," she insisted, hoping she sounded more convincing than she felt. "But it hurt Tristan and Deirdre a great deal. Not to mention

Benji and the other children at Willow Park who have always adored him."

She reached out with a gentle hand to rub her mare's velvety muzzle, and Artemis gave a soft nicker in response. "And then to find out that he's here to help with the investigation into the Oxfordshire thefts . . ." She shook her head. "Oh, Jenna, what are we going to do?"

When only silence greeted her, she whirled about once again to face her companion. "Jenna? Are you listening?"

The girl started and straightened from her nonchalant pose, reaching up to push her cap back from her forehead. "You're asking me? 'Ere I thought you'd forgotten I was even 'ere."

"Jenna, this is not a joking matter."

"Do I look like I'm joking?" Her friend sniffed and tossed her dark-brown braid over her shoulder. "I 'aven't exactly been enjoying myself while you've been nattering on about Peter Quick for the last hour. You've barely even stopped for breath, so I didn't think your question needed an answer. You seemed to be carrying on the conversation well enough on your own."

Emily bit her lip. Jenna was right. She'd done little else since she'd joined the younger girl here in the stables but fret over Peter's arrival. "You're right. I'm sorry. But I don't understand how they can all behave as if the last four years don't matter. We're just supposed to forget everything he's done to hurt us, I suppose."

"Don't you mean what 'e's done to 'urt *you*?"

"Yes. I mean no. I mean . . . Oh, I don't know what I mean!" With a frustrated huff, Emily tossed aside the currycomb and sank down onto a nearby stool. "Drat Peter Quick! The man scrambles my wits until I don't know which way is up."

"Maybe you should be considering why that is."

"I *know* why that is. He's a Bow Street Runner. One of the best, if the tales I've heard about him are true. If he finds out what I'm doing, who knows how he might react."

"Why don't you try telling 'im?"

The male voice had both women looking up in surprise to find a lean, gangly figure lounging just inside the stall, watching them with intent green eyes.

A cheerful young man with a shock of shaggy red hair and an open, freckled face, Miles Riley had been one of the original members of the Rag-Tag Bunch as well as one of Peter's good friends. Like the other children, he'd grown up at Willow Park, but unlike them he'd decided to stay in Little Haverton once he'd come of age to strike out on his own. His affinity for animals, especially horses, had prompted Lord Ellington to offer him a job in the stables at Knighthaven, and aside from Jenna, he was the only person who knew Emily's secret. More than once in the past few weeks she'd had cause to be thankful for the stable hand's help.

But now she found herself wondering at his sanity. "Tell him? Miles, are you mad?"

The young man lifted his chin in a defensive manner. "Well, we certainly 'aven't been able to discover a way out of this mess ourselves. Maybe 'e can."

"Or maybe he could toss us all in Newgate and throw away the key." Emily shot to her feet again and began to pace the stall, her movements agitated. "You know how he's changed in the past eight years, Miles. He'd never understand why we chose this path."

"I 'ate to admit it," Jenna said, shoving her hands in the pockets of her breeches and taking a step forward. "But maybe Miles is right. Maybe we *should* go to Peter."

Emily shook her head. "I don't know, Jenna. There's just no way to predict what he might do. Sometimes I think he's forgotten his old life. What it was like to be hungry and desperate and willing to do anything in order to get by."

Jenna's face closed up. "Believe me, you don't forget something like that."

Emily felt a pang of sympathy as she looked at her friend. A former pickpocket herself, the girl had more than a passing acquaintance with both hunger and desperation.

As a child, Jenna's very existence had been a daily struggle to stay alive. Her parents, Angus and Rachel McLean, were the caretakers of Willow Park now, thanks to the generosity of Lord and Lady Ellington. But at one time, the McLeans had simply been one of the hundreds of poverty-stricken families trying to survive in the rookeries of London. It had been Tristan who had offered them a home and a chance to make a better life for Jenna and their younger daughter, Gracie.

With an age difference of only two years between them, it hadn't taken long for Emily and Jenna to become fast friends. And though the younger girl's brusque manner could be somewhat irritating, Emily couldn't help but admire her bold, forthright attitude, and she had been grateful many times over the years for her friend's advice and support.

Especially recently. She didn't know what she would have done if she hadn't had Jenna and Miles to turn to for help when this whole ordeal had started.

"You know." Jenna's slow drawl drew her from her musings, and Emily looked up to find the girl watching her through narrowed brown eyes. "You never did tell us just what 'appened between you and Peter that night before 'e lit out."

"That's true," Miles mused, his expression curious. "Every time we've tried to ask you about it, you've put us off. Did you 'ave an argument or something?"

Emily quickly avoided their too-perceptive stares. "Not precisely," she murmured.

An argument. If only it had been that simple.

She had first met Peter Quick eight years ago, soon after the late earl's death and Tristan's return home. Angry with her brother for the years he'd stayed away and left her in the care of their indifferent father, she'd fought him at every turn, and had finally decided to teach him a lesson by running away.

It had been Peter along with his band of pickpockets, the Rag-Tag Bunch, who had taken her in off the streets, who had offered her shelter and taught her the art of picking pockets with the best of them. And it had been Peter who had listened to her endless complaints about Tristan and eventually made her see things from her brother's point of view. By the time Tristan had found her, she had come to the realization that he deserved a second chance and that she'd been far from innocent in their battle of wills.

It was through Tristan's search for her, she had discovered, that he had met Deirdre. He had enlisted the widow's aid to locate Emily, and the two had fallen in love. An angel of mercy for the people of the rookeries, Deirdre's past as a pickpocket had led to her dream of opening a home for former street urchins, and after her marriage to Tristan, that dream had become a reality.

And so Willow Park had been born, and the Rag-Tag Bunch had come to live there. From that moment on, Emily and Peter had been inseparable, and she had watched in awe as he had set out with fierce determination to better himself. Older than the rest of the children, he had found school lessons to be even more difficult for him than they were for the others, but he had never given up. Before long, he was reading and writing as well as Emily. He'd also managed to eradicate every last vestige of the Cockney accent he had spoken with for most of his life, though not without a struggle.

He had never seemed able to comprehend how very far he'd come, Emily thought now, resting her head against Artemis's side. But she'd seen it and had admired him all the more for it. And over time, their bond of friendship had grown and developed into something deeper, stronger.

In fact, she'd given him her heart.

She squeezed her eyes shut in remembered pain at how very foolish she'd been. She'd truly believed that

Peter had felt the same way, that all of the words of love they had exchanged, the sweet kisses and caresses they had shared, had meant just as much to him.

But in those last few weeks before Peter had left Willow Park, something had changed. She couldn't quite put her finger on the exact moment when it had happened, but suddenly he had become withdrawn, distant. She had felt him drifting away, and it had frightened her. Frightened her so much that it had tempted her into doing something altogether rash on the night of her eighteenth birthday. All in an effort to regain Peter's attention.

Well, she'd gotten his attention, that was certain. But it hadn't at all turned out the way she'd planned. They had come so close to making love that night, had shared the most passionate kiss she could ever remember indulging in.

Yet he'd slipped away before the dawn without even a farewell, leaving her heart shattered.

"What do you mean, not precisely?" Jenna's voice prompted with impatience. "Either you 'ad an argument or you didn't."

She waved her hand in a dismissive gesture, still not meeting her friend's eyes. She wasn't about to go into the details with Jenna and Miles. "Yes, I suppose you could say it was an argument. But I'd rather not talk about that now. I have far more important matters on my mind. Such as how I'm going to deal with all of this."

Miles shrugged. "I still think we should tell someone. Even if you don't trust Peter, you could still go to your brother. 'E'd know 'ow to take care of that devil."

Emily shook her head. "We can't do that, Miles, and

you know why." She was doing all this to protect Tristan. If he should find out that their whole lives might have been a lie . . .

Jenna laid a hand on her arm in sympathy. "Don't worry, Em. You'll find a way out of this. You always do."

"Right now I'd be happy just to figure out how to get through this evening." Emily looked up at the girl pleadingly. "I wish you'd change your mind and come with your parents tonight. It would make things much more bearable for me if you were going to be there."

"Sorry, but not bloody likely." Jenna gave her head a vehement shake. "There's no way in 'ell I'm getting all prettied up and prancing around like a blooming idiot."

"Why not?" Miles interjected, grinning wickedly in Jenna's direction. "It wouldn't 'urt you to act like a lady for once, you know. After all, you do tend to forget you're a female every now and again."

"Oh, bugger off!" Jenna groused, sending a fulminating glare in his direction. "Don't you 'ave better things to do than stand around offering unwanted advice?"

"It depends." He let his gaze travel down over her slender form clad in men's breeches and a simple broadcloth shirt. "But if you ask me, you need all the 'elp you can get."

Jenna started toward him in a menacing manner, but Emily caught her by the elbow, holding her back as the young man burst into laughter, then turned and strode out of the stall.

A growling noise emitted from deep in Jenna's throat as she pulled her arm from Emily's grasp and glowered after his departing form. "One of these days 'e's going to push me too far. As it is,'e's about to drive me bloody barmy. I don't know why 'e bothers to stick around 'ere instead of moving on like all the others."

Emily was relatively certain she knew why, though she doubted Jenna would want to hear it. Her friend had never seemed to have much use for men, and for the most part she acted as if she were completely oblivious to their charms. If Miles had any intentions in that direction, he would have his work cut out for him.

Turning with a sigh, she moved back to Artemis's side, raising a hand to pat the mare's neck. As if sensing her disquiet, the horse snorted and nudged her mistress's shoulder. "What am I going to do, Jenna? I have to figure out a way to avoid Peter as much as possible until this is all over. The less often I see him, the less chance there is that he'll catch on to what I'm up to."

Jenna eyed her doubtfully. "And just 'ow do you plan on doing that when 'e's right 'ere in the same 'ouse wiv you?"

That was a very good question, and one Emily currently had no answer for.

Why, oh, why had Tristan and Deirdre insisted upon him staying here at Knighthaven instead of at Willow Park as he had in the past? Having him underfoot was certain to make things that much more difficult for her, especially on the nights she had to slip out. Not to mention that having to see him every day was bound to stir up all of those old, tempestuous feelings she'd fought so long and so hard to forget. Feelings she had no desire to revisit.

"I have no idea, Jenna," she finally said aloud, lifting her chin with renewed resolve. "But I shall think of something."

She had to. She had no other choice.

Chapter 5

Peter reached up to give his cravat another impatient tug, then turned to face the mirror one last time, surveying his reflection with a critical eye.

Well, he wasn't precisely in the first stare of fashion, but he would do, he supposed, the corners of his mouth curving upward in a wry smile. The double-breasted coat of dark blue superfine and tan buckskin breeches had been purchased for the rare occasions when his job made it necessary for him to mingle with the more aristocratic members of society, but he had never felt comfortable wearing them, and tonight was no exception. They were the clothes of a gentleman, and that was something he had never professed to being.

He shook his head. If he had even half a mind, he would have continued to maintain that a dinner in his honor was not necessary, but one look at the countess's pleading expression and he'd been unable to say no.

"I want to thank you for going along with Deirdre's plans for this evening," Tristan had said to him once they had excused themselves and quit the parlor, leaving Lady Ellington and Lilah to their excited buzzing. "I know you've never enjoyed these sorts of things, but it's her way of distracting herself from her worry over the babe." The earl had given a rueful chuckle. "I've discovered it does little good to protest when she sets her mind to something. Far better to allow her to do as she wishes rather than fight it."

Perhaps that was true, Peter thought now with a slight grimace, but that didn't mean he was comfortable with the situation. At least tonight shouldn't be too much of a strain. He knew and liked everyone who would be present, and it might afford him the opportunity to speak with Benji and discover exactly what was going on in that quarter.

As for Emily, he hadn't seen a sign of her since they had all gone their separate ways earlier that morning, and he couldn't help but wonder if she might be deliberately avoiding him. If so, she likely had the right idea. They were both far better off if they stayed out of each other's way as much as possible.

Well, that was enough dragging his feet. The sooner he made his way downstairs to join the party, the sooner this evening would be over with. The sound of a carriage outside his bedroom window had signaled the arrival of the first of their guests a quarter of an hour ago, and he could not put it off any longer without seeming rude.

Straightening his shoulders, he turned on his heel and left the chamber.

The moment he stepped out into the hallway, the murmur of voices drifted up to him from downstairs, soft feminine laughter followed by a deep baritone. Hurrying his strides, he turned the corner onto the upstairs landing just in time to nearly run into someone coming from the opposite direction.

Words of apology hovering on his lips, he looked up to find himself staring into Emily's startled eyes. His breath left him in a rush, taking his request for forgiveness with it.

Dainty and delicate, she was a vision of beauty, as luminous as the moon that shone through the windows behind them, casting its pale light over her in an ethereal glow. Dressed in a full-skirted evening gown of palest blue silk shot through with strands of silver, and with her golden hair swept up in a mass of ringlets that tumbled about her heart-shaped face, she looked fey and innocent.

Untouchable.

He gave her a polite bow. "Lady Emily."

"Mr. Quick." The curtsy she offered him in return was stiff and not quite steady, and it gave him an odd feeling of satisfaction to know that he was capable of throwing her off balance. At least she wasn't indifferent to him. He thought he could stand anything but that. Even her hatred.

Unable to help himself, he let his gaze trail over her in a visual survey that was practically a caress, taking in the blond curls that clung to the slender line of her throat, the creamy expanse of skin bared by the low neckline of her gown. As he watched, a slow tide of pink crept into her cheeks, and he couldn't restrain the slight smile that curled his mouth at her response to his stare.

"You look lovely," he told her, his tone rife with a husky intimacy that he couldn't seem to quell.

She inclined her head in a gracious manner, though she continued to watch him with eyes that were shadowed with distrust. "Thank you, sir. You look quite dashing yourself."

He offered her his elbow. "Shall I escort you down, my lady?"

For a long moment, she didn't answer, merely stared at him with an unreadable expression. Then, just when he was certain she was going to refuse, she lifted her chin and slid her arm through his.

"Thank you, Mr. Quick," she murmured.

At her touch, Peter felt a sharp tingle shoot outward from the point of contact—even through the material of her glove. It spread throughout his body until every last one of his nerve endings seemed to be standing at attention, attuned to the woman next to him.

Sucking in a calming gust of air, he retreated behind a mask of reserve as he drew her with him down the stairs. "I trust you are quite recovered from your mishap this morning?" he inquired solicitously.

"Oh, yes. Quite. My ankle hasn't bothered me at all."

She paused for a moment, looking up at him from under lowered lashes. "By the way, I wanted to thank you for humoring Deirdre about tonight. I know you aren't looking forward to this, but it was most kind of you to agree to it."

The surprise in her voice annoyed him, and as a result he responded a bit more sharply than he intended. "I am capable of being kind, my lady. And I care for Lady Ellington a great deal. I would never do anything to hurt her."

She tensed next to him at the obvious reprimand, her eyes narrowing. "That's rather strange, Mr. Quick, considering that you've never seemed to be too concerned with those you've hurt in the past."

He winced. Damnation, but what was he to say to that? That he'd done it for her own good? She would never believe him.

As it happened, he didn't have to say anything at all. The two of them had reached the bottom of the stairs, and Emily dropped Peter's arm as if he were possessed of some contagious disease before sweeping off in the direction of the parlor, leaving him to trail along behind.

It was going to be a very long night.

Upon entering the parlor in Emily's wake, Peter was immediately greeted by Lilah, who waved him over to join her and her husband, Cullen.

"So,'ere is the guest of honor," the woman said with a wide smile. "I was beginning to think you'd run off again."

"Not yet," he said dryly, reaching out to shake Cullen's hand and exchange pleasantries before sending a glance in Emily's direction. As she stood chatting with Tristan, Deirdre, and the McLeans, the lamplight glittered in her golden hair and caressed the velvety curve of her cheek with a radiant glow, making her sparkle like the purest angel.

Too pure for the likes of you, Quick, he told himself firmly.

At that moment, Lady Ellington looked up and caught his eye. Smiling warmly, she excused herself from her husband's side before hurrying toward him.

"Benji is here," she informed Peter upon reaching him. She inclined her head in the direction of the fireplace, where a lone figure was ensconced in an armchair close to the hearth. "Perhaps you could go say hello."

Peter couldn't miss the hopeful look the countess sent him. So, Tristan was right. Deirdre was worried about the lad, as well.

He supposed he couldn't blame her. The brooding expression on Benji's face was so unlike his usual cheerful countenance that Peter couldn't help doing a double take. And if Deirdre hadn't pointed out his presence, he never would have noticed the boy was even there, he'd been so still and silent.

"Of course. I shall do so at once." Lowering his head in a brief nod to Deirdre, Lilah, and Cullen, he turned and approached Benji where he sat with his curly blond head bent over a book, his forehead wrinkled in concentration. Light from the lamp on the table next to him shone on the gilt lettering emblazoned across the cover.

A Detailed Accounting of Life in Ancient Rome.

Well, at least that much hadn't changed, Peter thought with some amusement. He couldn't remember the last time he'd seen the lad without his nose buried in a scholarly tome.

"Hello, Benji." He spoke in a low tone, his gaze never wavering from the gangly young figure slumped before him. In fact, he was watching so closely that he noticed the sudden stiffening of the boy's shoulders, the visible tightening of his fingers on the leather binding of the book.

Finally, after a pause of a second or two, the lad looked up at him, his brown eyes blinking in an owlish manner behind the lenses of his wire-framed spectacles, his face devoid of any emotion. "Hello, Peter."

Always before, Benji had greeted Peter as a much-loved elder brother, with hearty slaps on the back and excited exhortations to regale him with tales of his life as a Bow Street Runner. But not this time. The lad was cool, distant . . . and uneasy. It was there to see in his eyes, no matter how hard he tried to hide it.

Something was definitely wrong.

Unfolding his lanky frame from the depths of the armchair, the boy set aside his book and rose to his feet, studying Peter from under lowered lashes that conveniently veiled his thoughts. "It's been a while," he continued in a voice that had just started to deepen into the gravelly cadences of manhood.

"Yes, it has. I'm sorry for that."

"I expect you've been busy."

"And it seems you've been too busy to write."

Benji gave a careless shrug in answer. "Yes, I suppose so," he mumbled, glancing away.

When no further explanation was offered, Peter tried again. "I've missed your letters."

"I'm surprised you even noticed."

He had to suppress a guilty wince at the boy's words. "You know," he began, hoping that Benji could read the sincerity on his face, "just because I get a bit caught up in my work doesn't mean I don't care what is going on with you. And I hope you know that if anything is wrong—anything at all—you can always talk to me."

The lad's jaw set at a mutinous angle. "Who said anything was wrong?"

"No one in particular." Peter had to tread carefully here. He certainly didn't want Benji to resent Tristan or Deirdre for what he might interpret as their interference. "You just seem a bit . . . quiet."

"Well, everything is just fine. In fact, I've never been better."

"You're certain?"

"Of course. Wouldn't I say so if I wasn't?"

Peter didn't believe him for a moment, but before he could say anything else, Langley appeared in the doorway to announce that dinner was served.

As one, the others started to file out of the parlor, talking and laughing, though Deirdre cast one last concerned glance back at the two of them before she disappeared out the door on her husband's arm. Without hesitation, Benji took the opportunity to mutter an excuse and hurry after them as if the hounds of hell themselves were at his heels.

Oh, no, my good man, Peter thought with grim purpose. *I'm not done with you yet.*

Before he could take more than a step after the boy, however, Emily suddenly appeared in front of him, her dainty features pinched with anger.

"What did you say to him?" she hissed, her hands going to her hips in a defiant pose.

Peter's eyebrows rose. He had no desire to bicker with her, but Emily's accusatory tone put him on the defensive and prodded him into replying in a deliberately goading manner. "I'm sure I don't see where it's any business of yours."

Her cheeks pinkened with the flush of temper and she drew herself up, her violet eyes blazing. But instead of flying up into the boughs as he had expected, her voice when she spoke was soft and icy with disdain. "Benji is like a brother to me and I have every right to be concerned about your influence on him. I don't want to see him hurt. You must have said something to send him haring off in such a way."

Her words had him gritting his teeth against an overwhelming tide of frustration. Damn her, why must she always paint him as the villain? "I assure you, my lady, that I would never hurt Benji, and I said nothing of any importance. Perhaps he was hungry."

"Or perhaps he has finally discovered his hero is not the man he thought him to be."

"What are you talking about?"

"Heroes do not abandon the people they are supposed to care about. They do not go away and forget to write or forget to visit. Forget to care." Her voice quavered slightly and something vulnerable flashed in the depths of her eyes. Something that had him reaching out to her before he could help himself.

But she jerked back from his touch, her face hardening as she surveyed him with such scathing contempt that he flinched.

"Perhaps your defection has hurt more people than you know, Mr. Quick."

With that, she turned on her slippered heel and swept out of the room.

In the silence that lingered, Peter felt his pulse pounding in his ears and his breath escaped him in a rush.

It would be a long night, indeed.

Chapter 6

Would she never learn to control herself?

Quietly fuming, Emily sat at the dining room table, barely aware of the gay chatter going on around her as she thought back on her earlier encounter with Peter.

She had behaved like a child, she thought, feeling her cheeks heat with embarrassment. Hadn't she made up her mind that she wasn't going to let him goad her this evening? That she was going to be on her best behavior and ignore his presence as if it were of no consequence?

She should have known there would be no ignoring Peter.

She studied him where he sat at the far end of the table, deep in discussion with Tristan and the McLeans. Something her brother said must have struck him as humorous, because he threw his head back and laughed, a husky, pleasant sound that sent tingles running over her skin in reaction.

Dear Lord, did he have to be so very handsome? With his tawny hair tumbling over his brow in charming disarray, he possessed a boyish appeal that was hard to resist. But the way the soft blue material of his coat hugged his broad shoulders and leanly muscled physique like a second skin left little doubt that he was all man.

Her hands clenched into fists. She had to quit letting him stir up her emotions like this. Every time she allowed him to ruffle her calm façade, she wound up looking like a fool. Already tonight he'd managed to provoke her into confronting him like an irate fishwife over his interaction with Benji.

At the thought of the boy she'd always been so close to, she turned her attention to where he sat, using the silver tines of his fork to toy with the uneaten food on his plate. Like Tristan and Deirdre, Emily was concerned by his withdrawn behavior, but she was certain that badgering him about it would serve no useful purpose other than to alienate him further. It had been her fear that Peter had been doing just that, coupled with her worry over her own circumstances, that had led to her lashing out in such a manner.

You have to stop this, she scolded herself. *This is no way to convince the man that he no longer has the power to affect you!*

But she couldn't seem to help it.

"Tristan?" Deirdre suddenly spoke up from her seat next to Lilah, pulling Emily out of her ruminations.

"You never did tell us about your trip to London. Was it as terrible as you expected?"

"Worse, actually. Crowded and filthy and stifling." Tristan sent a smile in Emily's direction. "Not that I wouldn't like to see you find a husband, Em, but did I ever tell you how grateful I am to you for standing up to Aunt Rue and refusing a Season when she insisted on one for you?"

Emily squirmed in her seat as she felt Peter's eyes settle on her with unnerving intensity. "Yes, I do believe you've mentioned it once or twice."

Their father's sister, Ruella Palmer, Marchioness of Overton, was a stern lady who had never approved of Tristan as a guardian for Emily, or his marriage to Deirdre. But over the years, the woman had relented in her attitude and had tried to draw the family, especially Emily, back into London society. She had seemed determined to make an excellent match for her niece and had even offered to sponsor her for her expected comeout when she'd turned eighteen. But Emily had been just as determined not to be paraded before the eligible gentlemen of the *ton* like some brood mare up for auction. Wanting only her happiness, her brother had refused to coerce or pressure her in any way, and the marchioness had finally thrown her hands up in defeat.

"And Archer and Mrs. Godfrey?" the countess asked, raising an inquiring brow at her husband. "How are they?"

"The same as always." Tristan gave a reminiscent grin. "Each of them certain they are the one in charge and never hesitating to point it out to the other."

Elderly Archer had been the butler at the Ellington abode in London for as long as Emily could remember, and Mrs. Godfrey had been Deirdre's housekeeper when she'd first met Tristan. After the couple's marriage, Mrs. Godfrey had come to stay at the Ellington town house, and a battle of wills between the two stubborn retainers had ensued. Normally, Emily would have found her brother's tales of the servants' frequent standoffs amusing, but not now. At this moment, she was all too aware of Peter watching her, his expression unreadable.

As the meal progressed and the conversation continued, Emily found her attention drawn over and over again to the quiet, brooding man seated down the table from her. And by the time the ladies rose and excused themselves, leaving the gentlemen to their after-dinner port and cigars, she could only be grateful for the chance to escape. Unable to help herself, she cast one swift glance back over her shoulder as she departed the dining room, only to find Peter staring after her, the flickering of the candlelight that played over his lean visage giving his profile a hawklike appearance.

She suppressed a shiver.

Once back in the parlor, Lady Ellington led Lilah and Rachel McLean over to a grouping of chairs in front of the fireplace, where they seated themselves and continued their laughing conversation. Instead of joining them, however, Emily found herself wandering over to stare out the French doors, her mind a maelstrom of chaotic thoughts.

When had everything become so very complicated?

Up until a month ago, her life had been quiet and

fairly normal. She'd had her family and friends, as well as her work with the children of Willow Park. And if her existence in Little Haverton hadn't been all that exciting, at least she'd been content. But then her past had returned with a vengeance to turn her carefully ordered world upside down.

Now, on top of all that, she had Peter to contend with. Hugging herself against a sudden chill, she turned away from the window, only to find her attention caught and held by a portrait that hung above the sideboard on the far side of the room. Slowly, she drifted in that direction, her stare never wavering from the lines of the delicate face that had been so lovingly rendered.

It was a picture of her mother, Victoria Knight, the late Lady Ellington. Though she'd been only six-years of age at the time of her mother's murder, Emily could recall a laughing woman with violet eyes the same shade as her own and a gentle nature.

Much like Deirdre, the former countess had been a good Samaritan, using her spare time to minister to the needs of the poverty-stricken denizens of London's rookeries. It had been her work with these people that had led to her murder at the hands of street thieves, and the tragedy of her passing still affected all those who had known her, even after sixteen years.

By all accounts, Victoria Knight had been a kind and generous person, loving and unselfish. A veritable saint.

Dear Lord, had anyone ever truly known her? Was it possible that that innocent face had hidden a not-so-innocent heart?

"Emily?"

The soft voice at her elbow caused her to start and whirl about to find herself looking up at a concerned Deirdre.

"Emily, you've been standing here for quite some time. Are you all right, dear?"

Emily forced a smile to her face and quickly looked away, hoping her sister-in-law couldn't read the lie in her expression. "Yes. Yes, I'm fine." She gestured toward the portrait. "I was just thinking about my mother, wishing I could have known her better. Sometimes she seems so . . . distant to me. At least Tristan was older when she died. His memories of her are more clear than mine will ever be."

Deirdre joined her in studying the picture. "She was quite beautiful, wasn't she?" She reached out to tuck her arm through Emily's, drawing her close to her side. "According to your brother, she was just as beautiful on the inside. And she loved you both very much. You can take comfort in that."

There was a long silence, then Deirdre spoke again, her manner almost tentative. "Emily, dear, I don't want to pry, but I can't help but notice the strain between you and Peter whenever you're in each other's company."

Emily started to speak, but the countess forged onward, waving her free hand dismissively. "No. Please don't make excuses. I don't pretend to know what happened before he left for London that caused such a rift between the two of you, and I have no intention of asking, though it goes against my better judgment. However, I do want you to remember that he is here to help the people of Little Haverton, and if you could make some sort of effort, reach out to him just a little bit, then perhaps you could get past this initial . . . awkwardness."

Emily swallowed, casting her gaze down at the carpet as her heart seemed to suddenly increase its pace. "I rather doubt that, Deirdre."

The older woman turned and took a few steps away from the portrait, tugging Emily along with her. "Hadn't you mentioned earlier today that you planned on visiting Lord and Lady Tuttleston at some point tomorrow?"

"Yes, I did, but—"

"Perhaps if you would allow Peter to accompany you? He does need to speak with them regarding the break-in at their house, and they might be more comfortable answering his questions in your presence. You know how fond they are of you. And you might consider lending him your assistance in other aspects of his investigation, as well. I'm certain he could use your help, what with your knowledge of Little Haverton."

Emily stiffened. Deirdre wanted her to voluntarily spend time in Peter's company? She couldn't possibly know what she was asking. "That might not be such a good idea."

"Emily, please?" Deirdre's green eyes importuned her. "I hate to see you and Peter at odds when you used to be so close. Please, do this for your brother and me. We won't ask you for anything else, I promise."

Heavens, how could Emily possibly say no to such a heartfelt request? She took a fortifying breath. "Very well," she heard herself say, praying she was able to keep the trepidation she felt from coming through in her voice. "I'll speak to Peter about it when the opportunity presents itself. Perhaps after he's seen the constable in the morning."

"There's no time like the present." Deirdre inclined her head in the direction of the French doors. "He's out on the terrace."

Emily looked around, surprised to discover that she must have been so absorbed in her contemplation of her mother's portrait that she hadn't noticed when the gentlemen had rejoined them. Tristan, Cullen, and Angus McLean had seated themselves with the other ladies and were laughing at one of Lilah's remarks, while Benji had returned to the chair next to the fireplace and the book he'd been reading earlier.

The French doors where she'd been standing just a short time ago stood open to the warm night air.

Emily swallowed nervously. The mere thought of approaching Peter, alone on the terrace, in the dark, was enough to have gooseflesh breaking out across the exposed skin of her arms. "Perhaps this isn't the best time—"

Deirdre gave her a nudge toward the doors. "Go on. I'm sure he won't mind. He'll more than likely be grateful for your offer of help."

Emily wasn't so certain about that, but she started across the parlor with measured steps, mentally shoring up her courage. Maybe this wasn't such a bad idea, she tried to convince herself. After all, if she stuck close to Peter, accompanied him on his interviews, she could keep track of where he was in his investigation.

And make certain he didn't get too close to the truth.

She shrugged off another pang of guilt. She would not allow herself to feel ashamed over doing what needed to be done in order to preserve her family.

Straightening her shoulders, she stepped out onto the terrace.

Peter leaned back against the stone balustrade with an exhalation of air, enjoying the light breeze that brushed against his face. This was more like it. Out here he felt better able to breathe. Inside the house had been stifling.

Not that he hadn't been glad for the chance to catch up with the people who had made such a difference in his life. Lilah was as amusing as always, and it was nice to see the McLeans and Benji, despite the boy's less than receptive mood.

And Emily . . .

He closed his eyes and tilted his head back. Even with the resentful glares she had thrown his way throughout dinner, that lovely profile had drawn his gaze, and his pulse had sped up every time those misty violet eyes met his.

He couldn't deny he deserved her ire. Apparently he'd hurt her far more with his defection four years ago than he'd even suspected.

Turning, he gripped the railing with both hands, his hold tightening until his knuckles turned white. The smell of jasmine drifted to him from the garden beyond the terrace, teasing his senses with its exotic fragrance.

Out there, just past the expertly trimmed boxwood

hedges, near the copse of elms that stood sentinel next to the central fountain, was the spot where he had once almost made love to Emily.

His mouth went dry with remembrance. He could still visualize the way she had looked that night, with her hair tousled about her shoulders and her lips swollen by his savage kisses. The sound of her breathy moans and soft sighs echoed in his head as if it had happened only yesterday.

"Love me, Peter my darling . . ."

"Peter?"

The voice floated to him like a continuation of his memories, and for a brief moment he thought he was still lost in the past.

"Peter? Are you there?"

It was louder this time, jerking him from his haze, and as he whirled to face the house, he saw Emily step out of the darkness and into the path of a stray moonbeam that spilled across the terrace.

This was no memory. She was all too real.

Immediately, he smoothed his features into a mask of cool composure and shoved his hands in his pockets, attempting to project a façade of casual nonchalance that he was far from feeling. This woman had already proven that she was all too adept at stealing past his defenses, and he couldn't afford to let down his guard with her. Not even for an instant. "Lady Emily? What are you doing out here?"

"Looking for you." She moved toward him, her skirts making a hushed swishing sound on the stones beneath her feet. Coming to a halt not far away, she stared up at him with eyes that were opaque in the dimness, giving him no clue as to her thoughts. "I need to speak with you."

"And here you gave me the impression earlier that you'd be quite happy if you never had to speak to me again."

"Yes, well, that's what I wanted to talk to you about. My behavior this evening has been inexcusable, and I owe you an apology."

To say he was shocked would have been an understatement, and he knew his astonishment must show on his face despite his best efforts to hide it. *She* was apologizing to *him*? "Will wonders never cease?"

Emily's mouth tightened visibly at his reaction. "You needn't look so incredulous. I do know how to admit when I'm in the wrong. Regardless of our . . . differences, I know you would never deliberately set out to hurt Benji, and I had no right to accuse you of it. It's just—" She paused for a moment, glancing down at her hands clasped in front of her. "You were right this morning. Your presence here has made things a bit . . . awkward."

"It was never my intention—"

She halted him with a shake of her head. "I'm aware of that. The fact remains, however, that we've been placed in a rather uncomfortable situation, and we need to learn to deal with it—and each other—in a civilized manner. To that end, I have decided to lend you my assistance in your investigation."

What the bloody hell? "Your assistance?"

"Yes. I plan on visiting the Tuttlestons tomorrow, and I

know you'll need to interview them regarding the break-in. Deirdre thought they might be more comfortable if I was there when you questioned them, since I know them so well. And I might be able to ease your way with some of the other people you'll need to speak with."

It took a second for Peter to register what she was saying, for her words to finally come together to make some sort of sense in his mind. Emily help *him*? When they couldn't even be in the same room for more than five minutes without striking sparks off each other?

"I don't think that would be a good idea—" he began, but she cut him off before he could finish his protest, her tone firm.

"I do. This thief needs to be caught, and if I can help you in some way, then I would like to do so."

She took another step in his direction, and her scent wafted to him on the night air, a hint of roses that sent his blood racing through his veins in response. "Unless . . ." She drew the word out slowly, her prim expression changing to one of speculation as she looked up at him from under lowered lashes. "You can think of a reason why I shouldn't?"

He had to give her credit, Peter thought, studying her through narrowed eyes. She certainly didn't lack for audacity. But then, she never had. "It could be dangerous."

"Nonsense. I'm not suggesting that I be there when you track the man down. Only that I be present to help smooth things over when you're speaking to the witnesses and victims. You know how the citizens of Little Haverton can be, especially the local aristocracy." She tilted her head, the moonlight spilling across the fragile purity of her angelic features, giving her skin an alabaster glow. "And surely you can protect me in the unlikely circumstance that something should happen?"

Peter's hands tightened into fists in his pockets. As much as the thought of working with her troubled him, he knew she had a point about the people of Little Haverton. They more than likely would feel more comfortable answering his questions if she was at his side.

But just how was he supposed to be able to maintain his distance if she was constantly in his company, *helping* him with his investigation?

As if sensing his reluctance to agree, she reached out to lay a small hand on his arm. Though the touch was light and fleeting, it branded him as thoroughly as if she'd pressed a hot iron against his flesh. "Come now, Mr. Quick. We're both adults. Surely for Deirdre's sake we can manage to maintain a modicum of civility toward each other, at least long enough to see this through." A slight smile curved her rosy lips, teasing and almost seductive. "Of course, if you don't think you can handle working with me . . ."

That did it. Emily's coy manner and challenging words finally succeeded in bringing Peter's temper to the fore.

In an unexpected movement that had her eyes going wide in surprise, Peter closed the distance that remained between them and leaned over until his face was mere inches from hers. "I'm certain that I'm perfectly capable of handling any . . . difficulties which may arise," he assured her in a silken purr. "The question is, my lady, are you?"

He felt her stiffen, the material of her skirts brushing up against his breeches in a tantalizing fashion. He was so close he could see the rapid flutter of her pulse in the side of her throat, could feel the soft caress of her breath against his lips. If he lowered his head just the slightest fraction, he could discover for himself if she still tasted just as sweet as he recalled . . .

Emily blinked and jerked backward as if stung, breaking the spell, and Peter let her go. For a moment he'd gotten far too caught up for comfort in the sensual tension that arced between them.

Neither of them said a word for what seemed like a small eternity. Then Emily lifted her chin and spoke with a firm resolve. "I can handle anything you can, Mr. Quick."

He managed a careless shrug in response. "If you say so."

"Good. Then it's settled. We'll both head out tomorrow morning to see the Tuttlestons as soon as you finish with the constable." With a toss of her golden curls, she spun on her heel and marched away, sending him one last veiled glance over her shoulder before disappearing back through the French doors.

So much for staying out of each other's way.

Chapter 7

Emily descended the stairs early the next morning, filled with a renewed sense of purpose.

She had spent most of the night contemplating her new plan of attack, and the more she thought about it, the more she had come to believe it was the best option. If she was going to be forced into spending time with Peter, then she might as well use the opportunity to turn things to her own advantage.

Peter could not be allowed to discover her role as the Oxfordshire Thief. Not yet. Not until she, Jenna, and Miles had had a chance to ascertain once and for all if the piece of information her tormentor was holding over her head was the truth, or another lie. Once they had accomplished that, Emily had every intention of making certain that the Tuttlestons, the Fulberrys, and anyone else who had suffered at the thief's hands received their stolen property back, and that the villain who had caused all this pain was punished.

And then she would gladly accept the consequences of her own actions, whatever they may be.

In the meantime, she would have to get past the anger she still felt toward Peter and play the gracious companion. There could be no more tantrums, no more outbursts or accusations. She would be civil if it killed her!

A recollection of the way he had so gently explored her ankle yesterday morning rushed through her, making her shiver, and she pushed it away. It wasn't so easy, however, to rid herself of the memory of those blue eyes looking down on her on the terrace last night, full of a heated awareness and something else, something that had her heart skipping a beat in response.

Emily closed her eyes, giving her head a hard shake to dislodge her disconcerting thoughts. She couldn't afford to let herself think about Peter this way. Not now.

Not ever again.

As she reached the bottom of the stairs, the faint murmur of male voices drifted to her from the parlor, and she glanced in that direction. One of the voices seemed unfamiliar, and she couldn't help feeling a faint twinge of curiosity.

She hailed the butler as he entered the foyer. "Langley? Has the constable arrived?"

"Yes, my lady. He is with Lord Ellington and Master Peter in the parlor. I believe they are discussing the particulars of the thefts."

Emily bit her lip. Should she join them? She was dying to hear what the constable had uncovered in his investigation, but somehow she doubted the gentlemen would appreciate her presence.

Before she could come to a decision, there was a sharp rap at the front door, and Langley opened the heavy oak portal to admit Adam, Lord Moreland.

Adam Carver, Viscount Moreland, was the son of their neighbor, the Marquis of Brimley. Tall and handsome with thick, wavy blond hair and deep-set hazel eyes, the young lord had been a frequent visitor to Knighthaven since he'd returned from Oxford almost two years ago. Emily considered him a good friend, for he had always treated her with respect and had never seemed to judge her for her fierce need to be independent, as the rest of Little Haverton did.

However, in the past few months she'd noticed a slight change in Adam's attitude toward her. He'd become even more attentive than usual, and she'd caught him watching her more than once with an assessing expression. It was a well-known fact that Lord Brimley, an elderly gentleman of failing health, had been pressuring his son for some time now to choose a wife, and Emily was very much afraid that the viscount had settled on her as a likely candidate.

For some reason, the idea filled her with a sense of panic she couldn't explain. As fond as she was of Adam, she found she had no desire to wed him.

But then, she had no desire to wed anyone. Her heart had been far too trampled for her to ever trust a man that much again.

A smile tilted up the corners of Adam's chiseled

mouth as he caught sight of Emily hovering at the bottom of the stairs.

"There you are." Handing off his gloves and hat to Langley, he strode forward, catching her hands in his. "Just the person I wanted to see."

"Oh?" Emily returned his smile, for as much as his measured looks and hints at a marriage between them had plucked at her anxiety lately, she truly was glad to see him. Adam had always been good at taking her mind off her troubles, and right now that was just what she needed.

"I thought I'd come by and see if you would be interested in going for a ride in the phaeton with me. It's a perfect day to head down to the lake and perhaps have a picnic, and I know how much you enjoy that. We could stop by Brimley Hall on the way and have the cook pack us something if you'd like."

"I'm sorry, Adam, but I'm afraid I already have plans. I promised Lord and Lady Tuttleston I would pay them a call this morning, and I wouldn't want to disappoint them."

Something shifted in the viscount's expression and the smile faded from his face. "Instead you would rather disappoint me?"

"Of course not. You know—"

But Adam interrupted her, crossing his arms across his broad chest with a frown. "You know, Emily, I'm beginning to become quite put out with you. Every time I've asked you to accompany me somewhere in the last few weeks, you've had some excuse why you cannot do so. If I didn't know any better, I'd say you've been avoiding me."

Emily felt a sharp jab at his words. It was true. She *had* been avoiding him. But before she could think of a way to convince him otherwise and soothe his wounded ego, the door to the parlor suddenly flew open and Peter strode out into the foyer. He was followed by Lord Ellington and a thin stick of a man with straggly brown hair liberally streaked with gray and a bony face behind a pair of wire-framed spectacles.

Constable Jenkins.

"I appreciate your time, Constable, and the information," Peter was saying as he led the way to the door. "And I can assure you if I turn up anything at all in the investigation, I'll be certain to let you know."

The older man sent him a hooded glance, his eyebrows lowered in a fierce scowl. "I still say with a little more time we could have the scoundrel behind bars without any help from Bow Street."

"We do not doubt that, Constable Jenkins," Tristan interceded smoothly. "But at this point, I believe that the more men we have on the case, the better. After all, it is for the good of Little Haverton."

The constable sniffed. "If you ask me, you don't need to look any farther than the Park. Those children are former vagabonds and street thieves, all of them, and if one of those boys isn't responsible, I'll eat my hat."

Emily went cold all over with guilt. There it was again. The accusations against the children of Willow Park. She hated that her actions had turned the suspicious eyes of the law in their direction. They had enough problems getting past the time they had spent on the streets without having to deal with that, as well.

She watched as Peter's eyes narrowed and he took a step in the constable's direction, his manner menacing. "Do you have any proof of that, Jenkins?"

The man blinked and shifted his weight nervously. "No, I can't say that I do."

"Then it might be best if you don't go accusing anyone until you have all the facts. After all, I was once one of those *vagabonds* you mention, and I might take offense."

"Yes, well, er . . . As you say."

Tristan stepped past the two men to open the door, his countenance as dour as Peter's. "I'm certain you must have things you should be about, Constable. Don't let us keep you any longer. And as Mr. Quick said, we will keep you updated about the case if you will do the same."

"Of course, my lord. Good day to you. And to you, Mr. Quick." Constable Jenkins bowed his head to each of them in turn, his face mottled with suppressed anger, then took his leave.

As Tristan closed the door behind him, Peter turned away with a disgusted shake of his head. Good riddance! The man had been nothing but sullen and hostile since he'd arrived, and he had provided them with the requested information regarding the Oxfordshire thefts only grudgingly. Just as he had suspected in the beginning, the local authorities were not going to prove to be a source of much support in his investigation, especially if they had made up their minds that one of the boys at Willow Park was responsible for the crimes.

At that moment, as he raised his head to speak to Tristan, he noticed Emily and a blond gentleman standing at the foot of the staircase, observing the proceedings in silence. Emily's eyes were full of dismay, while her companion's were rife with speculation.

Peter disliked the man on sight. Tall and elegant, he was the utter personification of an arrogant young lord, and there was something about the way he hovered over Emily in such a proprietary and possessive fashion that put Peter's back up.

Tristan saw them at the same time and crossed the foyer with a smile of welcome, grasping the young man's hand in a firm handshake. "Hello, Moreland. I'm sorry. I didn't notice you standing there."

"That's quite all right, Lord Ellington. You were otherwise occupied." The gentleman cast a glance back over his shoulder at Emily before turning to Peter. "Em, aren't you going to introduce me to your . . . guest?"

"Of course." Though she appeared somewhat reluctant, Emily came forward to perform the introductions. "Mr. Quick, this is our good friend, the Viscount Moreland. His father is our neighbor, the Marquis of Brimley. And Adam, allow me to make known to you Mr. Peter Quick, a former resident of Willow Park."

"Ahhhh."

Peter clenched his teeth at the knowing tone. He wasn't certain what it was about the man's reaction that grated on his nerves. It wasn't as if he'd never run into that sort of attitude before. As a matter of fact, it was the usual response whenever someone realized he'd once lived in a home for former street children. But for some reason, Moreland's superior demeanor made him long to rearrange those bloody perfect features with a display of pugilistic expertise.

"Mr. Quick is a Bow Street Runner." Tristan stepped into the breach, the pride in his voice evident.

"A Runner, you say?" Moreland's interest seemed to perk up. "So you're the one the boy Benji is always talking about."

The viscount's statement piqued Peter's curiosity and he studied the other man closely. "You know Benji?"

"Of course. He's a frequent visitor to Knighthaven. As am I."

There was no mistaking the implication, or the subtle way the fellow shifted just a bit closer to Emily, almost as if staking a claim.

Peter's hands tightened into fists at his sides. He should be gladdened by this development, he thought. After all, Moreland was just the sort of man he'd always wanted for her. A true gentleman. A viscount and the future Marquis of Brimley.

But then why did the mere idea of the two of them together make his temper soar?

"Lord Moreland! What a pleasant surprise."

At the sound of the warm greeting, Peter looked up to see Lady Ellington making her way down the stairs, the mound of her belly preceding her like the prow of a ship. As she neared the bottom, she reached out to accept her husband's outstretched hand and stood on tiptoe to press a kiss on his cheek before facing the viscount once again. "How nice to see you. It's been too long since your last visit."

"Yes. Yes, it has." Lord Moreland looked at Emily, and Peter couldn't help but note the way she colored and glanced down at the floor. A tension seemed to vibrate in the air between the two of them, a tension that had Peter wondering just what he, Tristan, and the constable could have possibly interrupted with their entrance earlier.

His jaw tautened as a sudden vision of Emily and Moreland passionately entwined crossed his mind's eye, but he pushed it away with vehement force.

It's no longer any of your concern, a warning voice sounded in his head. But he knew convincing himself of that was another matter entirely.

"And how is your father?" the countess asked, drawing the man's attention away from Emily and back to her.

"Not well, I'm afraid. His health has deteriorated a great deal in recent weeks, and I must admit I've been concerned. His physician has given strict instructions that he is not to leave his bed."

"I'm so sorry to hear that. Please pass on my good wishes to him."

"I shall. Thank you, my lady."

Deirdre looked up at her husband. "Has the constable been here already?"

Tristan grimaced. "Unfortunately."

"Oh, dear. Was he uncooperative?"

"You might say that. He's still convinced one of the children at Willow Park is responsible, and he made it very clear that any help we receive from him will be reluctant, at best."

The countess turned troubled eyes on Peter. "I'm sorry, dear."

He gave a nonchalant shrug, though he couldn't deny he felt touched by her concern. "It's nothing less than I expected, my lady."

"Still, that's no excuse at all for the man's rudeness." Deirdre glanced at Lord Moreland. "We have asked Mr. Quick to look into the case of the Oxfordshire Thief."

The viscount's hazel eyes narrowed a fraction and he met Peter's gaze with an unreadable expression. "Really? How interesting."

Peter didn't bother to reply, merely returned the viscount's stare with a steady one of his own.

No, he did not like this man at all.

"Well, let us turn to more pleasant matters, shall we?" Deirdre said brightly. "Lord Moreland, perhaps you would like to join us for breakfast?"

Peter felt a surge of relief when the man shook his head. "I thank you for the offer, my lady, but I had a bite to eat before I left Brimley Hall this morning." He cast another hooded glance at Emily. "I truly only stopped by to see if Lady Emily would accompany me for a short ride, but as she appears to have other plans today, I suppose I should be on my way."

Emily, who had been a quiet, unobtrusive presence in the background all this time, took an abrupt step forward and slid her arm through Moreland's. "Please, Adam?" She glanced up at him from under lowered lashes, one corner of her lips turning up in an almost impish smile. "Won't you change your mind? You just got done saying we haven't had much of a chance to see each other lately. I would love to have you join us."

The viscount contemplated her for a long moment, then seemed to come to some sort of decision, for he inclined his head in a nod and gave her a charming grin that encompassed the earl and countess, as well.

And completely disregarded Peter.

"Since you ask so nicely, I'd be delighted to stay for breakfast," he replied, his gaze never wavering from Emily's piquant face.

"How marvelous!" Deirdre beamed. "I'll have a footman set an extra place at the table at once."

As she led Tristan off in the direction of the dining room and Emily fell in behind, still clinging to Lord Moreland's arm, Peter gritted his teeth and followed in their wake. Damnation! Emily was part of his past and he had accepted that long ago. It should no longer matter to him who she spent her time with, who she laughed and flirted with.

But it did. And as he saw her send the handsome viscount another brilliant smile, a small, undeniable flame of jealousy ignited in his heart.

Chapter 8

Over two hours later, as Peter trotted his horse along the road toward the home of Lord and Lady Tuttleston, he couldn't help studying Emily out of the corner of his eye as she rode beside him.

She had been strangely silent since they had departed Knighthaven, quite different from the laughing, animated creature who had chatted with Lord Moreland at the breakfast table. In fact, he didn't think she'd once met his eyes since they had all run into each other in the foyer and she had strolled off with the viscount in such a blithe fashion.

At the reminder of the haughty young lord, Peter felt his cheeks heat with temper once more and his hands tightened on the reins, causing his mount to do an impatient dance beneath him.

He drew in a deep, calming breath. He had to stop doing this. But no matter how often he tried to tell himself that Emily was no longer any of his business, it didn't seem to diminish his need to know just exactly what was going on between her and the viscount.

The question was out before he could call it back. "Have you known Lord Moreland long?"

Emily started as if she had forgotten his presence and looked up, blinking at him in an almost owlish manner. Then, reaching up to tuck a stray curl back behind her ear, she fixed her eyes on the road ahead when she replied, as if she couldn't bear to hold his gaze for too long. "I've known *of* him since I was a child. My father knew his father, Lord Brimley, very well, and our mothers were good friends. But Adam and I have only been personally acquainted for a couple of years now."

Adam. She had known the man for only two years and she called him Adam, while Peter was "Mr. Quick." Despite himself, that fact troubled him far more than it should.

"The two of you seem close."

"I suppose we are. He has been a good friend to me." She glanced down at her hands on the reins. "So many people can be kind to your face and then whisper about you behind your back. But Adam isn't like that."

Though her visage remained dispassionate, Peter could sense the hurt that lurked just beneath that impassive façade. Her family's unconventional past, as well as their connection to Willow Park, had always been prime fodder for gossip, and obviously it bothered Emily more than she would ever admit.

A part of him didn't want to know the answer, but something beyond his own volition seemed to be driving him. "And do you and Moreland have an . . . understanding?"

Emily paused for a second, appearing to be considering her answer as she nibbled on her lower lip, then shook her head. "I'm not certain."

Not certain? What the bloody hell did that mean?

Emily noticed the bemused expression that crossed Peter's face and couldn't blame him. She was feeling a bit bemused herself. What manner of devil had tempted her to flirt so shamelessly with Adam? For some reason, watching the two men size each other up like potential foes had set off a spark of mischief inside her and she had acted before she'd thought.

But she had forgotten that for every action there was a consequence, and now the viscount was certain to have all sorts of false expectations regarding their relationship, expectations she had no intention of fulfilling. She felt her cheeks flush. Somehow she would have to think of a way to explain her behavior to Adam and hope he would understand.

But that would come later. Right now she had to concentrate on dealing with Peter.

And it was time to change the subject. "You know, you haven't said much about your life in London."

Peter seemed surprised at the abrupt shift in the conversation, but he didn't bother to call her on it. He merely lifted one shoulder in a slight shrug. "That's because there's nothing much to say."

"Nothing much to say?" Emily gaped at him. "Come

now. Surely your life must be very exciting. Catching thieves and murderers and the like. Why, the boys at Willow Park think you're practically a hero."

When he said nothing in response, she pressed on, studying his profile intently. "Why a Bow Street Runner?"

"Why not?" Another shrug. "I just happened to be in the right place at the right time, I suppose."

"The right place?"

"When I first returned to London, I managed to find a job on the docks, loading cargo onto ships. I had a room at one of the boardinghouses nearby, and I was just leaving for work one morning when I walked right into the middle of a scuffle between a Bow Street officer and a fugitive he was trying to apprehend. I lent a hand, and I suppose the officer felt I showed an aptitude for the job. He offered to see if he could get me on at Bow Street, and here I am."

Emily suspected there was much more to the tale than that, but she didn't prod him any further. "You were very young."

"The youngest one in the office at the time. But they started me off as more of an errand boy, really. It wasn't until I was a little older and I had proven myself that they let me start taking on my own assignments."

"And is there anyone back in the city *you* have . . . an understanding with?"

She couldn't have halted herself from asking the question if she'd tried, and she felt her heart skip a beat as those blue eyes swung in her direction, searing her with their intensity.

For a long moment, there was nothing but silence between them. Then his mouth curved in a slow, taunting grin. "I'm not certain."

Emily gritted her teeth. Of course, the beast would throw her own answer back at her. Oh, well. It was not as if she truly cared to know.

Did she?

Peter's smile suddenly faded and he looked away. "How much farther is it to the Tuttleston estate?"

"Not far. Less than a mile, I would expect."

"Good. Perhaps we should pick up the pace a bit. I have much to do today."

Before she could say a word, he had nudged his horse into a faster trot and pulled ahead of her.

Oh, of all the— No. She would not let her temper be roused by his abruptness. It was better when he was like this, for it helped her to keep their association on a businesslike footing, to remember that he was not the man she'd once believed him to be.

But as she prodded Artemis to catch up to him, she found herself missing the warmth of that all too brief smile.

Emily and Peter arrived at the Tuttleston home to be greeted with genuine warmth by the viscount and viscountess. Having no children of their own, Lord and Lady Tuttleston were especially fond of Emily, and her weekly visits had become a ritual they all looked forward to.

After she had introduced Peter and explained his reason for accompanying her, the viscountess led the way to the sitting room, where a maid was busy laying out a tray of tea and buttered scones.

"I'm afraid I shall have to ask you to play mother and pour the tea, my dear," Lady Tuttleston told Emily as they all seated themselves and the servant departed. "My hands aren't quite as steady as they used to be."

Emily moved to comply with the woman's request, feeling her heart clutch with sympathy. Lord and Lady Tuttleston were kind people who didn't deserve the pain this theft had put them through. The necklace that had been stolen from them had been a much-prized family heirloom passed down through generations of Lord Tuttleston's family. Though it would bring thousands of pounds on the market, it was worth far more to the Tuttlestons than its mere monetary value.

Viscount Tuttleston, a rotund, jovial little man with a shock of pure white hair and twinkling blue eyes, interlocked his fingers on the pudgy mound of his belly and studied Peter over the tops of his spectacles. "So, you're a former Willow Park boy, eh?"

Emily couldn't help but notice the way Peter stiffened in his seat, the careful blankness that crossed his features before he nodded his head in the affirmative. "Yes, my lord, I am."

"A Bow Street Runner now, you say?"

"Yes, my lord."

"Good. Good for you. One of their elite, too, I hear." The elderly gentleman's tone was approving. "That's just what those children need to see. Someone like them who can rise above his past and make something of himself. It will give them something to strive for."

"Oh, yes." Lady Tuttleston gave an emphatic nod of agreement, her gray curls bouncing beneath the edge of her lace cap. "I can't tell you how much I admire your brother and his wife, Emily, for their determination to see Willow Park flourish. All those poor, dear children . . . And such a noble and worthy cause. I often say so, don't I, Henry?"

"Yes, indeed you do, my dear. And you're quite right. It's one of the reasons I make such a large donation to the home each year." The viscount winked at Emily.

She barely contained a flinch. It was true. When her family had first returned to Little Haverton, the proper funds for rebuilding and establishing Willow Park hadn't been easy to come by. The late earl had vastly depleted the Ellington coffers with his weakness for drinking and gambling, and it had taken several years for Tristan to recoup the wealth their father had lost. It had been people like the Tuttlestons, who had thrown their support behind the home and donated generously to the cause—and continued to do so—who had made it all possible and allowed Deirdre's dream to come true.

Just another reason for Emily to feel guilty.

She was grateful when Peter changed the subject. "My lord, my lady, as much as I hate to bring up a painful topic, I do need to ask you a few questions about the night of the theft."

Lady Tuttleston set aside her cup of tea and turned to face him. "Of course. Although I doubt we'll be of much help. And we've already told the constable every-thing we know."

Emily, seated next to the viscountess on the brocade-upholstered love seat, watched as Peter gave the woman a smile. "I'm sure you have, my lady. But some-times a fresh eye in these matters can be of help."

"Yes, yes. Quite right." Lord Tuttleston inclined his head in agreement. "Go right ahead, my lad."

"Perhaps you could start by filling me in on your whereabouts on the evening the theft occurred."

Lady Tuttleston pursed her lips. "Why, we were vis-iting Henry's sister in Compton, a few miles away." She leaned toward Emily in a confiding manner. "It was Wednesday evening, you know, and we always visit her on Wednesday evenings."

Peter's eyes narrowed. "So, this is a trip you make regularly?"

"Like clockwork for the last several years, ever since my sister's husband passed on," the viscount explained. "She gets lonely in that huge old house by herself, don't you know, so Roberta and I usually give the ser-vants Wednesday evening off, except for a mere skele-ton staff, and make the trek to Compton."

"So it's possible the thief was aware the house would be practically empty on a Wednesday night, with few servants about to stumble upon him as he went about his business," Peter mused, his forehead furrowing as he contemplated this bit of information. After a mo-ment, he swung his gaze from the viscountess to Lord Tuttleston. "And who was the first to discover the theft?"

"That would be Lady Tuttleston." The viscount gestured toward his wife. "As soon as we arrived home, she went upstairs to make ready for bed. The next thing I knew, she was screaming fit to wake the dead. Made my old heart skip a few beats, I can tell you that."

Lady Tuttleston's usually merry brown eyes suddenly swam with tears. "I saw the open window almost the moment I entered my bedchamber, and I knew I hadn't left it that way. It frightened me, and it didn't take me long to notice that the lid to the jewelry box that sat on my vanity was open, as well."

She sniffled, and Emily felt her throat constrict as she covered the elderly lady's hand with her own.

"I knew the necklace was gone as soon as I looked inside," the viscountess continued sorrowfully. "I blame myself. I should have let Henry put it in the safe long ago, but I so loved to wear it."

The viscount leaned forward in his seat and pressed a handkerchief into his wife's hands. "There, there, dear. You mustn't take on so. It isn't your fault."

"It is! Oh, Henry, your great-grandmother's necklace!"

As the tears slipped free and spilled down Lady Tuttleston's wrinkled cheeks, Emily felt helpless to do anything for the woman but pat her hand in a comforting manner.

After a moment of silence, Peter spoke again in a soft, soothing tone. "Lady Tuttleston, was anything else taken?"

The viscountess shook her head. "A few baubles, but

nothing of as much worth to us as the necklace. It's been in Henry's family for several generations, you see."

"And the authorities are certain the thief gained entry through the window?"

The viscount looked uncharacteristically grim as he watched his wife weep. "That's what the constable seems to believe. The vile devil apparently scaled the tree outside our bedchamber and picked the lock."

"Would you mind showing me this tree?" Peter asked, getting to his feet.

Lord Tuttleston started to rise, but Emily waved him back into his seat. "Please, my lord. Don't trouble yourself. I know where it is, and I'll be happy to show Mr. Quick the way."

The viscount gave a grateful sigh. "Thank you, Emily, my dear."

As Emily stood, Peter stopped for a moment in front of the viscountess and caught her hand in his, bowing low over it before pressing a kiss to the gnarled knuckles. "I thank you and your husband for indulging me today, my lady. And I promise you, I intend to bring this thief to justice. Your necklace will be found and returned to you. You have my word on that."

He brushed past Emily on his way to the sitting room door, and she cast one last glance back at the elderly couple as the viscount moved to sit next to his wife, wrapping an arm around her shaking shoulders.

Would they ever be able to forgive her?

Would anyone?

She turned and left the room.

*   *   *

"I still don't understand how actually seeing the tree is going to help you," Emily said for the second time in as many minutes as she led the way around the corner of the house. "The theft occurred weeks ago, so surely any evidence that might have been left behind would be long gone by now?"

Peter glanced at her rigid spine as she marched along in front of him. "Possibly. We shall see."

"And you must know the constable and his men have been over every inch of these grounds. If there was something to find, I'm certain they would have discovered it."

In Peter's opinion, Constable Jenkins couldn't have found his own nose in a dark room, even with a lantern and a mirror to aid him. He doubted any search the man had performed would have been very thorough, but he decided to keep that thought to himself. "Perhaps."

"Could you be any more vague?" Emily tossed over her shoulder in an irritated tone.

"That depends."

She stopped so abruptly he almost ran into her back, then she whirled to face him, crossing her arms over her chest. The action pulled the material of her lavender day dress taut across the mounds of her breasts, pressing the pale, rounded globes upward until they threatened to spill over the top of her normally modest, lace-edged neckline.

Peter's mouth went dry.

"You know, Mr. Quick," she told him, studying him

from under lowered lashes. "I have the distinct impression that you're making fun of me, and I don't like it."

"I would never make fun of you, Lady Emily," he said, his tone solemn. "I would never take my life in my hands in such a fashion."

She examined him for a long moment, then gave a sniff and started to turn back around. As she did so, however, her foot appeared to catch on something and she stumbled forward, a startled cry escaping her lips.

Reacting without thought, Peter reached out and caught her about the waist, hauling her to him in an attempt to steady her.

And knew immediately he'd made a mistake.

At the sensation of all those lush curves pressed up against him, he felt the breath seize in his chest and a surge of lust lick along his nerve endings. His hold on her tightened without his volition, and for just a second he was tempted to lay her down in a nearby patch of sunlight, peel off that gown, and cover her sweet body with his own.

Their gazes locked, and Peter could have sworn he saw an answering flare of desire in the depths of Emily's eyes before she quickly dropped a veil over them and lifted her chin with haughty aplomb.

"You can let me go now, Mr. Quick. I'm quite all right."

"Yes. Of course." He knew he should. He wanted to. But for some reason his hands were slow in receiving the message.

When he finally succeeded in convincing his fingers

to loosen their grip, Emily wasted no time in putting some much-needed distance between them. Casting him one last wary look, she dusted off her skirts, spun, and continued on her way.

Peter fell in behind her, letting the breath he'd been holding finally gust out from between his teeth in an inaudible whistle. This woman's effect on him was lethal!

Damnation, but what was it about Lady Emily Knight that made what had once passed between them so hard to forget?

It certainly wasn't as if he hadn't tried. Since his return to London, he'd lived a far from celibate lifestyle, and he'd been involved with several women over the years. But while they had relieved the physical ache of his body, they'd never come close to touching his heart.

The only woman who had ever been capable of doing that was right here with him.

But he could never let her know it.

"You'll never amount to anything, do you 'ear me? Never! I rue the day I ever gave birth to you."

The familiar voice from his past reverberated in his head, the cruel viciousness of the words enough to make him flinch, even now. It served to remind him that all of the reasons he'd had for pushing Emily away four years ago were still there, and they weren't going to go away. Nothing had changed.

Nothing.

"Here we are."

He was pulled out of his musings to find that Emily had come to a halt in front of a large oak tree that stood a few feet away from the side of the manor. Several thick branches protruded from its trunk, perfect for climbing on, and an especially sturdy-looking one stopped just short of the windows on the upper story of the house.

Focus on the investigation, Quick, he told himself sternly. He had made a promise to Tristan and Deirdre, and now to Lord and Lady Tuttleston, that he would catch this thief, and he intended to keep it. And he couldn't let his inconvenient feelings for Emily distract him.

With that thought uppermost in his mind, he stepped forward to examine the ground at the base of the tree.

Unfortunately, there was very little to be found. The carpet of grass that surrounded the oak would have concealed any footprints, and any inclement weather in the weeks since the theft would have washed away any other clues the intruder might have left behind.

Running a gloved hand over the rough bark of the trunk, he glanced upward toward the topmost branches, measuring the distance from the tree to the Tuttlestons' bedchamber window. Yes, it could have been done. In this instance, it looked as if Constable Jenkins had been correct. The thief had used this tree to enter and exit the house. Unless he had scaled the side of the manor itself, which seemed improbable, there was no other way the window could have been reached.

"Well?"

Emily's voice came from directly behind him, and he looked back at her over his shoulder to find her watching him with a strange expression, her violet eyes guarded.

"I shall most likely have to take a look at the bed-chamber," he informed her, turning back to his assess-ment of the tree, "and examine the window itself. If—"

At that moment, something high up in the tree caught his eye.

What the bloody hell . . . ?

Without a second thought, Peter caught hold of one of the lower branches and swung himself up in one smooth motion. A gasp came from behind him at his unexpected action, but he ignored it as he planted his booted feet on the branch and pushed himself to a standing position.

The object fluttered just a few inches above his head, concealed by the leaves that stirred in the slight spring breeze. Dark in color, it would have been well hidden from anyone who hadn't been studying the tree as closely as he had.

Reaching up, he wrapped his fingers about it and gave a tug. It was quite thoroughly caught, and it took several good yanks before it came free in his hand.

"What is it?" Emily called anxiously from the ground, shading her eyes with one hand to look up at him.

He dropped back down beside her and held his dis-covery out for her inspection.

It was a scrap of torn cloth.

Chapter 9

Emily sat ensconced on the window seat in her bedroom, staring out at the stars winking in the velvety night sky overhead and wondering if she would ever be able to fight her way out of the tangle her life had become.

"I intend to bring this thief to justice . . ."

Peter's words to Lady Tuttleston earlier that day echoed in her head like an indictment. He'd only been home for two days and already he'd made more progress in the case than the bumbling authorities in Little Haverton had in a month.

Dear Lord, he'd even found the torn scrap from the pants she'd been wearing that night!

Reaching down, she fingered the jagged hole in the leg of her dark brown breeches. She'd been so preoccupied lately, she'd almost forgotten how she'd become stuck in the oak tree on the Tuttleston estate the evening she'd embarked on her life of crime. It had been only later that she'd discovered the hole where the fabric had torn away, and by then it had been too late to do anything about it.

Of course, without anything to compare the scrap to, there was little chance Peter could ever connect it to her, but it was troubling nonetheless. She'd spent the rest of their time at Lord and Lady Tuttleston's home, as he'd questioned the couple's servants and examined their suite of rooms, trying to convince him that the piece of fabric could have come from anywhere, that it didn't necessarily have to belong to the thief.

She could tell she hadn't been very successful, however. Though he'd nodded and made noises of agreement to all of her comments, there'd been a gleam of purpose in his eyes that told her he'd already made up his mind that he had located his first clue in his search for the criminal.

Then, as if she didn't have enough to worry about, once they'd returned to Knighthaven, Miles had pulled her aside to remind her that she had an appointment to keep that evening. An appointment with the very man who had set this whole chain of events in motion.

How could she have allowed it to slip her mind, even for a second?

Now would come the first test. She would have to sneak out of the house, and she would have to manage to do so with Peter asleep in the guest bedchamber just a few doors down the hall. Something told her he would not be as sound a sleeper as Tristan and Deirdre were. And if he caught her . . .

Her hands tightened into fists on her lap. She would not panic, she decided with conviction. She had every reason to believe this would all soon be over. Tonight, she intended to demand some answers to questions she should have asked a long time ago. Once she knew the truth, she could finally call a halt to this charade and bring an end to her tormentor's machinations for good.

A low whistle from the darkness outside drew her out of her musings, and she looked out through the open casement to see Jenna standing below, wildly gesturing to her. Miles would be waiting with the horses, as usual.

It was much colder out than it had been the last few nights. Emily could feel the slight chill of the breeze as it swept through the window and brushed against her skin. Retrieving her cloak from where it lay across the back of a nearby chair, she swept it about her shoulders, covering her lad's clothing from head to toe. Then, with one last look around at her room, she swung her leg over the window ledge as quietly as possible and started the long climb down the rose trellis.

The gamekeeper's cottage nestled in a clearing deep in the woods on the Ellington estate. Abandoned and falling into a state of disrepair, its shutters hung limply from their hinges, and the path that led up to the sagging front door was cracked and overgrown with weeds.

The moon cast an almost eerie glow over the surrounding landscape as Emily, Jenna, and Miles pulled their horses to a halt at the edge of the tree line and swung down from their saddles. To Emily's relief, she had managed the escape from Knighthaven without rousing Peter or anyone else, at least as far as she knew, but she'd been well away from the house before she'd finally been able to convince herself of her success.

Other than the faint hum of night insects and the whisper of the wind through the leaves of the trees, there was no sound, no sign of any other presence save their own. But Emily wasn't fooled. She knew he was here, watching and waiting. He simply enjoyed toying with her.

With a slight nod of her head to her companions, she started toward the cottage with purposeful strides, and Miles fell into step behind her. Jenna remained with the horses.

She hadn't gone very far when a shadow suddenly materialized from around the side of the building and slunk forward to meet her at the head of the path. As she drew near, the moonlight illuminated a stocky figure with long, oily black hair framing a pale, bony face, thin lips twisted in a sneer.

Emily restrained a shiver of revulsion as she came to a stop in front of him. His was a face that, up until a month ago, she had believed she would never see again other than in her worst nightmares. "Jack."

Jack Barlow folded his arms across his chest and studied her with frosty gray eyes. "It's about time you got 'ere."

Eight years ago, when Emily had first met Peter and the Rag-Tag Bunch, Jack had been a member of the gang. A sullen, hostile boy who had been jealous of

Peter's authority over the others, resentful of Emily's intrusion into their lives, he'd done everything within his power to make them all miserable. He'd spent his days challenging Peter at every turn, questioning his decisions and instigating fights with alarming regularity.

There had been a bone-deep violence in Jack that had always frightened Emily, and she'd learned soon enough that she had every right to her fear. One evening, while the other boys had been asleep, he had cornered her in the dark alley behind the Rag-Tags' hideout and attacked her. There was no telling what he might have done if Peter hadn't come to the rescue. She felt a chill flood over her even now, just thinking about it. After that, Peter had kicked him out of the gang for good.

And in retaliation, Jack had betrayed them to their worst enemy, gang leader Barnaby Flynt.

It had been because of Jack that she had spent several terrifying hours in the hands of that monster Flynt. And it was only by the grace of God—and Peter—that Tristan had found her and gotten her away safely. But when the law had rounded up Barnaby's men, Jack hadn't been among them. He had escaped.

At the time, they'd all counted it a blessing that he was gone. Never could any of them have dreamed that he would be back years later, or that he would track them down in Little Haverton to exact his own brand of vengeance.

Struggling to keep her voice steady, she spoke from between clenched teeth. "I'm here, Jack. What do you want?"

"Now, is that any way to greet an old friend?"

"You're no friend of mine. Now quit playing with me and tell me why I'm here."

"I've chosen your next mark."

Emily's heart skipped a beat. She had come to dread this moment with every ounce of her being. "And? Who is it?"

Something cold and evil flashed in those eyes. "Why, your good neighbor, the Marquis of Brimley 'imself."

Emily felt every muscle in her body freeze into absolute paralysis. This monster couldn't actually expect her to steal from Adam's father!

"There's a certain brooch I 'ear the marquis is quite fond of," Jack was saying silkily. "I want it. Should bring in twice its weight in blunt."

The late Lady Brimley's brooch? She'd heard Adam talk about it several times, and she knew how much the marquis treasured it. She could never rob the poor, dear man of his one last remembrance of his wife.

"I can't do it. I won't."

The words were out before she could call them back, and Jack's eyes narrowed dangerously before he took a threatening step toward her. "You will, or you know what will 'appen."

At her side, Miles growled low in his throat and made an abrupt movement, as if to lunge at Jack, but Emily caught his elbow and held him back. "It's all right, Miles. Please."

The stable hand subsided, but continued to glare at the man in front of them with the light of battle in his eyes.

Emily turned back to Jack. "You know, you're going to use that threat once too often, and it's going to wind up losing its power over me."

"I doubt that." Jack leaned toward her, his lips peeling back from his yellowed teeth in a snarl. "Some'ow I don't think you want all of Little 'Averton knowing what a whore your mum was."

She winced at the harshness of the words and her hands tightened into fists at her sides. There it was. The accusation that had haunted her for the past month. The revelation that had made her start to doubt everything she remembered or had ever been told about her beloved mother.

Jack gave a casual shrug and shoved his hands in the pockets of his breeches. "Of course, if you don't care if everyone knows that the late Countess of Ellington diddled a mere servant before she married your father, I suppose that's your decision." He lowered his voice to a grating whisper. "But I 'ave to wonder 'ow your brother will take the news that 'e just might be the bastard son of a stable 'and."

Anger raced through Emily's veins, sharp and sweet. "And I have to wonder who would believe you. A wanted thief."

"Maybe no one." He shrugged again. "Or maybe everyone. Are you willing to find out? Why, at the very least it should cause quite the scandal. Society will be talking about it for months, if not years. 'Ow the countess slept wiv a stable 'and and passed 'er bastard child off as 'er new 'usband's son."

Is it possible? Emily wondered, not for the first time. Could there be any truth at all to what he said?

It was a puzzle she'd been tormenting herself with ever since Jack had first reappeared in her life.

She'd been shopping with Lilah in the village the day this whole nightmare had begun. While the older woman had been occupied chatting with the proprietor of the local millinery shop, Emily had been outside on the sidewalk, admiring a display of bonnets in the window, when a hand had grabbed her arm, pulling her into the alleyway behind the building.

And she had come face-to-face with Jack.

Stunned and outraged that he would dare to accost her after all these years, she had threatened to go straight to the authorities and report his presence in the village. It was then that he'd revealed the information he'd managed to stumble upon regarding her mother, and his intention of letting all of Little Haverton know what he'd discovered if she didn't do exactly what he said.

Initially, she had refused to believe him. But the more she'd thought about it, the more it had made a strange sort of sense. It would explain so much, including the late Lord Ellington's attitude toward Tristan. The earl and his son had never gotten along, and their relationship had been antagonistic, at best. Had their father somehow found out about their mother's affair and realized that his firstborn might not be his after all?

Jack was right. In a town the size of Little Haverton it would be the scandal of the decade. Dear God, how would Tristan react to the prospect that the mother he had so adored hadn't been the paragon he'd believed her to be? And not only that, but that he might not be the man he'd always believed *himself* to be?

The only son of the Earl of Ellington.

No, she couldn't allow Tristan to be hurt in such a way.

Jack jolted her back to the present by giving her a sly look and sidling away a step or two, glancing back at her over his shoulder. "Per'aps I'll approach your dear sister-in-law wiv the news first. Won't she be surprised to see me? I 'ope it's not too much of a shock. After all, she is carrying the possible 'eir to the earldom, and we wouldn't want anything to 'appen to the babe, would we?"

Icy cold fear lodged at the back of Emily's throat, but she fought through it and plunged forward to grasp Jack's sleeve. "You stay away from her!"

He shook her loose and turned back to face her. "If you don't follow through on our agreement, she's fair game. And what about that 'ome for wayward waifs?" His voice dripped with scorn. "'Ow long do you think it will last once word gets out?"

As much as she hated to admit it, Jack had a point. Most of Little Haverton would jump at whatever chance presented itself to get rid of Willow Park for good. With a scandal like this associated with it, her family could very well lose what little support they had. And if that happened . . .

"All it would take is for me to 'ead down to the local tavern and whisper the tale in the right ear," Jack told her, venomous glee clear in his expression. "And wiv my proof to back me up . . ." He let his words trail off meaningfully.

Emily swallowed and stepped back away from him. "You keep talking about this proof, but I have yet to see it."

"All in good time, my dear."

"No." Enough was enough. She'd made up her mind she would get some answers tonight, and she intended to do exactly that. "Now, Jack. I'm not doing any more of your dirty work until I see this so-called proof of yours for myself."

"My, my. Aren't we brave all of a sudden?"

"Not brave. Just tired of being endlessly led around by the nose on the strength of your threats alone. How do I know you haven't been bluffing this whole time?"

"I guess you'll just 'ave to take my word for it, won't you?"

"Your word? Hardly."

Jack's thick black brows lowered in a menacing manner. "I wouldn't be giving me any ultimatums, little girl. You'd best stick to the plan or I'll make sure you're good and sorry. You *and* your family."

"You bloody bastard!"

The words came from Miles, and this time Emily barely managed to restrain her friend before he got his hands around Jack's throat.

The older man sent him a disdainful glance. "Back off, stable boy. This is between me and 'er."

Still clinging to Miles's arm with all her might, Emily glared at Jack. "I could go to the law, you know."

"You could, but you won't. You're in this too deep now, princess. If I go to jail, so do you and your little friends."

Damnation, he was right again.

Realizing he had her over a barrel, Jack smiled grimly. " 'Ere now. Never let it be said I'm an unreasonable man. You do this next job, and it's possible I could be . . . persuaded to let you see what I've got. If I'm feeling generous, that is."

"And I'm just supposed to trust you?"

"What other choice do you 'ave?"

None. It galled Emily to no end, but she had no option but to continue to give in to his blackmail for now.

She couldn't take the chance that he might hurt someone she loved.

Straightening her shoulders, she leveled Jack with a look of pure loathing. "When do you want us to do it?"

"There now. I knew you'd see it my way." He gave her a smug, satisfied grin. One she longed to claw from his face. "The time isn't right to make our move yet. I'll send a message round as soon as I'm ready."

"Is that all?"

"Not quite. There is one more thing. Make sure you keep your trap shut and tell Peter Quick nothing."

Emily blinked at him in surprise.

"Yes, I know 'e's 'ere. I 'ave my ways. And I'm warning you to keep 'im away from this. I'd 'ate to see anything 'appen to my old friend Peter." Those chilly gray eyes bored into her, making her flinch. "But you know, accidents 'appen, even to the best of us. Remember that."

With those words, he spun on his heel and faded into the darkness.

Emily didn't hesitate, but turned and started toward Jenna and the horses with Miles trailing along behind. Damn Jack Barlow for coming back and turning her life upside down! Now he was not only threatening her family, but Peter as well.

And for some reason, that angered her more than ever.

She waited until they were mounted and had urged the horses back along the trail to Knighthaven before speaking again.

"This has gone too far. We must do something to stop him."

Jenna sent her a concerned glance. "Yes. But what? Nothing 'as changed. If we turn 'im in,'e'll just blurt out the whole sorry tale about your mum. Not to mention we would be arrested, too."

"I know." Emily tightened her grip on Artemis's reins. "If I could just manage to get my hands on this proof he keeps claiming he has, then we'd know once and for all whether there is any truth to what he says." She looked over at Miles. "Have you had any luck at all in your questioning of the servants at Knighthaven?"

He shook his head. "The few that were around back when your parents were in residence are very close-mouthed. And it's not easy to be subtle when asking about such a thing. I don't want to push too 'ard."

Emily nodded, then was quiet for a moment as she contemplated their options. Their current course had gained them nothing, and she could no longer afford to follow Jack's directives in hopes that sooner or later she would stumble across something that would help them.

They had to take more serious action.

"I want you to keep an eye on Jack for the next few days, Miles," she said finally, meeting the stable hand's eyes. "We know he's staying at the cottage. I want to know where he goes and who he sees. Perhaps he might give something away if we're patient enough. In the meantime, no matter how much I hate it, we may have to resign ourselves to breaking into Brimley Hall. We can't afford to anger Jack. Not at this point."

It was true, and Emily had to place one hand against her stomach to calm the roiling deep in her belly. Would Adam ever forgive her?

At that moment, the three of them reached the immediate environs of Knighthaven and dismounted.

Miles sent a surreptitious glance at Jenna. "You know, I could walk you 'ome, if you like."

The younger girl gave a start, then frowned at the stable hand. "I don't need you to walk me 'ome. It's not that far to Willow Park if I cut across the field instead of going by the road, and you need to get the 'orses back to the stables."

Miles visibly bristled at her superior tone. "It's not right for a woman to be out by 'erself after dark—"

"I'm perfectly capable of—"

"You're perfectly capable of annoying the bloody 'ell out of me!"

"Me? You're the one who—"

Emily winced. Leave it to the two of them to bicker

at a time like this. "If the two of you are going to fight, the least you can do is lower your voices."

They obliged, but continued to argue in hushed whispers.

It was useless trying to make either of them see reason when they were like this. They had their hackles up and Emily knew from personal experience that this could go on indefinitely. Shaking her head, she took a deep breath and began the walk back to the house, leaving her companions to their disagreement. She had faith Jenna and Miles had sense enough to call a halt to things before they either killed each other or someone stumbled upon them.

She didn't have far to go, and by keeping to the shadows of the numerous outbuildings scattered about the estate, she was able to reach the edge of the garden at the side of the house in no time at all. Peering from behind the safety of a large elm tree, she noted that all was peaceful and still. The moonlight cut a path through the hedges and neatly trimmed flowering bushes, illuminating the surroundings with a pale glow. From here, she could see the window of her bedroom and the candle she'd left burning on the sill to light her way.

She was almost safe.

She started forward, but she hadn't gone more than a few steps when a dark shape suddenly swooped out of the shadows, tackling her with enough force to knock the breath from her body and bear her to the ground.

There was no air left in her lungs for her to do more than let out a frightened squeak, and she reached up with desperate hands to attempt to push away the solid bulk that covered her, keeping her pinned to the ground.

Her fingers closed on broad, muscled shoulders.

"Just what the bloody hell are you doing out here?"

Oh, dear God, it was Peter!

Chapter 10

Peter had been unable to sleep.

That was not unusual, in and of itself. He'd never been a very sound sleeper. He supposed it came from all those years of having to keep one eye open, even at night, as a boy on the streets of London.

But he knew it wasn't entirely habit that had led to his restlessness tonight. The case of the Oxfordshire Thief was weighing heavily on him. And he had to admit that a certain angelic-looking, blond-haired young lady was on his mind far more than she should be.

He had paced his room for well over an hour, trying to concentrate on the facts that had been laid out before him that day. From what Lord and Lady Tuttleston had said, he couldn't help but draw the conclusion that whoever had stolen the necklace and other items knew the couple quite well, or at least was very familiar with their house and their routine.

As he'd turned that thought over and over, however, trying to come to some sort of conclusion, Emily's image had interfered with his usual cool rationality. Deciding to escape from the confines of his bedchamber, he'd made his way outside to the garden, where he had been grateful for the brisk night air that cleared his head.

If ever there had been a case that Peter felt compelled to solve, it was this one. From the moment he'd arrived at Knighthaven, he'd felt something stronger than his usual need to succeed pushing him onward. He had to catch this thief, to bring an end to the man's life of crime. He owed that much to Tristan and Deirdre. And meeting the kindly Lord and Lady Tuttleston today had only added to his determination.

He had no idea how long he'd been out here. It could have been mere minutes or more like hours. He'd lost track of the time as he'd wandered the moonlit pathways, and he'd just been contemplating returning to his room when he'd noticed the cloaked figure slinking from tree to tree, coming ever closer to the house.

The thief! a voice in his head had hissed. It seemed a definite possibility, for who else would be skulking about the grounds of Knighthaven so long after midnight?

His whole body went on immediate alert, and taking care to remain in the shadows where he could not be seen, he'd worked his way closer to the figure, then stationed himself at the edge of the copse of elms, waiting for the thief to make his move and step out into the open.

Surely it can't be this easy, Peter thought, the anticipation and the adrenaline pumping through his veins like sweet nectar. He damned himself for leaving his pistol in his room, but he'd never expected such an event to occur. Had never expected that the thief might try to break into Knighthaven right under his nose.

The bastard was in for a rude awakening.

When the shadowy form finally broke from the concealment of the trees, he didn't hesitate. He lunged forward, catching the intruder about the waist and knocking him to the ground.

But the moment he felt that soft body lying beneath his own, he knew this was no thief. The rounded curves pressed against him were much too familiar, the smell of roses making it nearly impossible to mistake her for anyone else.

Emily.

Anger at her foolishness blazed through him. "Just what the bloody hell are you doing out here?"

Hands clutched at his shoulders, and he waited for her to reply. But no explanation appeared to be forthcoming. The silence went on past all bearing, and just when he was ready to shake her in sheer frustration, he realized that she *couldn't* answer him.

He had managed to knock the wind from her.

His anger momentarily usurped by concern, he got to his feet in one swift motion and grasped her wrists, pulling her up next to him.

"Are you all right?" he demanded.

A second passed while Emily gasped for air, then she

gave an abrupt nod that had the hood of her cloak falling back and a spill of gold curls tumbling about her face.

She was so petite, so fragile. The thought of how easily he could have hurt her once again brought his anger to the forefront. "Are you mad? What are you doing wandering around out 'ere in the dark wiv a thief on the loose? Do you 'ave any idea what could 'ave 'appened to you?"

As always whenever he was emotional, the hint of Cockney he had tried so hard to get rid of crept back into his voice. But at this point he didn't care. The foolish woman had put her very life at risk by sneaking out of the house after dark, and for what? What could possibly be so important to her?

As he watched, he saw the hint of temper flare in the dusky purple of her eyes, and he had to stifle a groan when he noticed her chin go up in a haughty manner. She was going to be stubborn. He should have known.

"I couldn't sleep," she said, her voice filled with a distinct chill. "I simply needed to get away for a while, to get some fresh air, so I took a walk. And there was no risk. This thief hasn't hurt anyone that I'm aware of."

"There's always a first time," he told her, still tempted to shake her. He clenched his hands into impotent fists at his sides in order to restrain the urge to do so. "And you 'ave no idea what 'e might 'ave done if you'd stumbled across 'im in the act."

"Well, I have returned, safe and sound, so there's no need to belabor the point." She looked up at him from under lowered lashes. "And there's no need to bother Tristan and Deirdre with this little incident, is there?"

"No need—" Her gall astounded him. "I ought to turn you over my knee and deliver you the thrashing you deserve right now."

She took a step back from him. "You wouldn't dare!"

"At this point, I believe I'd dare anything where you're concerned, so I wouldn't push me." Taking a deep breath, he struggled to rein in his temper, and when he spoke again, he was gratified to note that he had managed to subdue that betraying trace of Cockney. "Where exactly did you walk to?"

"I don't believe that's any of your business."

"Until this case is solved, everything that goes on at Knighthaven is my business. Now, are you going to tell me where you went, or do I need to march you inside to Lord and Lady Ellington and have you tell them?"

Emily's defiant gaze abruptly skated away from his and she bowed her head, shifting her weight from one foot to the other in a rather agitated manner. "Nowhere in particular."

Peter frowned in sudden suspicion. Nowhere in particular? At that moment, a picture of Lord Moreland flashed across his mind's eye and his anger flared back to the surface. Was it possible . . . ? Could Emily have arranged some sort of illicit rendezvous with the man? All too easily he could envision the arrogant lord enfolding her in his arms in the moonlit garden, kissing her, touching her . . .

Taking a step toward her, he reached out to catch hold of her elbow in an unbreakable grip. "You weren't perhaps having a little tryst with Viscount Moreland, were you?"

"What?" Her eyes flew back to his and her mouth fell open in what appeared to be honest surprise. "Of course not! What would ever lead you to believe such a thing?"

"Well, it wouldn't be the first time, would it?"

Emily seemed momentarily at a loss for words, then she let out an outraged gasp and wrenched her arm from his grasp. "If you are speaking of Lord Percy, you know very well I never meant for things to go as far as they did that night. It was only a little harmless flirtation. I never thought . . ." She bit her lip and shrugged her shoulders in helpless entreaty. "I was young and it was long ago."

Not so long ago. At least, not for Peter.

It had been the evening of Emily's eighteenth birthday, and her family had arranged a ball in her honor. Though the Willow Park children had celebrated with her earlier in the day, he'd planned to slip over to Knighthaven that night long enough to wish her a happy birthday and to give her his gift in private.

He had saved up the money he had earned working in the stables at Willow Park for months, and had managed to come up with enough to buy her a pretty silk shawl he'd noticed her admiring in one of the shop windows in the village. It wasn't much, but he'd wanted to give her something. He'd hated the distance that had existed between them, and as he knew it was his fault, he'd wanted to make it up to her in some small way.

But by the time he'd arrived at Knighthaven and

peered through the French doors into the ballroom, hoping to catch her attention, he'd seen her dancing with Lord Percy. Whirling about the floor, fluttering her eyelashes in a most coquettish fashion, she'd held the young man spellbound. Peter had felt as if a knife had been plunged into his heart.

But before he could slink off to nurse his wounds, the dance had ended and the couple had come out to the garden.

From the shadows, he'd watched as they'd strolled the walkways, arm in arm. Every time Emily had laughed at something the young lord said, it had been like a mortal blow.

Then her companion had decided to become overly amorous in his attentions.

The two of them had come to a stop near the copse of elms close to the central fountain, and Lord Percy had pulled her into his arms and kissed her with fervent ardor. When Emily had pushed frantically at the man's shoulders and given a cry of distress, Peter hadn't hesitated. He'd leaped forward and gripped Percy by his collar, yanking him away from her with brutal force.

It hadn't taken more than a good shove and some threatening words to send the young lord on his way. And then Peter had turned on Emily and given her the tongue-lashing of her life for being foolish enough to allow Lord Percy to escort her out to the garden alone. But she had given back as good as she'd gotten, and her defiance had succeeded in rousing his passion as well as his temper.

Driven by anger and desperate need, they'd come together in a kiss of savage intensity, and from there things had spiraled quickly out of control. Before he'd known it, he'd had her pressed back against a tree with her skirts hiked up about her waist and his manhood poised to plunge into her.

It was only as he'd hovered there at the slick entrance to her womb that he had realized what he was about to do. He could only thank God that he'd managed to come to his senses in time, that he'd somehow found the strength to pull back from her.

And the next morning he'd gone to Lord and Lady Ellington and told them he was leaving Willow Park for good.

"I knew you were there."

Emily's words, softly spoken, drew him back to the present, and he stared down at her in surprise. "What?"

"The night of my birthday ball. I knew you were there the whole time," she repeated, peering up at him. In the dimness he couldn't be certain, but it looked as if she might be blushing. "I saw you the moment you peeked in through the terrace doors. Up until then, I'd been having a terrible time. But when I saw you . . . I don't know. You'd been so withdrawn, I suppose I just wanted to get a reaction from you. Any sort of reaction. That's why I flirted with Percy the way I did."

Peter raised an eyebrow. That was news to him. "And is that what tonight was all about?" He folded his arms across his chest. "Sneaking out of the house? Were you trying to get a reaction out of me?"

At the question, her chin went up and she glared at him. "Of course not. I have far better things to do with my time. To be truthful, I care little what you think of me now. It's not as if you have any say over my life."

For some reason, her words seemed to snap the final threads on his already frayed temper, and he acted before he thought, doing exactly what he had sworn he would never do again.

Reaching out, he caught her by her shoulders and pulled her to him, the feel of her soft curves coming into contact with his solid frame causing his breath to hiss out from between his teeth. Her startled expression was the last thing he saw before he leaned forward and took her mouth with his own.

And the feel of her silky lips beneath his after all of these years was enough to drive every rational thought right out of his head.

Emily was stunned, confused, unable to process what was happening or how it had happened. One moment she and Peter had been disagreeing in their usual vehement manner while she'd scrambled to come up with an explanation for her presence outside at this time of night, and the next he was kissing her with a fierceness that left her reeling.

She felt his hands leave her shoulders and smooth down over the slope of her back, his palms warm even through the material of her cloak as they settled at the base of her spine. Her pulse pounded in her ears as his warm, firm lips tasted hers deeply over and over, conquering their smooth surfaces as if staking a claim. And when his tongue flicked out to plunge into the warm cavern of her mouth, the heady flavor of brandy clouded her senses until she couldn't remember her own name, much less what they'd been arguing about.

Why was it only this man who did this to her? she wondered hazily as his lips finally left hers and skimmed down the underside of her jaw, his teeth nipping and his tongue soothing the sensitive skin in his path, wringing a moan from deep in her throat. It wasn't as if she'd never been kissed before, after all. Though most of Little Haverton considered her well on her way to spinsterhood, she'd had her share of suitors over the years. But none of them had ever held her attention for long, and none of them had ever made her feel like this.

None of them had been Peter.

She shivered as he nibbled at her collarbone, and her hands, which had been clutching her cloak, closed suddenly, released their convulsive grip, and settled on his broad chest, savoring the feel of sculpted muscle through his lawn shirt.

His hands moved once again, this time traveling downward to cup the rounded globes of her derriere and fit her more intimately against him. She stifled another moan as her most private place came into scorching contact with a thick, hard bulge that could not be mistaken. As heat flared through her, she gave a restless shift and rocked her pelvis forward, rubbing her suddenly moist cleft against the ridge of his arousal in an attempt to soothe the ache that pulsed there.

Peter groaned and raised his head to bury his lips in

the hair close to her temple, sounding like a man in torment. "Emily . . . Angel . . ."

His voice was a husky rasp, sending a shiver through her that left her weak and quivering. Letting her head fall back, she stared up at him, one hand sliding up over his shoulder to tangle in the long length of his tousled, tawny hair. "Oh, Peter. Please . . ."

Her words seemed to act like a dash of icy water. Peter abruptly froze and let his hold on her loosen bit by bit until his hands fell away and he stepped back, his expression cool and distant.

With him no longer supporting her, Emily's trembling legs caused her to stumble back a few paces, the night air rushing over her in a way that left her feeling bereft. "Peter—"

He shook his head, then reached out to catch her wrist in an unbreakable grip. "Come with me."

Before Emily could say a word, he started across the garden, tugging her along behind him like a recalcitrant child. Still off balance over their intense encounter, she didn't bother to protest. She was much too disconcerted to do more than follow him meekly.

Somehow, without her being quite aware of how they got there, they were standing beneath her bedroom window.

Peter let go of her arm and gestured to the rose trellis. "I'm assuming this is how you made your great escape?"

Emily nodded.

"Up with you, then."

When she didn't move or reply, merely gazed at him blankly, he gave her a gentle nudge in the direction of the trellis. "Go on. Climb up. And if you know what's good for you, you'll stay in your room after dark from now on, or the next time you'll be explaining yourself to your brother."

Emily felt her face heat in response to his patronizing tone. Of all the nerve! How dare he kiss her like that, then turn around and treat her as if she were little more than a nuisance to be dealt with! But instead of arguing with him, she gave a sniff, placed her foot on the first rung of the trellis, and began to climb.

By the time she reached the window ledge of her room and turned to look back over her shoulder, he was already gone.

Damn him!

She was very tempted to slam the window closed behind her in order to relieve some of her boiling frustration, but with the other occupants of the house still asleep, she realized that wasn't an option. Instead, she shut it as silently as possible and then slid down to sit on the carpeted floor, burying her flushed face in her upraised knees.

What on earth had come over her? How could she have allowed Peter to kiss her, to touch her like that? Had all reason deserted her? She should have slapped his face for his effrontery, or at the very least blistered his ears with a firm dressing-down. But she had behaved like an utter wanton. Had lost herself in the sensuality of the moment, in the feeling of his lips on hers after all these years . . .

Thank God Peter had called a halt before things went too far. But it rankled her pride that he had been the one to do so. That he still had such power over her defied all explanation. He had even managed to pull a confession from her regarding the incident with Lord Percy that night four years ago.

She sighed and lifted her head. Well, at least the kiss had served one useful purpose. It had made Peter abandon his quest to find out where she'd gone this evening. She could only be grateful she'd kept enough of her wits about her to make sure her clothing remained concealed by her cloak, or he would have been demanding an explanation for that, as well.

From now on, she would have to take extra precautions when coming and going from the house on her clandestine midnight missions. And she would have to make sure that she kept her distance from Peter. She couldn't allow him to touch her in such a way again, either physically . . . or emotionally.

For she knew without a doubt that she wouldn't be able to withstand the pain if she allowed him to get close and he left her again. She'd had her heart broken by Peter Quick once, and this time she was afraid the damage just might be irreparable.

Chapter 11

Peter awoke the next morning to sunlight streaming in through his bedchamber window. Wincing against the brightness, he let out a groan and flung his arm across his eyes to shield himself against the glare. Bloody hell, what time was it?

After his encounter with Emily last night, he'd returned to his room to find he was no less restless than he'd been when he'd left it. Even after stripping off his clothes and climbing under the covers, he'd tossed and turned for hours, until he'd finally drifted off sometime just before dawn.

At the memory of their passionate kiss, another groan escaped him and he rolled over to bury his head under his pillow. He could still hear Emily's low moans as he'd run his hands over her soft curves, picture the way she had looked when she gazed up at him, her violet eyes gone dark and dreamy with desire. And the way she had rubbed herself so sinuously against the hard ridge of his erection . . .

Feeling the lower part of his male anatomy stir in response to the vision, Peter pushed the image away.

What had he been thinking?

I still want her.

He squeezed his eyes shut at the thought, but there was no hiding from the truth. The moment his lips had touched hers he had known it could no longer be denied. Kissing her, holding her, had felt too much like coming home. But a former street thief had no business even imagining that he was worthy of the sister of an earl.

"You're a worthless little bastard."

It was his mother's voice, harsh and biting, throwing the same words at him that he'd heard so often as a boy. They were an ever-present mantra at the edges of his consciousness, an insidious whisper that taunted him whenever he started to think that he just might be able to finally leave his past behind him.

For the few short years he had lived at Willow Park, Peter had lulled himself into a false sense of security, allowing himself to be fooled into thinking that his background no longer mattered. He had opened his hardened heart to Emily and had even begun to believe that they could have a future together.

But he'd been wrong.

And after last night he owed her an apology.

The thought of facing her after what had passed between them was discomfiting, to say the least. But he couldn't deny he needed her help. There was no doubt in his mind that her presence yesterday had made his interview with Lord and Lady Tuttleston go much more smoothly than it might have otherwise, and if he planned on making the trip to Lord and Lady Fulberry's today, he needed Emily by his side.

Tossing aside his covers, he swung his legs out of bed and sat up, pushing a hank of hair off his forehead. From the angle of the sun outside his window, he would guess it must be close to noon. Already he'd wasted half the morning.

There was no use putting off the inevitable.

He rose and started to dress.

A short while later, having questioned Langley as to Lady Emily's whereabouts, Peter found himself traversing the long, tree-lined driveway that led to Willow Park. Apparently, this was Emily's regular day to visit with the children, and deciding that it was about time he paid his respects as well, he had set off on Champion.

The park wasn't more than a few miles away along the winding main thoroughfare that eventually ran through the village, and it had taken him less than half an hour to cover the distance between the two properties. Set back from the road behind a dense grove of oaks and maples, not even its tall chimneys could be seen above the tops of the uppermost branches.

Though not as large or majestic as Knighthaven, Willow Park was impressive enough in its own right, with a red-brick exterior and wide, stained-glass windows. Once, the house had belonged to the late Countess of Ellington, but it had passed to Tristan as part of his inheritance after her death and had sat neglected for several years. It hadn't been until Tristan and Deirdre had come to live permanently at Knighthaven that they had returned the Park to its former glory and started their home for wayward children there.

As Peter approached the circular drive in front of the house and pulled his horse to a halt, he became aware of the sound of a child's giggle, briefly echoing over the vast expanse of lawn. Swinging down from his saddle, he handed the gelding's reins to the groom who hurried forward and glanced about, trying to locate the source of the noise.

It didn't take long. From here, he could see a small group clustered about a willow tree next to the fish pond. And as he started across the grass toward them, he realized the identity of the person who was holding their rapt attention.

Emily.

She looked utterly enchanting, with her blond curls spilling from underneath the edge of her yellow, lace-edged bonnet and the sun gilding her animated features. She was reading from a storybook, and she held the children enthralled with the sheer magnetism of her voice.

Peter came to an abrupt halt a few feet away, frozen

in place as he recalled a similar scene, this one in a darkened corner of the Rag-Tag Bunch's hideout as she'd read to the boys gathered at her feet by the glow of one meager candle.

Dear God, she'd been their light in the darkness back then, her sweet and cheerful disposition making their lives a bit more bearable. And her friendship over the years had given Peter a sense of worth. The way she'd looked at him as if he were ten feet tall had made him believe he could do anything, regardless of his background.

At that moment, she caught sight of him and her smile faded. Though her voice stumbled a bit over the passage she was reading, she managed to regroup and bring the story to an end with little sign of her unease at his appearance. No one studying her would have ever guessed that she was even conscious of his presence. But he knew. He could feel the awareness vibrating between them like a wire strung too tautly.

As she closed the book, the children grumbled in disappointment.

"Oh, please, Lady Emily, couldn't we 'ear another story?" a young lad seated toward the front asked.

"I'm sorry, Will, but I'm afraid it's almost time for lunch." Her gaze went to Peter, cool and unreadable. "And it seems we have a visitor you might want to say hello to."

As one, the children all turned, and upon seeing Peter they let out glad cries and jumped to their feet.

Before he could move or say a word, he was instantly

surrounded by a laughing, chattering group of boys and girls, each one vying for his attention.

"Oh, Peter, you're 'ere!"

"Did you bring us anything, Peter?"

"I want to 'ear all about that murderer you captured! I bet you bloody well showed 'im not to mess wiv Bow Street, didn't you?"

"Children, please." Peter looked up to see Rachel McLean, a plump, dark-haired woman with kind brown eyes, coming toward them, shaking her head in fond exasperation. "You must give him a chance to breathe. I'm sure he'll be glad to answer all your questions. But Lady Emily is correct. Right now it is time for luncheon."

She turned to Peter with a warm smile. "I'm so glad you stopped by, dear. You will be joining us for lunch, won't you?"

He clasped her hand and raised it to his lips with a jaunty grin. "My dear lady, I assure you I would feel quite deprived if I wasn't invited." He winked at the children. "And I promise I shall fill you all in on every bloody detail of my London exploits. I'm sure you'll want to hear all about the time I chased the notorious Nine-fingered Ned into the sewers and brought him to justice with the business end of my trusty knife blade. I keep one of his nine fingers in a jar next to my bed, don't you know?"

They all cheered, and Mrs. McLean rolled her eyes. "Saints preserve us, they'll all be having nightmares." She shooed the group on their way with both hands. "All right, then. Back to the Park so we can all wash up."

They all started to troop up the lawn toward the house, their voices raised in excitement, and Peter turned to find Emily coming toward him, her storybook tucked under one arm.

Tilting her head, she looked up at him with a raised brow. "Nine-fingered Ned?"

He shrugged. "They're a bloodthirsty lot. I'm afraid they'd find the real tales of what I do rather boring."

"Somehow I doubt that."

There was an instant of silence, then Peter cleared his throat and shoved his hands in his pockets, not quite certain how to go about phrasing what he wanted to say next. "About last night . . . I want to apologize—"

Emily's expression closed up. "I'd rather not discuss last night, if you don't mind," she interrupted him, her jaw tightening visibly. "It would be better if we both put it in the past and pretend it never happened." She narrowed her eyes, holding his gaze with her own as if trying to convey the seriousness of her conviction. "And I'm certain we'll both make sure it *never* happens again."

Though he'd intended to tell her the very same thing, Peter couldn't help but feel a sharp spurt of anger at her words. She spoke with such assurance. Would it be that easy for her to forget what had passed between them? "Yes. Of course. I was just going to say that myself, as a matter of fact."

"Good. I'm glad we agree." There was another short span of silence, and when she spoke again some of the tension seemed to have seeped out of her. "Why are you here, Mr. Quick? Not that I'm unhappy you've stopped by to see the children, but I can't help but feel that's not the only reason you've come."

So they were back to Mr. Quick. Last night she'd called him Peter. "It's not. Langley said you would be here, and I was hoping to talk you into coming with me to visit Lord and Lady Fulberry later this afternoon. The sooner I interview them, the sooner I can start making some progress on this case."

Emily crossed her arms, hugging the book against her chest as she studied him. Then she gave an affirmative nod. "Certainly. We can depart first thing after lunch, if you would like."

She began to turn away, but before she'd gone more than a step or two after the others, something stronger than his need to keep distance between them compelled him to call her back, to hold on to her company for just a moment longer.

"Seeing you read to the children brings back memories."

She froze mid-step at his statement. "Oh?"

"Mmm." He strode forward to stand next to her once again. "I can remember watching you read to the Rag-Tags all those years ago, the looks on their faces as you carried them off to a different place and time with the power of your words. For just a short while they could believe they were someone else, living a better life." He paused, then took a deep breath. "You made a difference in our lives then, Emily, and I never thanked you for that."

He watched as pearly white teeth sank into her lower lip, her expression uncertain as she examined every inch of his features. Could she take nothing he said at face value?

As if she had finally determined the sincerity of his words, her mouth slowly curved in a genuine smile. "You don't need to thank me. It's something I enjoyed doing. Something I still enjoy doing." She indicated the book in her arms with an inclination of her head. "I try to come and read to the children here at Willow Park at least once a week. And I usually spend an hour or so working with a few of them on their reading and writing skills if I have the time. They're so eager to learn."

"I'm sure they all appreciate your help. I know the McLeans do. They were just telling me the other night at dinner that they didn't know what they would do without you, especially since Deirdre has been unable to be available as much of late due to her current difficulties."

Emily flushed and looked away. "Yes, well . . . thank you for saying so." Tightening her hold on her book, she glanced toward the house, where the rest of the group had just reached the circular drive. "I suppose we'd best hurry if we don't want to be late for luncheon."

Peter nodded, but just as he started to fall into step beside her, a slight movement out of the corner of his eye caught his attention. Looking back, he noticed for the first time that someone occupied a tree stump farther back in the grove of willows, several feet away from the place where the rest of the children had been sitting to listen to Emily's story.

Benji.

As usual, the young man's nose was buried in a book, but his posture was stiff and guarded, as if daring anyone to come near him.

"Why don't you go ahead, Lady Emily," Peter suggested, his brow furrowing as he studied the lad's closed expression. "I'll join you shortly, but I see someone I need to speak with first."

Emily took note of the direction of his gaze and her eyes clouded. Peter braced himself for her disapproval. After her reaction the other night, he was well aware how she felt about his interference in any matter involving Benji.

But she surprised him.

"If you can," she said softly, "please try to talk him into joining us for lunch? He's been avoiding the rest of the children for the last several weeks, and I can't believe that it's good for him to be alone so much."

He nodded, then waited for her to walk away before he started toward Benji.

The boy must have heard his footsteps in the grass, for he closed his book and looked up as Peter approached him, his eyebrows arching above his glasses in an expectant manner. "Finally decided to pay us a visit, did you?"

There was no missing the sarcasm in Benji's tone. Peter crouched down on his haunches next to the lad and propped his elbows on his knees, struggling to come up with the right words to say. "You should know

I would never return to Little Haverton without stopping by to see all of you. This is my home, my family."

Benji lifted a shoulder in a careless manner, but didn't reply.

For a second or two, all was quiet, the only sound the twitter of birds in the trees overhead. Then Peter spoke again. "You know, Lady Emily was hoping you'd join us for lunch."

"I'm not hungry."

"Perhaps not, but she says you've been keeping to yourself for the last few weeks, and she's worried about you. They all are. It might put their minds at ease if you would at least attempt to be a bit sociable. This separating yourself from everyone isn't like you."

A muscle tightened in Benji's jaw and he looked away, gazing out over the pond. The silence stretched, and Peter was just beginning to think he would have to prod the boy again when he spoke.

"I don't belong with them."

The words were said so inaudibly that at first Peter wasn't certain he'd heard correctly. When the statement finally registered, he felt his jaw drop in astonishment.

"Don't belong? Benji, you belong here just as much as anyone. Why would you say such a thing?"

The boy shook his head and reached up to rake his fingers through his blond curls. "It's just something I've always known. But lately—" He stopped, then gathered up his book and got to his feet, his eyes bleak behind the lenses of his spectacles. "Forget it. I don't want to talk about this."

"But it might help if—"

"I said I don't want to talk about it!"

With that, Benji stormed off in the direction of Willow Park, leaving Peter staring after him.

Chapter 12

Over two hours later, Emily found herself riding alongside Peter as they made their way toward Lord and Lady Fulberry's home on the outskirts of Little Haverton.

Reaching up with one hand, she brushed a stray curl back off her forehead, her bonnet having long ago tumbled off to hang down her back by its strings, and contemplated her companion from the corner of her eye.

He was such an enigma to her, she mused. Long ago she'd come to the conclusion that he couldn't possibly have been the sort of man her young heart had once believed him to be. That he couldn't honestly have cared for her and her family or anyone at Willow Park or he would never have left Oxfordshire—and her—the way that he had, without a word of explanation.

But observing him today, she'd been forced to concede that she just might have been mistaken in her assumptions. At least as far as the Willow Park residents were concerned. Talking and laughing with them at the lunch table, regaling them with tales of his life as a Bow Street runner, he'd seemed so happy, so content. To her consternation, he'd fit in as if he'd never left. And it was obvious the boys and girls adored him. To them, he was their hero. Just as he had once been hers.

Never before could Emily remember feeling so confused.

For the rest of their visit to the Park, she'd found herself unable to keep her eyes from this man who had caused such an upheaval in her life, both four years ago and in the last few days since his return. It was as if some strange magnetic pull beyond her control drew her gaze to him.

And more than one person had noticed her preoccupation with him. She'd seen Mrs. McLean send her several knowing looks, and Jenna had even pulled her aside before she and Peter had departed to comment on it.

"You keep staring at 'im like a cat at the cream," her friend had pointed out with a sly grin as they'd watched him saying good-bye to everyone.

"What utter nonsense," Emily had sniffed, deliberately turning her back on the sight of Peter as he'd shaken hands with Rachel McLean's big, redheaded husband, Angus. "I'm sure I don't know what you're talking about."

"Oh, I'm sure you don't. But you know, it might not be so terrible if you was to give 'im another chance."

"Another chance to what? Break my heart? Leave me behind again without a second thought? I don't think so."

Jenna's face had turned solemn. "Em, Peter's a good man. If nothing else, seeing 'im with the children today should 'ave proven that. Everyone seems to love 'im. Even your brother and 'is wife like 'im. Shouldn't that tell you something?"

It didn't matter that her friend had only been repeating what she herself had been thinking. She wasn't quite ready to accept that her judgment of him could have been so far off the mark. "I don't know, Jenna. I don't know what to think."

"I 'ate to say it, but maybe you ought to just come right out and ask 'im why 'e left." The younger girl had laid a sympathetic hand on Emily's arm. "Until you do, it will always be there between you. And you never know. 'E might 'ave 'ad a very good reason for what 'e did. Doesn't 'e at least deserve the benefit of the doubt?"

Jenna's words echoed in her head now, and Emily scowled, her hands tightening on her reins. There had been more than ample opportunity over the years for Peter to explain his actions to her, but he had never gone out of his way to do so. Obviously it hadn't been that important to him or he wouldn't have spent his past visits to Oxfordshire avoiding her.

But you never sought him out, either, Emily, a little voice in the back of her mind hissed. *You never bothered to ask him for his side of the story.*

But did she really want to know the answer? Did she

really want to find out that the reason behind his hasty departure from Little Haverton had nothing to do with a lack of caring on his part, and everything to do with her?

At one time, Peter had given her every reason to believe they would be spending the rest of their lives together. But somewhere along the way, things had come undone. Perhaps he had changed his mind and decided he didn't want her after all. But if that had been the case, why hadn't he come to her and told her the truth?

She didn't know. The only thing she was certain of was that it was getting harder and harder to ignore the feelings he was still capable of stirring in her. And after that kiss last night . . .

"Penny for your thoughts?"

Peter's warm, husky voice jolted Emily out of her reverie, and she gave a startled jump before taking a deep breath to steady her suddenly fluttering pulse. Certain her face must be an alarming shade of red, she turned to look at him, praying that he would think the sun was responsible for the color in her cheeks.

"I was just wondering about your conversation with Benji," she said, attempting to keep her voice calm and even. It wasn't a complete lie. She *had* been worrying about what had transpired between the two of them at the pond after she had left them. Peter hadn't mentioned it and the boy had never reappeared. "He never did join us for lunch."

"No. He made it clear he wasn't interested in doing so."

Glad to have something else to turn her mind to, she sighed and shook her head. "I just don't understand it.

Benji has always been so cheerful, so willing to spend time with the other children, especially the younger ones. Now, all of a sudden he can't stay far enough away from them." She bit her lip. "You don't suppose it has something to do with the robberies, do you?"

"I don't know. It could. I'm assuming Constable Jenkins has questioned him?"

"Once, along with a couple of the other older boys. But the odious man spent the whole time trying to intimidate one of them into confessing, so Tristan wouldn't allow it again." She would never forgive herself if what she was doing had led to Benji's present moroseness. She could well see how being suspected of a crime he'd had nothing to do with could make the boy resentful. Especially when he'd struggled so hard to better himself.

Peter frowned. "Sooner or later, I may have to question them again, if only to make sure I've covered all the same ground the constable has. But I don't believe for a minute that Benji had anything to do with it. Or any of the other children, for that matter. This thief is more than likely an adult. Someone who knows his marks personally and knows them well."

Emily felt herself go cold at his words. "What makes you say that?"

"For one, he seems to be well aware of the routines of his victims. He knew what night Lord and Lady Tuttleston would be away from home and used that to his advantage. And from what Constable Jenkins has told me, Lord and Lady Fulberry always throw a rather large dinner party the week before they are scheduled to depart for London every Season. I think the thief deliberately chose that night to break in knowing that they, as well as their servants, would be occupied seeing to their guests."

He was getting much too close, Emily thought with a flare of panic. Uncomfortably close. "But couldn't anyone determine that just by asking a few subtle questions here and there, or by observing the victims for a while? I mean, isn't it possible the culprit could be someone unknown to the victims?"

One of Peter's tawny eyebrows shot upward and he studied her with interest as he replied. "Perhaps. But there is also the fact that the thief appears to know exactly where each of the victims kept their valuables and went straight to their location, something that wouldn't be common knowledge. In the case of the Tuttlestons, he had something specific in mind. Lady Tuttleston's necklace. And whoever it was knew she kept it in her jewelry box, not her husband's safe."

"A servant might have that kind of information," Emily insisted, determined to offer up at least a measure of doubt as to his theory.

"True. And I haven't ruled them out. But all of Lord and Lady Tuttleston's servants have alibis for the time of the break-in. Of course, that doesn't eliminate the possibility that they could be working with someone on the outside, someone they passed their information on to. And if I can compare that scrap of cloth I found to some of their clothing, I might luck out and find a match. Although I doubt the thief will wear the same clothing during the day as he does during his break-ins."

"We still don't even know whether that scrap has anything to do with the thief," Emily argued. "It could have been blown there from somewhere else entirely."

"But it seems unlikely. It was stuck rather firmly to the branch, which I doubt could have happened if it had just been blown there by a passing breeze. I am well aware, however, that I can't rely solely on that to identify the culprit. You're right. Its presence in the tree can be too easily explained away by other means. But it *is* a place to start."

Peter's visage was filled with such grim purpose that Emily couldn't suppress a small shiver. "You seem so determined. Do you truly think you will be able to catch him?"

"Oh, I can assure you, I *am* determined. And there is no doubt in my mind that I will catch him." She watched him as his eyes narrowed and he gazed off into the distance. "Because of this criminal, my family has been threatened. The only family I have ever known. Not only have the children of Willow Park been badgered and accused of his crimes, but your brother and his wife have been forced to worry about the future of the home at a time when they should be concerning themselves with nothing but the arrival of their babe."

He paused, then looked back at her, his countenance rife with utter resolve. "I will not stand by and allow it to continue. I *will* track this miscreant down, and when I do he will be made to pay for the pain he has caused. I give you my word on that."

His voice was filled with such anger and assurance that Emily had to look away. She would not—could not—allow herself to be swayed by guilt. She had to remember her family was at stake. But if she'd had any uncertainty over how Peter would react if he ever discovered her unholy alliance with Jack, she didn't now.

He would hate her.

"Well," she said as Lord and Lady Fulberry's home came into view just up ahead, "here we are at our destination." The towers of Fulberry Manor were a welcome sight, and needing to put some distance between herself and Peter, she urged Artemis ahead with a small nudge of her heel, calling back to him over her shoulder. "We'd better hurry. It's getting late."

She caught a brief glimpse of his puzzled expression, but she brushed it aside as she trotted ahead of him up the drive. Better that she leave him wondering at her strange behavior than stay in his company and give herself away.

Deep down, she had known that his return to Knighthaven would cause her nothing but further heartache and pain. But never could she have guessed when she had run into him that morning in the woods that the man she had once loved might wind up holding her very future in his hands.

Chapter 13

By the time Peter and Emily departed the Fulberry residence late that afternoon, the sun that had been so bright earlier in the day was starting to disappear behind a layer of threatening gray clouds. The scent of rain on the air and the faint sound of thunder in the distance heralded a coming storm.

A groom brought their horses forward, and as Peter moved to assist Emily into her saddle, he studied her rather closed expression. She'd been quiet ever since they had arrived, and he couldn't help wondering what was troubling her.

Apart from being forced to spend time in his company, of course.

With a grimace, he swung up onto his own mount's

back and fell in next to her as she prodded her mare into a walk. She seemed eager to be on her way.

And he supposed he couldn't blame her. They had spent several hours at Fulberry Manor, and he felt no closer to putting a name to the Oxfordshire Thief than he had the first day he'd arrived.

Unlike the Tuttlestons, Lord and Lady Fulberry were a young couple who had been married just a few short years. When questioned about the robberies, the marquis had only been able to say that it seemed the thief had entered the study through the room's French doors and had known the precise location of the family safe: behind a portrait of the very first Marquis and Marchioness of Fulberry. Once again, the lock on the French doors had apparently been picked by an expert hand, and the safe itself showed no signs of forced entry.

Almost as if the thief had known the combination.

When Peter had asked the marquis if this were possible, the man had blinked and shaken his head. "I suppose anything is possible, but as far as I know, the only ones with the combination are myself and my wife."

Lady Fulberry, a flighty and high-strung young woman a few years older than Emily, had sobbed and dabbed at her eyes with a handkerchief. "This entire situation has been a nightmare! And now we shall have to delay our departure for London for the Season until this whole matter is settled. We shall have to miss the Duchess of Klein's ball this year, and I can't tell you what a disappointment that is."

Emily had made a sympathetic noise and patted the woman's arm, and Peter had found himself grateful once again for her presence. She alone had appeared to be holding the emotional marchioness in check, as Lord Fulberry himself had seemed at an utter loss as to how to deal with his weeping wife.

Peter could only breathe a sigh of relief when it was finally time to leave. The marquis had provided him with a list of guests that had attended their dinner party the evening of the break-in, as well as an itemized list of the valuables that had been taken, and after undertaking a thorough search of the premises and speaking with the staff, he could think of nothing more to be done.

He glanced over at Emily now where she trotted along beside him and cleared his throat, drawing her curious gaze to his.

"I want to thank you for your help today," he ventured. "I appreciate it."

She shrugged. "I didn't really do all that much."

"On the contrary. You did a great deal. You kept the marchioness calm and out of the way. I must confess, if I'd been forced to spend too much time in the lady's esteemed company, I might have been tempted to jump from the highest tower."

One corner of Emily's mouth curved in amusement. "Penelope isn't so bad. A bit shallow, it's true, but deep down she has a good heart."

When Peter raised an eyebrow at her in inquiry, she went on. "I've known her since we were quite young. We were never the best of friends, of course. More acquaintances. But she never treated me as if I were an outcast as some others in society did. She talked her husband into making a very generous donation to Willow Park recently, and I'll always be grateful to her for that."

"That was indeed kind of her."

"Yes. It was."

They rode on in silence for several minutes, and Peter found himself racking his brain for some other topic of conversation. When he opened his mouth again and his next words came out, however, he could have bitten his tongue off.

"You know, you never did explain where it was you went to last night."

Emily stiffened noticeably, and he stifled a curse. Of all the things he could have said, bringing up their run-in the evening before was the last one he should have mentioned. He was well aware of that, but the truth was, as hard as he'd tried, he had been unable to dismiss his curiosity as to where she had been before he'd stumbled across her in the garden. It had been weighing on his mind, and he couldn't seem to rid himself of the suspicion that it might have had something to do with the Viscount Moreland.

The very possibility was enough to make him see red.

"I told you, I went for a walk," she said, her tone stilted as she avoided his gaze. "And I thought we had agreed we weren't going to speak of it again."

"We agreed we wouldn't speak of what occurred between us. I never agreed not to question you as to your whereabouts." Some demon of jealousy inside of him would not let him drop the subject now that it had been brought up. "You're being so secretive about it, can you

blame me for wondering? Are you certain it has nothing to do with your . . . good friend Lord Moreland?"

Her face reddened and she faced him once more, her
violet eyes blazing. "I'm not being secretive. I've told
you exactly where I went and there is nothing more to
be said. And Lord Moreland is a gentleman who would
never think of luring a young lady out of her home in
the middle of the night for any reason." She lifted her
chin in a mutinous fashion. "But as I said last evening,
even if I had been sneaking out to meet him, I can't see
where it would be any business of yours. You gave up
the right to meddle in my affairs when you left us all."

A growl rumbled deep in his chest, aching to break
free. But before he could give voice to his anger, a drop
of rain splattered against his cheek and called his attention to the menacing sky above. The sun had long ago
disappeared, and the roiling black clouds overhead
looked ready to drop their heavy burden at any moment.

Brushing aside his temper, Peter indicated the darkness above them with a jerk of his head. "As much as I
would love to continue to argue the point with you, I'm
afraid we have a problem. It's going to rain at any moment, and from the looks of those clouds and the way
the wind is whipping up, it's not going to be any brief
spring shower. There's no way we're going to make it to
Knighthaven before it pours."

As if to punctuate his statement, a bolt of lightning
cut across the sky in front of them in a jagged arc, followed by a roll of thunder, and two more fat raindrops
pelted the side of his face. Damnation! They were still

on the outskirts of Little Haverton and had at least a mile or two to travel before they would even reach the village, much less Knighthaven.

Emily reached up and caught at the bonnet that hung down her back as a sudden gust of wind attempted to wrest it from her grasp, then looked over at Peter with apprehension, her earlier disagreement with him forgotten for the moment. "Should we go back to Fulberry Manor to wait it out?"

He shook his head. "It's almost as far to go back now as it would be to continue on to the village."

She bit her lip and studied the path ahead for a moment, then glanced back at him. "I believe there is a small cottage just a little farther ahead, set back off the road. It's abandoned and quite dilapidated, but it might offer us a bit of shelter from the storm."

Peter knew the building she was speaking of. The home of a previous tenant who had once resided on the Fulberry estate, it had been vacant for as long as he could remember, and it was indeed ramshackle at best. In fact, they would be lucky if it didn't fall down around their heads.

But as far as he could see, they didn't have much choice.

He nodded. "All right. Let's go."

No sooner had he come to that decision than the rain began to come down in earnest, and he and Emily urged their horses on to a faster pace, their clothes quickly becoming drenched with water as they struggled through the downpour.

After what seemed like a small eternity, Peter finally

caught sight of the cottage's roof through the trees and called out to his companion, signaling her to turn Artemis off the road. She did so and he followed, both of them coming to a halt in the weed-choked yard.

Swinging down from his saddle, he reached up to assist Emily and gave her a nudge in the direction of the building once she joined him on the ground. "Go ahead in," he told her. "I'll take care of the horses."

"But—"

"Go on. It shouldn't take long, and I'll be in shortly."

She hesitated for only a second, then obeyed, and he waited until he was certain she was safely inside before leading their mounts around to the rear of the dwelling. There, a squat wooden structure that must have once been used to house the former occupant's horses sat a short distance away from the cottage itself. Though it appeared to be in even worse shape than the rest of the property, at least the roof was still intact and should offer Champion and Artemis some measure of protection from the elements.

Once he had calmed the two animals and had made them as comfortable as possible in the circumstances, he retrieved his saddlebag and returned to Emily.

The interior of the cottage was cold and dark, and Peter had to pause for a moment in the doorway to give his eyes a chance to adjust to the dimness. A sudden flare of light from the far corner drew his attention, and as he saw Emily straighten away from the tumbledown fireplace, he was surprised to realize that she'd managed to start a small fire.

As she stood silhouetted by its glow, she had never

looked more like an angel. It took his breath away. Her long blond curls had come loose from their pins and fell about her shoulders in a damp mass of molten gold, and her sodden yellow gown clung to her ripe curves like a second skin, outlining her full breasts, slender waist, and rounded hips to perfection.

His mouth went dry. Perhaps not an angel. More like a seductive nymph sent to tempt him, despite all of his good intentions.

Taking note of him lingering on the threshold, she sent him a wry smile that he could see even in the half-light. "I could be wrong, but I doubt that you'll get very dry if you intend to remain out there in the storm."

He gave a start. She must think him mad to be standing here gaping at her like a complete lack-wit. Struggling to subdue his seething emotions, he came the rest of the way inside and closed the heavy wooden door behind him against the torrents of rain.

She came toward him, her head tilted as she examined him with veiled eyes. "Are the horses settled?"

Unable to speak, he nodded and turned his attention to their surroundings, faintly illuminated by the glow of the flames. The room was large and drafty with a hard-packed dirt floor and a low-beamed ceiling. It was also empty. There wasn't a lick of furniture in the place except for a rickety wooden stool set before the fire.

He jerked his head in that direction, needing a way to escape her disturbing proximity. "Why don't you go warm yourself by the flames? You need to let your clothes dry out or you'll be catching a fever, and your brother will never forgive me."

She studied him for a long, drawn-out moment, and just when he thought she wasn't going to comply, she shrugged and moved away, seating herself on the stool before the hearth.

With an inner sigh of relief, Peter hunched down on the dirt floor and started to unpack his saddlebag.

The first thing he withdrew was his pistol.

Hearing a slight gasp, he looked up to find Emily watching him with eyes as wide as saucers in her pale face. She was staring at the weapon, her expression apprehensive.

What? Did she think he was going to shoot her?

When she spoke, her voice was a hoarse whisper. "You know, I . . ." She stumbled to a halt and licked her lips, the action unknowingly sensuous, then tried again. "I've always been aware in some corner of my mind that your job involves a certain amount of danger, but I don't think I ever let myself truly consider just *how* dangerous it must be."

He ignored the jolt the sight of that pink tongue sweeping across her lips caused him and hefted the pistol in his hand, holding it up so the firelight flickered off the cold metal of the barrel. "Yes, well, luckily I've rarely been forced to use this." He shot her a censuring look. "Thank God I didn't have it with me last night."

She froze for an infinitesimal second, then her chin went up at a haughty angle and she looked away, staring into the orange flames next to her.

Would he never learn to keep his mouth shut? It seemed he always knew the right thing to say to put her back up. One minute they could be having a perfectly cordial conversation, and the next they were at each other's throats.

Smothering the frustration that boiled within him, Peter yanked a blanket from his bag and held it out toward Emily. "Here. You need to get out of that dress."

Her head jerked back in his direction with such force that her wet curls bounced on her shoulders. "I beg your pardon?"

One corner of his mouth quirked upward in amusement in spite of himself. "You're still shivering. You need to take off the gown and wrap yourself in this."

She hesitated, then stood and came forward to accept the blanket, eyeing him with a certain amount of distrust. "You won't look?"

"You know, I am capable of being a gentleman if the situation calls for it." And the last thing he needed was to see that luscious figure unclothed. "I promise I won't look."

To emphasize his point, he turned his back and busied himself emptying the rest of his pack, trying to ignore the sound of material rustling behind him. He could almost visualize the creamy skin that would be revealed as she peeled the muslin gown down over her body, the way the firelight would illuminate all her secret curves and hollows, gilding her with an ethereal glow . . .

Peter had to stifle a groan.

"I'm done." The voice came from behind him.

He turned to find her standing less than a foot away,

the blanket hugged about her, making her look small and helpless, like a child.

But she was no child.

Clearing his throat, he indicated the saddlebag with a jerk of his head. "Are you hungry? I have a half a loaf of bread with me that I snitched from the kitchen at Knighthaven. It isn't much and it's most likely a bit stale, but—"

"No, thank you." As he watched her, one side of the blanket slid down, and he caught sight of a pale shoulder barely covered by the lacy strap of her chemise before Emily tugged the covering back up. "What about you? Don't you have another blanket?"

He forced his gaze away from her and tried not to pray for the blanket to slip again—just a little bit farther this time. "No. But I don't need one. I'll be fine."

She nodded, then moved to drape her gown over the stool next to the fire to dry. Her movements were graceful and delicate, drawing his eyes back to her against his will, hypnotizing him.

Bloody hell, he should just hand her the pistol and let her put him out of his misery!

"You know, my reputation would be quite thoroughly compromised if anyone were to find us like this together."

Her comment pulled his gaze to her face, but he couldn't quite read her expression in the dimness.

"I don't think you need to worry about anyone stumbling across us here. And I won't tell anyone if you won't." Seeking to distract himself, he yanked off a hunk of bread and took a bite as he stuck the rest of the loaf back in his saddlebag. "Hopefully, we won't be here for long."

There came a small swish of sound, and he looked back up to find that she had crossed the room and stood once again at his side, staring down at him from under lowered lashes.

The silence lengthened, and just when he had started to believe she wasn't going to say anything, she spoke in a voice that was hardly more than a whisper. "Why, Peter?"

Something in the way she said it sent a chill up his spine. "Why what?"

"Why did you leave Little Haverton the way you did four years ago?" She paused, then tightened her hold on her blanket and took another step toward him, her eyes blazing with resolution, as if she had no intention of being dissuaded from gaining an answer. "Why did you leave me?"

Chapter 14

She'd made up her mind that she wasn't going to ask him, that she didn't want to hear what he might say in response. As she stood staring down at Peter, however, something beyond Emily's control seemed to drive her, forcing the question from her lips.

It might have been because Jenna's words had been swirling around inside her head the whole time they were visiting Fulberry Manor, replaying like a never-ending mantra until she was sure she would go mad. In spite of her worry about Jack and about Peter's investigation, she'd been unable to dismiss her friend's admonition from her thoughts.

"Doesn't 'e at least deserve the benefit of the doubt?"

Perhaps he did. Perhaps he'd truly had a good reason

for his departure from Oxfordshire. But she was tired of wondering. All she knew was that when he'd left, she'd lost not only the man she'd loved, but her best friend as well.

And she wanted to know why.

Maybe once she had the answer she could finally put it behind her.

For a long moment after she spoke, the only sound that could be heard was the pounding of the rain on the roof of the cottage. Peter seemed almost paralyzed, locked in place, as he returned her gaze with a carefully blank expression.

Then, rising to his feet, he brushed by her and strode over to the fireplace to stand with his back to the room, his stance rigid. "What can that possibly matter now?"

His distant tone roused her temper and she crossed the space between them, coming to a halt at his elbow and planting her hands on her hips in a belligerent manner. "It matters."

When he didn't reply, merely continued to stare into the flames, she reached out and caught his arm, her fingers digging into his sleeve. "Peter, please."

The desperation in her voice must have gotten through to him, for he finally turned to look at her. The firelight cast patterns of light and darkness over the hard angles of his face, giving him a vaguely saturnine appearance that sent a quiver throughout her body. Water dripped from the ends of his tawny, overlong hair, and Emily couldn't seem to help letting her eyes follow the trails of moisture as they slid down along the planes of his cheeks and the slope of his neck until they disappeared into the collar of his shirt. A very damp shirt that molded to his wide shoulders and lean, muscled arms and chest, leaving little to the imagination.

Closing her eyes to shut out the disconcerting sight of him for a moment, she took a deep breath, attempting to rein in her chaotic emotions before she met his stare and tried to speak again. "I have a right to know."

"I fail to see what difference it makes."

"I need to know—" In spite of herself, Emily's voice broke and she had to struggle to push the rest of the words out through her constricted throat. "I need to know it wasn't because of me. That it wasn't my fault."

Peter's visage suddenly seemed to pale in the dimness of the cottage and his jaw went slack, his expression one of honest astonishment. "Because of you? No!" Reaching up, he caught hold of her hand on his arm and twined his fingers through hers, his grip warm and gentle—and unexpected. "Is that what you've thought all this time?"

"What else was I to think? I make a fool of myself by trying to stir your jealousy, we come close to . . . to making love, and the next morning you're gone without a word and everything has changed between us. I must have done *something* wrong for you to react in such a way. Or perhaps—" She paused, fighting the tears that suddenly blurred her vision. "Or perhaps you never cared for me at all and our relationship was nothing but a lie."

"Emily, you mustn't believe that." He bowed his head, and she was certain she heard him give a low groan before he dropped her hand and began to pace in front of her. "I will always cherish the memories of our friendship. No one ever believed in me the way you did."

"Then why . . . ?"

"Damn it, how do I explain?" He pushed his fingers back through his hair in a frustrated motion, and when he met her eyes, his own were gleaming with a ferocity that startled her. "It was never *you,* Emily. It was us. Together."

"I don't understand."

Catching her hand again, he led her over to the stool and moved aside her damp gown before urging her to seat herself. Then he hunkered down next to her, propping his elbows on his knees. At first, he said nothing, then he heaved a breath and raked his free hand through his hair once more. "This isn't easy for me to talk about. I never planned on . . . But you . . . Bloody everlastin' 'ell!"

The fervor in his voice, his slippage into Cockney, was enough to tell Emily just how much this topic of conversation disturbed him. Before, she might have changed the subject, given up on prying the reason for his defection from him. But after her conversation with Jenna today, she had to know. She couldn't just forget about it and go on the way she had been. She was tired of feeling hurt and angry. It was well past time for her to learn to get on with her life without memories of what might have been to weigh her down.

Tightening her grip on Peter's hand, she wound her fingers through his and gave a slight squeeze. "Please go on. I have to know."

He looked down at her hand in his, and even in the

dark she could see a flash of something like pain in his eyes. "I've never told you—or anyone—much about my past. It's not something I like to be reminded of, so I don't speak of it."

It was true. Even after all these years, Emily knew little of Peter's background other than that his mother had been a prostitute and he'd lived most of his childhood on the streets of London. Whenever she'd been brave enough to ask him about it before, he'd brushed her questions aside, so she'd finally stopped asking.

"My mum . . . well, it's no secret she was a doxy," he went on, his firmly chiseled mouth twisting into a scowl. "She also . . . hated me. See, I was a reminder of what she did for a living, and she couldn't stomach it. She had no idea who my father was. He could have been any one of a hundred men, and the fact that she'd slipped up once and wound up with an unwanted child as a result stuck in her craw. When it came to me, she was quick with the back of her hand and a harsh word, and I was pretty much left to fend for myself."

He paused for a moment before looking up to meet Emily's gaze. "I experienced the worst of life before I'd even turned seven, Em. I lived in a whorehouse, and the dregs of society wandered in and out of its doors every day. My God, I had to sleep in the same room where my mum serviced her customers. Curled up in my corner, night after night, listening to those sounds . . ."

At the bleakness in his expression, Emily let out a small cry and leaned toward him, aching to comfort him in some way, but he evaded her touch by letting go of her hand and getting to his feet. He moved to stand before the fire once again, his profile cast in grim shadow by the flames.

"And that's not the worst of it. When I was seven, she finally got tired of providing a roof over my head. Never mind that I'd been feeding and caring for myself by picking pockets for longer than I could remember, that I rarely troubled her for a thing or even spoke to her. She wanted me gone, so she kicked me out onto the streets."

Emily stifled a gasp. She couldn't imagine a mother caring so little for her own child that she would cast him to the wolves without a second thought. But apparently Peter's mother had done so. Dear heavens, the woman must have been a monster! "Oh, Peter—"

But he kept talking, almost as if he hadn't heard her voice. He was too lost in his memories of the past. "And once I was on those streets, life didn't get any easier. I lived among murderers, thieves, the worst sort of criminals one can imagine." He looked back at her over his shoulder. "That's the sort of background I come from. I had to become one of them to survive, and until I found the Rag-Tag Bunch, I lived like an animal."

He took a step toward her. "That's why I left. What was happening between us . . ." He shook his head. "It was wrong, and I couldn't let it continue. You deserved better than a former guttersnipe who didn't even know what his father's name was. I knew I had to leave, to put distance between us, before something occurred that we would both regret."

Stunned, Emily clasped her hands together in her lap and studied every inch of his features, trying to read his thoughts by sheer force of will. "And you made this decision without even talking to me about it?"

"What was there to talk about? My mind was made up. I had to do what was best for you." A muscle tightened in his jaw. "Damn it, Emily, you know nothing could have come of it! The two of us together? The princess and the pickpocket? The daughter of an earl and the son of a harlot? What would society have said?"

He was right. Deep down she knew he was right. But it didn't lessen the pain. Nor did it make her any less angry that he had made the decision to sever their relationship without giving her any say in the matter.

Clutching her blanket about her, she lunged to her feet and crossed the room to his side, her temper seething just beneath the surface like a cauldron ready to boil over. She raised her chin and glared up at him. "Did you truly think I was that shallow? That your background mattered to me?"

"I knew it didn't matter to you, Em. That's why I had to make the decision for both of us. When we were children it wasn't so vital, but whether we wished it so or not, my background *did* matter. It *does* matter. And we can't let ourselves forget that again."

Emily's fury rose up, choking her. "You have no idea what it did to me when you left. I thought we loved each other, and when you were suddenly gone without a word . . ." She swallowed and blinked, once again feeling tears dangerously close. "I thought none of it had meant anything to you."

"I'm sorry for whatever pain I caused you. But you must see it was the right decision?"

"What I see is that you took it upon yourself to decide what was best for me when you had no right!"

Peter's face darkened. "Bloody hell, Em, you didn't hear the talk, the speculation going on around us. You were oblivious, but I wasn't. Every time I went into the village, I heard people whispering about the earl letting his sister run loose about the countryside with that worthless London 'street trash.' They said I would ruin you. *Ruin you*. And they were right, weren't they?" His tone turned bitter. "I almost did. I almost rutted with you up against a tree like you were a common dockside whore."

Emily didn't bother to reprimand him for his crudity. She was too busy recovering from his revelation. So that was why he had distanced himself from her in those final days before he'd left Willow Park! "I can't believe it. You let a few words of idle gossip drive a wedge between us, chase you away?"

"It was more than idle gossip. And it wasn't just that. It was the way I almost took you that last night. It reminded me of who—and what—I was. I knew if we had ever truly tried to make a go of it together, sooner or later you would have realized what a mistake you'd made. I decided to save us both the heartache and trouble."

"How dare you presume to judge how I would have felt? I didn't need your protection and I didn't ask for it." Emily glared at him. "But perhaps it wasn't me you feared for so much as yourself!"

Their eyes locked and held in challenge.

Emily wasn't certain which of them moved first. But

the next thing she knew, they were in each other's arms, and Peter's lips descended on her own.

The taste of her was like the sweetest of aphrodisiacs, the feel of her in his arms like his fondest dream come true.

With a gruff moan, Peter reached up a hand and speared his fingers through Emily's wet hair, tilting her head back for easier access as he thoroughly ravished her mouth. Her rounded curves fit against him to perfection, almost as if they were made for each other.

In some dim corner of his mind, he knew kissing her was a mistake. After last night, he had promised himself this would never happen again, but for once his lust had overcome his determination to do what was right. Lady Emily Knight had always been his Achilles' heel and it seemed she always would be.

Skimming his tongue over the velvety surface of her lips, he savored the sound of her soft sigh before lifting his head to bury his nose in the fragrant curls at her temple. Her arms slid upward to twine around his neck, and the feel of her delicate fingers sifting through the hair at his nape sent a shiver racing up his spine.

"My angel," he said huskly, closing his eyes for a fleeting moment, letting the ecstasy of her touch wash over him in waves. "Emily, my sweet, sweet angel . . ."

Peter brought his hands away from her face and let them glide down her body, passing over her shoulders, brushing down her arms, briefly resting on her slender waist before delving inside her shielding blanket to palm her bottom. He lifted her against himself, fitting her to the bold jut of his arousal.

At the contact, she gave a wavering cry and rocked her hips, the movement like a match to the flame of Peter's already rampant desire. With a deep growl, he turned with her in his arms to press her back against the wall of the cottage and took her lips once again in a devastating exchange.

Emily gasped and arched against him, the movement dislodging her blanket and sending it sliding down to pool on the dirt floor at her feet.

"Peter," she whispered once he released her mouth, her nails digging into his back through the lawn of his shirt, "Peter, please, I want . . ."

But she didn't finish the sentence. Instead, she gazed up at him in the dimness, her haunting purple eyes cloudy with passion and conveying an all too eloquent plea for him to continue.

He traced his hands up her sides in a slow stroke, taking satisfaction in the way she quivered beneath his touch. The firelight shone through the thin white linen of her chemise, delineating every curve of her lush form. Her breasts were high and firm, her rosy nipples taut and stabbing against the damp material.

It was more provocation than Peter could bear.

"Dear God, Emily. You are so beautiful," he said hoarsely, smoothing a hand over her shoulder. Slipping a finger under the strap of the chemise, he slid it down, his mouth following in its wake, tasting the creamy skin that was revealed to him.

Her head fell back against the wall, and she made no move to stop him as he reached up to peel aside the other strap as well. The chemise fell to her waist, baring her ripe breasts to the fire's glow and his reverent gaze.

Wrapping his arms around her, he leaned down to take one of the distended pink tips into the warm cavern of his mouth.

Emily was lost in the bliss of Peter's touch, unable to think of anything but the delight of being in his arms again. His hands on her sent bursts of sensation through her nerve endings, and the moment the heat of his mouth enclosed her naked breast, she went up on her toes in reaction, a keening cry falling from her lips. As he suckled her gently, his tongue plied her nipple, curling around the erect bud until it ached.

She had dreamed of him touching her this way. But never had she believed it could ever happen. Yet, here he was, caressing her, loving her, making her feel things she'd thought never to feel again.

Something niggled at the edges of her consciousness, but she pushed it away, determined to experience every bit of pleasure she could in the moment. Cupping the back of Peter's head, she held him to her as he nuzzled first one nipple, then the other, the edges of his teeth grazing the tender nubs before his tongue shot out to soothe them. She released another moan in response.

"If I'm dreaming, angel," he murmured, his breath fanning over sensitive flesh still moist from his attentions, "don't ever wake me. I want to stay in 'eaven wiv you forever."

His words were enough to send her pulse skyrocketing. The emotion in that Cockney-tinged voice told her he meant everything he said. To know that she affected him just as profoundly as he did her was heady knowledge.

Needing to feel his skin, to touch him in some way, she let her hands glide down over his broad shoulders and into the vee of his shirtfront. She felt his body shudder as her palms lingered on the solid wall of his chest, indulging in the feel of satiny flesh over hard muscle.

What would come next? she wondered as he lifted his mouth from her breasts to give her another soul-stealing kiss. Emily might have been a virgin, but she was well aware of what went on between a man and a woman, and she knew if they carried this through to the logical conclusion, there would be no going back.

No going back . . .

The thought was enough to arrest her movements and seize the air in her lungs. The vague shadow that had wavered at the back of her mind, disturbing her, took shape and had her suddenly shoving at Peter's shoulders in an attempt to push him away.

She couldn't do this! Too much stood between them. Not the least of which was the fact that *she* was the Oxfordshire Thief.

Seeming to become aware that she was no longer pulling him closer, but trying to hold him off, Peter tore his lips from hers and gazed down at her in confusion, his blue eyes unfocused and blazing with the depth of his need. "Emily?"

She barely managed to squeeze the words out through the lump in her throat. "Peter, we have to stop. Now."

Though her voice wasn't quite steady, he must have been able to read the seriousness in it, for he blinked and his expression instantly closed up. Wheeling about, he stalked across the room to stand with his back to her as he put up an obvious battle to regain control.

Pulling up the straps of her chemise to cover her swollen, aching breasts, Emily knelt down to retrieve her blanket and quickly wrapped it about herself. Dear God, what had she almost done?

Peter Quick was a dangerous man, and finally knowing why he had left her only made him that much more lethal to her peace of mind. She had believed for so long that he simply hadn't cared, but now she realized that he'd cared too much. He'd walked away from his home and all he'd known because he'd believed it was best for her.

Closing her eyes, she heaved a sigh and reached up to rub at her temples. Never mind that she was the one who had demanded the truth. She couldn't let any of it matter. Even if there was still some feeling between them, she couldn't afford to lose her heart to him. Not again. Regardless of his reasons, she'd put her faith in him once before and he'd left her.

How could she ever trust him again?

"I'm sorry."

His voice was low, almost inaudible over the ominous growls of thunder from outside, but she heard it nevertheless.

"It's my fault," he went on, turning to face her. The pain in his eyes was almost more than she could bear. "I never should have touched you, but when I'm around you I seem to have trouble remembering that."

Emily shook her head. She couldn't allow him to take all the blame. "No. I was just as responsible." She started forward, one hand outstretched as if to offer comfort, but came to an abrupt stop. He wouldn't want sympathy from her. Not after this.

Biting her lip, she looked down at the floor, struggling to find the right words to soothe the troubled waters between them. "Let's just put it down to talk of the past and the isolation of our surroundings. It's all too easy to forget things—important things—in a situation like this and to get swept up in the moment. It was an aberration, nothing more."

He laughed, but there was no humor in the sound. "An aberration. That sounds about right." Stalking over to his saddlebag, he lifted it off the floor and slung it over his shoulder before casting her a hooded look. "I'm going to go check on the horses."

Before she could say a word, he had pushed open the door and stepped out into the rain.

Emily hurried after him, coming to a halt on the threshold and watching as he splashed through the puddles in the muddy yard before disappearing around the side of the cottage.

As soon as he was out of sight, she collapsed against the doorframe, letting the weakness that had been hovering, ready to overtake her, have its way.

What have I done?

She shook her head. She knew the answer to that, even if she didn't want to admit it. She had reminded herself all too powerfully of what had first drawn her to Peter. Of the passion and emotion that was obviously still very much alive and well between them.

But it was of no consequence. No matter what she felt for Peter, nothing could come of it. Even if he should still care for her, any relationship was doomed to failure from the start.

Wasn't it?

Oh, this was getting her nowhere! Tightening her hold on her blanket, she glanced up at the gray sky, glad to see that at least the storm seemed to be over. The rain had slackened to a mere trickle, and the thunder had tapered off to an occasional grumble far in the distance.

Closing the door, she returned to the fire to lift her still-damp dress from the floor and shake it out, brushing off the particles of dirt that clung to the material before slipping it over her head. When Peter returned to the cottage, she would tell him it was best that they continue on their way to Knighthaven. Once they were away from this place, they could forget this incident and move on.

But despite her determination, a seed of doubt still remained. *Could* she forget what had passed between them here?

Could either of them?

Chapter 15

〜◯◯〜

"**Y**ou've been very quiet this morning, Em. Is everything all right?"

The soft query brought Emily out of her musings, and she looked up from her contemplation of a nearby patch of violets to meet her companion's concerned gaze.

"Of course, Adam," she said, forcing a note of lightness into her voice that she was far from feeling. "I was just daydreaming, I'm afraid."

The viscount shifted in his saddle, his expression unconvinced. "You've hardly said a word since we left Knighthaven."

Emily bit her lower lip and swiftly looked away. It was true, but what could she possibly say to explain her preoccupation?

It had been a need to clear her head and a large dose

of guilt that had led her to accept when Lord Moreland had dropped by the house early this morning to ask her to accompany him for a ride about the estate. After having turned down his previous invitation for an outing, she'd felt she couldn't say no without further widening the rift between them.

But things had been awkward, and for once she found herself at a loss as to what to say to him. He'd always been so easy to talk to before, but now that he seemed to have set his sights on her as a wife, she was afraid anything she said at this point could be construed as encouragement.

She glanced at him out of the corner of her eye. He looked especially handsome today with his golden-blond hair tumbling over his forehead in a rakish manner, his muscular form clad in close-fitting buckskin breeches and a bottle-green coat that outlined the width of his shoulders.

Why was it that the idea of wedding Adam filled her with a sudden desire to bolt for the hills with all due speed? Perhaps marriage wouldn't be such a bad thing to consider, especially to someone she liked as well as the viscount. She felt comfortable with him and they got along well. Of course, according to gossip he had a bit of a weakness when it came to the gaming tables, but no one was perfect, and there were certainly much worse faults to be had than a penchant for wagering.

But there was no spark between them, no attraction, no matter how much she might wish there was. If she was going to tie herself to someone for life, she wanted it to be someone who affected her both physically and emotionally. Someone who made her head spin and her heart beat faster.

Someone like Peter.

Emily's jaw tightened. She'd made up her mind she wasn't going to allow Peter Quick to cast a shadow over her time with Adam, but she was finding it difficult to keep exactly that from happening. Even when she wasn't in his company, he occupied her every thought. She couldn't seem to forget the feel of his hands smoothing over her skin, his mouth on her breasts . . .

Shivering, she took a deep breath and shoved him from her mind once again before turning back to Lord Moreland with what she hoped was a placating smile. "I'm sorry. I've been a bit troubled and haven't slept well lately, so I suppose I'm just tired."

"Troubled by what? Does it have anything to do with this Quick fellow?"

At his question, she started and couldn't help giving an inward groan. It seemed even in innocent conversation with another man, she couldn't escape Peter.

They had halted their horses next to a stream at the edge of the Ellington property, but needing to distract herself from the whirlwind of emotions that swept through her at the mention of Peter, Emily prodded Artemis forward into a walk and the viscount followed suit on his mount, falling in next to her.

She studied him over her shoulder. "What makes you ask that?" she queried, keeping her tone nonchalant.

Adam's chiseled mouth turned downward. "I don't like the way he looks at you. And he seems to put you on edge when you're around him. I noticed it the other day at breakfast."

Well, she couldn't deny that, Emily had to concede. And Lord Moreland was much too observant. More observant than she'd given him credit for.

Searching for some way to excuse her behavior, she shrugged and waved a careless hand. "Mr. Quick and I tend to put each other's backs up. We've had some . . . disagreements in the past, but we've come to terms with it and now we have an understanding of sorts."

That was true, as well. In the last few days since the incident in the abandoned cottage, she and Peter had somehow managed to continue to work together. She had accompanied him as he had questioned each of the people on the list of dinner-party guests Lord Fulberry had provided, and though their interaction had been strained at first, his investigation and her determination to keep him from finding out the truth had soon taken precedence.

And they hadn't spoken of what had passed between them again.

Adam's brow furrowed in obvious disapproval. "I'm certain that you believe that, Em, but I don't trust the man. He *is* a former pickpocket, after all. And to have him staying in your home with you . . . well, I can't imagine what Lord Ellington is thinking."

Emily took immediate exception to the viscount's condescending attitude. "He is a former pickpocket who is now an officer of the law. And my brother is *thinking* about the people of Little Haverton and catching this thief before he causes any more devastation."

"Of course." Lord Moreland looked suitably chastened, though something still lurked in the depths of his hazel eyes that tugged at her uneasiness. "I apologize. But you must understand, I'm just concerned."

She nodded, but found herself unable to reply. The man's criticism of Peter had angered her more than it should have, and that disturbed her. More than she was ready to admit.

At that moment, they trotted into the stable yard at Knighthaven, and Emily had to restrain a sigh of relief. Always before, she had enjoyed being with Adam, but today she was most anxious to part company with him. Had her friend always been so dictatorial, so arrogant? So proprietary where she was concerned?

It seemed Peter's return had opened her eyes to several things she'd once been blind to.

She started to slide down from her saddle, but the viscount appeared at her side before her feet could even touch the cobblestones and grasped her waist, lowering her next to him. Instead of letting her go once she was on the ground, however, he maintained his hold, staring down at her in a disconcerting manner.

"Why, Adam, whatever is wrong?" she asked, attempting to keep her tone light and amused. "Do I have a spot of dirt on my cheek?"

To her surprise, he let go of her waist to reach up and gather her hands in both of his. Oh, dear. Was he actually about to declare himself?

"Emily," he began earnestly, "I've been meaning to speak to you about something rather important. I'm certain you must know how I feel about you, and I—"

"I'm sorry. Am I interrupting something?"

At the sound of the deep voice, Emily glanced up to find Peter lounging in the entrance to the stables, arms crossed and eyebrows raised in silent inquiry. The sight of him had her heart giving a queer flutter in her chest, and she felt a surge of relief as she pulled her hands free from Adam's grip and took a step away from him. There was no mistaking the look of displeasure that crossed the viscount's face, but she could only be grateful for Peter's timely arrival. "Of course not, Mr. Quick. Lord Moreland and I were just . . . talking." She forced a smile. "Did you need something?"

He straightened and ambled toward them, his strides long and fluid. "As a matter of fact, Lady Emily, I was looking for you. I plan on going to see Baron Caulfield in a short while and was hoping you would have the time to come along."

"Certainly." A crony of Emily's father from long ago, Baron Caulfield had been one of the victims on Jack's list of marks. A stuffy, posturing man in his middle years, he had an attitude of preening arrogance that had made Emily feel a bit less guilty about the part she had played in the robbery of his home—though only a bit.

A slight sound drew her attention to Adam, who stood where she'd left him, a frown marring his handsome face. "I'm afraid I don't understand, Emily. Why should you need to accompany Mr. Quick to see Lord Caulfield?"

It was Peter who answered. "Lady Emily has been of great help to me in my questioning of the victims of the Oxfordshire thefts."

The viscount's mouth fell open and he sputtered for a moment, as if lost for words. When he finally managed to speak, his tone dripped with righteous indignation. "Quick, do you mean to tell me you've actually been allowing Lady Emily to take part in this investigation of yours? Do you realize what sort of danger you could be putting her in? Is Lord Ellington aware of this?"

Peter's countenance hardened and he took a step toward the other man. "Lord Ellington is quite aware of it, Moreland. In fact, his wife is the one who suggested Lady Emily might be of assistance. And I would never do anything to place her in any sort of jeopardy." He lifted his chin. "Never."

His voice was so fierce, the look in his eyes so challenging, that Emily feared fisticuffs might be imminent. Stepping swiftly between the two bristling adversaries, she placed a calming hand on Lord Moreland's arm. "Really, Adam. There is no need for this. I'm in no danger. It's not as if I am out chasing the thief down. I simply go with Pet—um, Mr. Quick—when he questions the victims and witnesses. They know me and my presence seems to put them at ease."

The viscount tore his gaze from Peter and folded his arms across his chest, giving her a belligerent scowl. "I still cannot approve of this, Emily. Not at all."

That did it. Emily's own temper flared to life and she fixed him with a stern glare. "It is not for you to approve or disapprove of anything I do, Adam," she informed him coolly. "Kindly remember that in the future."

For a long, awkward moment, no one said a word. Then, close enough to her ear that the warmth of his breath on her neck caused her to shiver, she heard Peter whisper, "Bravo."

She felt her cheeks heat in response.

It was obvious that Lord Moreland heard him as well. But other than sending another glower over Emily's shoulder in Peter's direction, the viscount didn't deign to reply. He merely gave a stiff bow, his pale lashes lowering to veil his eyes, effectively hiding his thoughts.

"Of course. I do apologize. It seems I've overstepped my bounds once again. But you are a good friend, Emily, and I can't help but worry."

"I appreciate your concern. But there is no reason for you to worry. I am quite safe in Mr. Quick's hands—er, care."

The slipup was telling, and Peter's soft chuckle had her seeing red. He *would* enjoy seeing her flounder like this!

"Yes, well, I suppose I'll just have to take your word for that." Seeming oblivious to Emily's discomfiture, Adam captured her hand again, raising it to his lips for a fervent kiss. Behind her, she could almost feel Peter stiffen. "I suppose I should take my leave now. But I do hope we will have a chance to finish our conversation later?"

She nodded, though the mere possibility of his proposing to her tied her stomach in knots. "I shall look forward to it."

As she and Peter watched, the viscount climbed on his horse, inclined his head to them, and cantered out of the stable yard.

After a second or two, Emily turned to face Peter, unable to help wondering if he could tell how glad she was that Adam was finally gone. The thought seemed disloyal somehow. "Well, if you don't mind waiting, it shouldn't take me long to make ready, and then I'll join you for the trip to Lord Caulfield's."

Peter examined her thoughtfully for a second. Then, shoving his hands in his pockets, he gave a casual shrug. "I don't mind waiting at all. If you're *sure* you want to go. Your Lord Moreland didn't seem to care for the idea."

"He's not *my* Lord Moreland, and as you heard me say to him, he has no authority over how I choose to spend my time. I've agreed to accompany you and I intend to do so."

As she finished speaking, a young groom came forward to take Artemis, but Emily waved him on his way. She needed some time alone, she decided, to rein in the chaos in her head. And taking care of her mare was always a soothing task that required little concentration on her part. Thank goodness. "It's quite all right, Tad. I'll get her settled."

"If you're certain, m'lady."

"I am." As the lad loped off, she wrapped the reins around her hand and cast Peter one last glance. "I'll be ready within the hour."

With that, she led Artemis into the darkness of the stables.

Once inside and out from under Peter's watchful eye, Emily felt herself relax, and her pent-up breath escaped her in a rush. It had been a trying morning, and she could only hope the day ahead would get better. Surely it couldn't get any worse.

Dutifully, Artemis allowed her mistress to lead her to her stall in the far corner. And it was only after Emily had removed the mare's saddle and bridle and turned to reach for the currycomb that she realized Peter had followed her. He stood just inside the stall, watching her with a quiet intensity.

Comb in hand, she froze mid-motion. She should have known it wouldn't be so easy to escape him.

"You know, nothing has changed."

His soft words had her narrowing her eyes in puzzlement. "Oh?"

"You always did like the stables. I can remember you used to come here whenever you were angry or upset."

That was true. The stable had been one of her favorite escapes for as long as she could recall. With its scents of hay and old leather, its sounds of horses snorting and snuffling in their stalls, it was a place of warmth and safety, somehow comforting to her senses.

"And I can remember the day your brother brought you Artemis." Peter crossed the stall to join her. "It was your sixteenth birthday. I don't think I'd ever seen you so happy."

He seemed more relaxed than he had since he'd returned to Oxfordshire, and his easy manner had Emily letting down her guard the slightest bit. Smiling in reminiscence, she ran the currycomb over the mare's side in a long, smooth stroke. "She was the first gift Tristan ever gave me after he returned home. The first *real* gift, other than impersonal, little-girl things. It meant a great deal to me. *She* means a great deal to me."

"I know." He reached up to give the horse's muzzle an affectionate rub, and Artemis whinnied in response, nudging his palm. "And I have no doubt she'd gallop through fire for you."

There was a beat of silence, then Peter's laughter floated through the space between them.

"What?" Emily eyed him askance, one hand going to her hip. "What's so funny?"

"I was just thinking about the afternoon you and I took some of the younger boys and girls from Willow Park on a picnic in the woods close to Knighthaven. It was soon after the earl gave you Artemis, and you brought her along. I think she enjoyed the experience as much as the children did."

Her own laughter mixed with his as her mind went back to the afternoon in question, picturing the way Artemis—who had been little more than a filly at the time—had frolicked and gamboled about, basking in the children's attention and making them squeal with delight at her antics.

"She *was* rather entertaining, as I recall," she agreed, meeting Peter's gaze.

"That she was." He paused for a moment, then went on, his tone introspective as he studied her upturned face. "I remember something else about that day, as well."

"Really?"

"Mmmm. It was the day I kissed you for the very first time."

Emily froze, his words catching her off guard. Why on earth would he bring up such a thing now?

A sudden energy seemed to crackle in the air around them, and she had to swallow several times before she could speak past the lump in her throat. "W-was it?"

Peter nodded, his eyes never leaving hers. "We were wading in the stream while the children were eating, and you slipped and lost your balance." One corner of his mouth quirked upward in an almost lazy grin. "I caught you, and when you looked up at me with those big violet eyes, I couldn't resist. Your mouth was practically begging to be kissed."

And what a kiss it had been, she thought dreamily. Slow and sweet and tender. Everything a first kiss should be. And the memory of it had the power to cause her heart to skip a beat even now.

But she had no intention of letting Peter know that.

Raising her chin, she struggled to keep her countenance as blank as possible. "I'm sorry, but I'm afraid I don't remember that."

His smile widened and he leaned forward until less than an inch of space separated them. Devilish sparks danced in those piercing blue eyes, stealing her breath. "You, Lady Emily, are a terrible liar."

She certainly was.

At that moment, the sound of someone clearing his throat had Emily drawing back in haste, her cheeks heating. Glancing up, she found Miles standing at the entrance to the stall, his expression apprehensive.

Oh, dear. What was wrong now? "Yes, Miles?"

"A lad just stopped by to drop off a message for you, m'lady." He took a step forward and held out a small, folded scrap of paper.

"A message?" As Emily met him halfway to take it from his grasp, she couldn't help but notice the troubled shadows that lurked in his usually merry eyes. She swallowed the sudden lump in her throat. If Miles was so disturbed, this couldn't be anything good.

She unfolded the scrap of paper and read the nearly illegible scrawl with growing horror: *Tomorow nite!*

It seemed Jack had decided the time had come for the Oxfordshire Thief to strike again.

Crumpling the note in her fist, she gave Miles a wan smile. "Thank you, Miles."

The stable hand nodded, his face full of a concern he couldn't quite hide, then spun on his heel and left the stall.

"A message from Lord Moreland?"

Peter had approached so quietly that she hadn't been aware he was standing right behind her until his query next to her ear caused her to give a cry of surprise. She spun to face him, her heart pounding fit to burst from her chest.

He studied her with hooded eyes. "I'm sorry. I didn't mean to startle you." All of the warmth that had vibrated between them just moments ago was gone. He gestured to the paper still clenched in her hand. "A message from Lord Moreland?"

Emily had just opened her mouth to deny it when it occurred to her that it was more than likely for the best if she let him go on believing that. After all, what was she going to tell him instead? That it was a note from their old friend Jack Barlow, letting her know it was time to put on her thief's cap and break into their neighbor's home?

Taking a deep breath and injecting a deliberate touch of coyness into her voice, she gazed up at him from under lowered lashes. "Perhaps."

She couldn't miss the shadow that passed over his features at her reply. "The two of you seemed rather cozy out there a little while ago. Are you certain I didn't interrupt anything . . . important?"

"Not at all." Some imp of mischief snapped at her heels, causing her to add questioningly, "Would it matter to you if you *had* interrupted something?"

"Only if he was trying to convince you to meet him for another midnight tryst. In which case I would feel it was my duty to point out to you that you've been advised not to leave the house or grounds after dark. So I would suggest you restrict your assignations with the viscount to daylight hours." He crossed his arms and leaned back against the door of the stall in a negligent pose. "After all, I would hate to have to stand guard beneath your window all night."

Oh, the nerve of him! He would, too. Emily barely restrained the childish urge to stamp her foot in frustration. So much for their earlier camaraderie.

Well, better that things remained this way for now, that he continued to believe she was attracted to Adam. As long as the two of them were on their guard with each other and she continued to keep her emotions at bay, she might at least come out of this sorry business with her heart intact.

She straightened her shoulders and faced him with disdainful hauteur. "I shall be sure to inform Lord Moreland of your dictates. Now, if you'll excuse me, I need to go change or I won't be ready in time to travel with you to Baron Caulfield's. And I certainly wouldn't want to deprive you of the pleasure of my company."

Leaving her final words hovering in the air, she whirled and marched off, feeling Peter's eyes burning into the back of her head the whole way.

Chapter 16

Emily pulled aside a low-hanging branch and peered through the trees at Brimley Hall, peaceful and basking in the pale light of the moon. All of the house's occupants were asleep in their beds, never suspecting what was going to occur or how they were about to be victimized.

A shaft of anguish pierced her.

"If we're going to do this, then we'd better get to it," Miles whispered from where he hunkered behind a nearby bush. "We've already lingered 'ere far too long and the 'orses are getting restless."

It was true. They'd been lying in wait for over an hour. Behind her, Emily could hear Artemis snorting and pawing the ground, and Jenna trying to calm her in a low, soothing tone. The other two horses stirred skittishly at the mare's agitation.

She could no longer afford to hesitate. If they tarried much longer, there was always the chance they could be discovered. It was time to act.

Placing a hand against her roiling stomach, she gazed heavenward. How she hated this. It was especially hard after having just spent yesterday morning in Lord Moreland's company, behaving as if everything were normal when it was far from it. But for now, she could see no other option. She could only pray that God—and eventually Adam and his father—would forgive her.

"All right." She looked back over her shoulder at her companions. "Jenna, you stay here with our mounts. Miles will come with me."

"Wait a minute." Jenna placed a hand on her hip and glared in the stable hand's direction. "Why do I 'ave to stay 'ere and Miles gets to go?"

Emily closed her eyes in weary frustration. "Jenna, we don't have time for this."

"I just don't understand, is all. I want to 'elp and—"

"Bloody 'ell, must you argue about everything, woman?" Miles rose and turned to face her, scowling. "You're staying wiv the 'orses because Lady Em asked you to. And it's not as if I 'aven't done my share of waiting wiv them while you two did all the skulking about. You don't 'ave to be in the middle of everything, you know."

Jenna lifted her chin in defiance. "I don't expect to be in the middle of everything. But I *do* want to be there if

Emily needs me. I don't see 'ow I can do that if I stay 'ere."

Emily watched in fascinated dismay as Miles took several steps forward until he was almost nose to nose with the bristling, dark-haired woman. The moonlight illuminated the angry red of his freckled face, the gleam of temper in his green eyes. "Believe me, you'll be the first to know if we need your 'elp. Now, stay wiv the 'orses and quit being so difficult."

"Difficult? Oh, I like that! All I want to do is 'elp and you're calling me difficult? Well, you're not my boss, Miles Riley, and I refuse to let you tell me what to do."

Emily closed her eyes and prayed once again—this time for patience. She loved both her friends dearly, but this was getting out of hand. They were behaving like children, and at the worst possible time.

She was just getting ready to intervene, to point out that it didn't matter who stayed with the horses as long as *someone* did, when Miles let out a growl.

"That bloody well tears it!" Seizing Jenna by the arms, he yanked her against him and brought his mouth down on hers in a hard, ruthless kiss.

It lasted for what seemed to the astonished Emily to be an endless moment. Then the stable hand put the girl from him and gave her a firm shake, his expression conveying absolute authority. "Now, are you going to stay wiv the 'orses, or do I need to tie you to a tree?"

Looking dazed as she gazed up at him, Jenna shook her head, nodded, then shook her head again before her fingers drifted up to touch her kiss-swollen mouth in obvious disbelief.

Emily shook off her temporary paralysis and cleared her throat. "Well, er . . . I suppose that settles it. Jenna, we shouldn't be too long. But if you notice anything amiss, I want you to take the horses and get out of here as fast as you can. Do you understand?"

The younger woman nodded again, but it was hard to tell whether she'd actually heard or not. She was too busy staring at Miles with wide, unfocused eyes.

As Emily led the way from their place of concealment, she glanced back at Jenna one last time to see her friend standing in the same spot, seeming stunned and unable to move.

She couldn't help the hint of amusement that crept into her voice as she looked at Miles. "Looks like you made your point."

"Yes." The frown faded from the stable hand's face to be replaced with a self-satisfied smile. "Looks like I did."

The two of them cut across the wide lawn at the rear of Brimley Hall, keeping to the shadows of the surrounding trees and bushes. All was quiet, not a sound penetrating the almost unearthly stillness.

If things went as planned, they should be able to carry this off with little difficulty. Having known Lord Brimley from childhood, Emily was aware the elderly marquis kept most of his valuables in his safe in the ground-floor library, but Adam had long ago mentioned that his mother's brooch still resided in her keepsake box in her old suite of rooms. Lord Brimley hadn't changed a thing in the marchioness's bedchamber since her death, and Emily was certain she would have no trouble attaining her objective and getting out of the house without detection. The viscount had told her yesterday morning that he would be out for the evening, attending a soiree at the home of Lord and Lady Beaumont, and with the marquis confined to his bed, there should be only the smallest chance she would run into anyone except perhaps a servant.

No, she concluded. The only thing she should have trouble dealing with was her conscience.

It stabbed at her now, and she couldn't suppress a wince. She tried not to think about how Lord Brimley would react if he discovered his beloved wife's favorite piece of jewelry was gone. Jack seemed to have an unerring knack for targeting the precise thing each of his marks prized the most. Exactly how was a mystery, but Emily felt sure his choices were deliberate. Anything to make it harder on her and her sense of integrity.

All the better to punish her.

Emily came to a halt next to the terrace doors that led into the library. Though she would be passing right by the location of the safe, she had no intention of breaking into it or taking anything else. Jack had specified nothing but the brooch, and she wasn't doing a thing more than he had instructed.

She refused to cause Adam and his father any more pain than necessary. She already felt guilty over the way she had treated the viscount lately, and she suspected there would be enough bad feelings on his part once she turned down his proposal.

If he ever got around to making it.

Withdrawing her pick from the pocket of her breeches, Emily had the lock on the doors sprung in only a matter of seconds. She eased them open, then turned to Miles.

"I want you to stay here," she instructed him in a hushed voice. "The fewer people traipsing through the house, the better. Keep an eye out and give me a signal if you notice anything out of the ordinary."

The stable hand's face creased with concern. "Are you certain? What if you need my 'elp?"

"I'll be fine. You'll do me more good standing watch." She forced a reassuring smile. "But I must warn you, I won't be kissing you to convince you of the fact."

Her attempt at levity had Miles relaxing slightly and giving a wry chuckle, but he still appeared doubtful.

She touched his shoulder. "I'll be back. Don't worry."

Wiping her sweaty palms on the seat of her breeches, she stepped inside and closed the doors behind her.

The only illumination came from a wall sconce out in the corridor as it spilled its fragile light through the partially open door of the library. Taking a deep breath, Emily made her stealthy way past the shelves of books and peeked out through the crack.

Nothing stirred beyond the threshold.

Pushing the portal the rest of the way open, she started along the dim hallway toward the front of the house. The back stairs would be much too close to the servants' quarters, and if she remembered correctly from previous visits, Lady Brimley's room had been the last door at the end of the corridor at the top of the main staircase. Of course, Lord Brimley's current bed-chamber was right next door, connected by a small combination sitting and dressing room, so she would have to be especially quiet.

She covered the distance on quick, silent feet, making no sound on the thick runner as she climbed the winding staircase and traversed the long, second-floor hallway.

You have to be careful, Emily, she told herself, approaching the marchioness's room with caution. *You mustn't forget who will be investigating this come the morning.*

Peter.

At the thought of the man who had caused her such confusion and dismay since his return, she felt her heart skip a beat.

What was she to do about him?

After their encounter in the stable yesterday, she was finding it more difficult than ever to keep up her previous façade of haughtiness and reserve. She was so tired of being on her guard, having to watch every word she said. How she wished they could talk as they had about Artemis, feel free to confide in each other about everything, the way they used to. She didn't want to fight with him anymore.

However, she wasn't certain what she *did* want from him.

She had spent the time on the journey to Lord Caulfield's yesterday afternoon contemplating this puzzle. As the baron resided several miles away in the town of Winterset, she and Peter had opted to travel by the Ellington coach rather than take their horses. The silence within had been oppressive and strained. Though she had tried a few times to start a casual conversation, he had seemed reluctant to talk, almost lost in his own thoughts, and she had finally given up in defeat.

And as it had turned out, her attendance hadn't been necessary. The baron had been as pompous and blustery as always, and far from cooperative. Emily's presence had done little to make the man more amenable.

"I fail to see why I need to answer questions that I've already been asked by the constable," he had barked impatiently. "I wasn't even home that evening, so I saw nothing and know nothing beyond the fact that the bounder broke into my study and my safe with hardly any trouble at all. Took everything that was in there, including my favorite pair of diamond cuff links." His chilly blue eyes had raked Peter with blatant contempt. "And if the magistrate has had no luck catching the thief, I doubt you will be able to manage it."

The baron had then turned to Emily. "I hate to say it, my dear, but I tend to agree with the local authorities. Most likely the culprit is one of those former thieves your family is housing at Willow Park." He'd shaken his head. "It is out of respect for your father that I've continued to support this home of yours, but should it turn out that one of the current residents is the guilty party . . . well, I shall have to withdraw my involvement. You understand, of course?"

Emily had made placating noises, but Peter had looked ready to explode. Fearing a confrontation, she'd made their excuses and they had departed as soon as possible.

Their visit had accomplished nothing, and she had spent the time since staying out of Peter's way, afraid her guilt over what she had planned to do tonight would show on her face. Not that he had noticed. He'd been closeted in the study with Tristan from the moment she'd arisen this morning, more than likely filling her brother in on how the case was progressing.

Or perhaps he was avoiding her, as well.

To her surprise, that possibility hurt.

She shook off the unwanted emotion and came back to the present. Now was not the time to get caught up in pondering her problems with Peter. She had to stay focused on the task at hand. It was much too dangerous to let her mind wander.

Putting her hand on the knob of Lady Brimley's former room, she pushed the door open and slipped inside.

The interior of the chamber was dark and musty-smelling, and Emily had to pause a moment to get her bearings. Tiptoeing over to the large casement window, she drew back the heavy draperies and allowed the moonlight to flood into the room. Then, turning, she placed her hands on her hips and surveyed her surroundings.

Now, if I were a brooch, she mused, *where would I be*?

A huge, ornately decorated bed took up much of the far wall, the mattress so high that a stool had been placed at the foot to aid the former occupant in climbing up onto it. A maple wood vanity sat opposite, close to the connecting door that led into the combination sitting and dressing room.

Hmmm. Perhaps . . .

Emily crossed to the piece of furniture and searched through the objects littering the top. She came across several dust-covered perfume bottles, a silver-backed brush, and an empty jewelry box, but no brooch.

She brushed her hands off with a grimace. Adam had been right about the marquis leaving things in here untouched. The chamber looked as if it hadn't been cleaned since Lady Brimley had passed on ten years ago.

Where on earth could the brooch be?

At that moment, she noticed a tall maple armoire in the corner next to the window and she hurried over to it, swinging the doors open with a creak that made her flinch. After waiting a moment to make sure she hadn't roused anyone, she began pushing aside the moth-eaten clothing that hung inside, pulling open drawers and searching the shelves with meticulous care.

It was as she shoved aside a shabby-looking portmanteau on the very top shelf that she discovered hidden behind it a small, lace-trimmed box.

The marchioness's keepsake box?

Emily plucked it from the shelf, her fingers trembling as she pried off the lid. Nestled inside were several odds and ends. A packet of yellowed letters tied with a red ribbon, a book of pressed flowers, a painted miniature of what was obviously Lord Brimley as a much younger man . . .

And a diamond-studded brooch.

Her pulse jumped and she lifted it from the box. As she turned it over in her palm, her gaze fell upon the writing that had been engraved on the back, just beneath the clasp.

To my darling wife, Lavinia. Mere words cannot express what I feel for you. Your loving husband, George.

Tears blurred Emily's vision and she clutched the brooch against her bosom. How Lord Brimley must have loved his wife.

I'll make sure you get this back, my lord, she vowed silently, glancing toward the connecting chamber. If luck was with her, the marquis might never even notice it had been taken.

Tucking the brooch into the pocket of her breeches, she placed the box back on the armoire shelf and closed the doors. Once again, they gave a loud squeak, but this time she barely noticed. She was already out of the room.

She started down the hallway toward the stairs, moving as soundlessly as before. But halfway there, she became aware of a faint noise from somewhere behind her. She turned just in time to see one of the doors along the way come flying open.

A frail, bent figure dressed in a nightshirt and tasseled cap limped out into the corridor.

It was Lord Brimley!

His cane pounding the floor, the elderly marquis called out in a tremulous voice. "Halt! Halt, I say, you miscreant! You'll not rob this house!"

Emily didn't pause, but whirled and began to run, her heart pounding with every step. She had to get out of here!

She could hear Lord Brimley's cane as he pursued her, continuing to yell as loudly as he could. "Help! Help! Stop, thief! Stop or I—"

His words choked to an abrupt, gurgling halt, and a sudden jarring thud followed by a gasp had her looking back over her shoulder just as she reached the top of the stairs.

The marquis lay in a heap several feet away, unmoving.

Emily let out a cry of distress, then covered her mouth with her hand. But it was too late to worry about giving herself away. Lord Brimley's shouts had awakened the servants, who were already bustling about below. The sound of frightened voices and running feet drifted up the stairs.

She couldn't be discovered. Not now. But she couldn't leave without knowing if the marquis was going to be all right.

Hurrying back to the elderly gentleman's side, she knelt next to him and felt for the pulse in his neck. It was there, weak but steady. A groan escaped his lips, but his eyes didn't open.

"I'm so sorry, my lord," she whispered, her heart squeezing at his helplessness. This was all her fault. Should anything happen to him . . . "I'm so sorry."

At that moment, a commotion from down in the foyer had her glancing up in alarm. She couldn't afford to linger. The staff would be arriving to investigate the fuss at any moment.

"I must go, but your servants are on their way to lend their aid, my lord," she told the marquis, patting his shoulder. "Just hold on. Please hold on."

Lunging to her feet, she scurried back down the hallway toward the marchioness's room. Obviously, her previous path through the house had been eliminated as an escape route, and she would have to come up with another way out.

She flung open Lady Brimley's door and ducked inside, closing it behind her just in time. Loud footsteps sounded on the front stairs and a chorus of startled cries echoed down the corridor.

"My lordship!"

"Someone send for the physician! Quickly!"

"What was he on about? Did I hear him yell something about a thief?"

Oh, dear heavens, they would be looking for her! There could be no delay. She *had* to get out at once.

Without hesitation, she raced to the window and pushed open the casement, then leaned far out over the sill, straining to see through the darkness to the ground below.

There. Just beneath the window was a large patch of bushes and flowering shrubs. It wouldn't be a comfortable landing, but it should be enough to cushion her fall, and keep her from breaking an arm or a leg.

Or her neck.

Closing her eyes, she slung a leg over the window ledge, whispered a quick prayer, and jumped.

Chapter 17

Over an hour later, Emily and her two companions limped into the clearing that housed the abandoned gamekeeper's cottage, exhausted and a bit the worse for wear.

After her miraculous jump from Lady Brimley's second-floor window, in which she had been lucky to receive nothing more than a few cuts and bruises, Emily had located Miles and dragged him with her to find Jenna and the horses. With Lord Brimley's staff combing every inch of the grounds, it had been no easy feat, but the three of them had managed to elude the searchers and disappear into the night.

Now, all she could do was hope that it had been too dark in the corridor and the marquis had been too far away to recognize her in her boy's clothing.

"Well, you certainly took your time about it."

Jack waited for them, leaning against the side of the cottage, arms crossed and lips twisted in a sneer.

"Best you be glad we got 'ere at all," Miles growled, making no attempt to hide his contempt for the other man. "We woke the whole 'ouse and almost got caught."

"Caught, you say?" Jack cocked his head and turned to Emily, his eyes gleaming with sudden interest. He seemed almost intrigued by the notion.

Yes, that would have been quite the coup for him, wouldn't it? she thought, her anger rising up to choke her. The younger sister of the Earl of Ellington being arrested for burglary would be the ultimate revenge as far as Jack was concerned.

She struggled to keep her voice even. "The marquis must have heard me prowling around. He came out of his room and saw me before I could get away."

"Did 'e recognize you?"

"I don't know. I didn't stay to ask him."

"But you got what I sent you for?"

Emily reached into the pocket of her breeches and withdrew the brooch, holding it out to him.

"Ahhh." Jack jerked it from her grasp, holding it up so that its diamonds winked in the moonlight, and she had to suppress the urge to wrest it back from him and run with it so fast and so far that he would never be able to catch her. "I knew you could do it. You make me proud, Lady Emily."

"Just what I've always aspired to." In spite of herself,

her words dripped with sarcasm, and he flung her a censuring look before tucking the piece of jewelry into his shirt pocket.

"We make a good team, princess." He gave her an infuriating smirk. "Next time—"

"There won't be a next time." She'd had it. This was the end. She couldn't do this any longer. Not after tonight.

Jack paused for a moment, then took a step closer to her, his eyebrows lowering. "What's that?"

"You heard what I said." Emily refused to back down. "And you might as well quit trying to intimidate me. It won't work. Perhaps you didn't understand Miles. We were almost caught tonight. And on top of that, Lord Brimley collapsed in the midst of our confrontation." Tears of shame and distress clouded her vision, and she struggled to hold them back. "Lord knows if he's even still alive."

"So? 'E's an old man. 'E most likely wouldn't 'ave been around much longer anyway."

Jack's complete disregard for human life shouldn't have shocked her, but it did. "You monster!" She started toward him, but Miles stepped into her path, bringing her to a halt.

"No, m'lady. Allow me." With an expression of almost predatory anticipation, the stable hand whirled without warning and his fist swung outward, connecting with Jack's chin in a solid blow. The force was enough to send the older man sprawling in the dust.

Emily's hand flew to her mouth to stifle a gasp—and

to cover the slight beginnings of a smile that came and went on her lips. It was oddly satisfying to see the scoundrel lying in the dirt where he belonged.

Jack's pale cheeks reddened and he sat up, fingering his jaw. "Consider that a free one, stable boy, 'cause the next time you 'it me, I guarantee I'll 'it back." He levered himself to his feet and faced Emily. "And as for you, princess, this ain't over until I say it is. You and I 'ave a lot more to do."

"I said it's over and I meant it." Facing him with fierce resolve, she held her hand out to him, palm up. "Now, if you would be so kind as to hand over this alleged proof you've been babbling about?"

He paused for a moment, then a slow, devilish grin spread across his face. "Proof?"

"Don't play dumb, Jack. You know very well what I'm talking about. This proof you've supposedly found that my mother had an affair. You said I could see it once I did this job for you, and I did it. So, where is it?"

"I said I *might* be persuaded to let you see it. And I'm not persuaded, especially not if you're going to leave me 'igh and dry before I say it's time to put an end to things."

Emily felt her face heat with anger. She should have known the knave would never keep his word. "Damn you, Jack!"

He gave a careless shrug. "Of course, I can't make you do anything you don't want to do, but I wonder . . . Do you 'appen to be familiar with the laws of in'eritance in England?" His gray eyes narrowed as he studied her. "If it could be proven that your brother wasn't the true son of the Earl of Ellington . . . well, it's possible 'e could lose everything, ain't it? 'Is title, 'is wealth, 'is lands and 'ome. All of it."

Emily's breath caught and her hand went to her abdomen, trying to calm the sudden pitching of her stomach. She had no idea whether what he said was true or not, but the mere possibility was enough to send her into a panic.

"And all I 'ave to do," Jack drew out in a slow, deliberate tone, the relish in his voice an indication of just how much delight he took in tormenting her, "is show a few little pieces of paper to the right person."

That was it! Emily was sick of the hints, the threats. She had to know just what sort of proof Jack was holding over her head. "What papers?" she demanded, her hands clenching into fists at her sides. "What are you talking about?"

He leaned toward her, his hot breath wafting across her ear, causing her to shiver in revulsion. "Letters," he said succinctly. "From your mum to a good friend of 'ers, admitting to 'er affair before she wed your father—and 'er pregnancy."

"That's not possible." She went cold all over and her pulse pounded in her ears. She could feel herself swaying, felt Jenna's arm wrap around her shoulders in comforting support. "I don't believe you. Where on earth could you possibly have gotten your hands on something like that?"

"I 'ave me ways."

"I want to see them now!"

"I already told you no. Maybe next time. It all depends on whether or not you continue to play nice and do as I say."

Emily's body quivered with rage and frustration. All she could think about was the pain this man had caused, all in the name of his revenge.

"You won't get away with this," she whispered, her words a mere rasp of suppressed emotion. "I swear to you, you won't."

"Oh, I won't, eh?" His cruel wink was like a dagger in her heart. "Well, we'll just see about that, won't we?"

"Oh, we will most definitely see about that!" She turned on her heel and marched off toward the horses with Miles and Jenna hurrying to catch up.

Flinging herself into the saddle, she cast one last glance back at Jack.

You'll pay for this, Jack Barlow, she swore to herself vehemently. *You'll pay for everything. And I'm just the person to make sure you do.*

Emily waited until they were quite a distance from the gamekeeper's cottage before she pulled Artemis to a stop on the moonlit path. She glanced over at her friends, who reined in their mounts as well and halted next to her.

"This is the end," she told them, her voice quiet and full of conviction. "After what happened with Lord Brimley this evening I can't continue to do this. My God, who knows what could have happened? He might have recognized me! And to see him lying on the floor, so pale and still . . ." She swallowed the fist-sized lump that tried to clog her throat. "If he's been harmed in any way, I'll never forgive myself."

Jenna patted her shoulder. "It wasn't your fault, Em. And I'm sure 'e's fine." But she didn't sound so certain.

"What do you plan on doing?" Miles asked, drawing her attention as he guided his horse a bit closer.

"You've been keeping an eye on the cottage, Miles. Has he done anything out of the ordinary, seen or spoken to anyone?"

The stable hand nodded. "The last few nights 'e's gone into the village to one of the local taverns, the 'Awk's Eye. From what I can see, it seems to be a pre-arranged meeting place of some sort. 'E sits at a table at the very back in the shadows, and after 'e's been there a while, a young lad approaches 'im, usually with some sort of written message."

Emily narrowed her eyes. "Did you recognize the lad?"

"Only to know that 'e's the one who delivered the message to you at the stables yesterday morning. Scrawny little scrapper. About twelve, brown 'air and brown eyes. Other than that, no. I don't remember ever seeing 'im around the village."

"So it's safe to say that Jack could be working with someone else, and this lad is more than likely an errand boy." Somehow the idea didn't surprise Emily. But she couldn't help but wonder who else would want to hurt her enough to fall in with the likes of the former street thief and his plans. "You say he's gone to this tavern every night?"

"That's right."

"But nowhere else?"

Miles shook his head. "Mostly 'e stays around the gamekeeper's cottage. I would imagine 'e's not too keen on 'aving anyone spy 'im."

"Then everything he's had us steal must still be with him at the cottage. He hasn't left town for any length of time, and he wouldn't risk pawning any of it around here for fear someone might recognize it." Emily felt a plan starting to take shape in her mind, and her hands tightened on her reins in growing excitement. "I would wager a guess that these letters of my mother's he claims he has are there, too—if they exist at all."

Jenna frowned. "Per'aps. But 'ow does that 'elp us?"

Emily turned back to Miles. "How long does he stay at the Hawk's Eye?"

"I'd say a couple of hours, maybe a little longer. 'E usually 'angs around for a short time after the lad delivers the message and orders a round or two."

"So we should have plenty of time to slip into the cottage while he's gone."

"What?" Jenna's shrill exclamation caused her horse to dance skittishly beneath her, and she took a second to calm her mount before facing Emily again, her eyes wide with trepidation. "Why would we want to do that?"

Emily gave her friend a beseeching look. "Don't you see? It's the only way to end this once and for all, Jenna. If we can find those letters, or prove that he never had them to begin with, we take away his power over us. And if we can recover everything he's had us steal, we can return it all to the true owners and finally turn Jack over to the law."

"I don't know. If 'e should come back and catch us . . ." Jenna still seemed doubtful.

"It's a chance we have to take. This *has* to end. And we're the ones who have to end it." Emily glanced at Miles, her expression pleading for his support. "What do you think?"

The stable hand was quiet for a long moment. Then he gave a single, abrupt nod. "I think you're right. I think it's time this stopped, and this plan is as good as any."

Breathing an inner sigh of relief, Emily waited for Jenna's decision. "Well?"

The younger girl bit her lip and closed her eyes, then inclined her head in agreement. "All right. I'm not sure whether I believe this is a good idea, but we're all in this together, and it's not as if I'd let you two go wivout me."

Emily felt a wave of gratefulness wash over her as she smiled at her two friends. Thank God for Miles and Jenna! She didn't know what she would have done without them.

She caught hold of Jenna's hand, gripping it tightly. "Good. We'll do it tomorrow night then, after he leaves for the tavern. We'll finish this once and for all, and we'll make sure Jack Barlow regrets ever threatening the likes of us."

"I'd say 'e already regrets it. Or if 'e doesn't, 'e should." Jenna sent Miles an admiring look from under lowered lashes. "That was some facer you planted on 'im."

The stable hand blushed under her intent regard. "You really think so?"

"I really do."

As Miles preened under Jenna's praise, Emily let her head fall back and stared up at the stars overhead, allowing the warm night breeze to caress her face. For the first time in over a month, she felt free.

By this time tomorrow, she thought with determination, she would have brought an end to Jack's reign of terror. She would see him pay for all he had put her through.

And maybe, just maybe, if she could accomplish what she hoped to, Peter might be a bit more understanding—and forgiving—when she finally had to tell him the truth about the way she had deceived him and what she had been forced to do.

But she wouldn't count on it.

Chapter 18

After another night spent tossing and turning with very little sleep, Peter rose and made his way downstairs long before the rest of Knighthaven's residents even began to stir. The sun had barely started to peek above the trees in the distance when he let himself out a side door, cut across the stable yard, and strode off along the trail that led into the woods. Perhaps a brisk walk about the estate would help to clear his head, or jar some obscure piece of information loose that might help him in his quest to unmask the Oxfordshire Thief.

He had been in Little Haverton for over a week now, and he was no closer to wrapping up this case than he'd been when he'd arrived. He had questioned all of the victims and their respective households—not to mention all of the guests who had been present at Lord and

Lady Fulberry's dinner party the night of the break-in at their home—and had nothing to show for his time but a scrap of cloth and a gut-level hunch that the culprit was someone the victims personally knew.

Taking a deep breath, Peter closed his eyes and made an attempt to sort out the muddled chaos of his thoughts.

Now, Quick, a voice in the back of his head whispered, *let's put this thing in perspective. Just what do you know about this criminal?*

He turned the facts over in his mind, examining them from all angles. First of all, the man seemed to be familiar with both the layout and the routines of each of the homes he'd broken into thus far. He'd also known exactly when the best time was to plan his attack and had been well aware of where his marks kept what he was looking for. And in each case, the thief had had something very specific in mind. At the Tuttlestons', he'd taken only the viscountess's necklace and the few baubles that had been in her jewelry box, but had made no attempt to break into Lord Tuttleston's safe downstairs.

To Peter, this alone seemed to point to some sort of acquaintance with the victims. He doubted any common thug off the street could have come by such knowledge, and though he supposed the culprit could be a servant on one of the estates, he had questioned each staff member in the employ of Lord and Lady Tuttleston, Lord and Lady Fulberry, and Lord Caulfield, and had run across nothing to arouse his suspicions.

The thief was also well versed in the art of housebreaking, he decided. He seemed to possess agility and stealth in abundance, as well as a true talent for lock-picking. So far, none of the locks on any of the means of entry the thief had used had posed any kind of challenge to him.

Unfortunately, that could be said for half the children at Willow Park, including Benji. More than one of them had been forced to try their hand at housebreaking at some time in the past, if only to steal food in order to feed themselves.

Why, even Emily had a passing skill at picking locks. He should know. He'd been the one who had taught her.

The memory of those long-ago lessons had the corner of Peter's mouth turning up in a slight smile. To his surprise, his well-bred pupil had displayed an amazing aptitude for a life of crime. During her time with the Rag-Tag Bunch, she had learned to pick pockets with ease, and even after she had returned to her brother and they had all made the permanent move to the country, she had continued to badger Peter for instruction. How to pick locks had been one of the last things he'd shown her before calling a halt to the proceedings in deference to the earl, who had seemed a bit alarmed by how well his sister appeared to be taking to it all.

A sudden bright glare in his eyes had Peter glancing up to see that the sun had finally risen above the tops of the trees in front of him and was casting its light across his path, dappling the forest floor with patterns of light and shadow. It was about time he started back to the house.

Doing an abrupt about-face, he began the return trek to Knighthaven as his mind mulled over the events of the last few days. More specifically, his interactions with Emily during that time. Or rather, his *lack* of interaction with her. Ever since their conversation in the stables and their visit to Lord Caulfield's, he'd found himself falling back on his original plan and going out of his way to avoid her. He wasn't certain what manner of devil had tempted him into teasing her about their very first kiss in such a way, but watching her read Moreland's note had only served to remind him once again of all the reasons to keep her out of arm's reach.

His hands tightened into fists in his pockets and he shook his head. He was well aware he couldn't avoid her forever. But he had felt the need for some space between them, a brief respite in order for him to gain control of the emotions that suddenly seemed so confusing.

Sooner or later, however, he would have to face her again. He may have finished interviewing the victims and potential witnesses, but that didn't mean he might not need her further input in the future.

At that moment, the trail broke from the trees, and as he approached Knighthaven, Peter turned off the path to take the shortcut through the garden. He had just reached the familiar patch of elms when he noticed a small figure seated on one of the benches that surrounded the central fountain, head bowed over a book. He stopped dead in his tracks in immediate recognition.

Emily.

As if suddenly becoming aware of his presence, she looked up and her eyes met his across the distance. Even from this far away, he could feel something warm and almost tangible arc through the air between them. It was enough to have his nerve endings standing at attention.

Well, there could be no running away now. She had spotted him, and he'd be damned if he'd let her see him turn tail and flee like a whipped hound. Surely he could manage a polite greeting and a few pleasantries without making a fool of himself.

But as he started across the grass toward her and felt his heart speed up its beat in direct proportion to each step he took in her direction, he knew he was only deceiving himself.

Emily closed the book in her lap and watched Peter draw closer to her, the air seizing in her lungs as she noted his lazy, loose-limbed stride, the casual grace that always seemed to surround him like a mantle. Her reaction to him disconcerted her, as always. Just the mere sight of him shouldn't rob her of her very breath or send her heart racing until she felt certain it would pound right out of her chest.

And yet it did.

She wasn't ready to face him. It was one of the reasons she had retreated to the garden this morning, thinking if she stayed out of the house there would be less chance of running into him. After the debacle at Lord Brimley's last night and the later meeting with Jack, it had been quite late when she'd finally slipped back into Knighthaven and retired to her bed. And the plan she had hatched with Miles and Jenna for this evening had kept her awake long into the wee hours of the morning, going over everything in her head to make sure there could be no mistakes.

Nothing could go wrong. She wouldn't allow it to. This was her one chance to bring an end to all of this, and she couldn't let herself forget that.

But whether she felt able to confront Peter or not, it seemed as if she had no choice now. She could only be grateful that she had remembered to cover the few cuts that had marred her cheeks—caused by her leap into Lord Brimley's bushes—with a faint dusting of powder before leaving the safety of her bedchamber. Unfortunately, she hadn't been able to conceal the dark circles under her eyes.

It was too late to worry about that now, however, for Peter stood before her. Forcing a smile to her lips, she nodded in greeting, praying her expression betrayed none of her disquiet. "Good morning, Mr. Quick."

He returned her nod. "Lady Emily."

They stared at each other in silence for a long moment, neither of them seeming to know what to say next. Then, Emily cleared her throat and ventured a question. "How is the investigation going? Any news?"

"I'm afraid not." Exhaling, Peter appeared to relax a bit and propped a booted foot on the bench next to her, leaning forward to rest an elbow on his knee. The action dislodged a lock of tawny hair, causing it to fall forward over his brow. "I spoke with Tristan about the case at length yesterday. He agrees with me that it is quite probable the thief is someone who knows each of the families who have been victimized. Other than that, I'm sure of nothing."

Emily's heart skipped a beat, but she smothered the burst of panic that raced through her at his words and managed to continue speaking in a calm tone. "I'm sorry to hear that. I know how much you and my brother want to see this criminal caught." She folded her hands on top of her book in an attempt to cease their trembling. "What are you going to do now?"

"I was planning to spend this afternoon paying calls on some of the pawnbrokers in the village and the surrounding towns, to see if anyone has attempted to pass off any of the stolen goods to one of them. But I can't help but believe it will be a waste of my time. Our man is too wily for that. He'd be well aware there's a good chance anyone local would recognize one of the pieces and report him to the law."

"Did you need me to accompany you?"

Peter's mouth curved in a grin as he looked down at her. "I thank you for the offer, but I'm afraid the areas I'll be frequenting aren't places where a lady should be seen."

"Oh, well . . . Of course." Feeling flustered at the way his smile spilled over her like warm honey, melting her insides into a puddle of tingling emotion, Emily ducked her head and reached up to push a stray curl back from her temple.

A callused hand snagged her wrist.

"Wh—what?" Startled, her eyes flew to his face to find that his smile had turned into a frown, and he was studying the hand he grasped in his with obvious concern.

"What's this?" he asked, holding her arm up for her inspection, his fingers gentle on her skin.

Tearing her gaze away from his face, Emily examined her wrist and had to stifle a gasp as she noticed the long, raw-looking scratch that marked the flesh on the inside of her lower forearm. Another telltale sign from her tangle with the Marquis of Brimley's bushes, she supposed.

"I don't know." She bit her lip and tugged her arm from his grip, covering the wound with her other hand. "I stopped to smell some of the roses earlier, when I first came out to the garden. I must have scratched myself without realizing it."

"You should have someone see to it. It looks rather angry, and it's never a good idea to leave a scratch like that untended." He paused for a moment. Then, in another unexpected movement that had her gasping, he reached out to cup her chin in his palm, tilting her head up until he could see into her eyes. "Come to think of it, you're looking a trifle peaked, as well. Didn't you sleep last night?"

She scrambled to think of something to say, but his steady regard seemed to render her incapable of rational thought, and she couldn't have come up with a lie to save her life. "I admit I did have a bit of trouble settling down." Heavens, but that was an understatement if she'd ever heard one!

His thumb smoothed over her lower lip. "You must take better care of yourself," he told her, his voice soft, his gaze never straying from hers. "What would the children of Willow Park do without their guardian angel and storyteller?"

Emily felt her body quiver in response to the underlying current of sensuality in his tone, and she felt herself drawn toward him as he leaned forward. Her eyes fell shut and her lips parted in anticipation—

"There you two are!"

The magical thread stretched so tautly between them snapped, and they both jerked away from each other like guilty children caught with their hands in the cookie jar.

Certain her face must be as red as a beet, Emily blinked and looked up to see Deirdre coming down the path toward them.

Dear Lord, how much had her sister-in-law seen?

"You're certainly both out and about early," the countess was saying as she approached, the serene mask of her features betraying not a hint as to what she may have witnessed. "Peter, I just passed Tristan in the foyer, and I believe he was looking for you. I promised him I would let you know if I saw you."

"Thank you for relaying the message, my lady." Peter lowered his foot from the bench and straightened, bowing to both of them. "More than likely he wishes to discuss the case. If you'll excuse me." With one last unreadable glance at Emily, he strolled off toward the house.

As soon as he was out of earshot, Emily took a deep breath and braced herself for the probing questions she was sure would come. But Deirdre surprised her by making no mention of the scene she had stumbled upon. Instead, she tilted her head back with a sigh, placing a hand on the large mound of her belly.

"It's such a beautiful day, and I've had little chance

to enjoy getting out and about lately. Tristan has become worse than a mother hen, not wanting to let me out of his sight. I must confess, I'm starting to feel claustrophobic." She sent Emily a pleading look from under lowered lashes. "Would you mind terribly taking a short stroll with me about the garden, dear? Perhaps if you're with me I shan't have to worry about my husband swooping down and declaring I'm much too delicate to be doing anything so strenuous as actually *walking*."

Relieved that she didn't appear to be in for an inquisition, Emily smothered a smile at the mental picture of her powerful giant of a brother fussing over his wife like an overlarge nanny. "He loves you, Deirdre," she pointed out in gentle amusement as she rose, tucked her book in the crook of her elbow, and looped her free arm through her sister-in-law's. "He's just trying to take care of you and the baby."

"I know. But the man has to understand that he can't wrap me in cotton wool. I'm much stronger than he gives me credit for. I've had to be, and he should be well aware of that."

As they started along the path at a leisurely pace, Emily studied the countess's stomach with concern. Was it just her imagination, or did it look twice as big as it had yesterday? "And how is the future Earl of Ellington?"

"As well as can be expected. According to the doctor, he should be making an appearance any day now."

"And you're so certain he's a boy?"

Deirdre gave a tinkling laugh. "He wouldn't dare be

anything else." She touched her belly again, a brief, loving caress. "He's been restless the last few days. Almost as restless as I am. It's as if he knows it's time."

Emily felt renewed determination stiffen her spine at her sister-in-law's words. If that were true, then it was all the more reason to put an end to Jack's machinations. When this child came into the world, she wanted Jack Barlow in jail, no longer able to threaten anything or anyone she loved.

It made what would happen tonight that much more important.

They had halted next to the fountain, and Deirdre's expression became serious as she turned to face Emily. "There is more than one reason I asked you to walk with me. I want you to know how glad I am to see that you've been able to put your differences with Peter aside and work with him on this investigation. It has meant a great deal to your brother and me, though I know it has been difficult for you."

"Yes, well, I've been glad to be of help. You know I would do anything for you and Tristan."

The countess's eyes narrowed in sudden shrewdness. "And what about Peter?"

The mere mention of the man's name was enough to bring to life all the confusing, mixed-up emotions that seemed to overwhelm Emily whenever she was in his presence, and just thinking about their near-kiss of only moments ago made her shiver. Struggling to appear unaffected, she gave a deliberate shrug. "What about him?"

"Oh, darling, I'm not blind. It used to be that you

would have done anything for him, as well. In fact, I would have wagered a guess that Peter was the most important person in your life. I know he hurt you when he left, but after spending time with him this past week, perhaps you've realized that not everything is what it seems."

Emily started to protest, to deny there was any truth to what Lady Ellington was saying, but somehow the words just wouldn't come. Her tongue cleaved to the roof of her mouth, arresting the lie before it could escape her lips. What was the use of denying something that had always been all too obvious?

"He believes he wasn't—isn't good enough for me," she finally whispered.

She felt Deirdre's fingers tighten on her arm, and she looked up to find the older woman watching her with a sympathetic countenance. "I'm going to let you in on a little secret, dear. Males don't always know everything. In fact, they are quite frequently wrong about a great many things, though they would never admit it. And that is when the female must learn to take matters into her own hands."

She began to walk again, tugging Emily along with her, this time toward Knighthaven. "By the way," she drew out slowly, one corner of her mouth curving upward in a significant smile. "You might be interested to know that Tristan and I have been invited to dinner at Cullen and Lilah's tonight, and after much pleading on my part, your brother has agreed to go. I expect that we shall be gone *most of the evening,* and the house should be quite . . . *empty.*"

Emily's feet froze to the cobblestones and she came

to an abrupt stop on the walkway, certain she must have misread the less than subtle hint in the woman's voice. "Deirdre, what are you saying?"

The countess let go of Emily's arm and placed her hands on her hips with an exasperated sniff. "Emily Knight, if you don't know, I'm certainly not going to tell you. But you've never been one to give up on something you really want, so if you love that man, you'd best figure it out. And quickly."

With that, she waddled off in the direction of the house.

Stunned, Emily stared after her, her mouth agape, clutching her book to her chest in an almost convulsive grip. Perhaps if she'd had her wits about her, she might have been more flabbergasted at the fact that her elegant sister-in-law had, for all intents and purposes, just given her permission to seduce Peter Quick right under Knighthaven's very roof, though in a rather roundabout fashion. But she was too caught up in the words Deirdre had spoken before she'd walked away.

"If you love that man, you'd best figure it out."

Love? She didn't *love* Peter. There was no denying she had in the past, of course, and it was true that there was still a certain amount of physical attraction between them, but love? No. She couldn't—she didn't—

Oh, dear God, she did!

A picture of Peter's smiling face flashed across her inner vision, and her mind went back over the last week since his return. She thought of the way he had been with the children the day they had visited Willow Park, so patient and kind, and the way he had talked and laughed with her in the stables the other day, his gentle teasing reminding her of the strength of their childhood bond. The way he had caressed her, kissed her in the abandoned cottage, with such worshipful reverence, as if she were infinitely precious to him . . .

Her knees suddenly felt like water and she had to clutch at a nearby statue for support. Despite the best of intentions and the defenses she had tried to erect between them, he'd somehow found his way past her wounded exterior to her heart again.

She still loved him. Perhaps she had never stopped.

Without conscious thought, her feet carried her in the direction of the house, her mind focused on the dilemma that lay before her. Never had she felt so lost. Acknowledging the true depth of her feelings for Peter could only cause her more heartache in the end. He had already made up his mind that he wasn't good enough for her, that a real relationship between them could never be. And once he discovered what she had done, how she had deceived him . . .

Dear God, what was she going to do?

Entering Knighthaven through the French doors into the parlor, Emily crossed the room and stepped out into the foyer, her mind still awhirl with the confusion of her thoughts. She had just made her way to the foot of the stairs when Tristan's study door opened and Peter emerged.

Seeing him so soon after becoming aware of her newly reawakened emotions left her feeling as if she had been punched in the stomach. Her breath seemed to leave her as their eyes met across the short distance separating them.

Say something, Emily, a voice scolded sternly in her head. *Quit standing here, staring at him like a ninny, and say something!*

She opened her mouth to speak, determined to force out some sort of polite pleasantry, no matter how banal it sounded. But before she could say a thing, there was a knock at the door.

Langley hurried past them on the way to open it, and Emily breathed an inner sigh of relief. She could only be grateful for the timely interruption, for she couldn't have guaranteed that any words she had spoken would have made sense.

But when the butler swung open the heavy oak portal and she saw who was standing on the other side, her relief turned to alarm.

"Constable Jenkins." Peter came forward to greet the man, his eyebrows raised in inquiry. "Has something untoward occurred?"

"I'm afraid so, Mr. Quick." The man glanced at Emily over Peter's shoulder, looking just as sullen and unhappy to be there as he had on his previous visit. "You asked me to keep you apprised of anything new in the case of the Oxfordshire thefts. Well, it seems there was a break-in at Brimley Hall last night. A very expensive brooch was stolen."

"Our man?"

"Appears to be. But this time someone got a look at him. Lord Brimley himself apparently stumbled upon the thief in the midst of the robbery."

Emily felt her stomach turn over and she took a step backward, glad that Peter's back was to her and he couldn't see her reaction. Had the marquis recognized her after all?

"Unfortunately, the marquis has suffered some sort of attack," the constable went on. "His heart, the physician seems to think. The man's not very lucid and I'm having a hard time getting anything out of him other than a lot of rambling nonsense. Lord Moreland suggested that you might be of help." His condescending tone clearly said that he rather doubted that.

This was it, Emily thought wildly. She would have to go back to Brimley Hall and face the very person who had seen her stealing from his home just a matter of hours before. Would he remember? Would he denounce her in front of Adam and the constable?

And Peter?

Guilt stabbed her in the heart. And how was she to deal with the fact that she was the cause of the poor man's current condition? Some sort of attack? Dear God, it was all her fault!

Peter spun to face her, the light of determination gleaming in his eyes. "This could be what we've been waiting for. Are you up for a visit to Brimley Hall, my lady?"

Struggling to keep her face expressionless, Emily nodded. It was a risk, but what else could she do? Adam was her friend, the marquis a close neighbor. After accompanying Peter to the homes of each of the previous victims, she would draw suspicions if she refused. And she *had* to find out for herself what he had seen. She would never rest easy otherwise.

She suppressed a shudder of fear and dread as Peter turned back to the constable. What would she do if Lord Brimley gave her away?

It didn't bear thinking about.

Chapter 19

From his seat across from Emily in the Ellington carriage, Peter studied her delicate profile as she peered out the window at the passing scenery on the way to Brimley Hall. He couldn't help but note that she'd been silent ever since they had departed Knighthaven.

Anyone who didn't know her well might have been fooled by the bland mask of her features into believing she was calm and composed, but the stiffness of her posture and the tightening of her full lips were clear indications to Peter of the disquiet that seethed just beneath the surface of that cool façade.

What could possibly be troubling her?

He couldn't help but wonder if their encounter in the garden had something to do with it. Damn it, he had never meant to touch her, but the paleness of her features, the weariness in her eyes, had made him long to comfort her. And his good intentions had gone right out the window the moment she had leaned toward him with her mouth temptingly parted. Though he should be grateful that Deirdre had interrupted them, he found that he couldn't quite manage to convince himself that tasting those sweet lips again would have been a mistake.

Had the incident left Emily as restless and aching as it had left him?

Feeling his body react in a predictable male fashion to the lustful direction of his thoughts, Peter shrugged off the vision of Emily in his arms and shifted in his seat, forcing himself to face her once again.

He schooled his own features into what he hoped was an unreadable expression and fought to keep his voice steady when he spoke to her. "Are you feeling all right? You've been very quiet since we left the house."

He saw her hands tighten into fists in her lap, and she paused for a moment before turning away from the window to send him a veiled look from under lowered lashes. "I'm fine. Just concerned about Lord Brimley, I suppose. He's been unwell for quite some time, but something like this . . ." She glanced away again, her jaw tautening. "Is it necessary for us to interview him now? I would hate to cause him any undue distress."

Peter leaned forward, silently willing her to meet his eyes. When she finally did, he offered her an understanding smile. "I dislike the prospect as much as you do, but I'm afraid this is the only lead we have at this point, and it's best that we speak with him while the incident is fresh in his mind. We can't afford to leave any stone unturned. I assure you, I have no wish to cause the marquis any further harm. We'll speak with his physician first, and I'll be as gentle and brief in my questioning as possible."

She gave him a timid smile in return, and the shy sweetness of it robbed him of breath. More and more often lately, the young girl he had once known was showing through that prickly exterior, making it difficult for him to distance himself from her in any way.

"I understand," she told him, her voice whisper soft. "I do. It's just that he's been through so much already."

The worry in her tone had Peter reaching out to her before he thought, his hand covering hers in her lap in what had been meant to be a comforting gesture.

He was immediately singed by the heat that arced between them.

Emily gave an audible gasp, and their gazes locked for a long, drawn-out moment. Time hung suspended.

And then the carriage lurched to a halt.

Breathing an inner sigh of relief, Peter removed his hand from its unnerving contact with hers and inclined his head in a brisk nod. "Right. It appears we have arrived."

Before he could think of anything else to say to help alleviate the sudden tension that seemed to suffuse the very air around them, the door of the coach swung outward and Lord Moreland appeared in the opening.

"You're here!" Ignoring Peter's presence, the man reached inside for Emily, who rose from her seat and accepted his help in alighting. "The constable returned just a short while ago. He said you were on your way, so I've been waiting."

"Oh, Adam, I was so sorry to hear about what happened. And your father . . ." Once Emily was on the ground next to him, she wrapped her arms about the viscount's neck in a brief, sympathetic hug. "How is he?"

Peter, climbing down from the carriage behind her, felt his blood start a slow, simmering boil through his veins as Moreland returned her hug. The way the man slipped his arms about Emily's waist seemed much too familiar, the look on that handsome face far too calculating for his liking.

"He's doing as well as can be expected," Moreland was saying in response to Emily's query. When she drew away and would have taken a step back, he halted her with one hand at her elbow, guiding her toward the stone steps that led up to the large front door in a proprietary manner that set Peter's teeth on edge. He was left to bring up the rear.

As usual, he thought darkly, falling into step behind them.

"The physician says he should recover," the viscount continued as they entered the house. Pausing in the polished marble entryway, he gestured to a hovering butler, who hurried forward to divest the new arrivals of their hats and gloves before fading away into the background again. "*If* he will start obeying instructions and remain in bed. However, you know Father. He never should have attempted to confront the thief on his own, but he's a stubborn old man."

Peter could remain quiet no longer. "Exactly what was taken, Lord Moreland?"

The viscount frowned in his direction, but Peter refused to back down. He had an investigation to run, and it was just too bloody damn bad if this dandified snob didn't like it.

Some of his determination must have shown on his face, for Moreland shrugged and relented. "A brooch that belonged to my late mother. Damned if I know how the bounder even found it. Father wanted to leave things in her room untouched, so it has remained in her keepsake box on the topmost shelf of her armoire ever since her death. He only rarely took it out."

"And who else would have occasion to know this?"

"Only those close to the family, and perhaps a few servants."

Peter furrowed his brow in thought. As he had suspected.

Emily, who had been silent all this time, finally took a step forward and spoke up. "And nothing else was taken?"

"Not that we can ascertain. It appears as if the thief picked the lock on the library doors and came in that way. Passed right by my father's safe and didn't even touch it."

Peter contemplated the winding staircase that led up toward the dark upper reaches of the house. "May we speak with the marquis?"

"You're welcome to try. The constable has spent

most of the morning doing just that, but every time he starts to get somewhere, Father drifts off into his own little world." The viscount's mouth tightened. "He's tended to ramble quite a bit in recent years, but it seems worse since last night."

"Oh, Adam, I'm so sorry." As Peter watched, a shadow seemed to cross Emily's face and her eyes glittered with unshed tears before she blinked them away and reached up to lay a hand on Moreland's arm. "So very sorry."

To Peter's ears, she sounded pained, almost tormented. It was more than mere sympathy that showed in her expression. It was grief, stark and unflinching.

Had she truly been that close to the Marquis of Brimley? Or was her agonized reaction due to her relationship with Lord Moreland?

The viscount waved a hand at the stairs. "You may go ahead up if you like. The constable is waiting, and I'm certain he's anxious for you to join him."

Peter gave him a curious look. "You aren't coming?"

"It's difficult for me to see him like this. The physician has suggested that I hire a round-the-clock nurse to sit with him. Father has resisted the idea in the past, but now . . ."

When his voice trailed off, Emily gave him a gentle smile and moved closer to him in a way that had Peter clenching his hands into fists in order to resist the urge to pull her away from the man.

"I understand," she said, her tone soothing.

"I only hope Father does." Lord Moreland patted Emily's hand, then sent Peter a hooded glare from narrowed hazel eyes. "You go on. I'll be up in a short while."

"Very well." Emily turned to Peter, raising her eyebrows expectantly. "Mr. Quick?"

He sketched her a slight bow, unable to resist goading her just a bit after all the attention she had given the viscount. He knew it was childish, but watching her fawn over the man had been too damn aggravating. "After you, my lady."

She pursed her lips and regarded him for a long moment, then swept past him on the way to the stairs. Peter followed, casting one last glance back at the viscount as he went.

Moreland stared after them, his visage devoid of emotion.

Peter shook his head. Maybe it was jealousy, plain and simple, but as Emily led the way up the stairs, he couldn't help but feel that the man was hiding something.

The second-floor hallway was dim and hushed, the draperies covering the windows at each end drawn against the morning sunlight. Standing before Lord Brimley's bedchamber door, the constable chatted with a balding, middle-aged man whom Peter took to be the marquis's physician.

As he and Emily approached, the two men ceased their conversation and the constable nodded stiffly to them both. "My lady. Mr. Quick."

The other gentleman was introduced as Dr. Billings, and after the customary pleasantries were exchanged, Peter posed his first question to him. "How fares the marquis? Is he well enough to be interviewed?"

The doctor surveyed them with disapproval, but gave his consent with a curt gesture. "I suppose it would be all right as long as you don't take long and don't over-tire him. But Constable Jenkins has spoken with his lordship at length and failed to gain anything of use from him, so I can't see how it will do you any good."

Jenkins's smug smirk infuriated Peter. But he merely drew a deep breath in order to gain control of his seething temper, letting one corner of his mouth curve upward slightly in a superior smile that was certain to irritate the man. "You may be surprised, Dr. Billings."

"Perhaps." The physician frowned, his eyebrows lowering in a censorious fashion as he turned from Peter to Emily. "My lady, are you certain you wish to go in as well? I can't help but believe it isn't at all proper."

If Dr. Billings had hoped to convince Emily to re-main outside the sickroom, he had chosen the wrong words to do so. Peter watched as her shoulders straight-ened and she leveled the doctor with a chilly stare.

"Nonsense," she informed the physician in a lofty tone, her violet eyes shooting sparks that had Peter sti-fling a chuckle. "The marquis is an old family friend, and what is *proper* doesn't enter into it. Besides, I'm certain having a bit of company can only do him good."

Dr. Billings puffed up in obvious displeasure, ap-pearing disgruntled and rather affronted by Emily's un-willingness to concede his point, but he backed down in the face of her determined ire. "Of course, my lady. As you say."

With a sniff, she pivoted and swept off toward Lord

Brimley's room, and Peter followed, still grinning. That was his Em, he mused with a definite touch of pride and—no matter how he tried to deny it—more than a hint of possessiveness.

Once inside the bedchamber with the door closed behind them, however, Emily's militant mien suddenly abandoned her. She came to a halt at the foot of the large, four-poster bed, and the same shadow that had crossed her face downstairs settled over her features once more, making her look pale and shaken.

Peter longed to hold her, to comfort her with the strength of his arms around her, but he resisted the urge and instead did nothing more than brush her arm in an all too brief caress.

"Would you like to speak to him first?" he asked in a whisper. "It might better prepare him for my questions if you were to smooth the way."

She bit her lip, then gave an abrupt nod in response.

The chamber was dark and still. As the curtains were tightly drawn, the only illumination came from the faint glow of a lamp on a nearby night table, and the only sound that could be heard was the raspy breathing of the room's frail occupant.

Emily moved to stand next to the bed, sinking down to sit on the edge of the mattress in a careful motion.

"Lord Brimley," she murmured, leaning over the elderly gentleman, her visage a mask of concern that Peter could read even in the dimness. "Lord Brimley, can you open your eyes?"

The figure on the bed twitched, then mumbled something incoherent before heavily veined eyelids fluttered open. They unveiled a pair of rheumy hazel irises, bloodshot and clouded with age.

"What—who—" the man gasped, his gnarled hand flying up off the mattress in alarm, palm outward as if to ward off an enemy.

Or a thief.

"Lord Brimley? It's all right. You're safe." Emily caught the marquis's hand in hers and spoke in a soothing tone as Peter crossed the chamber to stand at her elbow, trying his best to remain as unobtrusive as possible.

Brimley released a gusty sigh and seemed to calm a bit, those eyes struggling to focus on the person seated next to him. "Ah. Victoria, is that you? It's been so long since you came to see us. Lavinia will be glad you're here."

Peter felt Emily stiffen, but there was no trace of tension in her voice when she spoke again. "No, my lord. It is Emily, Victoria's daughter."

"Emily?" The man appeared confused for a moment, then his wrinkled countenance brightened. "Why, Emily, how you've grown. You're the picture of your mother."

"Thank you, my lord." She paused for a moment and glanced up at Peter before continuing. "Adam tells me you had a bit of a run-in with the Oxfordshire Thief last night, and there is someone here who would like to speak to you about it."

"Someone here?" The marquis squinted up at Peter

and his brow lowered in a fierce expression. "Here now! Who are you? If you're one of my son's creditors, I can tell you right now you'll get nothing from me! Nothing!"

Creditors?

As Emily rushed to reassure the elderly man, Peter found himself examining his surroundings with much more interest than he had before. Upon entering the room, he hadn't taken in the rather shabby state of the once expensive rug and furnishings, the lack of ornamentation and decorative knickknacks that most master suites in luxurious homes usually boasted. But he made note of it now with particular attention to detail.

Was it possible that the Marquis of Brimley and his son were in dun territory? He'd heard that the latter had quite a reputation in London for being a high-stakes gamester, but had the viscount actually managed to deplete the family coffers with his taste for the city's finer gambling establishments?

"Mr. Quick isn't a creditor, Lord Brimley," Emily was explaining, sounding vaguely nonplussed. "He's a Bow Street Runner, and he is here to ask you about the thief who broke into the house last night."

"Ah. The thief. Caught the blighter in the act, I did. Would have had him, too, if my old bones hadn't given out."

Peter's heart gave a skip, and he couldn't resist finally entering the conversation. He took a step closer to the bed, drawing the marquis's attention back to him. "Did you get a look at him, my lord?"

"I did, as a matter of fact." Brimley shook his head in a mournful manner. "He stole my Lavinia's brooch, you know."

"We know, and I am most sorry for your loss." Trying not to sound too impatient, Peter nevertheless couldn't help prodding the man a little. "But the thief, my lord. What did he look like?"

"It was too dark to make out much. He was a rather young fellow. Thin. He had a cap pulled low over his eyes, but I could see blond hair sticking out from under it." The marquis rolled his head on the pillow to stare up at Emily. "Blond hair just like yours, my dear."

Blond hair?

Peter hated himself for considering it, felt like a traitor that the thought even crossed his mind, but it hovered at the edges of his consciousness, tormenting him with the possibility.

Could Benji have been the one he'd been looking for after all?

He wanted to dismiss the idea out of hand, but somehow he couldn't seem to do so. The boy's behavior had been all too strange lately, and added to Lord Brimley's description of the thief . . . well, the matter boded further checking into.

"Yes." The marquis was still talking, his gaze growing dreamy and unfocused as he continued to peer up at Emily. "Blond hair just like yours, Victoria. You know, Lavinia has missed you dreadfully since you and Ellington made the decision to reside in London year-round." His eyes drifted shut, and his voice started to trail away. "She's kept . . . every one you . . . ever sent her . . ."

A frown marred Peter's face. Obviously, the elderly gent was rambling again and believed he was speaking to the late Countess of Ellington. He had no idea how to reply, and Emily appeared just as stumped and at a loss as he felt.

"Every one of what, my lord?" she asked, and Peter could hear the curiosity underlying her tone.

"The . . . letters." Lord Brimley's words were slow in coming and barely audible, and his eyes remained closed.

"I'm afraid I don't know what letters you're speaking of."

When the man said nothing further in response to Emily's statement, merely offered another unintelligible mutter, she reached out to touch his arm, her sudden urgency catching Peter by surprise. "Lord Brimley? What letters?"

"That's enough!"

The barked command came from the direction of the door, and Peter looked back over his shoulder to find Lord Moreland standing in the entrance to the room, arms crossed over his chest, as he took in the scene before him. Dr. Billings hovered at his elbow. Constable Jenkins was nowhere in sight.

Reacting without hesitation to the viscount's aggressive stance, Peter swung about and placed himself in front of Emily, leveling the man with a deliberately challenging stare. "Is there a problem, my lord?"

A muscle flexed in the man's jaw, and Peter took a grim satisfaction in knowing that he was capable of

piercing through that cool façade and pricking Moreland where it counted.

But before he had more than a second to bask in that
knowledge, Emily got to her feet and moved forward to
stand next to him, her swift action telling him more
clearly than words that she was hoping to circumvent
the confrontation that was brewing. "I'm sorry, Adam. I
didn't mean to pry."

Her eloquent apology did the trick. The viscount's
face softened and he turned to her, dismissing Peter
with one last frosty glare. "Please don't apologize. I'm
sorry for reacting the way I did. But I'm afraid I'll have
to call a halt to the questioning. After last night, I'm
sure you can understand why Father needs his rest. And
as you may have noticed, he's not quite himself. I can't
see how he could be of much help."

"Actually, my lord," Peter interjected with particular
relish, keeping his eyes fastened on the man's profile,
carefully gauging his reaction. "Your father just provided us with a rather good description of the thief."

"Really?" Blond eyebrows shot upward and the viscount subjected Peter to an enigmatic scrutiny before
facing Emily again. "I'm glad to hear that he's been of
help. But I believe it's time to let him sleep."

"Of course." Emily tucked her arm through Peter's
before he could say a word and tugged him toward the
door. "Come along, Mr. Quick. I'm sure we have other
things we'll need to accomplish while we're here."

Dr. Billings bustled by them to check on his patient,
grumbling under his breath, and Peter cast one final

look back at the bed. Lord Brimley was already snoring, his thin chest rising and falling under the covers, as his son led them out into the hallway and shut the door.

Once in the silent corridor, Lord Moreland stopped and raked a hand through his hair before facing Emily, his gaze skating over Peter as if he weren't even there. "Emily, would you mind joining me downstairs in my study for a moment? There is something of a rather personal nature I wish to discuss with you."

"I—I don't know." Emily regarded Peter questioningly over her shoulder. "Perhaps Mr. Quick might need my help."

To Peter's observant eye, the viscount's practiced smile seemed suddenly forced. "Nonsense. Mr. Quick is a Bow Street Runner, after all. I'm sure he can handle himself. Isn't that right, Mr. Quick?"

Moreland's query, posed to him in such an unexpected manner, caught Peter a bit off guard. So the man was actually going to acknowledge his existence, was he?

He met the viscount's stare with an arch one of his own. "Oh, I assure you, my lord, I can handle myself just fine. And there is little left to do but take a look at the late Lady Brimley's bedchamber and speak with the servants." He raised an eyebrow. "If that could be arranged?"

"Of course. Mother's room is right next door to Father's." Moreland gestured at the door to the right of Lord Brimley's. "Feel free to look around all you like, though the constable has already given it a thorough going-over. And on our way downstairs I'll have a word with the butler and see if he can't gather the staff for your . . . interrogation."

"Thank you, my lord."

Emily still looked uncertain as she examined Peter's features. There was something in her expression he couldn't quite read. Something almost pleading. But pleading with him for what? He had no way of knowing. "I still don't—"

The viscount interrupted her by putting a hand on her arm in supplication. "Please, Emily. I wouldn't ask if it weren't very important. It won't take long, and you'll be able to rejoin Mr. Quick shortly."

Her gaze went back and forth between the two men, full of equal parts consternation and concern. But she finally gave a reluctant nod. "Very well. If Mr. Quick is certain he doesn't need me . . . ?"

Now, how to answer that?

"I'm certain." He fought to keep his face expressionless, and after a moment, Emily allowed the viscount to lead her away.

Peter felt his heart give a particularly brutal squeeze as he watched them start down the stairs, their heads bent close in conversation. He hated the mere thought of the two of them alone together, but he was well aware there was nothing he could do about it.

Emily was not his to dictate to. Not his to protect.

But convincing himself of that was another matter.

Chapter 20

❦❦

"I beg your pardon?"

Stunned and more than a little overwhelmed, Emily gazed at Adam with her mouth agape, certain she must have misheard him.

"Come now, Emily, surely it can't come as that much of a shock." The viscount gave a wry chuckle, but the humor didn't quite reach his hazel eyes. They were narrowed, watchful, as he stood before her, both of her hands captured in his. "You must know how I feel about you. I've been trying to propose to you for weeks now."

It seemed her ears were in proper working order after all. Adam *had* asked her to marry him. She supposed she shouldn't have been so surprised. She'd suspected that things were leading in this direction, but she hadn't guessed that he would choose a moment like this to ask her to be his bride, when his family was in the midst of so much chaos.

For some reason, his attitude hit her as being just a trifle insensitive.

The proposal had seemed to come out of the blue. After leading her to his study, Adam had spent a moment out in the hallway, speaking with his butler, before joining Emily. Then, seating her in an overstuffed chair in front of his desk, he had caught her off guard by clasping her hands in a firm grip and asking her quite seriously to marry him.

Perhaps sensing her disquiet, he leveled her with an earnest look. "I may have been a bit abrupt, and for that I apologize. But I've decided the time for subtlety is past. Every time I've tried to ease into asking you to become my wife, something has happened to interrupt me. It seemed better to just come out and say it. Do you forgive me?"

"Of course. But—" She paused and licked her dry lips before continuing. "I don't know what to say."

"Say yes."

She avoided his disconcerting stare and let her gaze trail around the room. It was only now, as she sought to distract herself, that she noticed something she should have noticed upon first entering. Many of the pieces of furniture she could remember from previous visits were conspicuously absent, and there were several bare spaces on the wall where she was certain expensive paintings had once hung.

Lord Brimley's comments regarding his son's creditors suddenly seemed to make sense. Was Adam's gambling more of a problem than she'd believed? Was it bad enough that he'd had to start selling off their household possessions?

There was no way she could broach the subject without offending the viscount, so she resisted the impulse to question him and instead returned to the matter at hand.

"I'm afraid I can't just say yes, Adam," she ventured. "There is much to consider, and I can't help but feel this isn't the right time."

Lord Moreland's face flushed a deep red and he dropped her hands, crossing his arms in an almost defensive posture. "What is there to consider? And when would be the right time?"

"Adam, your father has just suffered an attack and is bedridden upstairs after coming face-to-face with the thief who stole your mother's prized possession! I should think you would have more pressing matters to concern yourself with."

Pivoting, he strode across the room to stand before the window, staring out at the sunny day beyond the glass. His back was stiff, his shoulders held rigidly, and just when she was beginning to think he wasn't going to speak again, he exhaled a breath of air and looked back at her over his shoulder. "You're right, of course. But you must understand how anxious I am about this. I've thought of little else for the past several weeks, and with Father in such poor health . . . well, to be honest, I could use someone to lean on."

Emily felt her heart give a tug of sympathy and she got to her feet, moving to stand next to him. "Adam, you know I will always be here for you. We're friends, after all, and that is what friends do for each other. And I will be glad to aid you and your father in any way I can."

He reached up to lay a hand on her cheek. His touch was so unexpected—and unnerving—that Emily had to fight the urge to put some distance between them. "I appreciate that, Emily. I truly do. And I know my father does, as well. He's always been fond of you, you know, and he'd be delighted to see us wed."

A shard of guilt pierced her as she recalled the marquis's pale face, the labored heave of his breathing. This was all her fault. And having the elderly man mistake her for her mother, hearing him talk about Victoria's friendship with his deceased wife, had made her feel twice as ashamed. She couldn't believe she'd been callous enough to continue to try to prod information from him even after he'd obviously had enough, but his mention of her mother's letters had made her wonder if perhaps some tie to the late Lady Ellington's past still existed. If so, then there might be a chance to prove whether or not Jack Barlow's claims were true.

But no. There could be no excuse for badgering someone in such a state, no matter her reasons. All she had succeeded in doing was arousing Peter's curiosity and tiring a poor old man.

The least Adam deserved from her was to be let down gently.

"Please, Emily," the viscount was saying, coming a step closer to her. "You must see how important this is to me. I've put off my usual departure to London for the Season, wanting to get this sorted out before I go." His palm fell away from her cheek and he reached for her hand once again. "As a matter of fact, I was hoping to persuade you and your family to come with me, so we can announce our betrothal. I care for you a great deal, and as we've been friends for so long, I feel that we would suit rather well. Surely you must agree?"

For the sake of the friendship she'd shared with Adam in the past, she forced herself to reply as cautiously as possible. "I don't know. Marriage is a rather large step and—"

"It appears I'm interrupting something important again."

The voice brought Emily's head jerking in the direction of the door to find Peter lounging in the entrance-way, arms crossed, his countenance cool and unreadable.

She'd never been so happy to see anyone in her life.

It was apparently a sentiment Lord Moreland didn't share. A scowl marred his handsome face as he glowered at Peter. "Are you already finished questioning the staff, Mr. Quick? I didn't expect you to be done so soon."

Peter shrugged, his perceptive gaze skimming over Emily's features in a way that led her to believe that every one of her confusing emotions must show on her face. "There wasn't much they could add to the story, I'm afraid. None of them saw the thief. It seems by the time they came upon Lord Brimley collapsed in the hallway, the man was long gone."

Emily tugged her hand free from Adam's grasp and sidled a step or two away from him, not realizing she'd been holding her breath until clean, fresh air raced into her lungs with her sharp inhalation.

"And you've examined Lady Brimley's chamber?" she asked. Though she was relieved by Peter's timely arrival, her interest in his answer wasn't feigned. She truly wished to know what he had discovered.

After all, keeping her double identity a secret could depend upon it.

"Thoroughly. The dust had been disturbed in a few places, as if in a hasty search. And the window was left open. There is no trellis or tree to climb, but some bushes close to the side of the house look as if something large was dragged through them recently. It appears our thief jumped to make his escape."

And had the bruises to prove it. Emily had to restrain the urge to rub her aching posterior.

"Well, I suppose that means our work is done here," she said brightly, starting toward Peter and the door. "We should most likely be off now. I know you had several things you needed to do with regard to the investigation, Mr. Quick, and I—"

"Emily, wait."

Drat and blast! She should have known Adam wouldn't let her escape that easily.

She stopped and turned with great reluctance, watching as the viscount approached her. As if sensing her trepidation, Peter moved up behind her, and she found herself grateful for his solid, warm presence looming at her back.

It was only Adam. She shouldn't feel this threatened.

But she did.

Nearing her side, the viscount caught her elbow in a firm grip and stared into her eyes, as if willing her to concede. "I hope you will promise me you will at least consider what I have proposed. I think we would make an excellent match, and if you will give it some thought, I'm sure you will agree."

Had Peter just growled in her ear? It wouldn't surprise her. She would have to be blind not to know that he didn't care for Lord Moreland, and the antipathy appeared to be mutual. Eager to flee Adam's unsettling presence and wanting to get Peter away before the two men came to blows, she gave a hasty nod. "Very well. I promise I will think about it."

With that, she pulled her arm free, whirled, and left the room with Peter at her heels.

But she couldn't help wondering as she made her escape what Adam would think if he knew he had just proposed marriage to the very woman who had stolen his mother's brooch and caused his father's attack.

Once in the carriage and on their way back to Knighthaven, Peter found himself unable to keep from studying Emily, trying to discern what she was feeling from the look on her face. But her expression was closed, leaving her eyes strangely blank as she stared off into space.

Lord Moreland had proposed to her.

Peter clenched his jaw against the anger that flared through him whenever he imagined her as the wife of the condescending viscount. Though he knew he would never be able to have Emily for his own, he still had a vested interest in her future happiness, and he found it hard to believe she could ever be happy with Moreland.

Not to mention the fact that the mere thought of the man touching, kissing, caressing her the way he himself had done was enough to madden him beyond reason.

"Well, Mr. Quick. Do you have any theories?"

So caught up was he in the troubling vision of Emily being made love to by Lord Moreland that it took Peter a moment to realize she was addressing him. Jerking himself from his disturbing thoughts, he faced her, hoping his countenance betrayed none of his roiling emotions. "I beg your pardon?"

"Theories, Mr. Quick. I was interested in whether you had any new ones regarding the Oxfordshire Thief now that you've spoken with Lord Brimley and had a chance to look over the scene of the crime."

As a matter of fact, he did. "Only one, I'm afraid. Is the marquis a frequent contributor to Willow Park?"

"I believe so. At least, he has been in the past. Why?"

"It occurred to me as I was examining Lady Brimley's old bedchamber that each of the victims of the thief has made some sort of monetary donation to the upkeep of the Park at one time or another. It's the only thing that ties the cases together that I've been able to pinpoint."

Emily's face whitened. "Oh, my God, that's true! I never even made the connection, but you're right." She appeared stunned by the revelation.

"It wouldn't be too out of line to assume that the culprit is someone who is associated with either Willow

Park or your family and holds a grudge. Can you think of anyone who fits that description?"

A frown marred her brow and she avoided his gaze. "It isn't a secret that most of Little Haverton would like to see Willow Park closed. But I can't think of anyone who could hate us so much that they would do such a thing, go to such lengths." She sighed and bowed her head. "Do you still plan on visiting the local pawnbrokers?"

Peter nodded. Something in her demeanor troubled him, but he couldn't quite put his finger on what it was. "While I'm doing that, you might try questioning your brother to see if he can think of anyone who has a personal vendetta against him or the Park."

"Of course. Anything I can do to help."

She didn't sound particularly enthusiastic, and he found himself perusing her visage, searching for some sign of what she might be hiding.

Was she bothered by what he had told her about the thief and the connection to Willow Park? Or was she thinking about Lord Moreland?

The possibility pricked at him, and he couldn't have called the words back that spilled from his lips if he had tried.

"You deserve better than Moreland, you know."

Obviously surprised by the change in subject, Emily's head flew up, her lashes fluttering as she focused on him with an intensity that pierced him. "Excuse me?"

He'd come this far. There was no use backing down

now. He took a deep breath and plunged onward. "Lord Moreland. He proposed to you, I assume?"

"If it's any business of yours, yes, he did."

"He isn't good enough for you, Em. You deserve someone who will love you and set you free to be yourself. Moreland would smother you inside of a week."

"And you're so concerned for my welfare and what sort of man I deserve? I'm certain I can't see why you should care." Her tone was haughty, leaving him in no doubt that she didn't appreciate his observation.

"I will always be concerned for your welfare, Emily. I will always care."

At that, some of the starch seemed to seep out of her. "I thank you for your concern. But I haven't exactly told him yes. I only said I would think about it."

Which meant she was considering it. Bloody hell.

Reaching out, Peter caught Emily by her elbow and pulled her toward him until only an inch of space separated them. "Do you love him?"

Her eyes widened and locked with his for a small eternity. Her hands fluttered up to rest against his chest, the warmth of her palms scorching him, even through the material of his shirt. "What?" she choked out.

"It's a simple question. Do. You. Love. Him."

Her chin went up at a mutinous angle and she tightened her mouth into a thin line, refusing to answer.

It was all the provocation Peter's temper needed. With a stifled curse, he hauled her onto his lap and kissed her with savage need.

Just that quickly, he was lost. Her taste, her scent, the feel of her in his embrace was enough to scatter his senses to the four winds.

She went still against him, and when a startled gasp escaped her, he immediately took advantage of it and plunged his tongue into her mouth, savoring her moist warmth and honeyed flavor with a fierce groan. After a second or two of hesitation, she slid her arms upward to wrap around his neck and returned his ardor, her tongue touching his at first timidly, then boldly.

Desire washed over him like a tidal wave, and unable to help himself, Peter lifted his hand to cup a plump breast, his thumb running over the beaded nipple through the fabric of her bodice. At the same time, his other hand moved to the hem of her gown, pushing the material upward, inch by inch, until his palm brushed against the silken flesh of her inner thigh.

The feel of that soft skin was enough to send him over the edge. "Emily," he breathed, tearing his lips from hers to skim them down the slope of her throat. "I want you so much . . ."

Her only reply was a quavering moan.

Encouraged, his fingers shifted the slightest bit, just barely grazing against the damp nest of curls that guarded the feminine heart of her. And like a dash of cold water, his action seemed to freeze her in place. Abruptly, the hands that had been urging him on were attempting to shove him away.

"Stop, Peter! Please!"

Her sudden panic penetrated his amorous fog, and he

raised his head with great reluctance, his hold on her loosening.

Jerking free, Emily flung herself back into her seat, and scooted as far from him as she could get without jumping from the moving carriage. Eyes large and turbulent with emotion, she crossed her arms in a defensive posture and took a deep breath before speaking in a trembling voice.

"We have to stop doing this. You were the one who decided four years ago that we were better off apart. Have you changed your mind?"

Yes! With all of his heart, Peter wanted to shout that he *had* changed his mind, that he would die before he allowed her to wed Moreland. But he couldn't.

His past stood like an insurmountable wall between them.

When he failed to reply, something dark and shadowed passed over her features and she shook her head. "Right. Well, then, it might be best if you keep your hands to yourself from now on. Don't touch me. Don't kiss me. Just . . . don't."

Peter felt his stomach lurch and he retreated to his own corner of the coach, taking a deep breath to calm his pounding heart. She was right. He knew that. But that didn't mean that he wasn't going to continue to look out for her best interests.

Full of resolve, he sent her a veiled glance as the carriage rolled to a halt in front of Knighthaven. If he had his way, a wedding between her and the viscount would never take place. By damn, he hadn't given her up so she could tie herself to someone who would never love or respect her the way she deserved. And he refused to stand by and watch her ruin her life by marrying a jack-ass like Moreland!

Chapter 21

Peter trotted Champion up the long, winding drive toward Willow Park. The sun was just starting to set in the distance, outlining the trees that surrounded the estate with a rosy glow and painting the house with an ethereal light.

It had still been rather early when he had finished his rounds of the surrounding pawnshops, of which there were very few, and he had uncovered exactly what he had expected. Nothing. None of the owners of the establishments had noticed anything untoward or seen anyone who had tried to pass off the stolen jewelry to them. He hadn't believed the thief would be that foolish, but it had been worth a try.

Still, the fruitless task had been discouraging, and he'd been left feeling frustrated. Surely by now he should be farther along in this case than he was? The more time that passed without the criminal being caught, the more chance there was he would strike again.

Needing something to keep his mind occupied after his earlier stand-off with Emily, he had decided stopping by the Park would be a good idea. He hadn't been out to visit in several days, and it would offer him the opportunity to question Benji a bit more. He needed to get to the bottom of what was troubling the lad once and for all. After hearing Lord Brimley's account of his confrontation with the thief, he believed that finding an answer was more important than ever, for Peter had to admit that the marquis's description of the culprit had been damning.

But Benji couldn't be responsible. He refused to believe it.

As he drew closer to the house, Peter let his gaze travel over his familiar surroundings. How he had missed all this, he mused with a fond smile. There, next to the pond beneath the willow trees, he and Emily had once walked hand in hand, basking in the glow of first love and sharing a joy and contentment he hadn't known since. And from here, he could just make out the second-floor window of what had once been his bedroom. A window that had served as a very handy escape route whenever he had felt the need to get away from the confines of the house and be alone for a while.

Even as he had the thought, he watched as that very same window slid slowly upward, and a leg swung over the sill.

What the bloody hell . . . ?

Halting Champion, Peter swung down from the horse's back and stood in the center of the drive, continuing to observe as the foot attached to the leg struggled for a toehold in the brickwork beneath the ledge.

Ah! It looked as if he were just in time.

Leading his gelding forward, Peter approached the side of the house and the tall, thin figure that was attempting to scramble down the brick façade in a rather clumsy fashion. He kept his footsteps as quiet as possible in the soft grass, for he certainly had no desire to startle the boy and send him plunging down to break his neck—or to warn him he was about to be caught.

He stopped beneath the window and waited until the figure had made it to the ground before speaking. "Hello, Benji."

The lad let out a yelp and jumped several inches in the air before whirling about, his face bright red.

"Isn't it a bit late to be heading out?" Peter went on, glancing up at the darkening sky. "By my estimation, the McLeans and the rest of the children should be just finishing up dinner."

Benji scowled and crossed his arms, leaning back against the side of the house in an effort to appear nonchalant that failed miserably. "I told them I wasn't hungry."

"That seems to be happening a lot lately." Peter wrapped his mount's reins around a nearby tree branch and sauntered over to stand next to the boy. "Do you want to tell me where you were going?"

"Nowhere special. Just out."

"That's not good enough." Taking a deep breath, Peter struggled to keep his tone as calm as possible. "I don't want to come across as heavy-handed, Benji, but you're not acting like yourself, and everyone is worried about you. Including me. Anyone who knows you knows you don't do this sort of thing. Distancing yourself from the others, sneaking out. I wish you would tell me what's wrong."

The lad's mouth clamped shut and he looked away, his jaw set at a stubborn angle.

Peter felt his temper flare. Damn it, one way or another, he was not leaving here without an explanation. "Look, you know I'm not one to badger you. I did more than my share of slipping out after dark at fourteen, and no mistake. But this situation is too precarious for you to keep things to yourself right now. I don't need to tell you about the thief who has been stealing from some of the families in the area, and I'm sure after being questioned you must know that Constable Jenkins has his suspicions about you and some of the other boys at Willow Park. The Marquis of Brimley was robbed last night, and the description he gave of the suspect sounds amazingly like you."

Benji gasped, his eyes widening behind his spectacles, and his expression convinced Peter once and for all that he'd had nothing to do with the thefts. The boy looked stunned, as if he'd been knocked completely off balance.

"You don't think—" The youth stumbled to a halt, his countenance suddenly almost pleading as he stared up at Peter.

"Of course not. But what I think may not hold much sway if the constable takes it into his head that you're the culprit. He'll be back to question you again, and maybe even haul you off to jail. And if that happens, the citizens of Little Haverton will have the excuse they need to shut down the Park for good. Is that what you want?"

Benji shook his head, then looked down at the ground, kicking at a clump of dirt with his toe. "I never meant to cause trouble for Willow Park."

Peter squeezed the boy's shoulder once, then let go. "Then you have to tell me the truth. Confide in me. Please, Benji. I want to help."

After a long moment of silence, the lad slumped and he met Peter's eyes with a resigned air. "Jack is here."

"Jack?"

"Jack Barlow."

The name was enough to send icy hot anger racing through Peter's veins. His gut clenched and his hands tightened into fists at his sides. Of all the things he had expected Benji to tell him, he certainly hadn't expected that.

"He's here? In Little Haverton?"

Benji nodded.

The bloody bastard! How dare he show his face here after all these years?

Jack Barlow had once been a member of the Rag-Tag Bunch and Peter's worst nemesis, and it was practically guaranteed that the man's presence in town spelled trouble. After all, "Trouble" had always been Jack's middle name.

Struggling to keep his anger in check, Peter looked down at the boy next to him, his mouth set in a grim line. "How long have you known about this?"

"I'm not sure. Maybe a month."

"And you've waited this long to let anyone know?"

"I didn't know what to do." Benji's expression became defensive, but guilt showed briefly in his eyes before he shuttered them and turned to walk a little distance away, standing with his back to Peter. "He said he would hurt one of the Willow Park children if I told. He snuck up on me one day when I was sitting out by the pond by myself, reading."

"And what did he say?"

"Not much. He made a bunch of threats. Said it would be easy to get to the people I cared about if I didn't do exactly as he said." The lad paused for a second, and when he continued his voice wasn't quite steady. "He said . . . he knew about my past, and if I ran a few errands for him he would make sure everyone at the Park stayed safe and he'd . . . he'd tell me where I came from."

"Where you came from? Benji—"

"You don't understand!" Benji whirled to face Peter, cutting him off. The look on the boy's face was agonized. "I've always wondered . . . well, bloody hell, Peter, you found me wandering in an alley when I was three years old! I don't know where I come from, who my parents were, why they left me alone on the streets of London. At least you and the other Rag-Tags had a sense of your past, even if you didn't come from the best of backgrounds." He shook his head glumly. "I don't even know who I am."

It was true. Peter had found Benji as little more than a babe, cowering behind a stack of crates and filthy debris in one of the dark back alleys of the rookery, and had taken him under his wing, offering him a home with the Rag-Tag Bunch. But never before had Peter realized that having no knowledge of his origins had bothered the lad so much. He had never shown the slightest sign of it.

Leave it to Jack to strike at the boy's weakest point.

"You're Benji," Peter told him, taking a step forward. "And that's all that's important."

"Easy for you to say," Benji grumbled in return, looking away again.

Peter raked his hands down his face, his frustration welling up to choke him. Please, God, help him to handle this the right way, to say the right things.

"So," he drew out slowly. "You went along with Jack to find out if he really knew anything about your past."

"I wouldn't say I went along with him. I told him I needed some time to think about it. He said he'd be back, but a couple of weeks passed and he didn't come. I was just beginning to think he'd given up and left Little Haverton when he showed up again."

"Here at Willow Park?"

"Yes. He said my time was up and I needed to make my decision."

"And?"

"I decided I couldn't take the chance that he might do

as he said and hurt someone. And I had to know whether he truly did know anything about my past. So I agreed to do as he asked."

"What does he want you to do?"

"I don't know. He hasn't told me. He said he'd be in touch, and yesterday he sent a boy with a message that I was to meet him tonight."

It couldn't be a coincidence that Jack, a former street thief with a grudge against those associated with Willow Park, had shown up in Little Haverton a little over a month ago—at precisely the same time the first of the Oxfordshire thefts had occurred.

Peter felt his heart pick up speed.

Was it possible that Jack Barlow was the man he was looking for? True, he didn't match the description Lord Brimley had given, but he could have been in disguise or in cahoots with someone else who had committed the actual crime. Or the marquis could have been mistaken. He wasn't exactly a reliable witness right now.

In any case, Jack's appearance fit too neatly into the entire puzzle.

"You realize that it's more than likely that Jack knows nothing at all about your past," he told Benji, moving to stand next to the boy again. "He'll say and do anything, use whatever he can, to get you under his thumb. But I doubt there's any truth to what he tells you."

Benji shrugged. "I know. But there's no telling what will happen if I don't do as he says. What other option do I have?"

"You can let me handle this."

When the youth started to protest, Peter halted him with a hand on his arm. "You trust me, don't you?"

There was nothing to answer him but silence.

He heaved a sigh. He supposed he couldn't blame the boy for doubting him. "Benji, I know I haven't been around much in the last few years. There have been some . . . circumstances of a rather personal nature that have kept me from visiting as much as I'd like. I'm aware that might have made you feel as if I didn't care about you or Willow Park, but I assure you that's not the case. I care very much, and I will do whatever I have to do to make sure you and everyone here remains safe."

Benji glanced up at him a bit uncertainly. "You'll—you'll find out if Jack really does know anything about me? Where I come from?"

"Once I have him in custody, I'll question him thoroughly. But the odds are he knows nothing. I want you to be prepared for that."

The lad inclined his head in an abrupt, affirmative nod, but the brown eyes behind the spectacles remained troubled.

At the pained look on Benji's face, Peter reined in a growl of frustrated anger. Barlow was going to pay for all he'd done. "All right. Where and when are you supposed to meet Jack?"

"At the old abandoned gamekeeper's cottage on Lord and Lady Ellington's property at sundown."

Which should be just about now. Well, Jack Barlow was in for a surprise.

"All right. I want you to go back inside—and this

time use the door. I'm going to look into this, and as soon as I have things under control I'll be in touch."

"Are you going to say anything to the McLeans or Lord and Lady Ellington?"

"Not right now. That's not to say I won't in the future. I may have to sooner or later in order to explain all of this. But they've been very worried about you, Benji. They all deserve to know what's been going on."

The boy swallowed visibly, but straightened his shoulders and started around the side of the house. He stopped and glanced back, however, when Peter called after him. "And, Benji? Try to remember that the past is behind you. It is who you are now and what you make of yourself in the future that's important."

Benji looked far from convinced, but he lifted a hand in acknowledgment and managed a smile that wobbled a bit at the corners before continuing on.

As soon as the boy disappeared out of sight, Peter strode for his horse, full of fury and a fierce resolve. It looked as if he might be on the verge of solving this case after all. If he was right, Barlow was behind everything, and it would be a privilege to make sure the man paid for his crimes——both past and present—once and for all.

Chapter 22

Emily knelt between Miles and Jenna behind the concealment of a pair of bushes and watched as Jack Barlow paced the clearing in front of the game-keeper's cottage, his strides swift and impatient.

He'd been doing this ever since they'd arrived over a quarter of an hour ago. And as time wore on, the scowl on his face grew more pronounced and he kept casting glances at the darkening sky, as if trying to judge the time.

Was he expecting someone?

"I thought you said he leaves for the tavern by sundown," Emily hissed at Miles, feeling her anxiety mount with every moment that passed. So much depended on what happened tonight, and Jack's continued presence threatened to ruin everything.

The stable hand shrugged. "'E's usually gone by now. Per'aps the boy is delivering tonight's message to 'im 'ere instead."

Alarm skittered through her. Dear Lord, she hoped not. She would never have a better chance to search the cottage.

There had been no difficulty in slipping away from Knighthaven this evening. In her eagerness to aid her young sister-in-law in her supposed seduction of Peter, Deirdre had given most of the servants, including Langley, the night off. And just before departing with Tristan for dinner at Lilah and Cullen's home, the countess had stopped long enough to give Emily a hug and a knowing wink.

But if Emily had been planning on taking advantage of the opportunity Lady Ellington had presented her with, she would have been doomed to disappointment. The sun had set, and Peter had yet to return from his sojourn to the local pawnshops. Jenna had mentioned earlier that she had passed him as she was making her way through the woods to Knighthaven. Apparently, he'd been on his way to Willow Park.

At the thought of Peter, she found her mind traveling back to earlier that afternoon, to his reaction to Adam's proposal. Though a part of her was appalled at the way she had allowed him to touch her in the carriage, she couldn't help but be pleased by his display of concern—and his obvious jealousy.

"Moreland isn't good enough for you, Emily."

And yet the stubborn fool would never admit that maybe—just maybe—*he* might be the man for her. In his mind, he was unworthy, merely by virtue of his background, and whatever Emily might think was beside the point.

But regardless of whether she could have Peter in her life or not, she would never marry Adam. She'd made up her mind about that once and for all when she'd entered the barn to meet Jenna and Miles before coming here and had walked in on them wrapped in each other's arms, kissing with a fierce passion.

Her two friends had sprung apart at her approach, red-faced and stammering, but she had waved off their excuses with an understanding smile. She was happy for them, glad that Jenna had finally realized what a good man Miles was, but she couldn't help but feel a sharp pang in the vicinity of her heart. No, she could never wed a man she did not love.

And the only man she would ever love was Peter Quick.

Now, however, was not the time to be thinking of this. She had to focus on the task at hand. Perhaps if she could accomplish what she hoped to tonight, she might be able to convince Peter to forgive her transgressions.

Her mind turned, instead, to his theory regarding the thefts and the connections between the victims. It had never occurred to her that each of Jack's marks had been contributors to Willow Park. Had the blackguard chosen them on purpose?

She answered her own question. Of course he had. It would be the ultimate revenge for Jack, once the victimized families found out who the thief was, to have them withdraw their support of the Park. And it was almost guaranteed that they would.

She had to put an end to Jack's schemes. She just had to!

At that moment, the object of her thoughts gave an irritated growl before throwing up his hands and stalking off around the side of the cottage.

"It looks like 'e's finally on 'is way," Jenna whispered.

Sure enough, a minute later Jack trotted back into view on a gray spotted gelding. With one last look around and a tap of his heels against the horse's flanks, he sent his mount galloping off down the path toward the edge of the woods and the main road.

"All right," Emily said as soon as he was out of sight. "Let's go."

If luck was with her, she just might be able to recover the stolen jewelry as well as the mysterious letters Jack was holding over her head and be back at Knighthaven before Peter returned and noticed anything amiss.

The three of them crept from their hiding place and stole swiftly across the clearing toward the cottage. There was no impediment to their entry, as the door was standing ajar, and Emily paused in the opening for a second in order to get her bearings.

Within, a lone candle had been left burning on the mantel above the crumbling fireplace. Its wavering light barely illuminated the interior of the small, one-room house, but there wasn't much to see. There was little in the way of furniture. Only a scarred wooden table and a single chair. A threadbare blanket had been spread out on the dirt floor before the fireplace, where the remains of a roasted hare hung on a spit over the hearth.

"Well, if 'e's 'idden the stuff 'ere, it shouldn't be too 'ard to find it," Jenna commented from behind her.

Miles stepped past them into the room. "We'd better start searching. We've only got a couple of hours at most before Jack comes back. And if 'e really was waiting for someone, there's no telling when they might decide to turn up."

He was right. Emily lifted her chin in determination. "Jenna, go get that candle and bring it here. Miles, help me check the walls for any holes or loose boards. Jack wouldn't leave any of the stolen goods out in plain sight. More than likely he has some sort of cubbyhole. We just have to find it."

As Jenna hurried to fetch the candle, Emily and the stable hand started to work their way around the room, knocking on walls, prying at the moldering wood and looking for any sort of chinks or cracks that might indicate a hiding place. It was slow going with only the glow of the candle to light their way, and by the time they were done, they were dusty and discouraged.

But Emily wasn't about to give up.

Placing her hands on her hips, she contemplated her surroundings with narrowed eyes. "It has to be here somewhere. There's no place else for him to hide any of it, and I can't believe he would have already pawned it."

Miles's brow furrowed in thought. "You know, 'e might have buried it outside somewhere."

"Possibly. But I doubt he would stray very far from

the cottage." She turned to the stable hand. "Why don't you go check around the clearing and see if you notice any signs of freshly dug earth. And keep an eye out for Jack. Jenna and I will keep looking in here."

Miles nodded and set off on his errand as the two women went back to poking and prodding into all of the dark corners of the room. Jenna moved to examine the fireplace, holding the sputtering candle aloft as she searched for loose bricks, while Emily sat down on the blanket and looked through the knapsack that Jack had obviously been using as a pillow.

It was empty except for a rather dull-bladed knife.

"This makes no sense," Emily said, unable to hide her growing frustration. "It *has* to be here somewhere."

She placed one hand on the blanket and started to push herself to her feet, but she paused for a moment when her fingers encountered a depression in the earth beneath it. Her heart speeding up a bit in response, she reached out to toss back the edge of the frayed material to find a shallow hole a little larger than a man's fist that had been dug into the dirt floor.

"Jenna! I think this is it!"

The younger girl hurried over to Emily, shining the meager light from the candle down into the darkness of the hole. Emily stuck a hand in and withdrew a small drawstring bag, uttering a quick, silent prayer as she loosened the string and dumped the contents out onto the blanket.

And there they were. Lady Tuttleston's cherished necklace, Lord Caulfield's diamond cuff links, the Fulberry jewels, and Lady Brimley's beloved brooch, all sparkling in the dimness like stars in the night sky.

"What about the letters?" Jenna asked anxiously, straining to see into the crevice. "Are they in there, too?"

Emily reached back into the hole and felt around. There wasn't much room to maneuver, and at first she felt nothing but loose dirt. After a second, however, her fingers brushed against something that made a hushed crinkling sound, and she pulled out two folded, yellowed pieces of stationery.

She stared down at them for a moment in consternation. Was this the proof Jack had been speaking of? Was she about to find out that her mother hadn't been the person that everyone had always believed her to be?

As if sensing her distress, Jenna laid a comforting hand on her shoulder and gave it a gentle squeeze. "I'll go let Miles know we found it," she murmured, then set the candle on the ground and quietly left the cottage.

Emily was grateful for her friend's sensitivity. Though she dreaded it, she knew she had to read the letters, and she would feel much better if she could do it in private. But she would have to do it quickly. She had no desire for Jack to return and find her here.

Her fingers trembling slightly, she unfolded the first paper and leaned in toward the candle so its faint glow spilled over the delicate handwriting on the page.

Her mother's handwriting. Her mouth went dry at the realization. She'd seen enough samples of the late Lady Ellington's writing over the years to recognize it now.

Dearest Lavinia,

Lavinia? Good heavens, this was a letter from her mother to the late Lady Brimley!

She continued to read.

You have been such a good friend to me over the years, and I hate to burden you further with my troubles, but I find I must share them with someone or I will burst.

I have ended my affair with Nick. Even though I know it was for the best, it was the hardest thing I have ever done. I will never forget the look of anguish on his face when I told him we could no longer be together. As much as I love him, I know that a true relationship would never work. You were right about that. Society would never accept it. I am the daughter of a viscount and he is a stable hand in my father's employ, and nothing will ever change that. I never should have allowed the physical side of things between us to evolve, but I couldn't seem to help myself. I am ashamed, but I find I can't be sorry for the time we had together.

Yet, it is time to move on and put all of this behind me. I have accepted Lord Ellington's offer of marriage. Sinclair is a good man and I care for him deeply, though I shall never love him the way I love my dear Nick. However, I couldn't wed him without telling him the truth about my affair. He was so very understanding, and he says he loves me. Perhaps everything will work out for the best.

The next page was another letter, dated three months later, and also addressed to Lady Brimley.

I am with child.

The words were enough to have Emily's stomach lurching.

I have suspected ever since Sinclair and I made the permanent move to London, and now I am certain. I would be so happy if I could only be sure of who the father is. Not that I could ever regret giving birth to any child of my darling Nick, but ever since I informed my husband of the news, he has been different. Quiet, withdrawn, almost brooding, and I've caught him staring at my stomach several times with a strange look in his eye. He, too, doubts that the baby is his, and I am so afraid he will be unable to love it.

If only I could be certain that Sinclair will eventually get past this difficulty and learn to treat my child as his own, regardless of his suspicions. I suppose I will know nothing until the babe's birth. Until then, I will hold out hope. Please pray for me.

Your dear friend, Victoria

Where on earth had Jack gotten his hands on such incriminating evidence?

The letters fell from Emily's nerveless fingers and

fluttered to the blanket as her eyes blurred with sudden moisture. Her poor mother. And father! He had known from the beginning that there was a chance that Tristan wasn't his. No wonder he had been so cold and forbidding with his only son. And no wonder he had become so very bitter. He had spent his life married to a woman whom he had loved fiercely, but who had never felt the same way about him. A woman who had loved someone else.

She closed her eyes, trying to picture her father's face, trying to match the features she could recall to those of her brother. The late Lord Ellington had been a big, dark-haired man and so was Tristan, but that wasn't necessarily proof that they were related. If this Nick had been large and dark in coloring, as well . . .

"So?"

At the sound of Jenna's voice, Emily looked up to find both the younger girl and Miles hovering in the doorway, their expressions full of concern.

"It's true." She forced the words out through a constricted throat. "All of it."

"Oh, Em. I'm so sorry."

Emily blinked back her tears, trying to gain control of her ragged emotions, then lifted her chin with firm purpose before picking up the pages, refolding them, and tucking them in the pocket of her breeches. There wasn't time for her to fall apart. Not now. "It doesn't matter. Jack can no longer use these to blackmail me." She gestured to the stolen goods lying on the blanket before her. "And we have what we were looking for, so I'd say our work here is done. We'll turn it all over to the law and explain what's been going on. Hopefully, Jack will be behind bars before the sun sets again."

"What about Peter?" Miles asked softly.

Emily took a deep breath. "I plan on speaking with him, but I want to make sure things are settled first. He deserves to know the truth about all of this." Regardless of how he might have reacted, she should have confided in Peter from the beginning. It had been wrong to keep him in the dark. Her initial anger toward him, her bitterness and hurt, had blinded her, but no longer.

Gathering up the jewels, she stuffed them back into the drawstring bag and handed it to Miles, then got to her feet. "Why don't you two go ahead? I'll hurry and put things to rights in here and join you in a moment."

The stable hand nodded, caught Jenna's hand, and tugged her out the door.

As soon as they were out of sight, Emily hastily set herself to the task of erasing all signs of their presence, reaching down to tug the blanket back over the hole in the floor and returning the candle to the mantel where it had been. But as she worked, her mind buzzed with the implications of all she had learned tonight. She still had to wonder how Jack had gotten hold of the letters in the first place. Had he broken into Brimley Hall himself and stolen them? Were these the letters the marquis had mentioned earlier today?

She firmly pushed away her worried musings. She didn't have time to think about that right now. Jack could be back any minute. She could only hope that he wouldn't notice that the letters and his cache of stolen goods were gone until she'd had a chance to explain everything to the local authorities.

And to make things right with Peter. *If* she ever could.

With one last glance back over her shoulder, she exited the cottage and started across the clearing.

Only to slam into a wall of solid muscle.

Her thoughts scattered like leaves on the wind as her heart flew into her throat, and her shocked gaze traveled up a pair of sculpted thighs encased in close-fitting breeches, past muscled arms crossed over a broad chest, to meet a pair of piercing blue eyes that stared down at her with obvious displeasure.

Peter!

His sudden appearance was enough to send her stumbling back a few steps, and he reached out and caught her by the elbows, preventing her from falling. Her mouth fell open, but nothing emerged except a startled gasp.

"What," Peter gritted out from between clenched teeth, his face red with fury, "are you doing here?"

What was *she* doing here? How had he even managed to find this place? Did he know about Jack?

Did he know about her?

No, he couldn't know. His countenance reflected anger, but not rage, as it would have done if he had discovered her connection to the thefts.

"Emily?"

The warning note in his voice told her she'd better come up with an answer to his question, and quickly. What on earth could she say to pacify him? Yes, she had planned on telling Peter the truth, but she had wanted to put things to rights before doing so, and she hadn't had a chance to do that yet. She looked past him to see a dark-haired head pop up from behind the bushes where she and her friends had concealed themselves earlier and prayed that Jenna and Miles knew to stay hidden.

"I, er . . . followed you," she finally managed to stutter, barely restraining a wince when Peter's brow lowered in an ominous manner. He didn't appear to be very happy with that explanation, but it had been the best she could think of on the spur of the moment, and it was better than the alternative.

The truth.

"You followed me?" He seemed almost incredulous as he pulled her closer, his grip tightening on her arms.

"I—I was worried about you when you didn't return from your visit to the pawnbrokers." Lies. More lies. But she comforted herself with the knowledge that come tomorrow morning, he would know everything. "Jenna said she saw you at Willow Park, so I thought I'd meet you there and see what you had found out." She made an attempt to shrug in a nonchalant fashion that didn't quite come off. "When I got there, I spotted you leaving and could tell you weren't headed home, so I followed you."

He closed his eyes and gazed heavenward for a brief moment, as if begging for divine intervention. When he met her gaze again, there could be no mistaking that he was waging a mighty battle to hold on to his temper, and his disbelieving visage told her more clearly than words that he didn't quite buy into her tale.

"Dressed like that?" he growled, indicating her lad's shirt and breeches with an inclination of his head. "Do you have any idea of the trouble you'd be inviting if some passing vagrant or vagabond had happened upon you looking like that? And I thought I said you were not to be out wandering about after dark anymore!"

His reminder of his ultimatum sparked Emily's own irritation and her chin went up. "What's wrong with the way I look? And I thought I told you that I don't take orders from you."

That did it. Peter's mouth tightened into a grim line and his eyes glittered with hostile annoyance as he sent a glance past her in the direction of the cottage. His gaze went back and forth between her and the small dwelling for a moment, as if he were trying to come to some sort of decision. Then, muttering an imprecation, he turned and marched off toward the far side of the clearing, dragging her behind him.

Emily breathed an inner sigh of relief as she stumbled along at his heels, trying to keep up with his longer strides. She might be in for the lecture of a lifetime, but at least she had managed to keep him from looking inside the cottage. She didn't doubt that Miles and Jenna would know what to do. They would keep the bag of stolen goods safe until she could meet with them again.

And in the meantime, she would have to figure out how to deal with Peter and the interrogation she knew was forthcoming once they returned to Knighthaven.

He led her to the rear of the cottage, where his mount was tethered just beyond the edge of the tree line, waiting placidly. As they approached, Peter pulled Emily forward and jerked his head at the horse. "Up."

"You expect me to ride with you?"

"It matters little to me. I suppose I could ride and you could run along beside me, but we *will* return to Knighthaven and we will do it *together*. I have no intention of letting you out of my sight until I have received a *satisfactory* explanation for your presence here tonight."

It seemed she had no choice.

With a shrug of resignation, Emily allowed Peter to help her into the saddle, then watched him climb up behind her. As he prodded the horse into motion, she resisted the urge to look back at the cottage one last time, to see if she could spot Jenna and Miles. If they had any sense at all, they would have already slipped away and be searching for a place to temporarily hide the stolen goods.

All she could do now was pray to find a way to put off telling Peter the truth just a little while longer.

But that, she thought with a shiver, craning her neck to study his set, tense expression, just might be easier said than done.

Chapter 23

❧

As Knighthaven came into view in the distance, Peter felt an overwhelming tide of relief wash over him. The ride from the gamekeeper's cottage had seemed to take twice as long as it should have. And all because of the infuriating bundle of femininity who rode before him.

Emily.

With her flowery fragrance filling his nostrils and her sweetly curved backside nestled against his manhood, it had taken every ounce of restraint he possessed to keep from giving in to his body's lustful urges. Not to mention the effort it was taking to keep from wrapping his hands around that creamy throat and throttling her.

What the bloody hell had she been doing in the clearing?

Never before could he recall feeling such a welter of confusing emotions. Anger, worry, fear. Good God, anything could have happened to her wandering around in the forest after dark! And he didn't for a moment believe she'd followed him, especially on foot. He was far too experienced not to have detected her presence if she'd been anywhere near. He supposed she could have been meeting Lord Moreland, despite her previous protests that she wouldn't do such a thing. After all, the abandoned cottage was an ideal trysting place, but somehow that scenario didn't quite ring true, either.

So what possible explanation could she have?

Well, regardless of her reasons, her intrusion had forced him to put off his confrontation with Jack Barlow. The thought of the former street thief anywhere near Emily made his blood boil.

At that moment, they trotted into Knighthaven's stable yard, and Peter pulled Champion to a halt. Without waiting for his assistance, Emily slid down from the saddle and started across the yard toward the house practically at a run, and he frowned at her retreating back.

Oh, no, my dear. You won't be avoiding me that easily.

Climbing down from his mount's back, Peter handed over the reins to the young groom who hurried forward, and went after Emily, catching up to her just as she rounded the corner of the house. She gave a visible start as he caught her arm, but said nothing, merely offered him a haughty glare.

He sent her one in return. He would not allow her to make him feel guilty. She was the one in the wrong, and he was certain her brother would be the first to agree.

Tightening his hold on her elbow, he led her up the front steps of Knighthaven and in through the front door. When the Ellington butler didn't immediately appear in the foyer at their entrance, he raised a brow at Emily in inquiry.

"Where is Langley?"

She pulled her arm from his grasp and moved a few steps away from him, meeting his gaze with violet eyes that snapped and crackled with irritation. "Deirdre gave him and the other house servants the evening off. They more than likely won't be back until late."

"Ah." Good. He had no desire for anyone to hear him giving Emily the scolding she deserved for her folly. He waved a hand at the parlor door. "Shall we?"

She sniffed, pivoted, and swept ahead of him into the room, and Peter followed, shaking his head.

She wasn't about to make this easy for him.

Once inside the chamber, Emily threw herself down on the love seat and crossed her arms in a defensive manner, her lowered lashes shielding her emotions from him. Peter remained in the doorway, surveying her mutinous expression.

How much should he tell her? he wondered, struggling to keep his own countenance cool and unruffled. She couldn't possibly have any idea of how close she'd been to coming face-to-face with Jack Barlow.

Peter had been on his way to the cottage after leaving Willow Park when he'd become aware of the sound of horse's hooves pounding toward him along the woodland trail. Something had prompted him to pull Champion off the path and into the bushes, and just in time, for Jack himself had come into view, galloping by on his way toward the edge of the woods and the main road.

Without a second thought, Peter had fallen in behind him, following discreetly as Jack had headed into town. Once in the village, the man had tethered his mount to a post outside a tavern called the Hawk's Eye and made his way inside. Leaving his own horse in the alley behind the tavern, Peter had slipped in through a rear door and watched from the shadows as Jack had ordered a pint of ale and settled into a chair at a table in the far corner of the room.

When the thief had reached out to pull a passing barmaid onto his lap with a leer, Peter had shaken his head. It hadn't looked as if Jack planned on going anywhere for a while. He supposed he could have confronted the man right at that moment, but it more than likely wouldn't have been a good idea in a tavern full of drunken fools just looking for an excuse to take part in a brawl. And he had no intention of going to Constable Jenkins. Not yet, anyway. He doubted the addled nitwit would have listened to a word he said.

Which had left going back to the cottage and waiting for Jack to return. It had seemed the best option at the time. That way, he would have the element of surprise on his side, not to mention he would have a chance to search the area to see if he could discover what the man had been up to. If his suspicions were correct and Barlow was the Oxfordshire Thief, perhaps he would come across the evidence needed to implicate the bastard.

So he had returned to the clearing, full of determined resolve and ready to tear the place apart to find the answers he sought. But his shock had known no bounds when he had rounded the corner of the cottage, only to run smack into Emily.

Anger had swiftly overcome him. Anger—and fear.

"If you're going to yell at me, I do wish you'd quit hovering in the doorway and get it over with."

Emily's words drew his gaze to hers, and he took a step into the room, pushing the door partially closed behind him before crossing the chamber to stand beside her. "You don't think you deserve to be yelled at?"

"I think you're not my keeper, and you have no right to lecture me as though you were."

Peter's temper sparked. "Damn it, Emily, *someone* has to rein you in if you're going to continue to behave in such a foolish manner. Do you give no thought to your own safety?"

"I can assure you that my safety was never in question. I know how to look after myself, and no one in Little Haverton would dare to accost me. Aside from you, that is."

"I'll dare much more than that if you don't tell me what the bloody hell you were doing at the gamekeeper's cottage at this time of night!"

Emily opened her mouth, but before she could say anything, Peter held up a hand. "And do not try to convince me that you were following me. I didn't believe that tale the first time around, and I'm not likely to change my mind now. However, you might try giving me the truth."

She was quiet for a long moment, then shook her head and turned away. "I can't tell you that."

"Can't, or won't?"

Emily shrugged and rose to her feet to pace across the room, coming to a halt in front of the French doors and standing with her back to him, her spine rigid. "What does it matter? The result is the same, in either case. I can't tell you."

The light from a lamp on a nearby side table shone on her, throwing her shadow onto the wall and outlining her rounded form. The men's breeches she wore hugged the heart-shaped curve of her derriere and the mouthwatering length of her legs, and the thin white lawn of her shirt did little to hide the fact that there was a female figure under the material.

Peter's breath seized in his throat.

Unaware of his distraction, Emily whirled and placed one hand on her hip, lowering her brow as she frowned at him. "And just what were *you* doing there?"

It was a struggle to even focus on what she was saying, much less form a reply, and his inability to switch off the emotions she aroused in him only served to increase his anger. "Don't try to turn this around. I'm a Bow Street Runner conducting an investigation, and what I was doing there is none of your concern. I'm the one asking the questions here and I expect some answers."

She crossed her arms and lifted her chin, refusing to reply.

That did it! Enough was enough!

Closing the distance between them with long, furious strides, he came to a halt next to her and seized her by the elbows, giving her a firm shake. "Bloody hell, why do you have to be so damned obstinate? What is so important to you that you insist on running about the countryside after dark, dressed in clothes that would be a temptation to any red-blooded man who happened to stumble across you?"

A stunned look passed over her face, and she glanced down at her outfit. "A temptation? Don't be ridiculous."

"You wouldn't think it so ridiculous if you had run across some stranger out there in the woods who refused to take no for an answer."

Emily's scornful snort pushed Peter right over the edge.

With a harshly grated expletive, he wrapped his arms about her waist, fitted her against him, and seized her lips with his own.

The moment Peter's mouth touched hers, Emily knew she was in trouble.

Every bit of her righteous indignation sailed right out the window, and suddenly all she was aware of was the feel of his arms about her, his warm, spicy scent surrounding her. Desire rose up, and instead of pushing him away, she lifted her hands to tangle her fingers in the front of his shirt and pulled him closer. So close that not an inch of space was left between them.

In response, that hard, hot male part of him sprang to instant life, nudging her belly, and she moved against him in a sinuous, provocative manner, spreading her legs just enough so that his erection nestled in the damp apex of her thighs. Even through the material of her breeches, she could feel the scorching heat of him. It was like two pieces of a puzzle coming together, and nothing had ever felt so right.

He groaned, stabbing his tongue into her mouth, deepening the kiss.

Dear God, she was so tired of fighting this, Emily thought dimly. Tired of keeping her distance. Of trying to pretend that she didn't have feelings for him. She couldn't go on this way.

She loved him, and she didn't want to deny it any longer. Forget all the obstacles that lay between them, the fact that he would hate her once he discovered her deceptions. Perhaps it was selfish, but if she could only have this one night with him, she intended to take what pleasure she could from it.

She wanted Peter to make love to her.

Her decision made, she slid her hands up his chest and went to work on the buttons of his shirt, slipping the topmost one from its hole with swift efficiency.

But as she moved on to the next one, Peter seemed to abruptly go still. The next thing she knew, he had pulled his lips from hers and reached up to grasp her wrists, halting her progress.

"Emily, stop."

His voice was hoarse, and she peered up at him from under lowered lashes, taking in the slight flush that stained his cheekbones, the passion simmering in the depths of his eyes. "Why? Don't you want me?"

"Of course I do. More than my next breath. But I shouldn't have started this. We can't let this happen."

"Why can't we? I know you believe that we could never have a life together, and perhaps you're right. Perhaps society would turn their backs on us and ostracize us and we would be miserable. But I'm not asking you to wed me." She rose on her toes, briefly nuzzling the wedge of bronzed skin she had exposed just below his collarbone, and felt his big body shudder in reaction. "I'm asking you to make love to me. To give me this one night. I'll never ask anything more of you."

"I can't dishonor you in such a way, Em. Your future husband—"

"There will be no future husband. I like my life the way it is. Why would I sacrifice my independence by tying myself to a man I feel nothing for?"

His face unreadable, Peter stared down at her, a muscle flexing in his jaw, and his grip on her wrists tightened. "What about Moreland?"

"What about him?" She met his gaze, hoping he could read the sincerity in her expression. She refused to allow him to deprive them of this one chance to experience the joy she knew they could bring each other. "I've said this before and apparently you didn't believe me. So listen and believe me now. I don't love Adam. He is a good friend, and I admit I considered his proposal for all of two seconds, but I could never marry a man I don't love."

She took a deep breath, attempting to calm her wildly racing heart, before freeing the words she'd been longing to say since this morning. "I love *you*."

Peter tensed, and for a long, drawn-out moment he was silent. Then, just as Emily was beginning to think she'd made an error in revealing her true feelings, a low, almost animalistic sound escaped him, and he dropped her wrists to cup her face in his hands.

And once again, his mouth came down on hers.

Peter was lost. Lost in the scent, the taste, the very essence of Emily. He couldn't believe she wanted him to make love to her. His head knew it would be a mistake, but he couldn't seem to convince his heart of that fact. She felt so good in his arms, as if she belonged there.

And perhaps she did.

But he didn't have time for this. He had to return to the cottage to confront Jack, to find out for certain if the man was the thief he'd been looking for. And he had to consider Tristan and Deirdre. If they were to come home and discover him with Emily . . .

Giving it one last valiant effort, he tore his mouth from hers and stared down into her eyes. "Are you sure, Em?"

"I've never been so sure of anything," she murmured, wrapping her arms about his neck. Her lips were kiss-swollen, her violet eyes unfocused and full of longing. "I want you, Peter. Please."

He couldn't. He had a duty to perform. He had to—

Her mouth brushed the underside of his jaw, her tongue feathering against the pulse that beat there, and he finally lost all control. Bloody hell, but he couldn't fight both her and his own feelings, as well! He wanted her, needed her too badly. He had for much too long.

Jack Barlow could wait.

Peter swept Emily up in his arms and bore her to the soft rug in front of the fireplace, following her down as he took her lips with his once more, plunging his tongue deep into the moist, sweet cavern of her mouth. He forgot the wall between them, the fact that they could never have a life together. He forgot everything except her.

His hands went to the front of her shirt and started to work on the buttons, undoing them with deft speed before pushing the material aside and sliding it down and off her arms. Underneath, to his delighted surprise, there was nothing but creamy skin. The sight of her pale, pink-tipped breasts was enough to set his mouth to watering.

In the meantime, Emily's hands had been busy as well. He was so caught up in the enchanting picture she presented that he didn't even realize she had unfastened the rest of his buttons until she peeled the edges of his shirt back, baring his wide chest and shoulders for her delectation. Her lips skimmed over his flesh, her tongue swirling over his pectorals in a bold, unexpected exploration that racked his body with shudders of need. Her fingers followed in the wake of her mouth, and as she flicked her thumbs over the flat discs of his male nipples, a guttural cry escaped him.

"Bloody 'ell, you're going to be the death of me, you are," he rasped, burying his face against her temple and winding one hand in the loosened strands of her blond hair, uncaring for once that he had slipped back into the Cockney dialect of his youth.

She emitted an almost feline purr and rubbed against him, her nails digging into his back. "Touch me, Peter."

"Where do you want me to touch you, darling?" He felt a devilish smile curl his mouth as he let his free hand travel downward, pausing just above the crest of her right breast, hovering in a teasing manner. "Right 'ere?"

"Yes! Oh, yes, Peter! Please!" Emily didn't wait for him to comply, but arched up off the rug, pressing the rounded globe into his palm. When his callused fingers came into contact with her silken flesh, any rationality he might have still possessed vanished. Molding the ripe orb to the shape of his hand, thumbing the hardened nipple, he savored her low moan as he leaned down and captured the tip of her other breast in his mouth, suckling with a savage intensity, nipping at it gently before soothing it with his tongue.

Emily's head fell back and she let loose a trembling cry that made his heart jump. Her hands locked in his hair, holding him to her as he treated both breasts to his loving attentions. She wanted him. His angel truly wanted him!

Unable to wait another second, Peter released her and got to his feet long enough to shed his breeches. Tossing them onto the nearby love seat, he took a moment to relish the picture she made lying on the carpet before him. She looked so beautiful in the lamplight. With her golden hair spread out about her head like a halo, she resembled the angel he'd always thought of her as. Her violet eyes were dreamy, her lids heavy and slumberous-looking, and her skin gleamed like porcelain.

He froze for a moment. He knew he didn't have the right to be touching her this way, making love to her, no matter what she said. It wasn't too late to call a halt.

But as if sensing his hesitation, Emily raised her arms to him in a supplicating manner, looking so winsome and adorable that he was lost once again.

There would be no turning back. Not now.

He came back down over her, naked and thoroughly aroused, his maleness coming to rest against the center of her desire. Her eyes widened and she bit her lip before wrapping her arms around him and rocking against him, sending his senses reeling. They kissed again and their tongues entwined in an imitation of the ultimate act of intimacy.

They were both too anxious to have each other to go slowly. Emily began to tear at the lacings of her breeches, but when she fumbled, Peter gently pushed her hands aside and loosened them himself before peeling them down her shapely legs and discarding them. Fascinated by the triangle of flaxen curls nestled between her thighs, he sifted his fingers through them. Then, a little bit at a time, he inserted the very tip of his forefinger into her narrow feminine opening.

She sucked in a breath, her eyes going wide once again, and he soothed her in a low croon. "It's all right, angel. I promise. I just need to make sure you're prepared for me, that I won't 'urt you." He had no doubt that she was an innocent, and if he was going to take her, he wanted to make sure she was ready, that there would be as little pain as possible and as much pleasure.

She was more than ready. Her channel was slick with

her juices in anticipation of his claiming. Filled with arrogant male satisfaction, he slipped another finger inside to join the first one, subtly widening the moist passage for his intrusion. His thumb brushed the small nub of her clitoris and she gave a shrill cry, bucking against him, her legs coming together to squeeze his hand almost spasmodically.

"Shhh." Removing his fingers, he reared up and fit himself against her, pushing the very tip of his shaft just inside her vaginal entrance. It was like gliding into warm satin, and he longed to slide the rest of the way home, but he forced himself to pause, to look down into her eyes. "Are you certain, Emily? There's no going back after this, and I don't want you to regret it."

She reached out and caught his hands, lacing her fingers through his and meeting his gaze with a seriousness that stole his breath. "I could never regret anything that passes between us, but most especially not this. I want you."

"Then take me, angel. Take all of me. And take me wiv you to 'eaven."

He thrust deep.

The moment was so right that Peter felt his whole body sing with the knowledge that she was finally his. They fit together almost perfectly, and as he set up a slow rhythm, Emily seemed to get past her initial discomfort at their joining and began to move in counterpoint to him. She let go of his hands and clutched at his taut hips, pulling him more closely to her. Her cheeks grew flushed and her head began to roll from side to side, small sounds of pleasure humming in her throat.

Peter could feel his own climax building. It was happening too fast, he knew, but there was nothing he could do about it. He'd wanted this for far too long, and he was lucky he hadn't lost it the moment he'd entered her. Her deliciously peaked nipples were a torment, brushing against his chest in a tantalizing contact as he pounded into her, and the tight walls of her sheath milked him with each thrust. He had wanted so badly to be gentle, but it seemed impossible now. Their passion was driving them, and it wouldn't allow either of them to slow down.

His teeth clenched. God, he was coming, and he didn't want to leave her behind. "Emily, angel—"

Before he could even finish the sentence, he felt her orgasm rip through her with the force of a tidal wave. She threw back her head and screamed her ecstasy, shuddering all over, her fingers digging into his hips.

Her climax triggered his and he exploded inside her with a hoarse shout of his own, spilling his seed deep within her womb.

He collapsed against her, drained, exhausted, and damp with perspiration, feeling as if he truly had been to heaven and back.

Chapter 24

Emily lay cradled in the circle of Peter's arms, her head resting on his chest, listening to the comforting thump of his heartbeat beneath her ear.

She couldn't believe that it had finally happened, that she and Peter had made love. And it had been perfect, everything she had always dreamed it would be. Their coming together had given her more pleasure than she could ever express in mere words. True, there had been a bit of pain at his initial penetration, but she had more or less expected that, and she had quickly gotten past it. He had carried her off to a never-before-imagined world of pure joy, lifting her to the very peak of ecstasy before they had both plunged over the edge together.

She wasn't certain how much time had passed since then. They were still entwined on the floor, naked as the day they were born, and she seemed to exist in a state of drowsy contentment. Soon after their soul-stirring climax, Peter had slipped free and slid off her to lie at her side, gathering her close with one arm around her shoulders. They might have dozed for a short while, but she couldn't be sure. Everything seemed to be moving in slow motion, and she prayed it would remain that way.

Her heart gave a painful squeeze. No matter how much she wished it wasn't so, she knew that sooner or later this blissful idyll would have to end. After she had handed over the stolen jewels to the authorities and told them about Jack, she would have to confess everything to Peter. If she didn't wind up behind bars it would be a miracle. At the very least he would never speak to her again.

But she would always have the memory of this night to sustain her.

Dear God, but he'd looked so utterly splendid standing nude before her in all his masculine glory, she thought with a sigh. His long, rangy body was sculpted with lean muscle, his hips and thighs taut and strong, his chest bronzed and sleek. He'd been a golden god, the blond streaks in his tawny hair gleaming in the lamplight.

She smoothed her hand over his chest, but her caressing fingers paused for a moment when they encountered a raised area of flesh. She traced it gently, her forehead furrowing, then lifted her head to study the pale, puckered line that slashed across his lower abdomen. She hadn't noticed it earlier in the dim lamp-light, and she couldn't help but be curious.

Her eyes flew to his face. He was watching her from under lowered lashes, his blue irises glittering.

"What's this?" she asked

"It's a scar."

She smacked his shoulder in exasperation. "I can see that. Where did you get it? It looks like a knife wound."

"It is." Seeming uncomfortable with the topic of conversation, he shifted a bit, dislodging her hand. "Do you remember me telling you about the fugitive I helped to apprehend soon after I first arrived in London?"

She nodded.

"Well, I neglected to mention that he had a knife, one he was prepared to use on the Runner chasing him until I stepped into the middle of things."

For Emily, the light dawned. Of course. He had gotten in between the knife and the Runner, more than likely preventing the man's death. No wonder he'd been offered a job at Bow Street! Leave it to her knight in shining armor to save someone's life without a thought to his own.

The mere possibility of what might have happened was enough to raise the hairs on the back of her neck, and she glared at him. "Don't ever do anything so foolish again. Do you hear me?"

He raised his eyebrows at her, a sardonic smile tilting one corner of his mouth, but she ignored him and settled back down at his side, resting her head on his chest once again. Truly, the man needed a keeper!

They didn't say anything for quite some time, and Emily was just getting ready to drift off into sleep when Peter finally spoke again.

"I'm sorry."

His voice floated to her as if from a great distance, and she was feeling so lethargic that it took a minute for his words to register. When they did, she craned her neck, straining to see his face in the dimness. "What?"

"I said I'm sor—"

She pinched his arm. "Don't you dare repeat it!" Raising herself to a sitting position, she pushed her tangled hair back behind her ears and glared down at him. "Don't you dare say you're sorry."

Looking affronted, he rubbed at the spot she'd injured. "How can I not be sorry, Em? My God, I took you on the floor!"

"And I loved every moment of it. So don't you dare ruin this for me by saying you're sorry." Leaning forward, she stared into his eyes with a piercing intensity, hoping he could read the sincerity in her gaze. "It was the most wonderful experience of my life and I will never be sorry for it."

Lifting a hand, he caressed the side of her face, his thumb tracing the seam of her lips tenderly. "You're certain? I didn't hurt you? I was rougher than I intended, but I wanted you so much . . ."

He looked so anxious that she felt her heart catch. Capturing his hand in hers, she bestowed a gentle kiss to his knuckles. "I'm certain. In fact . . ." A mischievous smile canted her lips and she lifted herself up to straddle him in a swift motion that had him giving a gasp of surprise. As far as she was concerned, she intended to take advantage of every second they had together. "I want to do it again."

His hands grasped her waist, and his cheeks flushed with renewed passion. She could feel his manhood already hardening and stiffening beneath her. But still he hesitated. "Again? Are you sure? So soon after the first time, you might be sore."

She bent over him, her breasts brushing his chest, her teeth nibbling at his earlobe in a way that wrung a harsh groan from him. "I'm sure."

"But what about your brother and his wife? And the staff? There's no telling when they might return and walk in on us."

"Then we'd best hurry, hadn't we?"

Pushing herself upright, she shifted her hips and came down over his thickening manhood without a second's pause, seating him to the hilt inside her.

They both held themselves still for a long, drawn-out moment. Emily had to admit she was more than a bit sore, but after giving herself a chance to adjust to his size and the feel of him inside her again, she began to move, rocking her hips languidly, rising and falling in counterpoint to his own slow, steady upward strokes. His eyes fell shut and his strong hands rose to cup her breasts where they dangled above him, his palms kneading and shaping the ripe mounds, his thumbs and forefingers rolling and flicking the distended tips, still slightly damp from his earlier ministrations.

She moaned, her soreness forgotten, and increased

the pace, clutching at his shoulders. He filled her to overflowing, stretching her slick inner walls to accommodate the length and breadth of his pulsating shaft, going deeper with each thrust. To have him so deep inside of her, a part of her, was the sweetest thrill she'd ever known, and the friction began to build toward the ultimate crescendo, carrying her higher and higher. Finally, without any warning, she plunged off the precipice and felt herself shatter, flying apart into a thousand tiny pieces of trembling delight.

"Peter!" she cried out, flinging her head back, pressing her breasts farther into his hands, her nipples stabbing his palms.

At her cry, he grunted and pumped into her one last time before his own orgasm overcame him, his big body shuddering once, twice, then going still.

She slumped against him, panting for breath, her blond curls falling into his face. She was so weak, so tired, and all she wanted to do was fall into a peaceful slumber here in his arms. But there was something she had to say first. Something she had to make sure he understood.

"I love you, Peter," she murmured as her eyes drifted closed, her lips buried in his neck. She didn't know if he'd heard her or not, and she lacked the energy to even lift her head to find out. "I'll always love you."

Rolling off him, she curled into his side and instantly fell asleep.

Peter stirred from his light doze and cracked his eyes, squinting around at the dimly lit environs. He was overcome by a momentary puzzlement as to how he'd happened to fall asleep on the parlor floor, until the soft, warm weight burrowed against his side shifted and emitted a small sigh that brought it all rushing back.

He'd made love to Emily.

Twice.

Reaching up with his free hand, he pinched the bridge of his nose and took a deep, calming breath. Dear God, it had been all he'd ever imagined it could be. And Emily had been a revelation.

He felt a slight smile curve the corner of his mouth in spite of himself as he recalled the way she'd ridden him to completion that second time, her supple body poised and taut, her head thrown back, her passionate moans echoing in his ears. His innocent angel had become a wanton, wringing the most powerful climax from him he could ever remember having.

But she had deserved better than a cold floor and a quick, clandestine coupling for her first time. She should have had a soft mattress and satin sheets. Her initiation into the world of erotic pleasure should have been slow and leisurely, lasting all night long.

And it should have been with her husband, something he could never aspire to be.

But she had said she loved him.

Easing his arm out from underneath her head, he rose up on his elbow to gaze down at her, looking so peaceful in slumber. He was well aware that, in the end, their feelings for each other didn't matter. They were too far apart in station, and society would never let them forget that. Regardless of what she thought, there could never be anything further between them. For her own good, he had to let her go.

Yes, their lovemaking had been a mistake. But somehow he couldn't quite bring himself to regret it. Emily had given him a night he would never forget.

Unable to help himself, he leaned over and pressed a soft kiss to her lips. She tasted like warm, sweet honey, and for a second he was tempted to take the kiss deeper. But he resisted. This had to end. Now.

With a feeling of regret, he pushed himself to his feet and crossed the room to retrieve his shirt and breeches. He still had work to do this night, and there was no more time to waste.

He had a thief to catch.

As he stepped into his pants, he cast a glance at the clock in the corner and was gratified to note that it wasn't as late as he'd surmised. It had barely gone ten. There was still every chance that he could make it back to the gamekeeper's cottage and commence with his investigation even before Jack returned from his evening at the Hawk's Eye.

Peter slipped into his shirt and quickly buttoned it, then sent Emily an indulgent look. He supposed he'd better wake her before he left. He doubted she would want one of the staff to return—or God forbid, Tristan and Deirdre—to find her sleeping naked on the parlor floor.

He started toward her, scooping up her shirt and pants as he went, shaking his head. He had to wonder how she'd even gotten hold of such clothing. If her brother ever found out she had a pair of men's breeches, much less wore them in public . . .

At that moment, something about the material he held struck him as familiar and he halted in the middle of the parlor, staring down at the pair of pants in his hands. He held them up so he could examine them more closely, and as he did, a light clicked on in his brain, filling him with stunned recognition.

No! It couldn't be!

Fumbling for his pocket, he shoved his hand in and withdrew the small scrap of fabric that he had discovered at the Tuttleston estate. It was the same color, the same material, but that didn't necessarily mean anything. Surely there were many pairs of men's trousers that were made from the same sort of cloth?

But as he turned the breeches over, holding them up to the light of a nearby lamp, its glow illuminated a gaping hole high up on the right leg.

And when he compared the scrap to it, it matched exactly.

At first, his mind refused to process what his eyes were seeing. When it finally registered, a burning, agonizing pain stole over him, gripping his chest and tightening with every ragged breath.

There had to be another explanation, another reason a torn scrap from Emily's pants had wound up in the tree outside of Lady Tuttleston's bedroom window. But if there was, he didn't know what it could be.

His sassy, stubborn angel was the Oxfordshire Thief.

* * *

Emily's eyes fluttered open to find Peter sitting on the floor next to her, his back against the love seat and his arms resting on his upraised knees. Fully dressed, he watched her with an unfathomable expression.

She yawned and stretched, unable to suppress a slight wince as the muscles in her body protested the movement. The floor was most certainly not conducive to sleeping comfortably. Pushing herself to a sitting position, unconcerned with her nudity, she sent Peter a small, seductive smile as memories of their lovemaking washed over her.

He didn't smile back.

Puzzled, she reached up to push a stray curl back behind her ear and scrutinized him with curiosity. What on earth could be the matter? Had she done something wrong? Had she failed to please him somehow?

The thought had heat rushing into her cheeks. Surely that couldn't be the case? Of course, she was far from experienced, but he had seemed more than satisfied to her. The joyous, blissful look on his face when he had climaxed beneath her that last time had said more than words could.

Perhaps he was feeling guilty. If so, she had to find a way to make him see that there was no reason for him to do so. She wasn't sorry for any of it. Not for a moment. If two people loved each other, there was nothing wrong with expressing that love. They—

She froze, squeezing her eyes shut for a brief moment. He had never said that he loved her. She had told him more than once, but he had never given the words back to her. The reminder was enough to make her heart ache. He might want her, but Peter would never allow himself to love her again. As far as he was concerned, tonight had been about satisfying their cravings for each other, and love didn't come into it. She had to remember that.

Feeling abruptly self-conscious, she drew up her knees and wrapped her arms around them, veiling her nakedness as best she could before venturing to speak in an almost timid voice. "Peter, what is it? What's wrong?"

Instead of answering, he tossed her shirt to her, his face devoid of any emotion. "Here. Put this on."

He rose and paced a short distance away, standing with his back to her as she shrugged into the shirt and buttoned it. It was long enough that it covered her to mid-thigh, and feeling not so diffident now that her nakedness was adequately concealed, she stood and crossed the room to lay a tentative hand on his shoulder. "Peter?"

At her touch, he whirled to face her, and his features were no longer unreadable. They were contorted with an anger he was trying hard to contain. His big body trembled with the force of it, and his eyes swirled with a plethora of feelings so potent that Emily gasped and took a stumbling step backward. Rage, confusion, disbelief, despair. But strongest of all was hurt. She could practically feel his pain, a tangible thing, vibrating in the air between them.

Desperate and quite suddenly afraid, she reached out and caught his arm. "Peter, please tell me what's wrong."

"Explain this."

His voice was low, barely more than a harsh whisper, his gaze piercing her with a savage intensity. His stare was so compelling, so full of wrath, that it took a second for her to realize that he had thrust something at her for her inspection.

She glanced down, and what she saw was enough to send the blood rushing from her head and a frigid coldness sluicing through her veins.

In one hand, he held her breeches with the gaping tear lying faceup. In the other was the scrap of fabric he had discovered last week in the tree at the Tuttleston home.

Even an untrained eye could have seen that they were a perfect match.

Oh, God, he knew!

Placing one hand over her stomach to calm the slow roll of nausea that churned deep within, she took another step backward, uncertain what to say, what to do. Just a few more hours and this would have all been over. Why did he have to discover her deception *now*?

"Please tell me this doesn't mean what I think it means, Emily. Please tell me that there is some other explanation, that you haven't been lying to me and deceiving me from the very beginning." He paused for a moment, his jaw visibly tightening. "Tell me you aren't the Oxfordshire Thief."

How she wanted to deny it. But she couldn't. After all they had shared tonight, she couldn't be less than truthful now. "I can't tell you that. Because I *am* the Oxfordshire Thief."

Fighting tears, she watched as his eyes fell shut for a brief moment and he swallowed almost convulsively. When he spoke again, his words sounded constricted. "God, Em, why? None of this makes sense."

"I'm so sorry."

"Sorry?" He looked incredulous. "Do you think being sorry makes up for what you've done? You've robbed from people who trusted you, cared about you! Do you think they'll accept a mere apology?"

His words were like blows, hitting Emily where she was most vulnerable. "I don't know. I hope they will, once I tell them why."

"You haven't even told *me* why yet!"

"I will. I just . . . It's difficult."

"Difficult?"

"Yes." In spite of herself, her tears finally slipped free and slid down her cheeks and she glanced away, biting her lip. "You're so angry."

"What did you expect, Em? Bloody congratulations? You've been nothing but dishonest since the day I arrived here. You pretended to help me, to aid my investigation, when all the while you were the one responsible."

"I never meant to hurt anyone, and I had reasons—"

"Then tell me what they are! Make me understand!"

He was shouting now, and Emily flinched at the sheer volume. Dear God, she had known his anger would hurt, but never had she suspected just how much. How could she explain? "It's a long story." She indicated the love seat with one hand, casting him a beseeching look.

"I'll tell you everything, but perhaps we should both sit down?"

Peter paused for an instant, then gave a single, abrupt nod.

He followed as she led the way across the room. But instead of seating himself next to her on the love seat, he leaned against the empty fireplace and crossed his arms. When she raised an inquiring brow at him, he shook his head.

"I'm fine here. Just go ahead. I'm listening, although I fail to see what you could possibly have to say that would excuse what you've done."

Taking in his closed-off expression with a sense of despair, Emily had to restrain a wince at his tone. She would never be able to make him understand, but she had to try. "I'm not excusing myself. I was wrong and I have no qualms about admitting it. But I do want to explain why and how I stumbled into such a mess. I had planned on telling you all of it in the morning, but . . ." She trailed off.

Peter said nothing. He didn't look as if he believed her, and she supposed she couldn't blame him. More than likely, he would never believe anything she said ever again.

Sucking in a gust of air, she twined her hands in her lap and prayed to the Lord above to give her the words to make things right. "It all began with Jack Barlow . . ."

She told him about Jack's arrival in Little Haverton and what had transpired between them on the day the thief had first approached her. She left nothing out,

telling him about Jack's threats against her family, what
he had discovered about the late Countess of Ellington,
and his attempt to use the tale to blackmail her and get
her to fall in with his plans.

"I know now I should have gone to the authorities
right away," she confessed. "Especially after he told me
what he wanted me to do, but I was so scared, so confused. I panicked, and I wasn't thinking very clearly.
All I knew was that I couldn't let Jack tell anyone what
he knew."

She paused and looked up at Peter, her chin quivering despite her determination to stay strong. "Because
I had been alone for so long as a child, the thought of
having my family torn apart was enough to terrify me.
The scandal Jack's story could have caused would
have been enough to do just that. And he threatened
Deirdre and the babe." Her hands tightened their grip
on each other. "It wasn't until after I committed the
first robbery at the Tuttlestons' that I realized I'd
made a mistake, but by then it was too late. I was already implicated in the crime. And it was like quick-
sand. I just seemed to fall in deeper and deeper. I tried
to figure out a way to stop it all, to foil Jack's scheme
without jeopardizing my mother's secret, but it was
no use."

"And you say Barlow had proof of your mother's
supposed affair?" Peter's voice was curt, his face a
granite mask, giving away nothing.

"Yes. Letters, written by my mother to her friend
Lady Brimley, admitting to the affair and her possible

pregnancy. I have no idea how he got them, but they're in her handwriting."

When Peter didn't speak again, Emily continued, desperate to get through to him. "That's why I was at the cottage tonight. To see if I could find the letters and retrieve the jewels. Without the letters, he has no proof of his claims, and I could turn him over to the law and return the stolen items to their owners without fear of what he might say to ruin my family."

"You must realize even if you had managed to do all of that, the law wouldn't have cared what reasons you had for being involved," Peter prompted with a hint of impatience. "They more than likely would have taken you into custody, as well."

"Yes, I was aware from the beginning what could happen. But I didn't care about me. I cared about my brother and sister-in-law, my future niece or nephew. You, more than anyone, should know how much they mean to me. I couldn't stand back and watch them be destroyed. Tristan would be devastated if he found out about Mother. He loved her so much. And I didn't know how much of what Jack said was true. As far as I knew, it was quite possible that he could lose his title, his lands, everything. Maybe even Willow Park. All because of those terrible letters. I couldn't take the chance."

Peter pushed away from the fireplace and began to pace the area in front of the love seat. "I can't help but wonder how you accomplished all of this. The breaking and entering? Lock-picking? I know I taught you a bit, but I called a halt to the lessons soon after we came to Little Haverton."

"After you refused to teach me anything else, I begged the rest of the Rag-Tags to continue with the lessons. Miles worked with me on lock-picking." Emily felt her face heat and she was certain it must be as red as a beet. "I got quite good at it."

"Obviously. Remind me to wring Miles's neck when we finish this conversation." Peter came to a halt and scrubbed a hand over his face before turning back to her with a frown. "And I suppose you knew the combinations to the safes at both the Fulberry and Caulfield residences?"

She nodded, her eyes never leaving him. He held himself so stiffly, as if he bore the weight of the world on his shoulders. Dear God, *she* had done this to him. "Penelope likes to talk, and she let it slip to me long ago that her husband had chosen the date of her birth as the combination to his safe. And Lord Caulfield keeps his written on a slip of paper in his desk drawer in his study, because he's always forgetting it. All I had to do was locate the piece of paper."

Silence stretched, and Emily began to fidget as Peter resumed his agitated strides, across the room and back. What would he say? What would he do?

"Damnation, Emily!"

His sudden outburst had her jumping in her seat, and she looked up to find him towering over her, his eyes blazing down at her.

"Why didn't you come to me? I might have been able

to figure out a way to resolve all of this long ago, *without* revealing your mother's secret."

Unsure how to answer him, she lifted one shoulder helplessly. "I . . . I didn't know what you would do."

For just an instant, Emily could clearly read the anguish in his gaze, then a curtain dropped down over his features, guarding his innermost thoughts from her. "I see. I should have known. You didn't trust me."

"It not that!" she protested. "It's just . . . Ever since you came to live at Willow Park you've tried so hard to always do what was right, no matter the consequences. I suppose it was your way of making up for your past. And you're a Runner, for heaven's sake! I was afraid if I told you, you would feel as if you *had* to turn me in, regardless of what might be revealed in the process."

"You didn't trust me."

Peter's tone as he repeated the statement was cold, emotionless. He turned away from her, and Emily shot to her feet, hating that she was causing him such pain, but not knowing quite how to make it up to him. She *should* have trusted him, should have realized he would never do anything to hurt her family. She knew that now. Now that it was too late.

"Peter, please listen to me. I swear, I was going to tell you in the morning. All of it. But I wanted a chance to make things right first. I wanted to hand the stolen items over to the law and make sure Jack was behind bars." She clasped her hands in front of her to still the trembling of her fingers, willing him to believe her. "I wanted to be able to tell you I'd done the right thing in the end."

He came to a stop in front of the fireplace again, running both hands through his hair before he spoke without turning to face her. "Did you get the letters?"

She eyed his back anxiously. "Yes. They're in the pocket of my breeches."

"And the jewels?"

"Miles and Jenna have them."

Peter glanced back over his shoulder, one corner of his mouth curled in a wry grimace. "So Jenna and Miles were in on this all along?"

"Don't blame them. They were just trying to help me, to keep me from getting into trouble. Miles wanted to tell you everything from the beginning."

"Smart man." There was another long silence, then Peter pivoted to meet her worried eyes. "Jack has been tormenting Benji as well."

Stunned at the revelation, Emily felt herself go cold all over. "What?"

"Barlow approached him several weeks ago and told Benji he had information about his past, information he would only reveal if Benji did as he said."

Aware of an alarming weakness in her knees, Emily sank down into a nearby chair, clutching at the cushioned armrests for support. "Do you think he really knows anything? About Benji's past, I mean?"

"I doubt it, but the boy believes he might. Apparently, not knowing anything about his background or where he comes from has been bothering Benji much more than any of us ever realized."

"No wonder he's been acting so strange lately."

"Well, this is all about to end. Right now. Jack Barlow will be sorry he ever thought to step foot in Little Haverton."

At Peter's angry, resolute words, Emily looked up to see him marching for the parlor door. Lunging to her feet, she reached out and caught his arm as he went by, fear for him setting her heart pounding. "Where are you going?"

"After Jack, of course. It's about time someone put a stop to his schemes once and for all, and I'm just the man to do it."

"Peter, you can't! He could be armed! Go to Constable Jenkins—"

"The time for bringing in the local authorities is past, Emily. Jack and I have a reckoning that is long overdue, and I can assure you that I'm more than capable of handling myself. I have a vested interest in making sure my family is safe." He leveled her with a scorching glare. "Whether some people believe that fact or not."

He shook her loose and left the room.

Emily started to follow, but realizing she was wearing nothing except a thin shirt, she hurried back to the love seat to retrieve her breeches and hastily stepped into them before rushing out into the foyer, lacing them up as she went.

She caught up with Peter just as he reached the front entrance.

"Peter, wait."

Before she could say anything else, however, there was a sudden loud pounding on the door, and Peter flung it open to find Miles and Jenna hovering on the top step, their expressions concerned.

Jenna pushed past the stable hand into the entry hall without even seeming to notice Peter and hurried toward Emily. "We 'id the jewels. We didn't know what else to do wiv them, and we were worried about you. Are you all right? Does Peter know? Did 'e . . ." She trailed off as her eyes followed Emily's to where Peter stood next to the door, arms crossed as he glowered at her. "Oh, bloody 'ell."

"Bloody hell, indeed," he intoned sarcastically. "And to answer your question, yes, I do know."

Miles nodded in satisfaction. "It's about time."

Peter turned to the stable hand. "I was just about to leave to go after Barlow. Do you want to accompany me?"

"No need to even ask, guv. I'd never turn down a chance to scrap wiv that bastard. 'E usually 'angs around the 'Awk's Eye for a couple of hours, so if we leave now, we should get there just as 'e's arriving back at the cottage."

"Let's go then."

Emily stepped forward and clutched at Peter's sleeve. "I'm going, too."

Peter's face darkened and he reached out to grip her arms, giving her a shake that had her teeth rattling. "Oh no you are not. You are staying right here with Jenna, or so help me . . ." He halted, closed his eyes, and took a deep breath before continuing in a slightly calmer tone. "You're in enough trouble as it is. I don't need you getting in the middle of things. For once, just trust me."

With that, he stalked from the house with Miles at his heels.

The door slammed behind them, and for a long moment neither woman spoke. Then Jenna planted her hands on her hips and sent Emily a knowing look. "You aren't staying 'ere, are you?"

"Of course not." Emily whirled and scurried back to the parlor, where she quickly slipped her feet into the riding boots she had discarded earlier. "Peter just doesn't understand. It's not that I don't trust him, but this is all my fault. It's my responsibility to take care of it, not his."

"I some'ow doubt Peter will see it that way."

"I can't help that. Jack is dangerous, and I refuse to stand by and watch Peter get hurt because I made a mess of things." Emily glanced over her shoulder at her friend. "You don't have to come with me if you don't want to."

"Of course I'm coming. What kind of friend would I be if I didn't?" Jenna paused for a second, studying Emily's flushed face and state of dishabille with growing interest. "What 'appened between the two of you, anyway?"

Emily was certain her cheeks must have reddened even more at the question. "Just never you mind."

The two women hurried back out to the foyer, intent on their mission. But when Emily swung open the door to find Lord Moreland on the other side, hand raised to knock, it was an unexpected—and unwelcome—surprise.

The viscount seemed just as shocked, and he stood taking in Emily's appearance for a moment with wide eyes before letting his hand fall and shaking his head in obvious consternation. "Emily, what on earth . . . ?"

Drat and blast, she didn't have time for this! Every second that passed was a second wasted. She had to get to Peter! "Adam, it's after eleven o'clock. What are you doing here at this time of night?"

"I'm sorry." He sounded contrite, but something about the way his stare passed over her made her feel a trifle uneasy. "I'm afraid I found myself too anxious to await your answer to my proposal any longer. I was hoping to catch you awake, but . . . it seems you're on the way out?"

He didn't wait for her to invite him in, but stepped over the threshold and swept his hat off his blond head, an eyebrow arched in inquiry. "Where are you off to so late? And dressed in such a manner? You look like a stable boy."

Emily exchanged glances with Jenna, who gave an unhelpful shrug. What should she do? Perhaps it might be a good idea to confide in Adam. He was her friend, after all, and if he went with them he might be able to help Peter in some way.

Of course, there was only so much she could tell him. She doubted that now was the time to admit that she was the one who had stolen his mother's brooch and caused his father's violent relapse. That confession might be better left for later.

She made a split-second decision.

"Adam, you have to come with us! Mr. Quick is on his way to apprehend the Oxfordshire Thief and we must go after him!"

Lord Moreland froze. "He has figured out who the scoundrel is?"

"Yes." She would have to tread carefully. She wouldn't tell any outright lies, but she couldn't be entirely truthful. "A man named Jack Barlow is responsible. He's been hiding in an abandoned cottage on my brother's estate, and Mr. Quick is on his way there now to confront him."

The viscount seemed to go pale, but Emily had only a moment to wonder at his reaction before she marched past him for the door, trailed by Jenna. "Hurry. We have to help Peter."

"I'm sorry, Emily."

At the strange note in Adam's voice, Emily whirled back to face him just in time to see him reach into an inner pocket of his coat and withdraw a small, lethal-looking pistol. He leveled it on her and Jenna with eyes that were suddenly cold with menace. "I'm afraid I can't allow you to do that."

Chapter 25

Jack Barlow would receive his comeuppance.

The very thought was enough to send a jolt of adrenaline rushing through Peter's veins as he crept closer to the cottage on silent feet. Approaching from the rear of the dilapidated structure, he and Miles had left their mounts tethered to a pair of bushes and had made their way around the outer edge of the clearing, making sure to keep to the concealment of the tree line. The gray horse Jack had been riding earlier was placidly munching on grass next to the partially open door, and the wavering light from a candle passed back and forth in front of the windows, a clear indication that the man had returned.

Aware of the reassuring weight of his pistol at his back, Peter felt one corner of his mouth kick upward in anticipation. Emily was right. Jack would most likely have some sort of weapon and wouldn't hesitate to use it, but Peter had no intention of using his unless he was forced to. Barlow deserved to languish behind prison bars, to suffer for his sins. Death would be too quick and merciful for him.

When he thought of the torment the man had put Benji through, it was enough to make Peter see red. And Emily . . .

It was true he had been furious when he'd first learned of her perfidy. A part of him was still angry. But he couldn't entirely blame her for what she had done. She'd been confused and afraid with no idea of which way to turn. And well he knew how much her family meant to her. When she loved someone, his fierce little angel loved with her whole heart and soul. There were no half-measures for her, and he knew she would have done anything asked of her to spare those she cared about from harm.

How could he continue to be angry at her for that when it was one of the qualities he'd always admired the most about her?

No, the most overwhelming emotion he felt right now was hurt. Hurt that she hadn't turned to him with her problems, that she had felt she had to deceive him rather than confide in him. She hadn't trusted him, and though he might understand why she had reacted the way she had, that didn't make it sting any less.

But he didn't have time to think about that right now. He would deal with Emily and his feelings regarding her deception later. Right now he had to focus on the task at hand.

Confronting Jack.

"Now?"

Miles's question coming from behind him had Peter looking back over his shoulder. The stable hand crouched behind a tree a few feet away, his expression tense.

"Yes, but I'm going in alone."

Miles started to protest, but Peter raised a quelling hand. "We have no idea what sort of situation we could be walking into, Miles. Jack is unpredictable at the best of times. You'll do me more good if you wait just outside the door without letting him know you're here. That way, you can step in if he happens to get past me."

The stable hand still didn't look happy, but he gave an abrupt nod of acquiescence.

Peter turned back to the cottage, took a deep breath, and started forward.

A few swift, stealthy strides brought him to the entrance of the dwelling, and he peered around the edge of the door into the dimly lit room beyond. A shadowy figure sat at a plank table next to the fireplace, his movements frantic as he stuffed items into a frayed knapsack.

So, it appeared he'd arrived just in time. Barlow had most likely discovered his stash was gone and was getting ready to either go after Emily or light out of town.

Peter wouldn't allow him to do either one.

Stepping across the threshold, he crossed his arms

and spoke in a low, harsh growl, fraught with menace. "Going somewhere, Jack?"

The man froze for a second, then lunged to his feet, whirling to face the door. The light from the candle on the fireplace mantel cast its sputtering glow over Jack Barlow's face, illuminating his startled countenance.

And Peter found himself face-to-face with his worst enemy for the first time in eight years.

Jack hadn't changed much. He was a bit taller and stockier, his black hair a bit longer, but he still possessed the same chilling pair of frosty gray eyes in a pale face that was marked by a perpetual sneer of cruelty. Peter would have recognized him anywhere.

The look of surprise faded from the man's face, to be replaced by a thin-lipped smile of pure evil. "Well, well. If it isn't my good friend Peter Quick."

"Hello, Jack."

In a deceptively casual posture, Barlow moved to lean against the plank table next to him. But Peter wasn't fooled. There was a tenseness, an alertness under that nonchalant pose that told him the thief was ready to spring if given the slightest chance. "I don't suppose you would 'appen to know where my jewels are?"

"In a safe place. Somewhere you'll never find them."

Something glinted briefly in the depths of those cold eyes, something that might have been fear. But it came and went quickly, and the thief raised his chin with a smirk. "I should 'ave known the princess would peach on me sooner or later."

"It wasn't Emily who told me. It was Benji."

"Ahhh. The brat. Of course." Barlow lifted one shoulder in a shrug. "I suppose it was pushing my luck to approach both of them, but I couldn't resist the opportunity."

"The opportunity for what?" Peter took another step into the room, his eyes never leaving his prey. "Just what did you hope to accomplish with this? If you wanted the jewels so badly, why didn't you just commit the robberies yourself? You're more than capable. Why rope Emily into doing your dirty work? Why try to involve Benji?"

Jack's eyes narrowed. "It was never about the jewels, you bloody idiot! It was about revenge."

"Revenge against whom? Emily and Benji?"

"Can't you guess?" Barlow laughed, but the sound was far from humorous. It sounded jagged and a bit less than sane. "Of course, making the princess and the brat suffer was a nice side benefit, but they were just pawns. This is about you, and it always 'as been."

He sidled forward a bit, a hank of greasy hair falling over his eyes as he tilted his head to study Peter with malevolence. "The Perfect Peter Quick. Do you 'ave any idea 'ow much I 'ate you? 'Ow much I've always 'ated you? All the Rag-Tags looked up to you as if you were a bloody saint. I was the oldest. *I* should 'ave been the leader. *I* should have been the one in charge, the one who gave them their orders. But it 'ad to be *you*. And then you 'ad the bloody nerve to turn around and kick me out of the gang!"

"You attacked Emily, Jack."

"So? I wasn't asking for anything more than what she was already giving you. She was, wasn't she? But the 'igh-and-mighty little bitch was too good for the likes of me!"

Peter barely held himself in check. He couldn't let his temper get the better of him, no matter what Jack said. He had to time this just right.

He sucked in a steadying breath of air and managed to school his features into a semblance of calmness that he was far from feeling. "You're right, Jack. Emily is far too good for the likes of you."

Jack growled and his hands fisted at his sides. "The honorable Peter Quick. I should 'ave known you'd wind up betraying your own kind, turning on all of us by going over to the side of the law. A Bow Street Runner." He spat the words with scorn. "'Ow many of your old friends 'ave you arrested, Peter? 'Ow many of the people you grew up wiv did you throw into Newgate?"

That evil grin returned, spreading across the thief's pale face in a way that had Peter itching to plant a fist in it. "I knew you couldn't resist poking your nose into what was going on around 'ere once you 'eard about the robberies. I knew you'd come back to town. And what better way to gain my revenge on you than to force the boy you've always thought of as a brother and your 'ighborn doxy into a life of crime?" He shook his head. "Of course, I didn't manage to rope Benji in, more's the pity. But Lady Emily fell in wiv my plans quite nicely. Tsk. Tsk. What a choice you 'ave. Love or duty. What do you plan to do, Mr. Bow Street Runner? Arrest 'er? Toss 'er be'ind bars and throw away the key?"

"The only one I plan to toss behind bars at this moment is you."

Jack gave a raspy chuckle, and in a flash of movement, he whipped a nasty-looking knife from the knapsack on the table next to him and brandished it before him in a threatening manner. "You're welcome to try."

It was the invitation Peter had been waiting for. He lunged forward and tackled Jack about the waist, knocking the shorter man off balance and sending the knife flying from his hand before they both went crashing to the ground.

The fight began in earnest, the two of them rolling about, grappling and exchanging blows, each of them trying to gain the upper hand. Jack was heavier, but Peter had height and righteous fury on his side, as well as four years of experience in apprehending dangerous criminals, and it wasn't long before he managed to subdue the smaller man, holding him still with an arm wrapped about Jack's neck.

Now that he had things under control, Peter let the rage he'd been holding at bay pour over him. At the thought of what this bastard had done to Emily and Benji, he was tempted to pound him into the dirt floor. But he had questions. Questions that couldn't be answered if Barlow was unconscious.

"Tell me, Jack," he gritted out close to the thief's ear as he hauled him to his feet. "Was anything you told them the truth?"

"Go to bloody 'ell."

"You first." Peter's arm tightened just the slightest bit, pressing against Jack's windpipe. "You know, I could snap your neck, right here and now. No one would ever need to know."

"You wouldn't do that. You're too bloody honorable, Saint Peter."

Barlow was right, but there was no reason he had to know that.

"Don't push me. After what you've done, you're lucky I didn't shoot you the minute I came in the door. If I got rid of you, I'd be doing the world a favor." Peter tightened his hold again, squeezing just enough to impede the thief's airway. "What a sad little life you must have led in the last eight years, Jack. Always running, always looking over your shoulder, wondering when the law was going to catch up to you, obsessed with finding a way to pay me back for my supposed sins against you."

Jack's face had started to turn red and real panic showed in his expression. A queer choking sound escaped him before he clutched at the arm around his neck, trying to pry it away, but Peter held fast. "Come now, Jack. Don't you want to meet your maker with a clear conscience? Tell me. Do you really know anything about Benji's past?"

The thief remained stubbornly silent.

Peter's voice rose to a dangerous level. "Do you?"

"Damn it, no!" Jack finally admitted, his voice barely more than a hoarse whisper as he struggled to breathe. "No, I don't know anything!"

Relaxing his grip, Peter allowed Jack to suck in a lungful of air. "And what about the letters? The letters you *say* Emily's mother wrote. Are they real, or did you have someone forge them for you?"

"Oh, they're real, all right. It's funny 'ow things like

that just 'appen to fall into your lap when you least expect it. They were just the leverage I needed to push Lady Emily into doing exactly what I wanted."

Peter restrained another growl of anger and frustration and let go of the thief's throat, jerking him around to face him. "Where did you get them?"

Once again, Jack's mouth clamped shut, and he gave Peter a mutinous look.

Peter's fist closed around the collar of Barlow's shirt, lifting him up onto his toes. "Where did you get them?" he repeated through clenched teeth.

"Now, if I told you that, it wouldn't be a surprise, would it?"

This was useless. Jack wasn't going to tell him what he wanted to know.

"That's it." Peter gave him a shove in the direction of the cottage door. "Let's go. Maybe a night spent in the local jail will make you more cooperative."

Jack stumbled, then started forward at a slow plod as Peter fell in behind him. But at the last second before he reached the door, the thief put on a burst of speed, swerved, and ducked, retrieving his knife from where it had landed on the dirt floor during their earlier altercation. He spun around to meet Peter's gaze, his features twisted into a mask of hatred and malicious intent.

"I ain't going anywhere. I didn't come this far just to get thrown into some dark, stinking cell. I'll kill you first!"

Peter had been expecting Jack to try something. Desperate and reckless people did desperate and reckless things, so he was prepared when the man launched himself at him, eyes wild and knife upraised. Peter could have reached for his pistol, but instead he waited until Jack was almost upon him before calmly stepping out of his path and sticking out a booted foot.

By the time it registered with Jack that Peter had moved out of the way, it was too late to do anything about it. The thief's momentum carried him onward. He tripped over Peter's foot and went sprawling in the dirt, hitting the ground with a jarring thud.

And he didn't get up.

Peter felt his blood run cold. Damn it, no!

Kneeling down, he rolled Jack over to find those gray eyes blinking up at him, looking dazed and confused. The man was alive, but barely.

And not for long.

The knife protruded from the thief's chest, a slowly growing stain of red spreading outward from the point of entry. The angle of the weapon when he had fallen on it had been such that the blade had sliced upward in a deadly arc, sliding under the ribs, and Peter didn't have to be a physician to know that the wound was mortal. The shrill whistle of air from a punctured lung could be heard as Jack struggled to speak, and his mouth was flecked with a frothy red foam.

Bloody hell, Peter thought grimly. He had wanted to bring Barlow in alive, to see the man brought to justice for what he had done. Now that wouldn't be possible.

But perhaps this was a far more fitting punishment.

"I'm dead, ain't I?" Jack was finally able to force the words out, though they sounded thick and garbled.

Peter paused for a moment, but there was no use lying to the man. He nodded.

Jack gave a watery chuckle, then coughed up a clot of blood. "Always knew . . . you'd be the death . . . of me, you bloody bastard."

"Why don't you come clean while you still can, Jack?" Peter suggested, almost gently. "Tell me where you got the letters. Did you rob Brimley Hall? Did you steal them from Lord Brimley?"

"'Course not. Someone . . . gave them to me." When Peter's eyebrows shot up in surprise, Jack gave a derisive snort that ended in another cough. "You didn't think . . . I was in this alone . . . did you? I 'ad 'elp almost from the beginning."

Peter felt a chill of foreboding trickle down his spine. "Who?" he demanded, digging his fingers into Jack's shoulders. "Damn you, don't you die on me until you tell me who!"

"Why, your . . . lady love's dear friend Viscount Moreland, of course."

Lord Moreland? But the man's own home had been robbed! It wasn't possible!

Was it?

"It seems 'e's desperate . . . for Lady Emily to marry 'im, and 'e'll do . . . just about anything to see that she does." One corner of Jack's bloodstained mouth curled upward in a taunting smile. "In fact, 'e sent me . . . a message tonight at . . . the 'Awk's Eye to let me know 'e was . . . 'eading over to Knight'aven this evening. Seems 'e's too anxious to wait . . . for 'er answer to 'is proposal. 'E should be arriving there just about . . . now."

Dear God! Peter's instincts had told him the viscount was up to no good, but he had put it down to jealousy. Now, because he had ignored the warning signs, Emily could very well be in danger.

"Ah, quite the . . . tangle, isn't it?" Jack's eyes were starting to glaze over and were becoming more and more unfocused with every second that passed, but the satisfaction in his voice was clear. "Will Prince Peter be . . . in time to . . . save the princess, I wonder?"

Peter stood and looked down at the man who had caused him and the people he cared about so much pain. "Too bad you won't be around to find out."

The thief started to speak again, but all of a sudden he gave a harsh gurgling sound and a stream of blood ran from the corner of his mouth. His eyes rolled back in his head and the shrill whistle of his breath stuttered once—then ceased altogether.

Jack Barlow was gone.

Without giving the man another thought, Peter whirled and headed for the door. He would have to worry about cleaning up this mess later. For now, he had more important things to concern himself with.

Like saving the life of the only woman he would ever love.

"Miles!"

The stable hand appeared in the entranceway, his curious stare taking in the still body of Jack Barlow before moving on to Peter's grim countenance. "Is everything taken care of?"

"No." Peter pushed past him and started around the side of the cottage toward where they had left their horses, his strides long and purposeful, and Miles fell in at his heels. "We have to hurry. Lord Moreland was in on the scheme all along. And if Jack was right, Emily and Jenna might very well be in his clutches right now."

Miles made a sound of distress, but he didn't say anything else. He didn't have to. His fear and worry were almost tangible.

Peter wanted to believe that the viscount truly cared about Emily, that their long-standing friendship would prevent him from harming her. But he could be certain of nothing. If the man discovered that his and Jack's plot had been uncovered, there was no telling what he might do.

Peter's heart clutched at the mere thought of losing Emily.

Please, God, let them be in time!

Chapter 26

Emily finished securing Jenna's wrists to the arms of the chair she sat in with the tasseled cords from the parlor draperies, aware the whole while of Lord Moreland standing behind her, the barrel of his pistol pointed at the back of her head.

"Make sure they're tight," he instructed, his voice flat and chilling. "If she should escape, I'll be forced to shoot her, and we wouldn't want that, would we?"

Emily obediently rechecked her friend's bonds as Jenna glared up at him, her brown eyes brimming with hatred. "You bloody bastard! I always knew you were no good, lord or no! You just wait until—"

The viscount shoved a handkerchief into Emily's hands. "And gag her. I refuse to listen to her prattle."

With an apologetic look at Jenna, she obeyed, her

336

mind awhirl with the implications of Adam's actions. Somehow, he was involved in all of this, but she was stumped as to how.

And why.

She finally turned to face him, unable to restrain a wince at the utter lack of feeling he displayed. Dear God, she'd thought she'd known him so well. How could she have been so wrong? "I don't understand any of this, Adam."

He raised his eyebrows at her in a haughty, condescending manner. "Yes, I know. And I regret the necessity for such deceit on my part. But one does what one must to look after one's best interests, wouldn't you agree? After all, isn't that what you've been doing by playing the part of the Oxfordshire Thief?"

"You knew about this all along, didn't you?" she accused. "You were in on Jack's plan."

"Guilty, I'm afraid."

Emily felt her heart lurch in her chest, the sense of betrayal staggering as the light suddenly dawned. "You were the one who gave Jack the letters my mother wrote!"

He inclined his head in a stiff nod.

"But why? Why would you do such a thing?"

"I fear I've managed to get myself into a spot of trouble at the gaming tables. The creditors are hounding my heels, and Father refuses to pay them off." Moreland's jaw tightened, and for the first time, a glint of true emotion flashed in his eyes, a spark of desperation. "I've done everything short of beg the man on bended knee, but he won't listen to reason. I may have reacted rashly, but his stubbornness forced me to it."

Still holding the pistol on her, he reached up with his free hand to rake his fingers through his hair, leaving the blond strands standing on end. "I thought to sell off a few of my mother's possessions, so I slipped into her room one night and stumbled across her keepsake box. You can imagine my surprise when I discovered your mother's letters, but I had no idea then that they could prove to be of use to me. At the time, I was only interested in those items that might be of monetary value."

"Such as your mother's brooch?" Emily prompted.

"Precisely. Unfortunately, my father brought a halt to the scheme. He caught me in Mother's room and rang a peal about my head. He was outraged that I would even dare to consider selling off anything that had belonged to her. Never mind that his only son could wind up being thrown in debtor's prison. So, I was forced to come up with another solution."

"Marriage to me?"

Moreland lifted a shoulder in a careless shrug. "I'm not sure when it first occurred to me, but one day I realized that if you and I were to wed, it would solve all my problems. Your brother was sure to settle a sizable dowry on you, more than enough to cover my debts. With that in mind, I set out to woo you." He frowned at her. "Of course, you had to make things difficult by refusing to cooperate. You started avoiding me, and I don't mind admitting that I grew quite frustrated with you."

Emily placed one hand against her midriff in an attempt to calm the churning in her belly. True, she had never planned on accepting his proposal, had never cared for him that way, but it hurt to know that he would have used her in such a fashion.

"I never would have married you," she whispered, her voice shaking with barely suppressed anger. "Never."

He laughed without mirth. "I don't doubt that, my dear. It was your obstinacy that drove me to the local tavern one night to drown some of my sorrows in a pint or two of ale. I wound up drunk and pouring my story out to the man who sat next to me at the bar." One corner of his mouth quirked in a wry grimace. "That man turned out to be Jack Barlow."

Emily's hands clenched into fists. So that was how such an unholy alliance had formed. "And?"

"And he admitted to me that he had a grudge against someone associated with you and your family, and that he was in Little Haverton trying to come up with a way to strike back at this person. He told me if I would help him with his revenge scheme, he could fix it so that sooner or later you would be guaranteed to accept my offer of marriage."

"You believed him?"

"What can I say? I was far from sober at the time, and his plan sounded plausible. The only thing he lacked was a means to force you into doing his bidding."

"So you thought of the letters."

"Of course. I slipped back into Mother's room and snatched a couple of them, two of the more incriminating ones, and handed them over to Barlow."

Emily shook her head. She felt numb all over and part of her wanted to just sit down and cry, to let out all of her sorrow and anger. But she wouldn't. She wouldn't give Adam the satisfaction. "And to think I was actually fool enough to believe you were my friend."

"You must understand, Emily." The viscount met her gaze, his expression touched with the faintest hint of regret. "I didn't want to hurt anyone, but I was desperate. Barlow kept saying that eventually you'd come around, that you would turn to me for comfort. And when you did, I was supposed to offer to make all of your troubles go away—for a price."

"Marriage?"

"Clever girl." His brow lowered in a fierce frown. "But then your Mr. Quick showed up and ruined everything. I'm not blind. I could see the way you looked at him, and I knew the moment I met him that he would throw a wrench into our plans."

Which must have been why he had stepped up the campaign to woo her and had become more aggressive in his pursuit so soon after Peter had arrived, Emily decided. The scoundrel had never truly cared for her at all!

Wrapping her arms about herself to ward off a chill, she glanced in the direction of the clock. It was after midnight. Surely Deirdre and Tristan should be home at any moment? If she could keep him talking, stall him just long enough . . .

"But what about the robbery at Brimley Hall?" she asked casually, praying that her face gave away none of her thoughts. "If you were involved in Jack's plot from the beginning, why would you allow your own home to be robbed?"

"Ah. A stroke of genius on my part." Moreland's smile was arrogant and assured. "A ploy to divert suspicion from myself, just in case your Mr. Quick should happen to catch on to things and start looking in my direction. And, of course, my mother's brooch was to have been my share of the spoils." The smile faded and he narrowed his eyes at her. "Now, however, I'm afraid Mr. Quick has more than put paid to that plan. If he hasn't arrested Barlow, then he's more than likely chased the bastard out of town along with all of the jewels. So, as it happens, I'm afraid I'll have to improvise."

He jerked the gun at Emily. "Come along, my dear. As much as I hate to do this, I'm afraid I'll have to take you with me."

She took a step away from him, shaking her head. "I'm not going anywhere with you."

"Oh, but you are." He reached out and snagged her wrist, jerking her toward him. "A bit of added insurance, you see, to make sure I get out of Little Haverton safely. Your Sir Galahad won't try to stop me so long as your life is in my hands, now will he?"

"But . . . Jenna . . ." She sent a worried glance in the direction of her friend, who wriggled in her chair, watching them with frightened dark eyes.

"She'll be fine. As soon as your brother and his wife arrive home, they'll release her, but by that time we'll be long gone. Now, hurry up. I want to be out of here before your Mr. Quick returns."

"Too late, Moreland."

The sound of the deep, calm voice sent a surge of relief through Emily, and she looked up to see Peter and Miles step in through the parlor door.

Adam quickly pulled her in front of him and pressed the pistol to her temple. "Why, it seems you've decided to join the party, Mr. Quick. Come ahead in. But please don't make any sudden moves. I would hate for anyone to get hurt."

Peter came forward, his hands raised, palms outward, to show he held no weapon. "Let her go, Moreland. You can't hope to accomplish anything this way."

"She'll see that I make it out of town without a bullet in my back." The viscount paused for a moment, and Emily could feel his breath on her neck, hot and damp. "Barlow?"

"Dead. We struggled and he fell on his knife, but not before he confessed to his crimes, and your part in them."

"I'm not surprised. The little weasel was only out for himself in the end." Moreland's hold on Emily tightened, and she barely restrained a wince. "Now, as I'm not the simpleton you seem to believe I am, Mr. Quick, I would like you to remove the pistol I know you're carrying and lay it on the floor in front of you, but slowly. Lady Emily wouldn't be nearly as pretty with a hole in her lovely head."

Without hesitation, Peter complied, withdrawing his weapon from the waistband of his breeches and placing it on the carpet before him.

"Good. Now, kick it over here."

Once again, Peter did as asked.

The viscount relaxed his grip on Emily the slightest fraction. "Emily, dearest," he said in her ear, "would you be so kind as to retrieve Mr. Quick's weapon for me, please?"

She wanted to spit in his eye, but as that wasn't an option, she leaned over and gingerly picked up the pistol, then craned her neck to look up at him, awaiting further instructions. His stare never wavered from Peter. "Now, open the window and throw it out."

Adam kept his own weapon trained on her as she took the two steps necessary to swing open the nearest casement and toss the gun out into the night.

He instantly reclaimed her arm and drew her back to his side. "There. I feel much better now, Mr. Quick. Much more comfortable. Don't you?" He gestured to Miles, who had remained in the doorway. "You. Stable boy. Go stand against the wall, where I can keep an eye on you."

Tearing his concerned gaze away from Jenna, Miles glared at the viscount as he moved to follow orders.

"Now then, Mr. Quick." Lord Moreland took a step forward, nudging Emily along in front of him, keeping his gun aimed at her head. "If you wouldn't mind clearing a path to the door, Lady Emily and I will be going. And if you want her to remain alive and well, I'd suggest you not follow me."

Peter didn't budge. Instead, he crossed his arms over his chest in a deceptively casual stance, his countenance almost dispassionate. But though he never looked at her, Emily knew him well enough to sense the fury that seethed just beneath the outwardly composed surface, the barely leashed energy he held in check. "I wouldn't do that if I were you, Moreland. Do you really want to add kidnapping to your list of crimes?"

"Do you think it matters? I'll wind up behind bars either way, and I'm not about to let that happen."

"What if I told you I had recovered the stolen items and was willing to make a trade? The jewels for Lady Emily."

Lord Moreland froze, his sudden stillness an indication of his shock. When he spoke, his voice was laced with suspicion. "And I'm supposed to believe that you, a Bow Street Runner, will just hand them over to me and let me go?"

Peter shrugged, but didn't reply.

Emily could almost hear Adam's mind working, ticking through the possibilities. "Where are they? I want to see them!"

Peter looked at Miles, who reached into his pocket and withdrew the drawstring bag they had found at the cottage earlier that evening. Careful to make no unexpected moves, the stable hand reached inside and withdrew Lady Brimley's brooch, holding it up for the viscount's inspection.

"Just think," Peter said softly. "You'll have the monetary means at your fingertips to go far away, to start a life somewhere else. Lady Emily would only be an encumbrance."

"Ahhh." Lord Moreland sounded well pleased, and

Emily longed to kick him in the shin, to yell at Miles to run and take the jewels with him. But she did neither of those things. She had to trust in Peter, had to believe that he knew what he was doing. "Well, as I am the one with a weapon, I don't imagine there is much you could do about it, Mr. Quick, should I decide I wanted the jewels *and* Lady Emily. And as it happens, that is exactly what I want. But I thank you for being so accommodating."

The viscount turned his burning stare on Miles. "Lay the bag on the floor and back away, stable boy."

The stable hand glanced at Peter, who gave an almost imperceptible nod, then returned the brooch to the bag and bent over to place it on the floor before returning to his spot by the wall.

"There. Now, I'll just retrieve the spoils and we'll be on our way." Moreland's fingers dug into Emily's arm, and this time she couldn't hold back a pained gasp.

Peter's head flew up, his gaze meeting hers for the first time since he'd entered the room, and she saw all the anger, fear, and concern for her welfare that he'd been hiding since he'd arrived. His fists clenched at his sides in a visible effort to rein himself in.

Emily's heart filled with warmth and love. No matter what happened, she had faith in Peter. He would rescue her. She had no doubt.

Praying he could read the sincerity in her expression, she gave him a shaky smile and mouthed the words *I trust you*.

His eyes blazed at her with a fierce light, and something passed between them in the second before Lord

Moreland pushed her forward toward the bag of jewels.

And in that instant, Emily slammed her elbow into Adam's gut and shoved at the hand holding the pistol as hard as she could.

The viscount cried out and clutched at his stomach, and his weapon went flying, hitting the floor and sliding across the carpet to disappear under the sideboard against the far wall.

And Peter exploded into action.

As the two men locked together in combat, Miles raced to untie Jenna and remove her from harm's way, while Emily ran across the room and dropped to her knees in front of the sideboard. If she could just get her hands on that gun . . .

But when she shoved her arm under the piece of furniture, her fingers closed on empty air.

Drat and blast, where was it?

She glanced over her shoulder. Behind her, the fight continued in earnest. There was no denying it was a life-or-death struggle, and both men were battered and bloody, each one determined to come out the victor. Even from this distance, Emily could see that one corner of Peter's lip was split and a nasty-looking bruise marred his cheekbone, while Lord Moreland sported a black eye that was already starting to swell.

As she watched, the viscount landed a particularly vicious blow that had Peter staggering backward, off balance, and she let out a cry of distress as he fell, landing on the carpet with a thud. Moreland took advantage of the opportunity to whirl around and withdraw a poker from the stand next to the fireplace. A glint of wildness blazed in the man's hazel eyes as he lifted it above his head and faced Peter.

"I believe it's time to say good-bye, Mr. Quick," he intoned with silky menace.

Frantically, Emily felt beneath the sideboard once again, and this time her groping fingers closed over cold metal. With a feeling of triumph, she withdrew the pistol and turned.

"Peter!" she shouted, and without hesitation she slid the weapon across the carpet toward him as hard as she could, just as the viscount launched himself forward, brandishing the poker.

In a flash of movement that was much too quick for Emily to even follow with her eyes, Peter snagged the gun, raised it, and fired.

Moreland jerked to a stop, the poker clattering to the ground. A splotch of red appeared on the front of his immaculate suit jacket, just above his heart, and he stared down at it in stunned silence for a long, drawn-out moment before his eyes rolled back in his head and he slumped to the floor, where he lay perfectly still.

For a second, no one moved. Then Emily shakily got to her feet and rushed to Peter, flinging her arms around his neck.

Dropping the still smoking pistol, he drew her down onto his lap, wrapping his arms around her in an unbreakable vise as he buried his face in her hair. She could feel his heart thumping at a frenetic pace beneath her ear.

"My hero," she whispered against his chest, and

though she tried to keep her voice light and teasing, it quavered ever so slightly.

"Oh, angel," he choked out. "When I saw 'im 'olding that gun on you, I—" He stumbled to a halt, and she felt his body shudder. "God, I never want to go through anything like that again!"

Leaving Jenna standing near the parlor door, Miles had hurried forward to bend over Moreland's body and had a hand pressed to the side of his neck to check for a pulse. Emily looked up, and she knew even before the stable hand shook his head that the viscount was dead.

She felt nothing. This man had once been her friend, and the only thing she felt at his death was a curious sort of numbness. Perhaps later, after the shock had worn off, she would grieve. But for now, all she wanted to do was to stay right here in Peter's arms.

Forever, if he would allow it.

But it seemed forever was not to be. The sound of the front door slamming open out in the foyer suddenly echoed throughout the house. In the next instant, Lord Ellington appeared in the parlor doorway with Lilah and Cullen right behind him, a pale Deirdre cradled in his arms.

Alarmed at her sister-in-law's pallor, Emily sat forward in Peter's lap, stifling a gasp of dismay and concern. "Tristan, what is it?"

"Someone fetch the physician," her brother croaked, his eyes wild and panicked. "She's having the baby!"

Chapter 27

L ate the next evening, Emily met with Peter and
Tristan in her brother's study, feeling as if she
were about to face a firing squad.

It had been a chaotic and draining twenty-four
hours. With the countess's labor lasting all through the
night and well into the morning, no one had gotten
much rest. Not that Emily could have slept even if
she'd attempted it after all that had happened. While
she, Tristan, Lilah, and Jenna had stayed close to
Deirdre's side, Peter, Miles, and Cullen had dealt with
the removal of Viscount Moreland's body as well as
contacting the authorities.

Emily had no notion of what Peter had told Tristan
about the events of that evening or her part in the Oxfordshire thefts. She only knew that he had pulled her

brother aside briefly for a hushed conversation soon after the physician had arrived, then had departed with Miles and Cullen. Surely Tristan must have had some inkling of what she had done, though, for she'd caught him studying her with hooded eyes more than once over the course of the long night.

Though part of her had longed to fling herself at him, to throw her arms around his neck and let her long list of sins come pouring out, she'd known it would be selfish to unburden herself at this point. Deirdre and the baby had to come first, so she had remained silent. But she hadn't been able to help worrying about what would happen once her crimes were revealed.

By the time the sun had shone in through her sister-in-law's bedchamber window early that morning, Emily had been mentally and physically exhausted. And when the countess had finally been delivered of a healthy baby boy just after noon, the entire household had breathed a collective sigh of relief. Emily had barely made it to her room before collapsing into a deep and dreamless slumber.

She had arisen before dinnertime, feeling only partially refreshed, and made her way downstairs to discover that Peter had come back to the house while she'd been asleep, only to depart again with Tristan. Not knowing what was happening was enough to make her want to pull out her hair in frustration, and she had decided to try and take her mind off things by visiting with Deirdre and her new nephew.

And that was where she had been, seated at the countess's bedside and cradling the heir to the earldom in her arms, when Langley had sought her out to let her know that Tristan and Peter had returned and were requesting her presence in the study.

This is it, she'd thought, her heart pounding with dread. Had they brought the law with them? Would they insist on arresting her? Would Tristan ever forgive her for what she'd done? Oh, she had no doubt her brother would fight to keep them from putting her in jail or hanging her, but that didn't mean that he wouldn't blame her deep down.

And what about Peter?

To be truthful, she was almost more afraid of him than she was of facing her brother. He'd been so caring after what had happened with Adam, holding her in his arms as if she truly mattered to him, but he'd also been very angry with her when he'd discovered her duplicity. She hadn't talked to him since Tristan and Deirdre had walked into the middle of things last night, and she had no idea what he was thinking.

Or feeling.

Deirdre must have seen the trepidation on her face, but misread it as a reluctance to leave her nephew.

"Go on, dear," the countess had said with a smile, taking the baby from Emily. "It's time for me to feed him anyway, and you can come and see him later. Jason will have plenty of time to get to know his aunt Emily."

Emily had smiled and nodded, letting her sister-in-law believe what she wanted. After all, it was easier than telling her the truth.

And now, here she was, seated in a chair before her

brother, hands anxiously clasped together in her lap as she met Tristan's steady regard across the polished surface of his desk. His countenance was composed, unreadable.

There was a long silence in which each tick of the clock in the far corner could be heard. Uncertain of what to do or say, Emily was all too aware of Peter leaning against the wall behind her, arms crossed in a casual pose, his eyes burning into the back of her head in a most disconcerting fashion. She'd glanced at him once when she'd first entered the study, but she'd been careful to avoid looking at him since. His impassivity had rattled nerves that were already strung too tautly.

Finally, Tristan spoke, his voice calm without a trace of anger. "I thought you might like to know that all of the stolen items have been returned to their rightful owners."

Emily felt a rush of relief at the same time as a sense of despair gripped her. So, the Tuttlestons, the Fulberrys, and Lord Caulfield would now all know what she had done.

But Tristan's next words surprised her. "They were delighted to have them back, of course. Right now they know nothing aside from the fact that the thief has been apprehended and the jewels recovered."

Emily's eyes widened. "But surely they'll have to know the truth sooner or later?"

"Peter and I have discussed it, and we have decided it's for the best if your name remains out of it."

"Out of it? How?"

"As far as the local authorities and the rest of Little Haverton are concerned, the sole perpetrator of the Oxfordshire thefts was a street thief named Jack Barlow. When the man was confronted last night regarding his crimes, he attempted to flee and was killed in the altercation. As was, sadly, the Viscount Moreland, who accompanied Peter in order to lend his aid in capturing the thief.

Emily shook her head, at a loss. None of what her brother was saying made sense. She couldn't help risking another glance back over her shoulder at Peter, who still stood in the same spot, his expression unchanged. "But I don't understand—"

"Peter gave me the letters you managed to . . . acquire from Barlow," Tristan explained, drawing her attention back to him, "and we paid a visit to Lord Brimley. He agreed to hand over the rest of our mother's letters in exchange for our agreement to keep his son's part in this sorry affair silent. Of course, as a result the whole village shall wind up regarding the vile miscreant as a bit of a tragic hero, but I'm afraid that can't be helped."

Rising, Tristan rounded his desk and stopped in front of Emily, catching her hands in his and drawing her to her feet. His face was no longer unreadable, but was full of warmth and concern. "I'm sorry, Emily," he told her softly, giving her fingers a sympathetic squeeze. "I know he was your friend. I can't believe he managed to fool everyone so completely."

She shook her head, still unable to believe that everything might work out for the best after all. Wasn't he going to yell at her, scold her? "But what about me? Don't I deserve some sort of punishment?"

For the first time since she'd entered the room, Tristan smiled. "I know you, sweetheart. I'm sure you've punished yourself far more than I ever could." He let go of her hands to grip her shoulders, giving her a little shake. "Surely you must have known Peter and I would never let them arrest you? Yes, what you did was wrong, but you did it with the best of intentions, to protect the people you love."

His smile faded to be replaced by a frown. "But don't believe for one minute that I'm not angry with you. Don't you ever dare keep such a thing from me again. Do you understand? We can weather any scandal, no matter what, so long as we stand together as a family."

Her heart full of joy, Emily threw her arms around her brother in a grateful hug. "I love you, Tristan," she whispered in a choked voice.

"I love you, too, sweetheart." Tristan returned the hug, then set her from him and turned back to his desk to retrieve a bundle of yellowed papers tied with a ribbon. Emily recognized them immediately as the letters that had been in Lady Brimley's keepsake box the night she'd stolen the brooch.

He held them out to her. "Now, I think you should read these. I believe you might find that the situation with our mother was not as dire as you had feared."

Emily eyed the letters askance for a moment, then

reached out and took them from her brother's hand before settling back into her chair to read.

The one on the top of the stack was dated two years after Tristan's birth.

Dearest Lavinia,

There can no longer be any doubt in my mind that my darling Tristan is Sinclair's son. And though I admit to being a trifle disappointed, I am relieved for my husband's sake. My Nick was slender and as fair as I am, while Tristan is a dark-haired and husky little boy who, at two years of age, already shows every sign that he will grow to be as large and powerfully built as the earl someday. Of course, Sinclair has not been so easily assured, and it breaks my heart that he cannot see how much his son looks like him. It is as if he has closed himself off from his own child. I can only hope that sooner or later he will realize how wrong he is, before Tristan is old enough to sense that his father holds him at a distance . . .

Emily laid the yellowed page in her lap and looked up at her brother. "So, you *are* the true Earl of Ellington."

Tristan shrugged. "At least as far as Mother was concerned. And I tend to agree. I look far too much like Father for me to ever believe otherwise, though it seems he was never entirely convinced of the fact. But that was his loss, I suppose." He paused for a moment, then inclined his head toward the letters she still held. "Why don't you keep those and read them when you have time? I've already looked through them, and it might help you feel a bit closer to Mother. I know you've always regretted the fact that your memories of her weren't as clear as mine."

Emily's eyes blurred with tears and she bit her lip to keep them from spilling. "Thank you."

He leaned over and pressed a kiss to her forehead. "You are very welcome. Now, if you'll excuse me, I believe I shall go spend some time with my wife and son. It's been a long day."

With a nod to Peter, he departed the room.

Leaving the two of them alone for the first time since last night.

Emily's pulse beat in her ears and she took a deep breath before forcing herself to turn in her chair and face the man she loved. He was still standing with his arms crossed, his gaze hooded as he studied her.

What was she to say to him? Was he still angry? It was impossible for her to tell from his detached expression.

"Are you all right?"

His quiet inquiry startled her, and she jumped in her seat. Surely he couldn't hate her too much or he wouldn't have asked her such a question, wouldn't have cared whether she was all right or not.

She inhaled another steadying gust of air and forced a slight smile to her lips, unable to quite meet his eyes. "I am fine, though a bit tired." Her fingers dug into the arms of her chair as she fought to slow the rapid pounding of her heart. "I want to thank you."

"For what?"

"For not turning me in to the law, when I know it must have gone against everything you believe in as a Runner."

An emotion she couldn't read flashed across his features and then was gone. "You were used, Emily. It's that simple."

He seemed so cold, so distant, and Emily hated it. Where was the man who had held her tenderly in his arms last night, who had called her his angel?

Seeking to bridge the gap between them, she tucked her mother's letters in the pocket of her day dress and stood, taking a step toward him. "So, what will you do now?" she asked, struggling to keep her tone light and even. "Will you stay and visit with the future Earl of Ellington for a while?"

"As a matter of fact, I just informed your brother that I shall be leaving in the morning."

Emily froze in place, certain she must have gone as white as a sheet. He was going away? After everything they had shared? He couldn't do this to her again!

Stunned, she forced herself to speak despite the sudden constriction of her throat. "Leaving? But why so soon?"

He lifted a shoulder in a careless manner and pushed himself away from the wall, striding over to stand before the window. "The case is solved and it is time for me to return to London. I've been here for almost a fortnight now, and I'm sure there must be important . . . matters awaiting my attention."

Emily knew she would be leaving herself open to

heartache beyond bearing if she asked the question that trembled on her lips, but she had to know. "And what about us?"

"There is no us. There can't be."

His reply left her feeling as if someone had reached into her chest and ripped out her heart, leaving a gaping hole in its place. "But . . . we made love last night."

"That was a mistake that never should have happened. Nothing has changed. We cannot be together and you know why."

"No, I don't know why!" Clenching her hands into fists at her sides, Emily made herself move forward once again until she stood directly behind him. She refused to let him throw away what they could have for the sake of what other people thought. "If we love each other, we should be willing to fight for what we want, and none of the rest matters."

When he didn't speak, she reached out and laid a hand on his shoulder. He stiffened under her touch, but she ignored it, desperate to get through to him, desperate to make him understand how she felt. "I love you, Peter. And I know you feel the same way."

Utter silence.

"Peter?"

He turned back toward the window.

Dear God, but he *didn't* feel the same! That could be the only explanation for his reticence, and Emily was quite suddenly sure she would die from the pain and humiliation that washed through her. Peter had never said anything about his feelings for her, and she never should have let herself forget that.

"I see." She backed away from him, unable to quell the slight hitch in her breathing. "I apologize for assuming you still had feelings for me. Obviously, I misunderstood what passed between us and was making far more of it than I should have." Despite herself, a sob escaped her. "Please do have a safe journey back to London."

With that, she fled, no longer able to hold back her tears.

Chapter 28

His mind and spirit numb, Peter sat ensconced in an armchair in Lord Ellington's study, staring out the window at the sunny day beyond the glass without really seeing it.

Exhaustion weighed heavily upon him. He had gotten very little sleep in the last two nights, and he'd arisen early this morning in order to make sure his belongings were packed for the return trip to London. Tristan had put the Ellington carriage at his disposal, and once he got around to saying his farewells, all should be in readiness for his departure. But somehow he couldn't quite bring himself to take the steps necessary to carry him out the door.

Emily.

The mere thought of her was enough to send a wave of anguish washing over him.

He loved her. He always had and he always would. He had known he could no longer deny it to himself the instant he had realized her life was in danger.

When he had walked into the parlor the other night to find Moreland holding a gun on her, fear such as he had never known had taken him over, making it practically impossible for him to think, much less function with his customary rationality. All that he'd been able to concentrate on had been freeing her, making sure she wasn't harmed. Nothing else had mattered. If she hadn't managed to get her hands on the viscount's weapon when she had . . . well, who knew what might have happened? He didn't even want to imagine the possible scenarios.

But now that things had all been settled, it was time to let his angel go.

Peter couldn't restrain a wince as he remembered the stricken look on her face when he had told her he was leaving. Having finally managed to regain the one thing he'd longed for most, her precious trust, he'd turned around and thrown it away. God, hurting her had been the hardest thing he'd ever done, and letting her believe he didn't care about her had been like a knife in his chest, but he knew it was for the best. Nothing had changed. He might love and want her more than his next breath, but he was still the son of a prostitute, a man who could never be worthy of her.

He never should have made love to her.

Throughout the night, he'd been haunted by images

of Emily naked in his arms, her skin gleaming in the lamplight, her violet eyes full of love and desire. All for him. Just knowing that he'd been the first to ever make her feel that way filled him with a fierce sense of satisfaction and possessiveness.

But it had been a mistake. Now that he'd had her, now that he knew what it was like to move deep inside her, a part of her, it would be harder than ever to stay away from her, to go back to pretending his love for her didn't exist. But he had no other choice. For her sake, he had to manage somehow.

He groaned and lowered his head into his hands. It felt as if he were being ripped apart from the inside out, and if he'd believed it would ease the ache, he might have been tempted to lose himself in a bottle of the earl's best brandy. He was well aware, however, that not even the haze of alcohol would be enough to drown out the pain of having to give Emily up. Again.

"I beg your pardon, Master Peter."

He looked up to find that Langley had appeared in the doorway.

"Master Benji is here to see you," the butler informed him. "He awaits you in the parlor."

"Thank you, Langley."

The butler inclined his head and disappeared from view.

Closing his eyes for a brief moment, Peter reached up to rub wearily at his temples. He had planned on stopping by the Park on his way out of town to say good-bye and let the boy know what he had learned from Jack, but he supposed now was as good a time as any. With a sharp exhalation of air, he pushed himself to his feet and strode from the study.

He found Benji standing before the French doors in the parlor, his shoulders stiff, his thin frame rigid with obvious tension.

Bloody hell, but how was he going to tell the lad he'd found out nothing? Peter wondered bleakly. "Hello, Benji."

The boy swung about and shoved his hands in his pockets, meeting Peter's gaze with eyes that swirled with a mixture of anxiety and uncertainty. "Mr. McLean told me last night that Jack Barlow was dead. Is that true?"

"Yes."

"What did he . . . What did he say? About me?"

"I'm sorry, Benji, but the man didn't know anything. It was a ploy to draw you in, nothing more."

Benji drew in a shaky breath and stared down at the floor. "I was afraid of that, but I just kept hoping . . ." In an abrupt move, he slammed a balled fist down on the back of the closest chair and turned away, a muscle working in his jaw. "Now I'll never know where I come from!"

"Don't be so quick to curse the fact. That might not be a bad thing."

The lad shook his head and glanced back at Peter over his shoulder. "How can you say that? My parents could have been the worst sort of criminals. Thieves, murderers. If nothing else, Jack Barlow's appearance only proves how the past can come back to haunt you. What if my mother or father should decide to turn up now?"

"It's highly doubtful after all these years, Benji."

"But it's possible. And what about what they say about bad blood? If my parents were truly evil people, how long will it be before those tendencies start showing up in me?"

Peter felt his heart contract at the utter despondency on the boy's face. "That's nonsense!"

"Is it? Do you know that for sure? I couldn't stand to disappoint the earl and countess after the faith they've put in me."

Taking a step forward, Peter reached out to grip Benji's arm, drawing him around to face him. "You are an exceptional young man, and I can guarantee that you will never disappoint Lord and Lady Ellington. You are who you are, Benji. The past has no bearing on today."

"I wish I could believe that."

"You can. My God, Benji, look at *me*. My mother was a prostitute, my father . . . well, I don't even know who the man was. I was a pickpocket, a thief, and I did some things I don't even want to remember in order to survive, things I will always regret. But I've made my life my own. I've risen above it. And if you take a good, hard look, I think you'll see that you have, too."

Something shifted in the boy's expression, some faint trace of hope that convinced Peter he was finally getting through to him. "You think so?"

"I *know* so. But if you don't believe me, ask Lord and Lady Ellington. I'm certain they'll agree. You have a wonderful future ahead of you, Benji. Don't let the past dictate the choices you make now."

Benji inclined his head, his countenance thoughtful, then crossed his arms and regarded Peter from under lowered brows. "Mr. McLean mentioned that you were leaving this morning."

"Yes, I'm afraid so."

"Why?"

Feeling awkward, Peter released the boy's arm and shrugged. What could he possibly say? "My work here is done, and I'll be needed back at Bow Street."

"Surely you could visit for a little while longer?"

"That wouldn't be a good idea, Benji."

"But why?"

Because he was letting the past dictate his choices.

Sudden insight slammed into Peter like a lightning bolt from the blue, and he almost reeled at the impact. My God, it was true! Here he was, counseling Benji to let go of the past, while he was holding on to his own with all of his might, using it as a barrier between him and Emily.

He loved Emily, and if he could believe what she'd said, she loved him, too. As far as she was concerned, his background didn't matter and it never had. No, he didn't like the thought of society ostracizing her, turning their backs on her because of him, but wasn't their love worth fighting for? Wasn't it worth the sacrifice if it meant they could be together?

Yes, by damn, it was!

Emily had tried to tell him that, had tried to make him see, but he hadn't wanted to listen. Now, he could only pray he wasn't too late.

"Benji, I'm afraid you'll have to excuse me now.

There is something rather important I need to do. But I will send Lord Ellington to you, and I want you to tell him exactly what you've told me. I'm certain he'll be more then willing to reassure you on all counts. All right?"

Benji nodded.

Peter offered the boy one last encouraging smile before leaving the room.

He ran into Tristan just outside the door. "My lord, Benji is awaiting you in the parlor. There is something he needs to speak to you about that has been troubling him for quite some time, and I believe you may be able to put his mind at ease on the issue."

"Of course." The earl glanced in the direction of the parlor, then raised an eyebrow at Peter in question. "But where are you off to in such a hurry?"

Now came the first test. He had always known that Tristan had the highest respect for him, but the man might feel differently when it came to a former street thief wedding his sister. Peter was willing to face anything for the woman he loved, however. Even the displeasure of the man who had given him so much. "I'm on my way to beg Emily's forgiveness on bended knee." He paused for a moment, then plunged onward. "And to ask for her hand in marriage."

There was a long, drawn-out silence, then a wide grin spread over Tristan's face. "Well, it's about time. Deirdre will be happy to hear it." He winked at Peter and clapped him on the back. "I believe Emily was in the garden the last time I saw her."

Peter's relief was staggering. "Thank you, my lord. I swear I'll make her happy."

"I never doubted it. Not for a second."

Would the pain never go away?

Seated on her favorite bench next to the fountain in the garden, Emily bent her head over her book, trying to ignore the soul-deep ache that plagued her and concentrate on the story. But the words were blurring on the page, making it impossible for her to see.

It might have been because her eyes kept filling with tears.

She had known from the beginning that it would be a mistake to trust Peter, to let him close again, but she had listened to her heart instead of her head, and look where it had gotten her!

When she had arisen this morning after a night spent tossing and turning, unable to sleep, she'd wasted no time in escaping the house. She didn't want to be present when Peter departed, to have to pretend it didn't matter that the only man she would ever love was leaving her again. All she wanted was to be left alone, to try to find some way to resign herself to the fact that Peter didn't want her.

But that was easier said than done.

With a sigh, Emily gave up on even attempting to make sense of what she was reading and closed the book in her lap, lifting a hand to pinch the bridge of her nose in sudden weariness. Hoping to raise her spirits, she had stopped by the stables earlier in order to visit with Artemis, but even being in the presence of her beloved horse hadn't helped, and watching Miles and Jenna together had been almost more than she could bear. Not that she begrudged her two friends their happiness, but they had spent most of the time holding hands, exchanging whispers and kisses in the far corner of the stall, and seeing the love in their eyes for each other had been like salt in a raw and gaping wound.

So she had retreated here to the garden, believing that the peacefulness and solitude might soothe her troubled thoughts. So far, however, she'd had no such luck.

Well, if Peter Quick was stupid enough to throw away what they could have, then he didn't deserve her love! Let him go back to London and get on with his life, just as she would get on with hers. She wouldn't waste another second of her valuable time mourning his loss.

And that had to be the biggest lie she'd ever told herself.

"Emily."

At first, she thought she was imagining things, that the soft voice calling her name came from the depths of her own subconscious. But when it drifted to her again, sounding gently insistent, she looked up to find Peter standing a few feet away, watching her with an unreadable expression.

Oh, no! Had he purposely sought her out to say good-bye? What should she do? What would she say?

Taking a deep breath and bracing herself, she laid her book aside and returned his stare with a steady one of her own. "What do you want?" she asked, struggling to keep her tone even. "I thought you were leaving."

He took a deliberate step forward, his gaze never wavering from her face. "I was. But it occurred to me that there was something important I needed to tell you first."

Emily swallowed the lump in her throat and forced herself to give a haughty sniff. "I'm certain I don't know what you could possibly have to say that I would care to hear."

"I love you."

She froze, every muscle in her body rendered immobile at the stunning impact of his words. Surely she must have misunderstood? "I beg your pardon?"

In a swift motion that had her stifling a gasp, Peter closed the space left between them and stood before her, his blue eyes suddenly blazing with a fierce light that caused her heart to skip a beat and her mouth to go dry in response. "I said I love you, and I'm willing to do whatever I need to do, whatever you want me to do, to prove it to you."

He couldn't mean it! He'd made it quite clear last evening how he felt about her.

"What am I supposed to say, Peter?" Despite herself, her voice quavered. "How can I believe you? We made love, but you insisted it was a mistake. You took me in your arms after the incident with Adam as if I truly meant something to you, yet you all but turned your back on me last night. Every time I let myself trust you, every time I let myself care, I wind up getting hurt. I can't risk that again. I won't."

At her obvious agony, Peter flinched, then reached

out to catch her by the elbows, drawing her up off the bench. "I'm so sorry, angel. I deserve your anger. I know I do. And I hate like hell that I hurt you. My only excuse is that I was doing what I thought was best." He paused for a moment, then sucked in an audible gust of air. "Will you at least let me try to explain?"

At the eloquent plea, Emily couldn't deny him, no matter how much she might wish she could. With a single, abrupt nod, she pulled away from his grasp, crossed her arms, and waited for him to speak.

He let go of her and scrubbed a hand over his face before pacing a short distance away. "I told you about my background, about my mother and about my past before I met you. Whether it shows or not, it affected me. It still does."

There was a pause, then he glanced back at her over his shoulder. "No matter how much I've accomplished with my life, there's always been a part of me that sees myself as unworthy. Unworthy of my place at Willow Park. Unworthy of all the support I received from your brother and his wife. But most of all, unworthy of you."

The pain on his face was stark and intense, and Emily felt her heart give a sympathetic squeeze, her love for him softening her in spite of her resolve not to be swayed. "Oh, Peter. You *are* worthy. You must know that."

He shook his head. "You don't understand, Em. Deep down inside, I'll always be that vagabond street thief, the son of a whore who doesn't even know what his real last name is."

"None of that matters!" she protested, moving toward him, unable to resist the need to reassure him, to offer him comfort. "I've tried to tell you that over and over. And you are not unworthy. Just look at what you've become. You're one of the best men I know."

When he didn't answer, merely looked down at the ground, she laid a hand on his arm, drawing his attention back to her. "Think about it, Peter. Lord Moreland had every advantage money could buy, and look what sort of human being he turned out to be. But you . . . It's a testament to your strength of character that you are the man I see before me. I've always known that."

Peter captured her free hand in his, lacing his fingers through hers. "But *I* had to know it. I had to believe that I deserved you, and I didn't. Until today." He lifted her hand to his lips, brushing a kiss across her knuckles that managed to wring a shiver from her before offering her a slight smile. "I was talking to Benji when I realized something. All along I've tried to tell myself that I was pushing you away because of what other people might think, what they would say about us together. But it was what I thought of myself that was the true barrier. And somehow I just couldn't get past that."

He turned, reaching up to cup her cheek in his palm. "And then I remembered the look on your face the other night when I found Moreland holding that pistol on you. In that instant, I saw all the love in the world on your face. You believed in me, had faith in me to rescue you. You thought I was worthy enough to give me your trust."

His smile widened, and he leaned forward to bestow

a brief kiss upon the tip of her nose. "And if my angel thinks I'm worthy, who am I to argue?"

Warmth and hope flooded through Emily. Did Peter truly mean it? Was he saying what she thought he was saying?

His next words confirmed it. "Em, if you still want me, if you truly don't care what society or anyone else thinks, then I'm all yours. Your brother has already given his blessing." He wrapped his arms around her waist and tugged her close, staring into her eyes with so much love it took her breath away. "Say you'll forgive me for being a stubborn fool. I love you more than you will ever know, angel. I want to marry you, have babies with you, and spend the rest of my life with you. I promise I'll never push you away again."

How could a woman resist such a moving proposal?

"Very well," she breathed, going up on tiptoe and framing his face in her hands. "But first, I want you to repeat after me." She traced the seam of his lips with her tongue. "I."

He groaned, his hold on her waist tightening. "I."

"Am." Emily punctuated the word with a slow, deep kiss.

"Am."

"Worthy."

"Worthy . . ." Peter barely managed to whisper it before she plunged her tongue into his mouth, tasting him with voracious need before finally tearing her lips from his. A shaky laugh escaped him. "And the luckiest bastard I know."

She giggled and rested her head against his chest, soothed by the thump of his heart beneath her ear. It was a sound she wanted to go on hearing for the rest of her life. "I love you, too, Peter."

"I know, angel. It's the one thing I can always count on."

They were quiet for a long moment, then he spoke again. "You'll be all right with living at least part of the year in London? I know you love the country, and we'll visit as often as we can, but I'll be needed at Bow Street."

"Of course. I would never expect you to give up your position as a Runner. Not when you've worked so hard to get where you are. But I will insist that we make use of the Ellington town house when we're in the city. It seems silly for it to sit there empty so much of the time."

Emily felt him bury his face in her hair. "Hmmmm. That might be a good idea. My flat certainly isn't big enough for a family, and it occurs to me that we might already have a babe on the way."

She gave a jolt and pushed herself away from him, staring down at her stomach with a mixture of consternation and joy. Such a thing had never crossed her mind. "Peter . . . A baby . . ."

He tilted her face up with a hand beneath her chin and gave her that seductive smile again. "I like the idea of a beautiful little girl with her mother's eyes. Although I am putting my foot down now. There will be no lessons in picking pockets—or locks—for this one."

Emily felt a smile spread over her own face. "Come

now, darling. Don't you want our daughter's education to be well-rounded?"

"Not if it means that I'll have to worry about her slipping in through other people's windows on a lark." He stroked her bottom lip with his thumb. "And I expect her mother to behave, as well. Though I might not mind if you should decide to wear those breeches for me again. In private, of course."

"Of course. And speaking of privacy . . ."

She led him with her into the copse of elms, where they were shielded from prying eyes by the thick foliage and the surrounding hedges. Overcome by their passion and not caring who might stumble across them, they began to shed their clothes, exchanging kisses and caresses in between untying laces and undoing buttons.

When they were naked, Peter drew her down with him to the warm, soft grass, fitting her intimately against him. She felt him shift his hips and gave a soft gasp as the thick hard length of his manhood entered her, sliding deep into her feminine core.

He began to move inside her, and she rose to meet him, their shared pleasure gradually building until it reached the peak and they both shattered, wave after wave of ecstasy sweeping over them.

When the tempest had passed and they lay close together, spent and sated, Emily raised her head from his chest and gazed up at him from under lowered lashes. "So . . ." she ventured, almost timidly, "you're not angry with me anymore?"

His brow lowered in a frown. "I won't lie and say I wasn't at first, Em. You should have gone to someone, anyone. As your brother said, you went about things the wrong way, and I hope you've learned a lesson from it." The frown faded away and he captured her lips in a brief, yet tender kiss.

"But how could I stay mad at you when you were only trying to protect the ones you love?" he continued huskily. "Just as you've always done from the day the Rag-Tags met you. It's why I fell in love with you, you know. That urge you have to take care of everyone and everything around you. You were our guardian angel then, Em. You still are."

She smiled, a genuine smile of pure joy and contentment. Finally they would have the future they'd once envisioned so long ago.

Leaning forward, she pressed a kiss to his temple before whispering close to his ear, "I'll always be *your* angel, Peter. Only yours."

Who wants to be cold anyway? Start the new year right with these sizzling new romances coming in January from Avon Books . . . and you'll be feeling the heat in no time.

An Unlikely Governess by Karen Ranney

An Avon Romantic Treasure

Beatrice Sinclair, forced to accept a post as governess, never expects to be tempted by the seductive pleasures Devlen Gordon offers her. While she strives to draw her young charge out of his shell, she must also confront the passion she soon feels for Devlen . . . but is he her lover—or her enemy?

Sleeping With the Agent by Gennita Low

An Avon Contemporary Romance

Navy SEAL Reed Vincenzio must eliminate Lily Noretski . . . by *any* means possible. Lily is as beautiful as she is dangerous, and in possession of a devastating weapon. He must win her confidence, find the weapon . . . and put everything on the line for a woman he soon loves but cannot trust.

The Bride Hunt by Margo Maguire

An Avon Romance

Lady Isabel Louvet is a kidnapped bride, stolen by a Scottish chieftan to warm his bed! But she is rescued by a feared warrior of legend—the brave hearted Anvrai d'Arques. Isabel's fierce spirit stirs his passion, her touch makes him wild. And her love will set him free . . .

A Forbidden Love by Alexandra Benedict

An Avon Romance

The Viscount Hastings is the most scandalous man in all England! So when he discovers Sabrina, a Gypsy in danger, he spirits her away to the most *unsafe* place in the land . . . his bed. He longs to join her there, but instead vows to uncover the secrets this beautiful woman hides . . .